ALSO BY JOSH EMMONS

The Loss of Leon Meed

Prescription

for a

Superior Existence

A NOVEL

JOSH EMMONS

SCRIBNER

New York London Toronto Sydney

SCRIBNER
A Division of Simon & Schuster, Inc.
1230 Avenue of the Americas
New York, NY 10020

First Scribner hardcover edition June 2008

SCRIBNER and design are trademarks of
The Gale Group, Inc., used under license
by Simon & Schuster, Inc., the publisher of this work.

For information about special discounts for bulk purchases,
please contact Simon & Schuster Special Sales:
1-800-456-6798 or business@simonandschuster.com.

Designed by Kyoko Watanabe
Text set in Aldine 401

Manufactured in the United States of America

1   3   5   7   9   10   8   6   4   2

Library of Congress Control Number: 2007038164

ISBN-13: 978-1-4165-6105-7
ISBN-10: 1-4165-6105-6

*Prescription
for a
Superior Existence*

In this part of the world it is light for half the year and dark the other half. Sometimes at night I look at the halos around the window blinds and breathe in salty air redolent of afternoon trips to the beach I took as a boy, my hands enclosed in my parents', my feet leaving collapsed imprints in the sand, my mind a whirl of whitewashed images. I remember how the shaded bodies lying under candy-cane umbrellas groped for one another, and how I pulled my mother and father toward the ice-cream vendors, and how I fell in love with the girls who slouched beside their crumbling sandcastles. The sun an unblinking eye on our actions. The waves forever trying to reach us. From the beginning there was so much longing, and from the beginning I could hardly bear it.

I used to think that with enough scrutiny I would discover a moment to explain what happened later. Not anymore. Now the idea that a Big Bang in my youth caused the events that have sent me here—or that with enough focus I could recall the incident, like an amnesiac witness during cross-examination recollecting how and where and by whom a murder was committed—seems absurd. Now I know that I was always on a collision course with Prescription for a Superior Existence, that it couldn't have been otherwise.

To pass time I walk around this nightbright Scandinavian village, past seafood grottos and tackle and bait shops and thatched Viking ruins with pockmarked, briny walls blanched the color of dead fish. Bjorn Bjornson, a cod oil wholesaler who joins me sometimes in order to practice his English, though it is already better than most

Americans', says that the village has changed radically since he was young, noting that the citizens didn't have cellular phones, personal audio devices, satellite receivers, or sustainable fishing laws, that as always in the past many indispensable things did not exist.

He imagines that growing up in California I witnessed even more incredible developments. "Your state is rushing ahead of everywhere else," he says. "In Europe the conviction is that this is terrible, and we are expected to fear and disdain it. But I have met your countrymen and seen your films and read your literature, and I want to visit to make up my own mind. Consensus is sometimes no more than shared folly."

Given more time in each other's company, Bjorn and I might become friends. He is a patient, thoughtful man who considers every angle of a problem without being paralyzed by indecision. If it weren't dangerous, if information didn't travel so quickly and unpredictably, I would explain to him why I'm here and ask for his advice; instead I've told him I'm a tourist, come to take pictures of the glaciated fjords before they disappear.

And so I have to decide without his or anyone else's counsel if the past month, and before that all of history, justifies my presence in a remote northern village where it has been decreed that at midnight on Sunday I will, after delivering a eulogy that is both inspirational and absolute, with a solemnity great enough for the occasion, conduct and preside over—I am choosing my words carefully and none other will do—the end of the world.

This is as strange for me to say as it must be to hear, and I should add that I'm not yet certain that the end is coming; it could be a grand deception, or sincerely but wrongly delineated, like the edges of the world on a fifteenth-century map. There are compelling arguments for and against each possibility, and I change my mind about them so often that on Sunday, instead of having discovered the truth, I may be as confused as a pilot with spatial disorientation, in danger of mistaking a graveyard spiral for a safe landing, when up is really down, sky is really earth, and life—suddenly and irreversibly—is really death.

CHAPTER 1

A month ago I thought we all had too much rather than too little time, and that like one of Zeno's paradoxes its end couldn't be reached. The future looked as though it would stretch out forever with no single moment more or less significant than any other—with a basic equilibrium underlying its progress—not because time was fair but because it was neutral, as disinterested and limitless a dimension as length and depth.

What I thought turned out to be meaningless, however, the sort of frangible wisdom that can't survive large or even small cataclysms of the spirit, when during the course of two days in mid-February I lost my job and fell in love.

Neither event was extraordinary and together they might have struck the sort of balance I believed in, with the good and bad canceling each other out, except that the woman I fell in love with, Mary Shoale, was the only daughter of Montgomery Shoale, founder of the antisex religion Prescription for a Superior Existence. Looking back I see the unwisdom of getting involved with someone whose family ties were so forbidding, and even then I knew I should pursue a more available woman, but I was convinced that she and I were soul mates who belonged together at any cost, proof that love emboldens as much as misleads us.

The fallout came quickly. On the afternoon we first got together, an anonymous note was slipped under my front door warning me to stay away from Mary or face swift and severe retaliation. Not knowing if it was serious, I called her but couldn't get through, and so spent the next few hours debating the question. Either she didn't actually have to follow PASE precepts just because her father had invented them, or she was obliged to do so for that very reason; either I had nothing to worry about, or I had everything to worry about. The answer arrived later that evening when a Paser broke into my apartment to carry out the note's threat. He was a large man, a giant, but with the help of my neighbor Conrad, who happened to be over, I prevailed in the resulting skirmish. Afterward, while waiting for the police to take him away, I understood that Mary and I would have to proceed on a cautious footing, that we couldn't be careless about our affair with zealots like the giant running around. But in the calm of that moment, as I swelled with resolve and relief that the worst was over, shaken but guardedly hopeful, five more Pasers entered the room and took up positions around us, and when one of them pointed her gun at me I saw that the worst had yet to come.

Before she fired many things occurred to me, the most important of which was that I had never thought much about the afterlife. Conrad began to protest and was told to be quiet. I stared at the gun. My adoptive parents, Rick and Ann, who were artists, had reared me without religion and the incentives of heaven or hell or purgatory or nirvana, and I'd not gone out of my way to fill in the blanks. Which isn't to say they opposed religion; rather they thought of it as an inheritance that other people made the best of or discarded. They didn't dismiss it out of hand and they weren't uninterested in the soul. Ann had once even described art as a pathway to joy more honest than religion—it admitted, after all, to being a human invention—but not better. In her view, art's only advantage was that it didn't tell a purportedly true story that science could disprove, which religion did only because it was so old, because in the past people had had to grope blindly for explanations of life and death and pain and love, which they called Judaism or Hinduism or animism. Happily, science had since come up with a version of how the cosmos worked that rendered the seven-day theories and turtles resting atop turtles all the way down quaint and irrelevant.

Bjorn Bjornson, who like most of the villagers here has a trace of the poet-philosopher in him—something about living so far from the planet's nerve centers and being preoccupied with the great cycles of sky and ocean, where the human drama is contained in an unvarying population of 1,400 villagers among whom one is both participant and anthropologist, gives one access to more sweeping thoughts and ambitious language than the rest of us possess, which has led me to think that if we all lived as these people do, and as our ancestors did for millennia, rarely straying more than twelve miles from our birthplace, we might be better prepared for what is to come—phrased it as I would have liked to at the time, when I told him yesterday about Prescription for a Superior Existence. Shaking his great blond equine head Bjorn said, "In religion, in the end, the new is neither better nor worse than the old; beliefs and insights swirl and constellate over time without shedding any greater light than what has pulsed weakly throughout the ages. Reason and passion enact a tortoise and hare race in our hearts, and what seems true and beautiful today may seem false and hideous tomorrow."

So I can't adequately explain what happened in my living room, with Conrad and the giant and the five paratroopers standing around like Roman senators on the Ides of March, a moment heavy with anticipated violence. Whereas I might have thought, "Here it is at last, what we are all marked for from the beginning," and seen it as a pointless conclusion to what had been a cosmically pointless existence—though able to obsess me for thirty-four years with the same resolute focus everyone pays to his or her own being—I felt that it shouldn't end there, and that I would do anything to extend it long enough to determine its why and wherefore, which I knew then were not matters of insignificance or superstition but actually more important than work and friendship and the romantic impulse and whatever else I'd slotted into my viewfinder and looked at with such keen interest. I seemed to have gotten everything wrong, and I wished for a speech or action that would arrest the woman with the gun.

This is only worth mentioning because after being shot I did not die. Instead I opened my eyes in what appeared to be a hospital recovery ward on a hard bed beneath a thin sheet and thick downy comforter that smelled of unscented soap, as dawn glowed through three triangular skylights above me. Repudiating everything I'd thought about misunderstanding life, I sat up and looked around. The room and its contents were white: the sheet, ceiling, end table, linoleum floor, dust particles in the air. My head felt both weightless and heavy, like a stone held under water, and I craved coffee and food and any of the painkillers a hospital of this size would stock in unregulated doses. Nine beds were lined up on either side of mine and another ten along the opposite wall, in all of which men were sleeping, a mishmash of ethnicities and ages, though most looked younger than forty. I swung my feet onto the floor's warm tiles and was about to stand up when an alarm clock rang and everyone opened their eyes at once, as if they'd been feigning sleep.

Next to me a tall stout Indian folded on a pair of thick plastic glasses, yawned widely, and said, "You must be Jack. I'm Mihir, and I will be your mentor here. Those are for you to wear." He pointed to powder blue cotton pants and a collarless long-sleeved shirt stacked in a tidy pile at the foot of my bed. Everyone was dressing in the same outfit and folding their bed sheets so vigorously that they might not have been convalescents. Some hummed high-energy pop tunes. "I hope you slept comfortably and are fully rested. These mattresses are firm, yes, perhaps too much so for your taste, but the firmness is part of the treatment. Did your wife send you?"

"I'm not married."

"Parents?"

"What kind of hospital is this?"

"Hospital? We are at the PASE Wellness Center. Please put on your exercise garments."

"I have to get out of here."

"Yes, naturally, after you have improved. In a moment we are due at Elysian Field, so we haven't time for a full conversation."

A man about my age entered the room dressed in a navy blue version of our outfit, wearing a whistle around his neck and holding a palm-sized stopwatch. The beds were all made up and crisply smoothed out; the men stood beside them proudly. "Good morning," he said in an Alabaman drawl, making eye contact with each of us in turn. "You'll be glad to know that Paul Davies and Thabo Ombassa were granted savant status yesterday and arrived home safely last night. They send their regards and expect all of you to be home soon. Also, as you can see, two new guests are joining us today, Shang-lee Ho and Jack Smith. Please make them feel welcome."

"Excuse me!" I said, holding up my hand as he turned and walked out.

Mihir tugged gently on my sleeve and said, "Our schedule, as I said, is very tight and allows no time at present for questions or comments. That man was Mr. Israel, by the way. He's a facilitator and neither the smartest nor the most advanced, which is why he's assigned to exercises. Most facilitators, however, are very kind, very wise persons, and even Mr. Israel has his good qualities."

"What the hell is going on?"

"Yes at first it is overwhelming, but that is why I have been assigned as your mentor. I will help you through this adjustment period and soon you will be as confident as I am, knowing just what to do and when. The learning curve is steep but short. Now, stand behind me."

A perfectly straight line had formed at the door. I seemed to be in a dream that combined Prescription for a Superior Existence with boot camp, featuring people I'd never seen before and too-real set pieces. Through the skylights morning advanced timidly. Mihir went to the end of the line and signaled for me to follow him, which I did half-consciously, too bewildered to protest. From this room—this barracks or ward or whatever it was—we entered a classical Grecian hallway as ersatz and authentic as a Las Vegas hotel, with ceramic amphorae and bronze goblets lit up in display cases inlaid in its ocher walls, and walked to a lobby forested with Doric colonnades and painted marble vases and, in one corner, a large limestone replica of the Colossus of Rhodes. I seemed to be the only one paying attention to our fantastic surroundings, and then we were outside in a courtyard studded with young eucalyptus trees and straight-backed wooden benches painted volcanic red. To our left a round pond thirty feet in diameter steadily overflowed its edges, and a trio of stone seraphim at its center blew misty water into the air through copper trumpets. We kept walking and I kept gaping. Ivy-covered Corinthian and Tuscan buildings enclosed the courtyard; in the entablature above the doorway of each a name was carved: Shoale Hall, Celestial Commons, The Synergy Station. We followed a pathway out of the courtyard and passed between other buildings and a tennis court and a scale imitation of the Citadel and a menagerie of topiary animals, until finally we stopped at an acre of landscaped lawn bordered on its far side by a fifteen-foot, gleaming white wall. There we separated into two rows and spread out at arm's length. When Mr. Israel instructed us to do fifty jumping jacks I came to attention.

"Why am I here?" I shouted, taking a step out of formation.

Mihir shook his head at me, and the others, already jumping in unison like young cadets, stopped and looked at Mr. Israel, who came toward me with a concerned expression, as if I were choking and needed his help. Up close his face was dotted with razor nicks that had stopped bleeding in the cold. He was younger than I'd originally thought, no more than twenty-five, and hid whatever Southern amiability was native to him beneath a mask of critical authority.

"Morning exercises," he said, a vertical crease deepening between his eyebrows, "are how we begin the day."

"I mean why am I at this PASE Wellness Center? I didn't ask to come and I want to be returned home." I looked around for sympathy, but with the exception of Mihir, who looked pained on my behalf, everyone shared Mr. Israel's frown.

"You're here like the other guests, to improve."

"But I don't want to improve."

Someone yelled out "Ha!" and Mr. Israel's body tensed and his right arm bowed like a gunslinger's preparing to draw—he looked ready to hit me—but then he pulled a phone from his utility belt and asked for an escort team to come to Elysian Field. He signaled for everyone else to resume their jumping jacks, but their coordination was off now and they resembled windmills out of sync. Mr. Israel regarded me coolly until two men dressed in navy blue tunics approached and, with a nod from him, led me back to Shoale Hall. I asked them questions on the way, but they were as silent and formal as beefeaters, betraying no hint that they either heard or understood me. My back, which like most parts of my body ached, felt a little better for the brisk walking, and I would have liked to keep up the pace even after we entered the building. Instead they delivered me to the Red Room, which was painted beige and smelled of cinnamon and was furnished with a desk, silver suede sofa, and glass-topped coffee table, on which a pristine copy of *The Prescription for a Superior Existence,* the religion's holy book, rested solemnly, thick enough on first glance to seem like a stack of individual books. I sat on the sofa for several minutes, my back and wrists and stomach and head all competing for my attention, like patients crowding a doctor late for his morning appointments, and I wanted a cigarette and drink and muscle relaxant, which is to say I wanted clarity, but a look around the room revealed nothing that could provide it.

"Not a reader?" The door shut behind a matronly woman in her midfifties wearing a feminine version of the navy blue tunic that seemed to be the uniform. Her hair was short and layered and gray, as thick as sheep's wool, and she wore a pair of silver-colored feather earrings. Touching her nose with a tissue and then tucking it into her sleeve, she said, "My name is Ms. Anderson, and I'm director of this PASE Wellness Center. I've been watching you through the two-way mirror; you didn't once flip open *The Prescription*."

"I'm not supposed to be here."

"Yes you are." She crossed the room to a shelf laid out with a pitcher of orange juice and a bowl of green and red fruit, from which she took two pears and handed me one. "I signed your involuntary admission papers when you came in. You were unconscious."

"Someone shot me."

"It was only a tranquilizer gun. Physically you're fine, if a little weak. One of our resident physicians monitored your reaction to the drug and found it satisfactory; in fact your system was so suffused already with similar substances that he thought it shouldn't have affected you at all."

"That's—Why was I shot and brought here?"

Although I spoke with a demanding, inquisitive tone, like my earlier protest this question was disingenuous, for I thought I knew the answer.

She polished her pear on her sleeve. "Let me ask you a question: Did you consent to go to school when you were a boy?"

"Excuse me?"

"When your parents took you to kindergarten on the first day, did you run willingly into what must've seemed the confinement of the classroom, or did you beg to go back home to all that was familiar?"

"That's not the point. I'm an American adult and my rights have been violated."

She sat in a wingback chair that would have engulfed a smaller woman. "Mr. Smith, you are being given a great opportunity, a chance to escape from the prison you're in. And I don't mean this Center. I mean the larger prison of your desires, the one that makes you so unhappy so regularly."

"I'm not unhappy."

She folded her ring-laden hands together. "Forgive my bluntness, but you certainly are. You overeat and are obsessed with work and can't maintain romantic relationships. You take pills to fall asleep and wake up and calm down and get energized. You drink too much alcohol and watch too much television and are terrified of being left alone with your thoughts for more than a few minutes at a time."

The room's lights didn't change, but everything seemed to rise and then drop a shade in brightness, as though an electrical surge had passed through the wiring. "Who told you that?"

Ms. Anderson sneezed without breaking eye contact with me. "Like most people, you are unhappy because you aren't fulfilled by what you have. You always want more, and that more is never enough. Throughout your life you've desired things, only to find after getting them that contentment lies in the *next* thing. And the next and the next and the next. Sadly but predictably, the result of all this deferred satisfaction for you and others has been the same: anxiety and depression. And if allowed to continue it will lead finally to the crowning tragedy, ambivalence."

"This has nothing to do with me and I want to leave right now."

"Some people say the cycle of desire is human nature. They point out that before we can speak we cry for milk and human contact and toys and dry diapers and relief from teething pain, that infancy is little more than *I want!,* that childhood is no better, that adolescence is worse, and that adulthood is a full-blown epidemic of insatiable neediness. But does it follow that we should forgive desire just because it's human nature, in spite of its cost? Think of the old people you know, so beaten down by years of disappointment that they have no interests or passions or convictions left, who are content to let television mark time until they die. We at the PASE Wellness Center want to spare you that fate."

I shook my head. "You're trying to kill me."

"No." She smiled beatifically. "We are trying to save you."

I opened my mouth to speak and at first nothing came out. "But I've become close with Mary Shoale. Aren't I here because her father thinks I pose a threat to PASE?"

"It's safe to say that Mr. Shoale considers you a friend. Besides, although Mary is at heart a good girl, she's addicted to gratifying her own desires. PASE wouldn't punish someone else for her folly. No, the man who broke into your apartment was a renegade Paser acting entirely on his own and without the administration's knowledge. He has since been disciplined."

"The giant?"

"We do not condone or practice violence. Our religion is neither a cult nor simply a nice philosophy to live by. It values all human life and does its best to protect rather than endanger people. You don't need to look skeptical. Mary's other playmates have sat where you are now and been just as suspicious and later emerged transformed, improved in every way. I don't doubt that you will be equally successful. Now eat your pear."

My wrists radiated pain and I hyperextended my back as recommended by physical therapists. When I turned around the two escorts leaned in toward each other at the door, blocking passage in or out. The room's single window, although large enough to jump through, was one story above ground that, from the angle where I sat, appeared to be concrete.

"So you know about the men she's been with? And you've abducted them all so they don't embarrass your public relations department?"

She bit into her own pear and spoke while chewing. "Let's concentrate on you so that we don't waste your valuable time here. At this hour you should already be showering after exercises, though I understand that because this is your first morning at the Center, especially given the state in which you arrived, you have questions and concerns that might interfere with your improvement. The orientation session we've set up for you and the other new guests after breakfast will address those more fully, but we can touch on some of them now."

I scratched off a section of wax from my pear and said, "This is illegal and you'll go to jail for keeping me here against my will. I have an excellent lawyer who will destroy you in a civil suit once the state finishes with you."

"Please don't worry about us. We are well aware of the court's attitude and behavior in California. You need to concentrate on learning about Prescription for a Superior Existence, for that, despite your disinclination, is why you're here."

"I'm here because I was kidnapped. I don't want to know anything more about PASE."

She took another bite of her pear and it was half gone. "What do you think about God?"

I glanced back again at the escorts, who hadn't moved.

She said, "I presume that as an atheist you think of him as a fanciful idea man came up with to get through all the terrors of prehistory. 'If God didn't exist we'd have to invent him,' and that sort of thing. This doesn't necessarily make you a cynic, but on the measuring stick of faith your notch is nearer the closed than the open end. In a way, we don't blame you. The god that most of the world recognizes is schizophrenic: either angry, wrathful, and genocidal, or subservient, meek, and fond of easy bromides. We Pasers see through that god, as well, and if we didn't know about UR God, we might be atheists too."

I thought about getting up to run and crash through the window with the hope of landing on the ground outside with a mere sprained ankle and skinned palms, but when I considered the lacerations this would also incur, provided the glass pane was thin enough to break through and the unlikelihood that I could then reach and scale the perimeter wall, I decided against it. "Ergod?"

"Ultimate Reality God. Media stories are always so concerned with our stance on sex or our charitable activities that they often neglect to mention Him. When they do, He is wrongly described as 'a deity without any defining qualities,' as though we were too lazy to give Him a deep voice or a long white beard. Journalists can be as inattentive as toddlers and as sex-crazed as teenagers. But you will shortly discover that UR God is our focus and that He is the supreme generative force who, cognizant of the Earth's imminent collapse, gave us the book *The Prescription for a Superior Existence* so that we can improve enough to fuse into Him."

"I thought Montgomery Shoale wrote it."

"UR God used him to convey His message."

"Did that happen on a mountain?"

"As I said, a certain amount of cynicism is healthy, but there comes a point where it causes more harm than good. All we ask is that you pay attention and keep an open mind during your stay with us, the length of which depends entirely on you. Put simply, by the time you leave here you will be free from anxiety and depression and anger and self-destructive tendencies, ready to know UR God. This freedom is in you now, buried like a precious metal; we will show you how to mine it." Ms. Anderson looked at her watch and stood up. She'd eaten her entire pear, including its core. "Now you'd better go; it's breakfast time."

CHAPTER 2

B efore the events leading up to my abduction and placement at the PASE Wellness Center, I had been a capital growth assessment manager at Couvade Incorporated, a midsized financing firm in San Francisco. After eight years with the company I was, as my performance reviews put it, "a self-starting team player who [thought] outside the box but within the realm of possibility." The case for my promotion to senior manager was therefore strong, and I had, with others' encouragement, begun to court and, in certain exuberant moments, expect the position. I ran a quick and efficient squad, never took sick days, and had the highest client satisfaction ratings of my peer group. I voluntarily fact-checked other squads' work and was friendly yet professional with the interns. Following my surgery in December my boss, Mr. Raven, a reserved and laconic man to whom I'd worked hard to draw close during the previous year, and whose passion for presidential biographies and Latin jazz I had come to share, said that I appeared to be as healthy as my best reports and that he looked forward to working in closer tandem with me.

So when in early February, nearly one month ago from today, my squad was given the Danforth Ltd. project, a standard client profile that would take no more than a week, it seemed to be a victory lap at the finish line of which I would be promoted to senior manager. Passing from Juan to Dexter to Philippe, the file reached me on a Monday, two days before it was due. I opened it at six, after most people had gone home, and, chain-smoking into my air purifier and snacking from a box of shortbread, made great progress. An hour later I ordered Chinese takeout and a six-pack of beer. At eight, already a quarter done, I took a break and lost a game of speed chess to Alfredo, the janitor for my floor, and then spent ten minutes emptying the cubicle trash bins while he read online Mexican newspapers at my desk.

At 10:30 I made an error—I transposed a 6 into 9—so I packed up and went home. There I took four ibuprofens, three sleeping pills, a muscle relaxant, a shot of whiskey, and four green capsules a homeopath friend had given me for joint trouble in my wrists. My ex-girlfriend Camilla had stopped by to look for a sweater she thought might be there and to write a note on the dry-erase board saying she'd heard about my surgery and wanted to get together for a drink. I rubbed out the note and my surroundings began to spin as gently as a carnival ride beginning its cycle.

In the living room I landed on my red velvet couch, which just then felt like a flying carpet, but instead of falling asleep I heard broken snatches of piano music coming from the apartment next door. I struggled to sit up and listen. Scales. *Do-re-mi-fa-sol-la-ti. Do-re-fa. Stop. Start over.* This was interesting because Conrad, who was a piano teacher, had not had a student in the three years he'd lived there. He blamed this dry spell on the rising quality and falling prices of piano lesson software—people, he said, would rather learn from a computer program than from a live human being, resulting in the spread of rote, mechanical musicians who hadn't had the individual instruction necessary to play Chopin or Satie with integrity and impact—but the more likely reason was that he charged two hundred dollars an hour. It was too much for someone as unknown as him. I'd recommended that he lower his rate to be competitive with other nonprofessional teachers', but he thought that the more expensive a service was, the more people would value it; until this happened he was content to live on monthly disability checks from the military for an injury he'd sustained to his right leg in Iraq.

Hearing the scales, I was glad for Conrad and hoped this would begin a busy chapter in his career, but I also needed sleep and could easily be kept awake by the noise, so I went over to ask him to end the lesson. What remained of his dyed-blond hair was slicked back in a casino operator clamp, and he leaned against his doorway with a new ivory-handled cane in his right hand. Just thirty more minutes, he said, looking over his shoulder and thanking me for my patience. He would have closed the door then had not a young woman, the student, appeared behind him and said she was ready to quit. Conrad gripped the handle of his cane tightly. I mumbled thanks and retreated to my apartment and in a wobbly swoon lost consciousness at the foot of my bed.

I could do this—black out in the middle of a room at midnight—because I lived alone, as I had ever since taking my first one-bedroom apartment, in San Francisco's Hayes Valley, because neither of the two women I'd dated seriously in that period had wanted to move in with me. Supritha, the first, had ended our seven-month relationship over a fiery south Indian breakfast when I mentioned the time and money we would save—not to mention the love we would generate—by living together. "I don't know why," she'd explained, ladling *dal* over a pancake and frowning as though her fickleness were as mysterious to her as to me. I died a little. The second, Camilla, had in the six months we dated cheated on me "with tons of guys," which was, she decided, given that I hadn't been enough for her sexually, partly or perhaps largely my fault. I died a little again.

What brought me back to life on both occasions was the thought that someday I would meet the woman of my dreams and we would fall in love and these early false starts would provide all the contrast I needed to appreciate what at last I had found.

In the meantime I tried to make the best of being a bachelor. My married or otherwise engaged friends put a positive spin on it by pointing out that I never had to eat with boring couples, bicker, clean up after myself, shop, talk about my feelings, talk about her feelings, or be anywhere besides work and home. I didn't have to remember birthdays or anniversaries or Valentine's Day, nor did I have to think about the toilet bowl lid or hide my pornography or apologize. This last point was especially important to them. Being alone, they said, meant never having to say you were sorry.

But I would gladly have paid for the upsides of romance with its downsides, because to me, in addition to being a source of human connection and joy and security, relationships were a health matter—almost a survival issue—and I looked and hoped for one constantly. That is, on my own, undisturbed and unapologetic, I had a dangerous amount of freedom that allowed for all kinds of abuses that, even while committing them, I regretted but could not stop. There were points on which Ms. Anderson would later be correct. Alone and without the regulatory oversight of a companion, I had license to eat, drink, and watch anything at any time. I could treat my body as a chemical processing plant or a temple, filling it with whatever brought relief from or an end to my daily stresses, which led to grand solitary debauches, nights when I would stare at an empty pizza box or *Playboy* care package ordered by and for myself, in a drug- and alcohol-induced fugue, forced to consider that overeating and binge drinking and perpetual masturbation were signs of deep and abiding unhappiness, and that I ought to do something about them right away. At those times I would say aloud, "If I keep doing this I won't last much longer," without daring to answer the follow-up question: "Would that be any great loss?" A little while later, calmed by the exhaustion that follows worry, I would find myself seminaked on the couch with five barbiturates and a half-bottle of scotch sluicing through my bloodstream, watching East European adult television at four A.M., and I would tell myself that there were many versions of a full life and this was mine. Nothing is good or bad but thinking makes it so, said Shakespeare.

In several respects, though, I was doing poorly and getting worse. My insomnia, for example, was out of control. I'd always had trouble sleeping, but since receiving an email in November from my biological mother, I'd found it nearly impossible. Then came an unfortunate work-related incident in Chicago. Then my break-up with Camilla. Then my surgery, which I feared meant that at heart I was vain and shallow, a slave to the body image stereotypes I'd rejected for so long as demeaning and oppressive. Then my back and wrist pain increased. Then I realized that, unable to change my diet following the surgery, I was on course to quickly regain every one of the eighty pounds I'd lost, that the case for my guilt was about to get stronger.

And my real troubles had not even begun.

On Tuesday, after finishing and sending the Danforth file to Mr. Raven, I asked my coworkers if they wanted to go to a bar after work to unwind, but everyone either had plans or was too tired or had stopped drinking. At eight o'clock, with nothing left to do at the office, which was empty—Alfredo had come and gone early—I went home and downed three tall whiskeys and put a corned beef in the oven, along with rice on the stove. A radio show broadcasted news that Greenland was splitting apart due to softened permafrost from rising annual temperatures; the war had claimed another 107 lives; an earthquake near Seattle was reported, the size and effects of which weren't known; and there was now consensus among economists that we were in the middle of a recession, housing market slump, and dollar devaluation that hadn't spurred a consequent rise in demand for U.S. exports. A terrible trifecta. The alcohol relaxed me, and the hours until I could return to work in the morning—when I would again be around people, with a purpose, liberated from my own thoughts—seemed endurable.

As I refilled my glass with ice, the doorbell rang. I thought it might be my brother, Sid, stopping by to borrow money or set me up with another of his girlfriend's friends (as payback or pay forward), but it was Conrad's student from the night before. She wore tight brown slacks and a short white blouse with stressed buttons, and her shiny straight black hair brushed the top of her shoulders and cut across her forehead with Cleopatra precision. Her name was Teresa, and she had come to apologize for keeping me awake during her lesson. She knew what I'd suffered because a neighbor of hers who built birdhouses was always hammering something at odd hours. She shouldn't have agreed to a lesson so late at night.

"It's not your fault for agreeing," I said. "It's Conrad's for suggesting."

She tugged on the bottom of her blouse, bringing her nipples into bas relief, and wedged a thumb into her front pants pocket. "Thanks for understanding."

"Sure."

"I was afraid I'd have to beg."

"No."

"Can I use your bathroom?"

"Right now?"

"I just drank a big bottle of water."

Although I usually welcomed the chance to let beautiful young women into my apartment—despite its rarely, actually never, happening—I hesitated. She was lying. I couldn't say how or why I knew this, only that it was so. Heat gathered around my neck and crept slowly up my face like an allergic reaction.

"I'm in the middle of making dinner," I said, not widening the door.

"I'll be half a minute."

"My toilet isn't completely reliable."

"Please." She smiled and revealed two rows of evenly set, glistening white teeth, evidence of great luck or money or discipline as a child. The radio was an indistinct babble in the background. Maybe, I thought, I was being irrational and drunk, and there was nothing suspicious about this woman or her request. She bit her lower lip and I stepped aside to make way for her.

Back in the kitchen I found milky water bubbling from the rice pot into a moat around the burner's flame. This was typical of how ineptly I cooked, because of which I had recently contracted with the woman who cleaned my apartment every other week to make and deliver frozen batches of food—enchiladas, chicken mole, lasagnas—on her workdays. The last of her latest delivery was gone, though, and I didn't remember when she was scheduled to return.

A minute later Teresa stood framed in the kitchen's entrance, wiping wet hands on her hips, imprinting black finger marks on her slacks like daguerreotype shadows. "I hate leaving someplace and then realizing I should have used the bathroom. My family never went on vacations, so as a kid I wasn't trained to always go before getting in the car. A lot of what we do instinctively comes from our nine-year-old self."

Again I felt a slurred apprehension and concentrated on cleaning the stovetop. The water had evaporated to leave a layer of dried white froth like old sea foam cobwebbed on the beach. From the beginning there had been so much longing that I could hardly bear it. "You remembered to use my bathroom."

"That's because of the water. It's like an alarm clock for me. Did you know that on nights before they were going to wage battle, Native American warriors drank gallons of water so they'd wake up early and get the jump on their enemies?"

I grunted no and pulled from the oven the corned beef, a loaf of grayish meat with a scrim of yellow fat around its sides, as the radio announced that an Amazon-born virus with a thirty-six-hour incubation period had killed twelve people in the last week. Epidemiologists expected it to travel far and wide over the coming months. I flipped on the stove fan and trimmed off the fat and sipped at my whiskey while Teresa picked up a piece of junk mail lying on the counter.

Burning my thumb on the oven pan, I turned to her and shouted, "What are you doing?"

"Nothing."

"That's my mail."

"It's just a PASE brochure."

"Please leave it alone."

"Are you a Paser?"

"That's— Why are you still here?"

"I want to help you clean up." She indicated the dishes in the sink, torn seasoning packets by the cutting board, blackened hand towels, and a grease-spattered calendar tacked above a sink full of brackish water.

"Why would you do that?"

"To make up for last night. Because I'm nice."

"I don't think so."

She let go of the brochure and lost her veneer of friendliness and the pain in my thumb seemed unimportant. Conrad, when talking on the phone to his first-ever student, would not have vetted her closely, and in the final analysis nobody could safely say what another person wasn't capable of. She stepped forward and I braced myself, my right hand a foot from the knife block, ready for what might follow, be it loud or quiet, and the moment was starting to feel very drawn out when she leaned in and kissed me. A button of her blouse came undone at the sternum, pressed against my chest.

"There's no need to be hostile," she said, pulling back as a thread of saliva bridged our lips, her green eyes as limpid as a secluded pool. She held the intimacy for twenty seconds and I grew painfully erect. "That's why I came over, so we could be friends."

"I don't understand," I said, wiping my mouth.

"Yes, you do."

"Women don't just walk into strangers' apartments and kiss them."

"How do you know?"

"Everyone knows."

"Maybe everyone's not as smart as they think they are." She turned around. "At this rate, you have a minute to stop me from reaching the front door."

She walked carefully, one foot precisely in front of the other, as though on a gymnast's beam, out of the kitchen. A voice told me to let her go and lock the door behind her and return to my dinner and later fall asleep on the couch. In the morning I would go to work and, except for five or ten solitary adventures, forget Teresa as easily as I'd forgotten all the other women who'd taken friendliness with me only so far. You learn to release because otherwise you're pulled in directions you can't go. But even as I registered this warning, wondered if being thin could make so much difference in my attractiveness to women, and thought about newspaper accounts of femmes fatales who seduced men in order to rob them or turn their bodies over to the internal organ black market, as well as about the venereal risks involved in sleeping with someone so brazenly pursuing anonymous sex, I ran to the living room and then the front door and then the common space from which both the stairwell entry and the elevator were visible. I was too late. She'd gone.

When I got to work late the next morning at 9:45, having dozed off just before my alarm sounded and then slept for an hour, most of my coworkers were putting on their coats and crowding around the elevator, making quiet conversation and picking hairs from their clothing. One stood motionless off to the side with his eyes closed, leaning against the wall as if asleep or recovering from a dizzy spell. They were all men.

The office, despite its vaulted ceilings with propeller fans, felt particularly warm and close that day, like a ship hold. My cubicle mate, Max, talked on the phone and stared at the kidney-shaped glass bowl between his desk and mine, in which a Japanese fighting fish swam through Neptune reefs and arched castle gates, trailing a gossamer of skin. I loosened my tie and unbuttoned the top of my starched yellow shirt and, feeling the nausea pangs that stabbed me every morning, held my stomach as if to keep it from swelling back to its former size.

"Max," I said. He shook his head, switched the phone to his left hand, and wrote "angry girlfriend" on a piece of paper.

Across the room Elizabeth, Mr. Raven's secretary, waved me over to her desk. I had invited her out to dinner the week before, and although she'd begun refusing before I'd finished asking, it seemed possible as I walked across the houndstooth carpet that she was one of those women with a default no response that, although it cost her a few good dates, saved her from the many undesirable men who saw deliberation as foreplay, and that, breaking character, she had reconsidered me. In a flattering blue pantsuit, she smiled and poured steaming water from a tulip-decorated teakettle into a matching cup.

"Are those new earrings?" I asked.

"You're late and—"

"They bring out the auburn in your hair. Where's everyone going?"

"The sexual harassment sensitivity course at the Prescription for a Superior Existence Station," she said.

"I forgot that was today. Only men seem to be leaving."

"That's the directive." She squeezed a lemon wedge into her teacup, beside which a pewter condiment caddy held honey, sugar, cream, and echinacea powder. "Mr. Raven asked me to remind you that he needs the Danforth file by four o'clock." Her eyebrows, sharpened and defined and darkened since I'd last seen them, came together as she looked up and curled a ginger lock of hair behind her ear. She had not reconsidered me.

"I emailed it to him yesterday," I said.

"He must not have gotten it."

"I'll send it again."

She nodded and I returned to my computer, where I found no record of the email in question. Also, the Danforth file I opened was not the one I'd worked on for eight hours. The date and time of its last modification was Monday afternoon, when Philippe had given it to me.

"We broke up again," said Max, shutting off his phone.

"My Danforth file has been replaced with an older version," I said.

"She thinks I hate her brother."

"This is impossible."

"Everybody hates him. She says other people just don't understand him, and since I've spent so much time with her family I'm supposed to see past his unattractive qualities, but it's precisely because I've been around him so much that I can't stand him and don't want him over for Seder." He turned off his computer and desk lamp. "Come on, let's go. We're the last guys here."

"I can't redo Danforth today and go to a training seminar at the same time."

"You have to go. You're a man."

"Mr. Raven wants the file by four."

"Your absence would be noticed in a big way."

Discreetly but unmistakably Max was referring to the conference in Chicago I had attended in January with my squadmates, one of whom, Juan, had used a company credit card for our six-thousand-dollar gentlemen's club bill. Although he later called and finessed the charge down to a more realistic thirty-seven hundred dollars, and in spite of company policy not to reveal employee money matters, the story got out and the four of us were forced to give the Employee Conduct Board a lurid and damning account of our trip.

"Is Mr. Raven still here?"

"He left twenty minutes ago."

"What about Mr. Grobalski?"

"Gone too."

Max handed me my coat and I followed him out slowly.

It's hard to say if I would have been more open to the seminar if Danforth hadn't hung over me that morning. I knew I could be more sensitive—as much as the next man, certainly—but I was wary of the involvement of Prescription for a Superior Existence. Maybe I shouldn't have been. Beyond what was common knowledge, all I knew then about PASE was that its founder, Montgomery Shoale, a rich venture capitalist, had self-published *The Prescription for a Superior Existence,* a thousand-page book that introduced and explained the eponymous religion, nearly two decades ago, when it was widely considered a vanity project designed to lend depth and credibility to his company training seminars—he had built a reputation around the Bay Area for speaking about intra-office social cohesion and running more time-efficient meetings—until eventually PASE's religious bona fides were established and the IRS granted it tax-exempt status as a faith-based organization. When the Citadel, the flagship building of its Portrero Hill headquarters called the PASE Station, became the sixth-tallest structure in San Francisco, there was speculation that Shoale would go bankrupt, but instead he expanded the operation by building the Wellness Center, a four-acre campus in Daly City where people could study PASE intensively. Then he started the PASE Process, a charitable organization that infused money and crackerjack administrative staffs into underfunded soup kitchens, homeless shelters, and daycare centers in low-income areas of the city. It also gave grants to arts companies, medical research labs, and neighborhood development centers. At some point within the last couple of years a small but high-profile group of celebrities had begun talking in interviews about their conversion to PASE, and it had made international headlines the previous spring when the French government objected to its building a Wellness Center in Marseilles. That surprised me because I'd thought PASE was strictly a California phenomenon.

In general, though, I didn't think about it. The West Coast gives birth to several religions annually, and although PASE had lasted longer and was better financed and more diversified than most, like them it seemed destined to struggle for a place on the country's spiritual landscape before fading into the same horizon that had swallowed New Thought, the I AM movement, and hundreds of indigenous American faiths before it. If anything, it was at a disadvantage to the others because it condemned sex in every form; I couldn't imagine it attracting more than a few thousand followers at any one time. Yes, PASE looked likely to burn through a dry distant swath of the population without threatening the green habitable land in which I lived.

Max and I pulled into a thirty-story parking garage at the Station and found a space sliced thin by two flanking armor-plated vans on the top floor. In the street-level lobby of the adjacent Citadel we joined our coworkers grazing on donuts and coffee, waiting for the seminar to begin. Max stopped to talk to someone and I went in search of the bathroom, along the way grabbing two maple bars and an apple strudel from the buffet table, which I ate crouched down in a stall. I returned to find Max with Dexter and Ravi at the orientation booth discussing the unemployment figures that had just been released and the crippling effect these would have on next quarter's accounts retention.

"You guys seen Mr. Raven?" I asked.

Max pointed to a wall covered with pamphlets and book displays, beneath a giant video banner that said "Keep the PASE," where Mr. Raven was talking to a member of the board of directors I'd only seen at weekend retreats and regional conferences. He was walking two fingers across his open palm as if to illustrate a story about someone running.

Deciding to wait for a more private moment to talk to him, I studied an orientation packet until the loudspeakers announced that the seminar was about to begin, whereupon we filed into a vast auditorium with sloped stadium seating that ringed an oval stage on which a thick wooden podium stood like a tree trunk. I sat between Max and Ravi and arranged my handheld devices on the pull-out desktop. Calibrated the personal light settings. Stretched and cracked my neck. Max ate a thick chocolate donut and held a cheese Danish in his lap.

"What?" he asked.

"Nothing," I said.

"You could have gotten your own."

"I've quit eating sweets as part of my post-surgery diet."

On the stage down below a man in a dark brown suit approached the podium and clipped a microphone to his tie just below the knot. Tapping it twice, he said, "Good morning. My name is Denver Stevens, and I'm the PASE corporate activities director. I'd like to begin today's events by saying that although they are open to men of all faiths and creeds, our approach will use techniques and ideas developed in Prescription for a Superior Existence. This powerful spiritual system, parts of which will become familiar to you today, can help liberate you from the dangers of overintimacy at the workplace."

There was so much work to do on Danforth in so little time. Either my computer and email programs had randomly and momentarily malfunctioned or someone had sabotaged them. If the latter, who would do it and why? No one personally benefited if the report was late. Our computer system's firewall was the best in the industry. I had no enemies.

When Denver Stevens stopped talking and left the stage to respectful applause, the lights dimmed and people shifted around in their seats. I began to feel panicky, as though stuck in traffic going to the airport, and I might have snuck back to the office if at that moment a spotlight hadn't interrupted the darkness to shine on a man climbing the steps to the stage. Like a wax figure, Montgomery Shoale too perfectly resembled images of him I'd seen in the media: short and barrel-chested, wearing a perfectly tailored suit, with a relaxed executive presence. Around the base of his bald skull a two-inch band of white hair angled down into a trim Viennese beard.

"Hello," he said in a soft baritone that through the room's space-age acoustics sounded everywhere at once. "We're delighted to have you with us today. When your chief executive operator, Mr. Hof-brau, called me to arrange this seminar, I was saddened but not surprised to hear about recent events at Couvade, and I assured him that our primary concern here is with helping people—with helping you—more fully appreciate what it means to have a personal and a professional self, and how to improve in each until perfection is inevitable. As the great Russian doctor and writer Anton Chekhov once observed, 'Man will become better when you show him what he is like.' We hope that after today's activities you will know yourselves better and so *be* better."

One of the other candidates for the senior manager promotion might have wanted to hurt my prospects in order to bolster his or her own, but I couldn't think of any who had both the refined Machiavellian instincts and the technological skill to intercept my email and override my password file protection.

"I don't know you all as individuals. Sitting beside a vegetarian might be a carnivore. Next to a pacifist, a war-supporter. There may be two men among you who claim nothing in common but an employer, and even that may be a bone of contention. As human beings, however—and more specifically as men—you are in many crucial ways the same. You eat and sleep and wear clothes. You use language to communicate. You feel joy and anger and love. You were born and you are going to die." He took a sip of water. "From these common traits we can draw certain conclusions: eating reflects a common desire for food, sleep meets a desire for rest, and clothes answer a desire for warmth and propriety." He paused and I looked for Mr. Raven in the audience. "We could spend a whole day—a whole lifetime, perhaps—talking about your desires and what is done to gratify them, but today we're interested in one in particular: your desire for sex."

I asked Max in a low voice if he would give me the Danish, and he said no.

"You might ask what is wrong with sex and point out that no one, with the exception of a few test-tube babies, would be here without it. You might say that it is a fundamental part of us. That would be understandable. At one time I myself would have said the same things, for I too once knew the full force and function of sexual desire, the urge that begins with the sight of a pair of legs or a bawdy joke or a warm object held in one's lap, and grows until nothing matters but the satisfaction of that urge. And like many of you here today, I believed that I was fine." Shoale took another sip of water. "But was that true? Are you fine? Your eyes, like mine were, are forever restless in their sockets; you covet your neighbors' wives and sisters and daughters and mothers; you fidget from the time you wake up until you go to sleep, and even then the fidgeting doesn't stop. You're like live wires that can't be grounded for more than a few hours at a time." He let this sink in for a moment. "The majority of sexual attraction takes place in the mind, where you are, in a word, distracted. Deeply so. And what are the consequences of this distraction?" A few hands rose timidly in the air. "You contract costly, disfiguring, sometimes even deadly diseases; your marriages break up; your job performance suffers; you hurt others and subsidize prostitution and make false promises. You become dissatisfied with life and lose the respect of your friends, families, and coworkers. You don't say hello to someone without figuring the odds of getting them into your useworn bed. You spend idle, obsessive hours poring over Internet pornography like prospectors burning with gold fever, and in the end a sad onanist looks out at you from the mirror." Next to me, Max was breathing heavily. "This is a sickness as debilitating as tuberculosis or emphysema. You are aware of its symptoms, yet you don't try to get well."

My thoughts swung between Danforth and Shoale's speech and my fatigue from not having had any replenishing sleep in three months. With a small cough Max stood up and stalked out to the aisle, ignoring the grunts of men whose knees he banged.

"Is he okay?" I whispered to Dexter, who'd sat on the other side of him.

Dexter shrugged.

Max ran up the aisle and out the door. I thought about going after him but spotted Mr. Raven seven rows down and twelve columns over, staring at me with eyes as dark and cold as two black moons, so I returned my focus to the stage and tried to concentrate on what was being said.

This opening speech made me wonder why our CEO thought the seminar would be helpful. Some of the incidents Shoale had alluded to at Couvade were serious—a vice-president was being sued by his secretary for telling her inappropriate jokes, an accounts manager had downloaded a virus-infected pornography file onto his work computer that immobilized our entire system for two days, a field representative had been arrested for buying a child bride in Indonesia, and of course there was my squad's own ill-executed trip to Chicago—but such a stridently antisex message seemed farcical and doomed to fail with the men of Couvade, whom I'd seen at bachelor parties and after-work clubs and company retreats to Florida.

The rest of the day's content, however, was more effective. After Shoale's talk we watched a documentary about sex crimes and one about the ravages of sexually transmitted diseases that featured disturbing footage of a syphilitic man having his nose surgically removed. Then we had lunch and came back to form small discussion groups and role-play exercises—when alone with someone we found attractive, we were to talk only about work-related subjects, even if that person tried to make things personal—before concluding the day with a lecture from Shoale that took a more positive, empowering tone than his first: "You have the ability to be as great as anyone who ever walked the Earth," he said. "Gandhi, Buddha, and even Jesus suffered the same temptations and trembled from the same desires that you do. What made them different—what can make you different—is that they heeded the call of their best selves. They made the choice, as you can, to rise above the squalor of desire."

Several men around me nodded thoughtfully while gathering together their things.

From there I raced back to the office and finished Danforth at four A.M. Then I went home, slept for three hours, and by nine the next morning was seated at my cubicle, where I opened an email from Mr. Raven. I felt a burning sensation in my right wrist and popped two homeopathic pills that went on to have no effect.

"Mr. Raven?" I knocked lightly on his door.

"Come in," he said, pushing aside his keyboard. Commemorative posters of marathons and charity races covered the wall space not taken up with shelves of corporate histories, mambo primers, and presidential biographies. Through the window I could see latticed scaffolding in front of a former hotel being converted to office space. Mr. Raven patted his gelled gray hair, which lay frozen across his scalp like a winter stream.

"Sit down," he said, moving things around on his desk—a box of chocolate mints, a pair of Mongolian relaxation balls, a penknife—and fingering a reddish birthmark on his chin. "I assume you know why I want to see you."

"Is it about Danforth Ltd.?"

Mr. Raven appreciated candor about painful or difficult subjects, as well as when bold action was required. We'd discussed Harry Truman once and, while acknowledging and finding fault with his faults, we'd approvingly measured the strength of his character—its unflinching directness—because of which he could say without hypocrisy that the buck stopped with him. A true leader saw, identified, and accepted mistakes while learning how not to repeat them.

"Please tell me why it was late."

"I first sent it to you on Tuesday and didn't know that you hadn't received it until yesterday morning. I would have done it again right away except that the sensitivity training seminar was about to start."

"Which your actions largely occasioned."

"That's—"

A questioning look settled on Mr. Raven's face.

I drew my left ankle up onto my right knee and pulled at the pant leg material. "As you know, there were four of us in Chicago. I didn't see the credit card Juan used and figured it was his personal one, and we'd pay him back later. This isn't to say I'm blameless— the whole thing reflected bad judgment, including my own—but I've already had my wages garnished to make up my quarter of the expense account item, and I formally addressed the Employee Conduct Board last week and volunteered to do community service as well as—"

Mr. Raven leaned forward with a hard, penetrating look and said, "Let's cut the folderol."

"Excuse me?"

"We both know you're a sick man."

"Excuse me?"

"Your performance at Couvade has been greatly compromised lately, and you now have a choice. You can take a leave of absence and get healthy. Check into a sex addiction clinic like the PASE Wellness Center in Daly City. Work on this problem and beat it. Or you can accept the ten demerit points I'll have to issue you for Danforth Ltd., which combined with your ten demerits from the Employee Conduct Board would total the twenty required for me to fire you."

I swallowed thickly and felt the beginning of a sinus headache, of my tear ducts opening and throat constricting. Mr. Raven pushed a box of tissues toward me. I rose and then sat back down.

"The Board is giving us ten demerits?"

"You'll get a copy of their written decision."

"I don't understand."

Mr. Raven's voice softened and his forehead relaxed, lowering his hair a quarter inch. "It's going to be okay. You'll undergo treatment and then, following a probationary period of not less than eighteen months, I'll review your case and consider your coming back to work for Couvade."

"No, this is wrong. Danforth was a mysterious accident, and I'd like to appeal to the Conduct Board for a reduced penalty."

"It's too late for that."

"You're telling me this for the first time right now!"

Mr. Raven, still holding the base of the tissue box, pulled it away from me and then picked up his phone. "Don't make me call security."

"But I'm being railroaded. You can't—What if you call the system administration department and ask them to recover my Tuesday computer profile and they'll tell you that I'm not lying about Danforth? In a situation this serious, you have to!"

I quit yelling and Mr. Raven set down his phone and we stared at a midway point between us for the seventy-three seconds it took two building security officers to arrive and lift me to my feet. I weighed a thousand pounds in their arms.

CHAPTER 3

Following my meeting with Ms. Anderson at the Wellness Center, the escorts took me to the dining hall, a high-ceilinged oval room with rectangular metal tables, where, arriving as the others were finishing, I ate a four-egg omelet with sausage links and home fries. Nothing tasted as good as it looked, being made of the sort of low-fat, low-cholesterol ingredients that I'd bought after my surgery and then never again, but I took comfort in the act of eating and didn't get up from the table until my escorts said that the orientation meeting was about to start in the Celestial Commons building. I would have argued that I didn't care about missing the beginning—or the middle or the end—if I thought they'd care that I didn't care; instead I followed them out.

Having felt like an animal caught in a steel trap during my conversation with Ms. Anderson—when I discovered that I lacked the strength to chew off my own foot—just then I felt calm and self-possessed. I walked steadily between my escorts. This was all temporary. Conrad must have understood PASE's role in my being shot and taken away, meaning either the police or FBI would arrive at any minute to rescue me from this horrible compound. It was important that I not panic, that I keep my wits and be ready to level sane and convincing charges against my captors. A cigarette would have helped, or a stick of nicotine gum, or an assortment of pills with something liquid to chase them, but I made tight fists and clenched my jaw and knew that this was about to be over. Back in the courtyard I looked for signs of disturbance, not knowing if the authorities would drop from a helicopter in a SWAT team raid or storm the front gate, or if their warrant and tact would help them avoid an open and violent confrontation with the Center's security guards. Everything was quiet. The escorts looked straight ahead, one in front and the other behind me. As a giant clock tower struck eight A.M., I tried not to think of what was delaying my rescuers.

The orientation meeting, in a room on the first floor of the Celestial Commons building, was led by Mr. and Mrs. Rubin—a small, round couple with nearly identical bodies, like two pieces in a Russian doll sequence, Mrs. Rubin could have nested snugly inside her husband—who handed me a notebook and a small bottled water and introduced me to the four other new arrivals at the Wellness Center: Rema, a tax assessor from Seattle; Shang-lee, a chemical engineering graduate student at Stanford; Alice, an obstetrician from Alameda; and Star, a retired "friend to gentlemen" from Key West. I sat in the chair closest to the door and waited for the door behind me to open and my release to be effected.

Mrs. Rubin rolled up her tunic sleeves and stepped forward. "Does anyone have a question before we begin?"

"No," answered Mr. Rubin immediately. "Okay, first of all, congratulations on taking the first, most difficult step toward improving. The worst is already behind you. From now on, each successive step will be easier than the last until, near the end, your feet will hardly touch the ground as you bound toward the perfection of UR God. But I must warn you that this won't come at the same time for everyone. Just because you're here in orientation together does not mean you will progress with identical speed. Some Pasers advance quickly and others slowly, which is okay because we are not in a race. UR God will be as ready for you in fifty years as in fifty days."

A short but purposeful knock came at the door. Mr. and Mrs. Rubin looked at each other quizzically and then moved in concert toward it. Trembling with relief, I envisioned the squad of armed men about to enter, call my name or even recognize my face, and lead me back to my apartment, where I could expect the law's full protection until my safety was established. Which wouldn't take long. Once PASE's criminal intentions toward me were proven beyond question—a day? two days?—my only concern would be how much to ask for in damages. As far as I knew, Shoale's private fortune had been blended into PASE's coffers, meaning I might expect millions—perhaps tens of millions—of dollars, depending on how sympathetic a jury I got. Couvade would probably offer me a vice-presidency or some equally nice sinecure to restore its main-stream image and distance itself from the PASE fallout. Women from all over the Bay Area and beyond would read about me and, their interest piqued in someone who had almost been murdered before being forced into a celibacy camp and then awarded an enor-mous compensation settlement, seek me out. Yes, for several sec-onds in that orientation room, at the end of a row of desperately gullible people from whose rank I was about to escape, I foresaw a hasty and lucrative resolution to all of my problems. Part of me even dared to imagine Mary Shoale, whom I loved more with every passing second, seizing the moment to break from her father and make me the happiest of men. What had been my terrible luck was going to be flipped around and turned right side up.

Except that it wasn't. Mr. and Mrs. Rubin cautiously opened the door, consulted in whispers with a young man and woman in regu-lation tunics, and then returned to the center of the room, smiling as though they had swallowed a bottle of Percodan.

"Sorry for the interruption," Mr. Rubin said, "but we've just received wonderful news. Tonight, following Synergy, Montgomery Shoale will make a major announcement via a live video address that we'll watch at the Prescription Palace. You are new here and so can't appreciate how rare and magnificent an event this is, but to give you some perspective I'll say that it's been many months since Mr. Shoale last spoke to us."

"Five months," said Mrs. Rubin gently, though with a correcting tone.

"He is close to becoming an ur-savant, and this could be his last public appearance. You will witness history in the making."

Shang-lee, whose unlined face and glinting gray hairs placed him between twenty and fifty, and who, besides me, was the only one not reflecting the Rubins' smile, adjusted his small round spectacles, raised a bony hand, and said, "What's an ur-savant?"

"You will learn about the savant stages later today in class," said Mrs. Rubin. "Our purpose now is to provide you with background on the Wellness Center, its history and aims and rules of conduct, so that you'll know what to expect and how to behave while here."

During the ensuing account, told in alternating sections by the Rubins, I fought against the fear that every passing minute made my rescue less likely, that if the police weren't there yet it was because Conrad hadn't told them. Or they disbelieved him. Or they were in league with PASE and, even given proof that I was being held against my will, not going to help me. I closed my eyes and willed the door to open, an amateur's telekinesis. At nine A.M.—twelve hours since I'd been shot and kidnapped—full of disappointment and desire for pills and alcohol and tobacco, I wiped away two tears caught in my eyelashes and fought down a rumbling nausea.

Mr. and Mrs. Rubin explained that this Wellness Center, a mere three miles from the San Francisco PASE Station, had been built eight years earlier based on a blueprint drawn up by Montgomery Shoale and provided through revelation by UR God. The first of its kind, it provided the model for the other Wellness Centers subsequently established in Los Angeles, Houston, Chicago, and New York, as well as for those planned in or near Buenos Aires, São Paulo, Edinburgh, Cornwall, Tangiers, Marseilles, Utrecht, Riga, Seoul, and Sidney. Mrs. Rubin punched something into a laptop computer and a montage of photos blanketed the wall behind her showing the various stages of each new Center's completion. Like the Daly City original, they were all set on four acres and would, when completed, have an outdoor park with a botanical garden, a meditation post, two residential dormitories (one for men and one for women), an education building (Celestial Commons), a screening facility (Prescription Palace), a hospital (Freedom Place), a library and administration building (Shoale Hall), a recreation building, a dining hall, and a church (Synergy Station). They would all house forty guests at a time, an even number of men and women, whose activities would be fully integrated.

Although the architecture varied slightly from one Center to another, as did the flowers in the botanical garden and the food served in the dining halls to reflect local produce and culinary traditions, life would follow a set schedule at all of them: 6 A.M. wake up. 6:30 A.M. exercises. 7:15 A.M. breakfast. 8 A.M. reading/studying. 10 A.M. counseling. 12 P.M. lunch. 1 P.M. class. 3:30 P.M. individual research. 4:30 P.M. recreation. 6 P.M. dinner. 7:30 P.M. all-guest activity. 10 P.M. lights-out. On Sundays there was a thirty-minute Synergy session at 7 P.M.

And what exactly was the purpose of a Wellness Center? What did Montgomery Shoale hope it would accomplish? Although in practice its functions and benefits were too many to count, it was designed to speed along neophytes' and longtime Pasers' journey toward permanent synergy with UR God, the fusion of everyone into His vast being and thus the end of human strife on Earth. Shoale's goal was our own. He personally interviewed all the doctors and staff, who then underwent a rigorous training program and six-month probation period before being brought to work at a Center full-time. He kept in close contact with all the individual directors and monitored the progress of their operations worldwide.

In addition to treating the normal range of behaviors that had to be modified and/or eliminated—sexuality, rage, material greed, television, Internet abuse, etc.—the Center was equipped to help people with problems involving addiction, extreme emotional imbalance, and psychiatric disorders. According to its strictly refined physical and spiritual practices, it helped these unfortunate guests using a holistic approach to mind and body and soul wellness taken from *The Prescription,* which, in its wisdom, recognized that while everyone needed to improve, some were, at the time they reached adolescence or adulthood, at such a deficit that they required extreme and immediate preimprovement treatment. For example, the Center's hospital included a Seclusion Ward that provided twenty-four-hour care for sufferers from drug withdrawal, during which the guests' isolation was leavened by audio recordings of Montgomery Shoale lectures, as well as by frequent use of a Synergy device and special stretching techniques favored by UR God and interpreted by Mr. Shoale. PASE enjoyed a hundred percent success rate in curing heroin, cocaine, and methamphetamine addiction, as it did with freeing guests of anger, violent tendencies, schizophrenia, bipolar disorder, depression, generalized anxiety, misanthropy, boredom, acute narcissism, and—

"What are you doing, Mr. Smith?" Mr. Rubin asked, cutting off his wife's speech.

I'd gotten up from my seat and walked to a window overlooking the courtyard. "Just checking something." As when I'd crossed it earlier, there were no policemen or FBI agents visible, though I told myself that they could be talking to Ms. Anderson or some other administration figure, trying to ascertain where I was being kept, on the verge of taking the noncooperative Pasers into custody and beginning an exhaustive hunt around the premises for me. I looked for a latch or lever with which to open the window—thinking I would scream out for help and catch the attention of either the law or someone passing by on the other side of the Center wall—but it was sealed shut.

I heard Mr. Rubin take a few steps toward me and then stop. "During instructional sessions like this one, there is a basic protocol for being excused from your seat to go to the bathroom or attend to another Center-approved activity. Please sit back down and I'll explain it to you."

"I'd rather stand here, if you don't mind."

Mrs. Rubin said, "We do. We mind very much."

A door opened in the building across the courtyard and two men emerged, one of whom wasn't wearing a blue tunic. I tried to make out whether he had a metallic badge on his breast or walked as officiously as someone in the intelligence community, but at that distance I couldn't tell.

"We really must insist," said Mr. Rubin. "Please don't make this difficult for us and yourself."

The two men walked in my direction and disappeared under the foliage of a pair of eucalyptus trees shooting up like twin geysers in the middle of the courtyard.

"Go on with what you were saying," I said, waiting for the non-tunic man to come back into view, when he would be close enough for me to make out his clothing and features. But then four meaty hands gripped my arms, turned me around, and roughly pulled me back to my seat. My escorts withdrew from the room after nodding tersely to Mrs. Rubin, who bit her lower lip and looked at me pityingly.

I stared with dull hatred at the Rubins, who said that they would now go over the basic rules of conduct so that such disciplinary measures wouldn't be necessary again. Anarchy did not reign at the PASE Wellness Center. Some actions were forbidden and others encouraged. In the first category, we were not allowed to leave the Center or receive visitors without permission. Television, books, and the Internet were okay with some built-in restrictions, for which reason certain programs and periodicals and websites were blocked or made inaccessible. We could not drink alcohol, take non-prescribed drugs, or engage in any sexual activity, including with ourselves. Profanity was prohibited, as was licentious talk and any attempt to leave the Center grounds before the facilitators deemed it appropriate. Disputes between guests were to be taken to a facilitator and should not involve violence or violent intent.

I thought I heard footsteps in the hall outside but it was just my teeth grinding.

Mr. and Mrs. Rubin knew that these restrictions sounded harsh. No one liked to be told they couldn't do something. But Montgomery Shoale had devised them for our health and safety; otherwise our improvement would be no more possible than rain without clouds. Much was asked of guests at the Center, and in return much was given. We were worthy, infinitely capable people, for we came from UR God and would be with Him again someday. We had to bear in mind that reaching this destination was the most difficult, rewarding journey we would ever undertake.

"Did you say there's going to be Synergy tonight?" I asked.

"Yes," said Mr. Rubin.

"What is Synergy?" asked Shang-lee.

"So today is Sunday?"

"Synergy," said Mrs. Rubin, while smoothing out a kerchief she'd held bunched in her left hand, "is the feeling of being fused into UR God."

Mr. Rubin added, "It can be had on this planet in one of two ways. The first is with a Synergy device, which is like a big gyroscope that you stand in with electrodes connected to your temples. Synergy is, you'll find, the most wonderful feeling imaginable, and when you become an ur-savant it is the only one you will ever experience again."

"Sunday the nineteenth?" I said.

Mr. Rubin nodded and I leaned over and tried to throw up. I had been shot on Friday the seventeenth, meaning I had been unconscious for an entire day, meaning any immediate attempt to rescue me from the Wellness Center would already have ended. There was no cavalry on the way, no quick response to my dilemma. And this whole situation was neither a joke nor a social experiment. A camera crew was not filming behind a fake wall, ready to ask me how it felt to believe that I'd been forced into a PASE indoctrination camp. There was no winking host or thoughtful documentarian orchestrating my deception in a cruel and elaborate prank, and I would not have the chance to talk about how similar it was to my childhood fear of being sent to an orphanage full of seemingly well-intentioned people who were in fact bent on destroying my will. This was real.

Unable to vomit, I sat back and the orientation session ended. The Rubins thanked us for being good listeners and handed out information packets with a map of the Center grounds, a personalized schedule listing our counseling session and class locations, a rulebook, a pocket-sized edition of *The Prescription for a Superior Existence,* and a personal digital assistant with electronic copies of everything. The other guests, eyes on their packets, rose and filed out of the room, and Mrs. Rubin asked me civilly if I needed assistance in getting to my next event.

My itinerary said I was supposed to be in Room 227 of the Celestial Commons building, one floor above, so I left the room and paused to look up and down the hallway, where Shang-lee's back was receding toward an Exit sign that marked the stairwell and elevator. Single escorts were placed at fifty-foot intervals between us, as motionless and erect as suits of armor. I passed these hollow men in their blue tunics, reached the stairs, and climbed them deliberately, going over problems that configured themselves in my head as a tetrahedron, with my separation from Mary on one side, my present incarceration on a second, my forced sobriety on a third, and my unemployment—with its implications for my debts—on a fourth. The first and fourth sides existed in the outside world, to which I didn't have access presently, while the second and third affected me then and there, and had to be overcome. Which I didn't know how to do. Shang-lee, Rema, Alice, and Star were out of sight when I got to the second-floor landing, apparently already in their counseling rooms.

A short man in his midforties with a flat nose, sparse hair, and ruddy complexion met me at the door of Room 227. His name was Mr. Ramsted, and he invited me to sit at an oblong mahogany table with attached seats that slid back and forth on floor tracks, where the other guests—Ang, Brian, Eli, Rema, Quenlon, Amanda, Tyrone, Helmut, Sarah, Summer, and Mihir—introduced themselves. For the benefit of Rema and me, the only newcomers to counseling, Mr. Ramsted explained the sessions' format: on days not designated for group discussion, a guest told the story of how his or her problem developed up until the time they chose to enter the Wellness Center. Then the other guests would make observations and suggestions and corroborations, and Mr. Ramsted—who throughout his twenties had been a sex addict, practically living in the Castro's bathhouses, and who therefore possessed authority beyond that of just being an actuated savant—would provide his own insights into what was wrong with us and how we could improve.

"Jack," he said, "since this is your first day, why don't you start our session by telling us the history of your problem?"

"What problem?"

"With sex."

"I don't have one."

"You do."

"I don't."

"Let's not waste everyone's time, please."

This echo of my exchange with Ms. Anderson was an effective piece of psychological torture. I slid my chair back to the end of its groove. The faces around the table looked at me impatiently, as though I were an actor who'd come onstage in costume and makeup to say that the evening's performance would not go on because I didn't look the part.

"I don't belong here," I said.

Addressing the rest of the table as a prosecutor would a jury, Mr. Ramsted said, "Are you saying you're completely satisfied with your sexual history?"

"Yes," I answered.

"All of it."

"Yes."

"That's amazing. I've met confirmed libertines, people who would rather have sex than bring about world peace, who can't say as much."

The walls were a creamy orange and air ducts in the ceiling circulated a cool breeze. The windows' shades were drawn and I pictured what was happening on the other side of them—nothing. I felt as though I were tumbling down a mountain while the static world spun around me. My lower back was alight with discomfort and I placed my wrists gingerly on the tabletop, where they glowed yellow in the reflected varnish, thinking that if I remained completely still the pain in them would settle down to an acceptable throb.

"What do you want to hear?"

Mr. Ramsted pursed his lips and rubbed his nose, the divot in the bridge of which suggested an old fracture. "I want an explanation of the incredible statement you just made. I want you to confirm that you've never made an unwanted pass or offended a partner in bed. That you've never had an inappropriate dream about a family member or friend. That you've never lusted after someone too young or too old. That you've never had erectile dysfunction or gotten an erection when you shouldn't have. That you don't fantasize too much or too intensely. And that you think back on all your sexual encounters with approval and sanguinity."

"I do."

After a pause Mr. Ramsted said, "Rema, let's hear about your experiences."

"From the time I was a kid?" she said.

He rose and began slowly circling the table. "Just be honest. Without honesty no one can hope to grow or improve or come to know the truth." He looked at me and continued his orbit. "You know what Alexander Pope said: 'An honest Man's the noblest work of God.' And Emily Dickinson wisely wrote: 'Truth is as old as God, / His twin identity—and will endure as long as He, / A co-eternity . . .' And Jesus said, 'You will know the truth, and the truth will set you free.' Honesty is the bedrock of Prescription for a Superior Existence, as it is the policy of every right-thinking adult who aspires to succeed in this life and the next."

Rema then gave a nearly two-hour account of her sexual biography, starting full throttle at age thirteen and accelerating through twenty years of rogue-gallery men and dithyrambic women, in bedrooms and public parks and water closets and interstate train bathrooms, in and out of schools, in and out of jobs, in and out of in and out. It was a smoldering, exhaustive, unpredictable, and inventive monologue that, had it been told breathily instead of with evident pain and shame and self-censure, could have been turned into a podcast sensation. I was enthralled and uncomfortably aroused throughout most of it, and my problems seemed as small as dust mites.

"I have to cut this short," Mr. Ramsted finally said, giving me another reason to resent him, "and forgo our chance to comment, which is unfortunate because this tragic story puts into stark relief the misery caused by our libidos, in exemplary fashion, but it's time for lunch. I'd like to thank Rema for her brave, unstinting account of two decades' worth of mistakes. I asked for honesty and she provided it generously."

Mihir fell in line beside me on the way to the dining hall and said that despite my obstinate behavior during exercises and counseling, I hadn't ruined my chances at the Wellness Center. I could yet make up for it. At the serving line as I selected six pieces of pepperoni pizza and a tall fruit juice, he said he understood my attitude, which, although counterproductive and immature, was to be expected at first. Men were brought up to brag about their exploits, not confess them, so we felt cognitive dissonance when learning that our every sexual thought from the moment puberty stretched and dropped our genitals was a debasement of our truest self. It had taken him five days to work up the courage and to develop the perspective to tell his story.

"Is that right?" I said, disappointed by the pizza before even tasting it.

He ladled salad dressing over a plate of tomatoes. "Now I love to tell my story. Every time I do I feel such relief and gratitude that I changed before it was too late. As recently as one month ago I was like a person eating red meat three meals a day without any thought for his cholesterol level, as though I had a good reason to be cavalier about my diet, as though heart attacks were as uncommon as Huntington's disease! One month. Perhaps you would like to hear my story now."

We stopped, holding our trays of food, to look around the room for a place to sit.

"I just want to eat."

"That is not a problem. I will give you the abridged version, not go into the painstaking exact details. You will get more from it than you did from Rema's, because as a woman her methods and goals of seduction were necessarily different from yours, her experience more complicated and harder to relate to. My story, on the other hand, coming from a man's perspective, will show that you aren't alone in your depravity, that sex does not actually prove your power and virility, and that you must step out of the orgasm rut."

We found an empty table beside a bay window facing the Center entrance, and Mihir shook the salt and pepper dispensers over his plate. "I am married," he said, "and have cheated on my wife, according to a conservative estimate I made just last Tuesday, more than eight hundred times in the twelve years of our marriage, beginning within twenty-four hours of our wedding vows, when my driver's daughter took me to the office while her father saw a dentist, and ending the day before I came here. I intimately knew a dozen prostitutes in my neighborhood and fathered seven children out of wedlock, one of whom is the finest junior cricketer in southeast New Delhi. All seemed to be going well, with of course some minor problems, until three weeks ago, when after an afternoon dalliance with two British backpackers I came home from work and found my wife threatening to castrate my eldest son, who shares my name, unless I agreed never to have sex with anyone but her again. You should have seen the cold resolve of this woman, such as she had never shown before, ready to mutilate her own child to restore a fidelity that I considered to be an impossible dream. Well, here, look, this is a picture of her taken at the airport the next day. She made calm accusations that were all true and I denied them fiercely—I tell you I felt no guilt about my past behavior or my present lies and thought that the only injustice would be if I were forced to admit wrongdoing and then forswear doing it again, for yes I was a sociopath!—but she had hired a private detective, and she produced video footage and compiled written testimony from my disgruntled former mistresses. I was caught and would you believe that even then I feebly tried to explain away the evidence as either having happened before our marriage or been part of my job? According to my pathetic story many women clients of my company would have gone with a rival had I refused to sleep with them. My wife grabbed the knife sharpener in the middle of these excuses and my son cried and swayed in place like a hungry beggar. Ten minutes later, with my son's pants around his ankles and his penis pulled taut in her hand, seeing that she was not bluffing, I acknowledged everything. I told her about all the women and all the occasions and do you know what, instantly this had a remarkable effect on both of us. She went from composed resolution to tears, and I went from being an indignant child weighed down by complicated lies and self-justifications to being for the first time in my life an adult able to look at myself, if not dispassionately, at least from another's point of view. I felt a type of levity then, almost an ecstasy, and as my wife's tears fell I apologized and comforted her and explained truthfully that my former life was over, that I would not go back to covering up and misleading and hurting those who meant most to me. By decree I ended the lies and recriminations and performance enhancement supplements that had compromised me for years, during which time sex had so darkened my perspective that I felt just then as if I were stepping out of a cave and into the light of day. By evening time we were discussing our future together, and my son was happily doing his homework. It was the rebirth of our love. Yet I knew even as we made new pledges that my body could betray me and my resolve could falter and that I needed more than self-help, so I looked into programs that fostered celibacy and found information about the PASE Wellness Center."

The pizza tasted like air. "Your wife must be happy."

"At first, yes, she was overjoyed, but now that I have learned the truth of PASE and know that all sex is unnecessary, including with her, she is less supportive. In fact we have had some trying conversations on the phone and it's clear to me that she must come here herself, for I am worried about her own salvation. At present, however, she refuses to even consider it. This causes me great disquietude."

By then five other people had joined our table. One of them, seventeen-year-old Tyrone, who was in our counseling group, said that he wished to have a tenth of Mihir's resolve. A pimply boy with crowded teeth and a slightly hunched back, he confessed that he was a chronic masturbator who had backslid the day before and been forced, as part of the treatment, to send a picture of himself in midact—taken by one of the microscopic cameras planted all over the Wellness Center—to everyone in his email address book, with exaggerated close-ups of his face and hands reserved for his teachers, grandparents, and parents' friends. If he slipped again the picture would be delivered to any schools and employers he approached in the future.

"Why don't you take an inhibitor?" asked Warren, a dark-haired Bostonian with a sharp widow's peak who, Mihir whispered to me, due to his rage issues had beaten up a small Filipino woman for not crediting his expired coupon at a supermarket, and was at the Wellness Center in lieu of serving half his prison sentence.

"As if they're around," said Tyrone, forking a cherry tomato that squirted onto his hand.

"What's an inhibitor?" I asked.

"A chemical injection that lowers your sperm count and prevents you from achieving and sustaining an erection," said Mihir, with a forbidding shake of his head. "It's a type of antiaphrodisiac and PASE does not allow it."

"Out of fear," said Warren.

Mihir said, looking at Warren as he would a stranger cutting ahead in line, "One doesn't conquer desire and become compatible with UR God by taking inhibitors."

"UR God cares about ends, not means."

Mihir raised his voice. "You can't achieve lasting synergy with Him if you've merely put desire into a closet instead of throwing it out for good. Any declared Paser can tell you that; it is basic teaching."

Warren cut the remainder of his steak into diamond-shaped bites, the muscles of his forearms moving independently like machine parts. "If you don't get in fights or have sex or whatever, you're going to mainline UR God without any problem. It's all about results and there's no point in having this debate like we're too stupid to know as much."

Mihir set down his clean silverware, folded his napkin, and said, dropping his voice to a chilly undertone, "You are prattling on stupidly in front of a new guest who is my mentee. I'd rather you not confuse or dishearten him, so if you must speak rubbish perhaps you could do it at another table."

"Are you going to say that when someone on the outside challenges you? Are you going to ask them to go away? That won't bring one more person to UR God."

"As if you care about Him or yourself or the goal of improving! You care only for appearances, not substance. Reality Fact Number Thirty-two in *The Prescription* states clearly: 'Not everyone will embrace the truth.' On the outside I will not bother trying to convince such persons as yourself, who are incapable of the necessary sacrifices."

Warren smiled. "I think you're forgetting Reality Fact Number Twelve: 'He who thinks he knows the nature of UR God is like a child convinced he can speak a foreign language after hearing it once.'"

"Reality Fact Number Eight: 'The way to UR God can no more be shortened than can a ladder stretching from the ground to the moon.'"

"Reality Fact Number Five: 'There is room for every aspirant in the body of UR God, as there is for every note in the body of music.'"

"Reality Fact Number Three: 'Desire has a thousand faces; take care to destroy the one that most resembles yours.'"

"All right," said Eli, a leathery old man from our counseling group, a retired fisherman from the Puget Sound area who'd built a crystal meth lab in his basement and blown off all his left-hand fingers in an explosion the year before, and who'd managed to keep using the drug for a week before someone found him sleeping in their driveway and sent him to the first of four rehabilitation centers he would attend in advance of this Wellness Center. "Let's just enjoy our food. We can settle this in class."

Mihir leaned over and told me that nearly everyone—99 percent of the guests—would and could improve, but that sometimes a wastrel such as Warren came through who was doomed to failure and I was to ignore him and his crude, perhaps intentional misunderstandings. Those full of poison delight in infecting others. Just ask the scorpion.

Mihir seemed in earnest and no more open to talk of escape or insurrection than a freshman at Harvard. I tried catching Warren's eye to see if by a wink or glance he might acknowledge that we were on the other side of the looking glass, but, however heretical Mihir considered him, he had a serene expression, as though internecine squabbles at the Center—and PASE itself—were great fun and in no way a sign of the religion's inanity.

When a Brazilian man named Caetano, sitting to Tyrone's left, launched into a description of how his former girlfriend had wanted him to do "unspeakable" things to her, which at first he had done willingly, thereby eclipsing his best self behind a "grunting, squealing" animal self, and which set in motion a sense of defilement that "spread like a cancer" and made part of him feel relieved when her death the previous December in a car crash released both of them from their sick physical entente—although she, dying without any contact with PASE, was suffering the agonies of non-being—a bizarre declaration that ought to have repelled everyone at the table but instead brought out their warmest sympathy, I concentrated on my pizza.

After lunch came the class period. While walking together to Celestial Commons, where all classes were held on the third floor, Mihir told me that I was in Introductory Level A with Mr. Ortega, who focused on the mechanics of the PASE hierarchy and simple exegeses of *The Prescription,* things that were self-evident and not challenging to intelligent persons such as ourselves. Luckily, it lasted for only five days and then I would move on to Introductory Level B, helmed by the inspiring, ethereally beautiful Ms. Webley, to whom I, like all guests, would form an intense nonsexual attachment that might show up in my dreams.

When I got to class, Mr. Ortega, a potbellied man with oversized hands and head, rolled up his sleeves and crossed his bandy legs and took no notice of me. Instead of sitting around an oblong table, we— all four guests from my orientation, a freckled and too-muscular Englishman named Alastair, a slender black woman with tight corn- rows named Tonya, a skinny Italian woman named Suzanne, and a zaftig blonde named Emma—sat in fold-out chairs arranged in a semicircle, with Mr. Ortega at the opening. If the seating arrange- ment was meant to satisfy our need for variety, it failed, but I was determined to treat this class like a work seminar, an occupational hazard to be endured quiescently, signifying nothing in itself. I may have been tumbling down a mountain but I would not worry any- more about the ground below. I was collecting my bearings.

"Today," Mr. Ortega said, tugging on his thick forearm hair— for this and his sloping forehead, rounded shoulders, and other simian qualities I felt a kinship with him—"we're going to talk about the six Paser stages. Can anyone begin by describing the dif- ference between a declared Paser and a savant?"

Everyone looked at their hands or laps uncomfortably until Alastair, in the posh accent that Americans affect to tell British jokes, said, "Isn't a savant basically like a more advanced declared Paser, in that he professes faith in UR God but takes it a step further by giving up sex? He walks the walk, in other words."

"Correct," said Mr. Ortega, "*if* sex is his or her favorite activity. It's important to note that you become a savant by giving up what- ever you most love to do, which isn't always sex. Many people live happily without that and therefore renounce nothing by renounc- ing sex. They need to look elsewhere in order to achieve savant sta- tus, such as to chocolate or gambling or cocaine or shoe shopping. The essence of being a savant is self-control; it demonstrates the beginning of your independence from the false joys of this world and shows your affinity with UR God."

This was all very boring and I remembered counseling wistfully and with a new fondness. I thought about Rema's various exploits, their audacity and imaginativeness, which, now that she'd joined PASE, would cease, and I grieved for their passing. Then, despite my earlier conclusion that half of what had gone wrong in my life was externally unchangeable and the other half internally so, and that I should not worry about where I was going—the bottom of the mountain toward which I was barreling—the tetrahedron of my problems rose up in my mind's landscape like a terrible portentous obelisk. It eclipsed everything else in my line of sight, so that I barely saw Shang-lee sitting next to me, his hands folded in his lap in bodhisattva fashion, and feared that I might pass out from terror at any minute. I badly wanted—I needed—a sedative and drink and cigarette and pornography and coffee and chocolate and lasagna and assurance that I would not languish here forever, that my absence meant something in the world at large.

Shang-lee asked me if I was all right and I nodded.

Mr. Ortega opened his hands questioningly at us, cocked an eyebrow, and then continued, "After you're a savant you become a functioning savant. In this stage you branch out beyond desire in its most active sense to work on curtailing your vanity and self-focus, the two biggest impediments to improvement. As a functioning savant you will think less about yourself and how others perceive you. To do this requires reducing the time and money you spend on clothes, cosmetics, hair care, entertainment, etc., and at the same time increasing your charitable contributions and your study of *The Prescription*. Both your reductions and your increases need to be substantial. For example, you can't buy four lipsticks instead of five and call that cutting back, nor can you spend eight hundred instead of nine hundred dollars on a new season's wardrobe. You must feel the deprivation of having less than you used to."

"How long does it take to go from being a savant to a functioning savant?" asked Tonya. Midway through Mr. Ortega's speech she had put down the emery board with which she'd been filing her nails, as though even this act of grooming might be unPASElike.

"The Rubins must have told you in orientation," said Mr. Ortega, "that everyone advances at their own speed, but I'll warn you that it's possible to go too slowly or too quickly. You can't become a functioning savant overnight, nor can you drag it out over ten years. The good news is that when you reenter the outside world you'll be able to consult with advanced Pasers at any PASE Station to come up with an appropriate timeline. Just remember that your improvement has to be real and consistent. You can't take breaks to do things you're not supposed to."

"Do you get a badge or a certificate when you move up a level?" Tonya asked.

"No."

"Then how's anyone supposed to know you're a functioning savant and not some starting-out type?"

"UR God will know and you will know. Nothing else matters."

"But it wouldn't be bad—you wouldn't get in trouble, right—if you wore a shirt that said 'functioning savant' on it or a button or a belt buckle."

"That would be fine. Now, after the functioning savant stage you will graduate to the master savant stage, which is defined by fewer desires, smaller meal portions, a commitment to buying only used clothes and no-brand hygienic items, further engagement with *The Prescription,* taking a leadership role in a local Paser study group, and active volunteering with the PASE Process, such as at one of its soup kitchens or homeless shelters or hospital terminal wards."

"I'd like to do something with the blind," said Alastair. "I'd like to read to them or take them to a museum."

Mr. Ortega made a displeased face and said, "Next you'll become an actuated savant. I, for example, got to this stage a year ago by memorizing large sections of *The Prescription,* whittling down my desire, eating modest meals without appetizers or desserts or alcohol, dressing mainly in my tunic, and making large contributions to the PASE Process."

"Does everyone have to be an actuated type to get a job here?" asked Tonya.

"It's a necessary prerequisite, yes, for becoming a facilitator, along with taking a test and undergoing an apprenticeship training program. The whole process takes about two months, and only a third of the applicants are then hired to be on staff."

"Are the tests hard?"

"They're challenging, yes."

"Did you have to know lots of names and dates? Because my intelligence isn't geared toward those per se. I'm more of a conceptual thinker, and I'm wondering if there's a type of test that would capitalize on that aspect of the mind as opposed to the dates."

"The tests are very concept-oriented, yes."

Mr. Ortega and Tonya went on for a while and to distract myself I drew up a mental list of people from whom I might ask to borrow money to pay my creditors until I found a job: my parents, though they'd retired the year before and were cash poor; my brother, Sid, who owed me three thousand dollars but wouldn't have it; Max, who carried almost as much credit card debt as I did; Supritha, whose family was wealthy but not fond of me; and Juan, who, having sold me out at Couvade, would probably avoid me forever. Mr. Ortega was nodding at Tonya and Alastair was scrawling notes and I was having revelations I'd had many times before. At age thirty-four you don't have the thousand options you had at twenty-four. If barred from the world of capital growth assessment, I effectively had none. Anxiety fell on me in droplets as corrosive as acid rain, and Mr. Ortega told a joke that made everyone laugh, and I saw no shelter big enough to cover me.

"Next," Mr. Ortega said, "comes the master actuated savant stage. This is the penultimate step you take before becoming an ur-savant. In it you renounce all desires beyond those necessary for maintaining a physical body, such as for food, water, heat, sleep, and oxygen. You have to know *The Prescription* backward and forward, give away whatever money and objects you don't immediately need, work with the sickest and most hobbled people in the vicinity, advocate nonviolence and universal tolerance, and take care of any unfinished business you may have in anticipation of becoming an ur-savant." He paused and cracked his knuckles. "I'm not going to lie or sugarcoat it: this is a difficult level. It requires a great deal of commitment—a superhuman control over your corporeal reality—so don't worry if it sounds impossible to you right now. No one when they first start jogging attempts an ultra marathon."

Normally when a person in a meeting lays out a preposterously hopeful forecast, when they talk about doubling a company's clients or tripling its revenue in a year, the realists in the room hasten to point out the obstacles to such a development, from the scarcity of potential new clients to increased competition to insufficient staffing, and quash the fantasy before anyone besides the initial speaker decides to believe in such nonsense. I listened to this description of a master actuated savant and expected someone to point out the patent absurdity of anyone—much less hundreds or thousands of Pasers—fulfilling its ascetic criteria, and when Alastair raised his hand, I looked to him as a mute would his advocate.

"That does sound like a difficult level," he said, tightening his mouth and closing his eyes halfway to suggest deep concentration. "One really has to change one's life around, it seems. More so than on the previous levels."

"That's what PASE is about," said Suzanne, tapping her foot against the leg of her chair. "If you're too weak or noncommittal to make it, you drop out and that's that. No one's forcing you to fuse into UR God."

"I'm not weak or noncommittal," said Alastair. "I'll make the changes necessary to improve; I'm just pointing out that there's a wider chasm between the actuated and the master actuated stages than what's come before."

"That's a defeatist's point."

Mr. Ortega cut in by saying, "Then, lastly, most wonderfully, you will attain ur-savant status and be ready for eternal synergy with UR God. At this stage you will be totally self-contained and perfect in every way. You will have no more need of this planet or your body. You will be what you were in the beginning and will be forever after, a wand waving about inside of UR God as an ecstatic part of the truth, a sliver of true harmolodic vibration."

Silence followed. I pulled at a thread coming from my chair's seat cushion and the clock ticked as loudly as a metronome. It became clear after a minute that no one would respond, that Alastair had been at best a semirealist and was now, following Suzanne's comment, even less of one. My standard aches and pains performed their dirge and my need for alcohol and a sealed bottle of anything swelled in my head and I knew not to speak—it didn't matter what these people told themselves, and I didn't want a repeat of my confrontation with Mr. Ramsted—but as the silence continued I couldn't stand it any longer.

"Are you saying," I asked, "that ur-savants don't eat or drink or breathe?"

"That's correct."

I yanked the thread free and wrapped it around my left pinkie, turning its tip pink. A fly landed on Alastair's knee, and he slapped his hand down and missed and it buzzed away at an angry pitch. "Then they must be dead."

"On the contrary, it is they who are truly alive, as part of UR God, fused synergistically into His being."

"But to everyone on planet Earth they must appear to be corpses."

The fly landed on Mr. Ortega's knee and was not lucky a second time. "You must understand that our bodies are holding vessels that no more own our spirit forever than a balloon does the air it contains. For example, you, Jack Smith, consider sex to be an integral part of yourself, whereas really it's a pointless pressure that, once released, will leave you free in its absence."

"I don't see how you can say that, or how you can say that an ur-savant isn't just a dead person. If sex isn't an integral part of me, nothing is." I was beginning to feel engaged and defensive against my will, for it seemed that this was more than a bidding war between common sense and uncommon belief; I wished someone else would play my part.

"You only think so because you've been brought up to expect to feel that way. Surely you know by now that much of what we're taught is wrong or misleading, that there are specious biological justifications floating around for our worst behavior."

"That's—I don't know what exactly you're talking about."

"Take meat eating, for example. People say our incisors are designed for cutting and our molars for crushing and tearing meat, which supposedly gives us the right to inhumanely raise and then slaughter millions of animals a year."

"What does that have to do with people deciding not to breathe or drink anymore?"

"I presume you haven't read *The Prescription*."

"No."

"It explains exactly what happens when we break free of our bodies and, if we've proven ourselves worthy of UR God, rise into Him. Its eloquence and truth are irrefutable."

"I refute them."

"You haven't read them yet."

"I refute *Mein Kampf* and a hundred other stupid manifestos I've never read."

"Those were all written by mortals. *The Prescription* was written by UR God."

"The Bible was written by the regular God, and I imagine it contradicts *The Prescription* all over the place."

"The temptation to endow a man-made book with legitimacy by saying that a higher power wrote it—whether it's the Bible, the Koran, *The Book of Mormon,* or what have you—has often tempted its authors."

"Like it did Montgomery Shoale."

"I recommend that you read *The Prescription* and then tell us what you think. That's not too much to ask, is it?"

When class ended Mr. Ortega took me aside and said he appreciated my dynamism in class, the way I fought to understand what PASE was really about and challenged hearsay. Most guests quibbled over trivia or blindly accepted whatever he said, which was fine at the Center, but later, when back among the general population, they would be vulnerable to others' lies and misinformation. Because I poked and prodded PASE, my belief would be deeper, more substantial and harder won. I would be immune to the hucksters and charlatans who preyed on the spiritually defenseless and only cared about power and money and their own aggrandizement. I would earn my place in PASE hierarchy and would see clearly how false prophets and gurus and religious leaders in the so-called real world plied their sham religions and took advantage of everyone they could. He said that I would be a savant before I knew it.

After wading through a cold undercurrent of criticism all day, Mr. Ortega's warmth was a welcome change. His conclusions—like everything he'd said on every subject—were wrong, but I liked his kindliness and support, like that of a math teacher for a student who, despite his indifference or even hostility to calculus, instinctually gets at the heart of a problem. I decided I liked Mr. Ortega, and for that matter I also liked Mihir, whose friendliness, however stained by zealotry, was genuine. I made another resolution on the spot to treat my time there as no more than a minor inconvenience. Perhaps I should even view it as an opportunity to study, at a proximity not allowed to nonbelievers, a strange and soon-to-be-short-lived subculture. Yes, I faced loneliness, professional uncertainty, and prolonged abstinence from painkillers—which would lead to both withdrawal symptoms and a bold reassertion of my body's underlying pain, and which had been perpetrated on me by this selfsame subculture that had in its brief lifespan done a great deal of damage—but I would also witness firsthand how a small portion of Americans were going crazy. Someday I would have an interesting story to tell.

My schedule listed the individual research period next, at the library. I followed my map and was met at the building's Gothic entrance, a great Carnegian archway, by a facilitator, the willowy Ms. Kim, who explained that I was free during research to explore the book collection and media center, both of which had rich educational tools covering every aspect of PASE's history and practice. Or I could work on my own or join a small study group. Or collaborate with others on projects like planning PASE parties for the outside world. Or write letters to newspaper and magazine editors in defense or celebration of PASE. Or send personal emails to friends and family, pending approval by Center officials. Basically, the time was mine to do what I wanted. She left and I wandered toward the videos, next to which several people sat upright in deep-cushioned downy chairs, watching portable viewing screens while wearing headphones. One held a magazine with dog-eared pages. I grabbed a viewing screen and sat among them and closed my eyes to take a quick nap.

After a minute, however, I felt someone's presence and looked up to see Ms. Anderson standing in front of me, her feather earrings illuminated from the ceiling light shining above her. She squatted down, rested a hand on each of my armrests, so that I was enclosed by her, and said in a gentle voice, such as nurses adopt in triage, "How are you doing?"

"Fine."

"I heard you chose not to share in counseling."

"Right."

"And that you asked some tough questions in class."

I shrugged.

"Perhaps it'll ease your mind a little to know that we've talked to your boss at Couvade, Mr. Raven, and he has agreed to rehire you at a promoted level as soon as you're back on the outside. Should you want to return to work, that is."

"You're kidding."

"No."

"As a senior capital growth assessment manager?"

"Yes."

My aches all subsided at once, as though the switch connected to my pain receptors had been thrown, and my eyes moistened and I grabbed and squeezed Ms. Anderson's hand before quickly releasing it. Her smile grew in radiance and I shared it, letting the video screen fall into a crack between the bottom seat cushion and the chair's arm. For ten seconds we grinned at each other like children in a staring contest, as though this were an elective game that we both might win.

Then she stood up and walked away, saying hello to the guests and facilitators she passed, gliding out of the room like a fairy god-mother. I was employed again. And promoted. I wanted to shout and slap people on the back but took a minute to let my giddiness settle; I was impressed, almost overwhelmed, by PASE's benevolence and power, by the thought that rather than crush me it had decided to protect me. The tetrahedron lost a side and became a simple triangle. I would be able to continue paying off my debts and not go bankrupt and resume my professional climb to Couvade's upper ranks. I was 25 percent better.

Of course this spasm of gratitude didn't erase my feelings of disorientation and impotence as an internee at the Wellness Center, nor did I forget the grievous wrong being done to me, or the fact that PASE was responsible for my having been fired in the first place, meaning I should no more thank it than I should someone who'd struck me on the head and then force-fed me an aspirin. And yet PASE hadn't *had* to help me out with Mr. Raven. It could have withheld its influence at Couvade and allowed me after my release to scramble for rent and food money while looking, perhaps forever, for an elusive job. Nor was it under any obligation to save me from my sex drive, which, however errant a crusade, was, from PASE's perspective, an act of kindness. They believed they were helping me and I, although fundamentally against such help, appreciated the sentiment.

Yet I hadn't asked for any of its attentions, which had been, on balance, more destructive than constructive, a series of interferences that, even if I were allowed to go home and start working the next day, had already wounded me so much that I might never wholly recover. Just two nights before, for example, they'd broken open my door to drug and abduct me. And I had to bear in mind that they wanted to keep me from Mary Shoale, with whom I'd had a deep, albeit brief, interaction, and about whom I harbored long-term hopes and fantasies. And if they had their way with my beliefs I would never again do anything enjoyable; I would become a sort of urban gelding bent on eliminating my appetite for life.

So the situation was not entirely black or white—forces of good and evil that originated from the same pool were swimming beside one another—but it did, in the final analysis, speak against PASE, and I took Ms. Anderson's news like a prisoner of war hearing that peace talks were about to commence, as helpful signs that were not helpful enough.

When a bell sounded in the library, Ms. Kim announced that research period was over and we were to go to the Festival Parlor for recreation. I walked with Tyrone and Mihir to a large slate-floored room in Shoale Hall where seven small workstations were set up in a star pattern. The greeting facilitator, Mr. Hirotaka, found my name on a list and sent me to a station near the far corner of the room beside the walk-in airport-style bathrooms, where Ms. Bentham, a bony facilitator in her early sixties with shiny brown hair that lay like an animal pelt over her left shoulder, gave me an easel, paint palette, and cup full of brushes. Today's recreation activity was freestyle painting, she said. Two women I'd seen at lunch were already sketching outlines, studiously absorbed in their creations. I sat across from them and had a vivid, disturbing flashback of sitting on the hard, splintery wood stool Rick and Ann gave me as a child during our two-hour family paint-alongs, when I had to draw fruit bowls and ballerinas that ended up looking like no fruit or dancer on Earth, before enduring technical criticism from my parents that was both incomprehensible and demoralizing. This recreation period was mandatory, though, so I went through the motions by running a few brushstrokes over the canvas, waiting for it to end.

An hour later Ms. Bentham went around examining our work. I'd dabbed on small clumps of Maimeri oils and mixed and smeared them together in a cornucopian swirl—a few dozen overlapping circles—and when she saw it she choked on thin air and said, "Your color combination is superb." Then, leaning in closer so that her hair crawled onto my shoulder, she said, in a confidential whisper that tickled my ear, her breath herring-like, "That's UR God, isn't it?" I started to answer but she interrupted me, standing up as if jolted by electricity. "It's the most extraordinary likeness I've ever seen!" She stepped back and called for the other facilitators to come over. I explained that the painting was nothing, the visual equivalent of radio static, a doodle not meant to represent UR God or anything else, but she was lost in the mess and not listening. Four facilitators arrived and, after a mute appraisal from up close and far away and then one side and the other, excitedly agreed that this was the UR God they'd always envisioned, His apotheosis in art. One wondered if, as in the Jewish mythology, one would not be allowed to live after seeing Him. Ms. Bentham assured them that there was no such precedent in *The Prescription*.

How do you feel? they asked, crowding around my wooden artisan's chair. *Inhabited by truth? Bowed toward the infinite?* I said I would love a few extra-strength ibuprofens and told them that my painting was meaningless, that it deserved the disclaimer novels had about any resemblance to people living or dead being entirely coincidental. But one by one, hesitantly at first and then with growing conviction, the facilitators, with Ms. Bentham directing their line of thought, decided that I didn't know what I'd done, that like the poets whom Plato asked to explain their work and who obliged with boorish dilettantism—bards who hadn't the faintest idea of what their work actually signified—I was the last person to be trusted about my accomplishment. A whiskery redhead noted that Montgomery Shoale, when sitting down to write *The Prescription for a Superior Existence,* had originally thought it would be a self-help book for business executives. He had not known at first that UR God wanted him to be His spokesman, that everything he would write would come from Him.

I wanted them to go away and forget their embarrassing projection, but instead by dinner, forty-five minutes later, they had spread the word and the other guests, with their mouths full of bland food, looked at me curiously and with some dubiousness, as bodybuilders would at an apparent weakling said to have benched six hundred pounds. A few pointed. Less hungry than I'd been at lunch, I nibbled at a lean ham sandwich and stared at my table. When Tyrone asked me if he could see the portrait, I repeated for the last time that it was a nonsense painting, conceived and executed without thought or skill, and that he should ignore what the facilitators were saying, for it wasn't true. I had neither the desire nor the presumption to paint UR God.

"You are a sly one," said Mihir with an admiring grin that seemed like a leer. "All day long you act so detached and even opposed to PASE, as though nothing could be less palatable to you, and then you channel UR God during recreation. Oh yes, I can see our relationship is about to change. The student will teach the teacher, the son becomes father to the man, etcetera."

Shang-lee said, "You don't need to deny it because you're afraid we'll be jealous. We're all just trying to improve, and if you have special talents or insights you should share them."

The others at the table nodded in agreement, and Eli, placing his fingerless hand atop mine solicitously, said, his eyes as cloudy as if he'd been high all day, "Those blessed with gifts should give them away freely."

"Aren't you listening?" I yelled, unable to control myself any longer, dropping my sandwich into a dollop of no-calorie mayonnaise on my plate. "I'm not being deceitful or modest because I have nothing to be deceitful or modest about! If my scribbling looks like UR God it's an accident, a coincidence!"

"That's just your conscious mind talking," said Mihir. "Perhaps your unconscious guided your brush, and you do not know about it even now. You think it was all just claptrap; you are ignorant of your own design. And of UR God's."

Unable to respond, boxed in by twilight zone reasoning, I put my sandwich back together and tried eating, though I had even less appetite than before. The coping strategies I'd come up with during the day—treating the Center like work, approaching it as a sociologist would, going into mental hibernation—were buckling and faced collapse. The dam was under too much strain, and soon I would crack and my sanity would gush out by the gallon. *For what purpose?* A question asked too much and answered too little.

With dinner ending the table talk turned to the evening's activities, first Synergy and then Montgomery Shoale's live broadcast.

A double feature of concentrated bliss and unmediated wisdom awaited us, by far the high point of our stay at the Center. After building on one another's excitement, Mihir and Tyrone and the others sprang from the table like schoolboys on a field trip, and raced to drop off their trays on the conveyor belt that rotated into the kitchen. I let a few seconds pass before following suit, and when I got outside they were already off in the distance. I walked by myself until Warren appeared next to me.

"Beautiful night," he said, craning his head back. "There's not a lot of city glare and you can see Cassiopeia, Orion, everything. Do you know the constellations?"

"No," I said.

"You can learn them from a guidebook, real easy. I recommend it, gives extra value to stargazing when there's nothing else to do."

"I'm sure."

"Learning keeps the mind fresh and agile. That's the general motto around here, in case you haven't noticed. Gather the right knowledge and your mind can fit into anything."

"I guess." I looked at him but his chin-length hair curtained his eyes.

"From what I hear you made a pretty good guess of what UR God looks like," he said. "Yelling a denial of it at dinner isn't going to help you get out of here, though. Word to the wise."

"I'm not getting out of here anytime soon."

"You sound pretty sure of that."

"I am."

"But you never know when an opportunity will present itself."

"What kind of opportunity?"

He blew on his bangs with a long low-pitched whistle that got lost in a far-off dog's howl. "You're going to like Synergy," he said.

"Do you know of an opportunity?"

We had passed Elysian Field, along the edge of which were small lawn torches lighting our path like a luau, and come to the doors leading into the Synergy Station, a hangar-sized building big enough to swallow a small plane.

"That's the North Star right there," he said, pointing to a crater of light in the firmament brighter than all the others, a droplet of marigold in a black field of white specks. "From it you can find everything else."

I would have pressed him for an answer, but we were already in front of two facilitators, on the other side of whom, forming a perfect circle around the inside of the building, were forty Synergy devices spaced at five-foot intervals. Mrs. Rubin had said they looked like gyroscopes, but they more resembled transparent cocoons with gauzy flaps of skin surrounding open fronts through which you could see body-sized holsters. A facilitator directed me to one marked Number 38 and showed me how to board it and then adjust the web of straps and buckles that fastened me as tightly as an astronaut in a space shuttle. After attaching electrodes to my temples and inner wrists, he walked away and I hung suspended in the device alongside the thirty-nine other guests, dangling like a baby in a nursery crib, losing a tiny amount of blood circulation to my extremities.

Ms. Anderson entered the circle of devices and said, "As many of you know already and some of you are about to discover, Synergy will last for exactly thirty minutes from the time the meditation warm-up ends. It requires no effort on your part, except to stay still. Moving or thrashing about before it begins could give you bruises or skin burns, so just relax and ready your mind. Are there any questions before we get started? No? Good."

She raised and then lowered her hand. The lights slowly faded to black, and the walls, floor, and ceiling turned into giant surroundscope video screens, so that every square inch of the building's interior reflected an unbroken, three-hundred-and-sixty-degree, continuous filmed image of the sky taken from over the cloudline. The effect was that we were a mile above the ground, looking at a piercingly thin blue in every direction but down, where a carpet of fleecy white cumuli spread out to infinity. From one corner of the ceiling a pale yellow sun shone brilliantly, gilding the clouds below so that they glowed and sparkled like wet snow. A warm breeze caressed us with a refreshing mist that dried on impact. It was like we were hang gliding at an impossible height, or flying like birds, or floating like gods while Ms. Anderson walked around as a messenger from Hyperion. A thrilling vertigo shot up my spine and then was gone, leaving me empty and cold.

Ms. Anderson said, in the commanding tone of a high school tennis coach, "The weight of your body is no weight at all, just as the burden of your consciousness is no burden. The world is spinning far below you like it has since the beginning of time. It is a toy top, and its troubles are no more consequential than those in a storybook. The heavens above are swirling like dust in a sunbeam, and whether they collide or spiral off into darkness doesn't matter, for all of this is a daydream from which you are about to awake restored and, for the first time in what you've mistakenly considered your life, truly alive. For you are not of this world or bound to it; your sorrows and pains and disappointments are simple illusions, lies you invented when you forgot the truth so very long ago. Now you are on your way to knowing better. Now you are prepared to know best. UR God is waiting for you to put this knowledge to use, to set aside the cares and concerns of ignorance and fuse into the truth of Him like so many tributaries flowing into the ocean."

A slight vibration began in my machine, a tremor that at first seemed like a malfunction, as when a car sputters after running out of gas, but when I saw the other guests' devices also vibrating I realized that they had been programmed to do so. It was pleasant. Ms. Anderson led the facilitators out through a side door—what appeared to be a tractable rectangle of sky—leaving us in a simulated midair environment without further instructions. I didn't know what to think about the stratosphere and clouds and sun stuttering all around for no purpose. A minute went by and I began to feel embarrassed for PASE. Mrs. Rubin had said that Synergy was the most wonderful feeling imaginable, and although it was no surprise that she'd oversold the experience, in keeping with the Center's habit of overselling everything, this seemed especially silly and one-dimensional and cheap. I felt a headache coming on and would have called for a facilitator to return and take me down—I would have explained about my back and nausea and asked them to make an exception in the no-nonprescription drugs rule for me, if only for tonight—but just then a tingling started in my toes and spread from my feet to my legs to my torso to my neck and finally bloomed in my head like fireworks. I felt, in a euphoric rush, Synergy, which worried me for about two seconds, until I abandoned thought and gave myself over to it and lost all track of time and space.

Most religions, like most societies, use a combination of reward and punishment to keep their followers in line, variations on heaven and hell that I'd always discounted because the first seemed like a fairy tale and the second a nightmare. Both represented farcical extremes, with seventy-two willing virgins awaiting the righteous in heaven and an ever-ablaze landscape of torture awaiting infidels. With the gold carrot and the spiky stick. It seemed as if many of religion's architects had figured that a desire for happiness and fear of pain, along with a childlike devotion, at least in theory, to fairness, were enough to compel people's faith and obedience, that ultimately few would risk damnation when for the small price of faith they might receive eternal blessedness after death. Standing inside the Synergy device while Ms. Anderson talked I had expected, at best, a parlor trick, something like the sensation of flight mixed with aural stimulation, an episode that might impress the video game set but couldn't have lasting appeal for normal people. When, a half hour after she left the room and Synergy began, a facilitator turned off my device and helped me down, I said nothing. I needed to recover. I needed to pry loose the smile from my face and make my peace with the suddenly vacant walls and floor and ceiling and people and devices all around, the vertiginous return to Earth after soaring so far above it.

Mrs. Rubin had, if anything, been conservative in her praise of Synergy. Every atom of my mind and body tingled from the incomparable depth and profundity and ecstasy and joy and wonder of it. The other guests and I rubbed our arms and stumbled around like survivors of a plane crash, recognizing one another as so many walking miracles. My only negative thought was that I didn't think there should be an afterward to Synergy, that what went up should not have to come down. For it had been—to provide a list of inadequate comparisons—like coming home from a war, an infatuation, slaked thirst, a nighttime massage, floating on a river, winning a prize, a third drink, rescue from drowning, an inspired joke, being forgiven, sated hunger, offering forgiveness, falling asleep, a cup of coffee, the applause of an audience, cool water on a hot day, found art, a Christmas bonus, and being born with an idea of what it all means. It was as though the division I'd always felt between me and other people, objects, and ideas was a great misunderstanding, that the truth consisted of unity and belonging and intense encapsulating thankfulness. I wanted to laugh and prostrate myself and swear allegiance to the confraternity of humankind. For the first time all day—for the first time in years—I didn't need or want alcohol and painkillers. I was wholly content.

"What did Warren say to you before Synergy?" Although I hadn't seen him coming, Mihir was standing in front of me, the concern in his voice as jarring as a sharp note at the end of a lullaby. "I thought it was clear that you are to avoid him. He is guilty at least of irreverence and carelessness, and perhaps of worse things besides. We are the company we keep, you know, and as your mentor I don't want to see your improvement imperiled by bad influences."

We were being swept along with the crowd outside the Synergy Station, where Shoale's name was on everyone's tongues, a great rustling leaves-across-the-forest-floor sound, and then toward the Prescription Palace to hear his address.

"Is it true that we only use the Synergy device once a week?" I asked.

"He mistakenly sees in you an ally, which he will try to exploit. You must be too vigilant against such a maneuver. You must guard your mind against men like him the way young women should guard their chastity against base seducers."

"In orientation Mrs. Rubin said that there's another way besides the device to feel Synergy."

"You should think more about what I said concerning the scorpion." He let out a sigh and stepped on the heel of a man walking in front of us, who sped up. "I am serious."

We came to a halt as a bottleneck formed up ahead in line.

"Can the other way be done alone, or is it a group thing?"

"Through meditation one can tap into Synergy," Mihir relented. "It requires enormous effort and doesn't last much longer than you can hold your breath—it is really a mere stopgap for the device, not a replacement—but as you progress through the savant stages you will develop the ability. Just don't get the idea that here on Earth you can be always in the happy throes of Synergy, for that will be so only when you become an ur-savant."

We were moving again, and found ourselves next to Tyrone, who picked at a swollen pimple on his neck. "Have you heard?" he said. "Montgomery Shoale is going to talk about the Last Day."

In the distance I saw an ornate building with a striking Pekingese façade; its bronze roof was supported by two gigantic coral red columns, between which a wrought-iron dragon mask was stretched. At the base of each column sat stone replicas of the Heaven Dog statues that guard Mann Chinese Theatre in Hollywood. Searchlights swerved back and forth from the ground, bathing the building's copper-topped turrets in soft yellow, adding luster to the arabesque neon marquee. It was a glamorous sight.

"Who told you that?" asked Mihir.

"Everyone's saying it."

"What last day?" I asked.

"The cutoff point in time for fusing into UR God," Mihir said.

"I didn't know there was one."

"Officially there isn't, but rumors from the PASE Station say that Montgomery Shoale has received a further revelation from UR God reversing this."

On our way into the Palace a facilitator gave us a small fig bar and a cup of pomegranate juice, and another shone a flashlight on the seats we were to take, three adjoining chairs upholstered with green brushed velvet. I leaned back and a spring-loaded footrest popped up to support my legs, and as I sipped my juice a holographic image of Montgomery Shoale standing at a podium flickered into view on the stage in front of us, giving me an unwelcome déjà vu of the sexual harassment training seminar. Next to me Mihir cleared his throat.

"It was the best of times, it was the worst of times." Shoale looked thinner than he had the previous week, and despite the theater's crystalline sound system his words ended with a strange tremolo effect. "Written seventy years after the French Revolution began in 1789, this famous first sentence of Charles Dickens's *A Tale of Two Cities* recognizes truths that are too rarely acknowledged: namely, that the past has never been a Golden Age, that progress always coexists with its opposite, and that in every era going back to the dawn of mankind there has been as much reason to be optimistic as to be pessimistic. Those of us who reach a certain age in life often lose sight of these truths, however, and oppress the young with rosy-hued reminiscences of a better, kinder, cleaner world than the one in which we now live. Time polishes our rough memories into smooth sleek surfaces, like a pumice stone removing unsightly skin from our hands, giving them the appearance of being healthier and more attractive than in fact they are. This is a tragedy because it nurtures nostalgia for periods and places that did not exist; it asks us to believe that society was once marked by political wisdom and aesthetic greatness and moral distinction, that in every important way it was once better than it is.

"Any trained historian will tell you that their period of expertise, be it revolutionary France or Aztec Mexico or Ancient Greece, flourished with medical and scientific and artistic advances at the same time that it rotted with pestilence and war and political corruption. No civilization has ever achieved greatness without demonstrating that it was just as barbarous as the savage lands beyond its borders. After the French Revolution swept away the excesses of the aristocracy and the Catholic Church, for example, and introduced the metric system and made education gratis and instituted a thousand positive reforms for the proletariat, it began a Reign of Terror against three hundred thousand political dissidents that bathed the streets of Paris in guillotined blood, launched a vicious assault on organized religion, and set in motion a power grab that allowed Napoleon to crush the country's fragile democracy, declare himself emperor, and conduct a fifteen-year war that engulfed all of Europe and killed millions of men, women, and children."

He put a hand to his temple and lowered his head. "If looked at from a far enough remove in time and space, any era can be shown to have been a seamless blend of good and bad. But when it is nearer at hand, when it falls within our personal past or present, we tend to overlook its nuances. We say things like, 'The 1960s were a time of war and protest,' and 'The 1980s were soaked in greed and nuclear fears,' and 'The world today is defined by ideological conflict between the Middle East and the West, the threat of environmental disaster, and a deep cultural divide within individual countries.' It's as though our species suffers from a historical farsightedness and ought to wear reading glasses to see clearly what's going on right in front of it.

"Unfortunately, religious eccentrics have long been able to take advantage of this collective hyperopia. Using obscure mathematical formulas from the Book of Revelation or their own supposed clairvoyance, they have at various times convinced people that on a specific date, at a specific hour, the world would come to an end. They've pointed out unmistakable signs and told whomever would listen to prepare their hearts and minds, that soon everyone would be destroyed save for the righteous among them. This phenomenon, called millennialism, always seemed amusing to people outside its sway, but to those trusting souls who sold their houses and cut off ties to their families and got ready for the planet's dramatic finale, the uneventful passing of this or that specific date and hour was a terrible disappointment. The world, to which they had already said good-bye, kept on turning, and by doing so proved, again and again, that it could not have been otherwise. Millennialism has always been wrong, and it has always inspired mixed feelings in observers, for while every disgrace of a deluded religious leader is an unqualified good, one must at the same time pity those who were taken in.

"What does this mean for us here tonight? Why should we care about past hysteria surrounding the dreaded end of the world? Surely not to emulate it. No, given that history shows civilization never to have been uniformly damned or blessed, to always have hung in a delicate balance; given our resilience as both a species and a planet; and given the numerous occasions on which the end has been prophesied without coming to pass, it would seem prudent never again to speak in apocalyptic terms. It would seem like the essence of sense to reserve judgment on our own age, to acknowledge the visual impairment that prevents us from seeing it in focus, and, if pressed for specifics, to point out that for every terrorist attack on the United States, thousands of people work to promote understanding and peace between observant Islam and the secular West, and that for every newly discovered disease a scientist concocts a vaccine to eradicate an old one, and that for every freshly extinct animal species redoubled efforts are made to protect and secure the habitats of those that remain. Because there have always been natural disasters like hurricanes and earthquakes and droughts. And there have always been heroes and villains in positions of power. And the poor, as Jesus pointed out two thousand years ago, have always been with us.

"Yes, until recently this equivocal response would not only have been prudent, it would have been necessary. Too often, those not anticipating a wild conclusion like the Rapture have used fearmongering and faulty logic to promote their destabilizing ideas. 'Invade any country that has powerful weapons and dislikes America,' these opportunists have said. 'Ban all fossil fuels. Bomb societies that have a different god or tolerate moral laxity or give women too much freedom. Imprison people who question a government's right to do whatever it pleases.' Until recently we would all have done well to step back from the precipice and acknowledge that we, like everyone everywhere, are too strongly guided by self-interest, and that it is foolish to blame others for the very actions we would take in their place. Until recently we ought to have advocated understanding, restraint, and relativity.

"I stand before you tonight, however, with a heavy heart because our situation has changed. The sidewinding march of time is drawing to a close, and we can no longer justify such guarded hopefulness for our present and future. No, we now find ourselves irreversibly embarked on a road to self-annihilation, and we lack the ability to stop. Because of us, the polar ice caps are melting, the coral infrastructure of the Great Barrier Reef is dying, and severe deadly weather is becoming normal. Temperatures are soaring and plummeting to dangerous extremes. Hitherto forest-bound viruses are, through deforestation, entering the human population. Vital links in the global food chain are going extinct, the ripple effect of which will cause starvation among animals we care about while doing nothing to stop disease-carrying insects.

"In what seems like the blink of an eye to history, the human race has multiplied so quickly—we have gone so far along the road—that the world soon will not be able to support us. We are becoming too many and we are wanting too much. Whereas in the past our insatiable desire for more—more food, more clothes, more land, more money, more toys, more leisure—could be met by the provisions of planet Earth, those provisions will soon reach the point of exhaustion. The world then will not end in a fireball or with God lifting up the faithful and casting down the sinners—no—it will slowly and painfully turn barren, and with this turn will come a scene too terrible to contemplate, for as people eat and consume what's left they will gradually behave as animals do whenever demand overtakes supply: They will turn on themselves and fight and to the victor will go the spoils, until those too are depleted. Then they will one by one disappear, and nothing will be left of our tenure here but ruins."

He looked directly at whatever camera was recording this address, and his eyes were sorrowful. "Some among you are perhaps asking yourselves if this doomsday scenario must come to pass. Perhaps you think we'll devise a solution or series of solutions to our problems, just as we always have. Surely, you'll say, our planet's dire fate can be avoided, if not as easily as former prophecies of doom then at least with great effort and determination, of which our species is more than capable. It is true that such efforts are being applied even at this very moment, and I wouldn't blame you for thinking that ultimately they will work, that they simply have to. We are hardwired with the notion that everything will turn out all right. For this reason children's stories have happy endings. For this reason we are drawn to the idea that good will win out over evil; for this reason we believe a touching, beautiful lie.

"The reality is that we have careened off track and don't have much time before we smash into the hard unforgiving wall of our selfishness and mutual distrust. We are now well past the best and worst of times, and we must decide as individuals whether to achieve eternal happiness through Prescription for a Superior Existence or give in to the forces of entropy and dissolution that are set to destroy the material world.

"Not long ago UR God communicated with me directly for the first time since dictating *The Prescription*. He said that the window of opportunity that He opened seventeen years ago is about to close due to our expedited waste. Originally He had hoped this would not be necessary, but we are fast approaching a tipping point beyond which so many will perish that He feels He must give us an ultimatum. We don't have much more time to improve and become worthy of Him. The Last Day will soon be here. After it passes those who haven't become ur-savants will continue to live as they always have, but in a rapidly decaying world from which they will not be able to escape. As many of you know, I am almost an ur-savant, and so almost gone. I will not personally oversee the conversion of every single one of you into ur-savants, but someone else will. Do not despair; if you continue to improve you will be with Him. UR God told me that although it is too late for our planet, it is not too late for our souls."

Like a spell breaking, the end of Shoale's speech tore me out of the horrified, credulous lull I'd slipped into. My mental fog lifted with the lights coming up, and the clatter of applause from my fellow guests sounded as foolish and even repugnant as a Nuremberg rally. Why had I listened so raptly to that paranoia? Shoale had a certain charisma—his face and voice improved in my estimation the more I saw and heard them—but his message had been ludicrous, as rhetorically flimsy and self-serving as any plutocrat's op-ed piece in the company newsletter. The sky was falling? In T-minus so many years it would all be over? Admitting that end-of-the-world proclamations were as common as miracle diets and get-rich-quick schemes, that spiritual mountebanks going back to the first bipeds had used them to sway fearful hearts and minds didn't mean he wasn't their latest incarnation. He couldn't dismiss the charge that he was naked by merely acknowledging that past emperors had also thought they were wearing new clothes. Mihir and Tyrone and everyone else around me seemed to be both troubled and grimly determined, as though what they'd heard, while alarming, had only strengthened their prior resolve. Facilitators greeted us as we filed out of the theater with somber good-night wishes.

After returning to the residence hall and brushing my teeth, I lay in my cot as the men around me began to snore, building in variety and volume like crickets at dusk, and the stars glimmered around a satellite inching across the skylights, cutting through stellar figures I could not name. Shoale's impersonation of Cassandra had lent new urgency to my plight. I needed to do something. I needed to formulate a plan that would propel me beyond the past forty-eight hours and out of my captivity at the PASE Wellness Center, where I was drifting away from the realm of normal experience toward one that claimed to be superior but was really group madness. That everyone saw UR God as real and hoped in the immediate future to starve to death as a way of joining him, proved that reason and sense, my primary survival tools in life until then, were as worthless there as foreign currency. I couldn't hope to argue or cajole or reason my way out, nor could I appeal to anyone's sense of fairness and compassion.

Having seen the Center's perimeter walls and entryways, I figured escape was impossible. Which meant I had to be rescued or let
go naturally. Which meant, since rescue seemed unlikely, I had to act
wisely. I thought about movies and books featuring people wrongly
accused of being crazy, and how their insistence on being sane usually strengthened their captors' decision to keep them locked up, following the Catch-22 idea that denial is the surest sign of a problem.
It had always seemed obvious that they should have done whatever
was expected of them, bidden their time until, satisfied with their
progress, the people in power restored their freedom. That, clearly,
was what I had to do. Like a possum playing dead in order to stay
alive, I would drop my objections and questions and incredulity
toward PASE, and adopt in their place a grudging respect that would
then harden into an inviolable faith—stretching my conversion over
a few days to make it believable—and thus appear to be a naturalized
savant who had earned his release.

With this resolution I felt better, with the right exit strategy from
this surreal detour, but as sleep came on despite my not having
taken any pills or drunk alcohol, I began thinking about the Synergy
device and my relief and joy and absence of worry on it, and as my
snore joined the others' chorus I ransacked my unconscious for a
way to feel those things again.

CHAPTER 4

Although I said before that nothing from my past could explain what brought me to this northern village and my part in the end of the world, the truth isn't so simple. Or rather, it's simple in a complicated way. My adoptive parents explain part of it, not because they played a direct role, but because if Heraclitus was right that character is destiny, then a look at the contributors to one will provide insight into the other.

What's odd is that I used to think destiny applied only to heroes of fairy tales and science fiction sagas, and that, unlike character, which was evident in everyone on Earth, it didn't exist in the real world. As a child, therefore, I spent more time thinking about character than destiny, and I decided—before carrying the decision with me through the summer and fall of my adolescence and early adulthood—that my own owed little, perhaps nothing, to Rick and Ann. Consequently, I ascribed all of my strengths and weaknesses to my genes—the sources of which, my biological parents, I knew nothing about—like a rose giving full credit for its blossoms and thorns to the anonymous pollination that produced the seed from which it grew, as though sunlight, soil, and rain had been as incidental as a gardener's conversation.

I had good reasons for doing this. Rick and Ann and I were very different people. When at age twelve I compared their appearance, interests, moods, dispositions, mannerisms, and prejudices with mine, I discovered almost no areas of agreement. For example, they were tall, thin towheads with smooth, round faces and no body hair, whereas I was dark and pimply and already previewed the over-weight, furry little man I was to become.

I accepted these differences as conditions that strained but didn't break our relationship, while—even this shows our opposite temperaments—Rick and Ann wanted to get rid of them. They thought I could, by following a strict diet and exercising constantly, become as skinny as a natural child of theirs would have been. To this end they barred most sugars and fats from our kitchen, installed a tread-mill in my bedroom, and volunteered me to do yardwork all over the neighborhood. They gave me tiny meals and bought me clothes a half-size too small, so that the suction fit of my pants and shirts would, like a cilice, remind me of a higher goal. In eighth grade they insisted that I sign up for two sports, tennis and water polo—I had the perfect build for football, but they dismissed the game as dan-gerous and primitive—at which I did badly until the summer after my sophomore year in high school, when I could no longer meet my coaches' basic stamina requirements. Rick and Ann felt vindi-cated and defeated at once. They sat me down and said that in a cou-ple of years they would not be able to moderate what I ate and did, and that I would then be faced with a choice. I could either suc-cumb to or rise above my generation's excesses. Life, they said, without irony or melodrama, was short and probably meaningless, and by continuing to get bigger I was ensuring that mine would be even shorter and probably more meaningless. Which would be sad for a dozen reasons, they said, not least of which was that if chiseled free from my extra weight I might become handsome and able to secure a partner with whom to enjoy my time here.

But this is not the place to dwell on our struggle over my body, the tug-of-war I couldn't help but win, because it was trivial beside the issue that most divided us: their devotion and my indifference to art. As with my weight, they thought I could and should become more like them—they were both painters—so from an early age I had to draw and paint for two hours every Sunday, as well as submit to lessons in mixing colors and dead-artist biographies. I had to read classic works of literature and go to the symphony and listen to opera and watch ballet. And sit through documentaries about the Renaissance and study the nuances of Doric versus Ionic architecture. I had to understand the mechanics of villanelles, sestinas, and roundels; the properties of mobiles and stabiles; and the tyrannical hold representational painting had on Western Europe before Cubism.

Although I was uninterested in all of it, I especially disliked the summer arts camps they sent me to between the ages of five and eighteen. Run by stringy exiles from Bay Area repertory theaters and dance troupes and artist collectives, these places were devoted to singing, drawing, acting, writing, photography, and dancing, to jam sessions and improvisation nights and scaled-down productions of *Cyrano de Bergerac* and Handel's *Messiah* and *The Nutcracker*. Hundreds of dream-addled children from all over the state—who shone at the camps but must have been persecuted elsewhere for being so fantastically weird—came to have their abilities encouraged. They overperformed; they developed medieval grudges against one another; they salted their conversation with French and German and Italian expressions, using *le mot juste* to describe the *Sturm und Drang* of their *cuore aperto*. I barely survived those summers, when, on good terms only with the one or two other miserable children who looked forward to the day they could reject their parents' interests in favor of their own, I was the outcast of outcasts.

Every year Rick and Ann hoped that I would come home transformed, my inner artist found and nurtured. When I never did— when at last I went off to college and majored in business administration—their feeling was that I had willfully and stubbornly grown into an unimaginative adult, that I had squandered the advantages they'd given me as a child, and that I'd chosen to measure life in numbers rather than epiphanies. They ruefully concluded that nature played a greater role than nurture in human development, which, being the very conclusion I'd come to as a child, made me respect their judgment and even partly regret disappointing them.

*　*　*

Deposited outside the Couvade building after being fired, I walked around a raised concrete flower bed empty of the nasturtiums and irises and roses that in gentler seasons colorized that stretch of monochrome sidewalk. To steady my heartbeat, which pounded at half-second intervals like something trying to escape, I stopped and looked up at the grid-plotted windows of 595 Market Street, a thousand apertures in a great amethyst chain mail protecting the building from—what? Me. I'd been let go. Made redundant. After seventeen tax-paying years, first as a sales assistant and then as a busboy, waiter, sales associate, bank greeter, bank teller, loan officer, research analyst, and finally capital growth assessment manager, I had no professional identity. I was utterly and fiscally alone.

While the terror of this sank in I climbed aboard a crosstown bus and slumped into a cat-clawed vinyl seat beside a tiny old Chinese man wearing a tie-dyed poncho and teal lederhosen, who inched away from me. The Couvade building receded behind us and everything was a blur until we reached the Sutro Baths, which before the 1906 earthquake reduced them to ruins had resembled Rome's baths of Caracalla, where I disembarked and walked to the jagged remains of its stone embankment, on a cliff overlooking the gunmetal blast of the Pacific Ocean. The sky was marbled with formless clouds grayed by time and indolence. On the sandy shore below, a family in matching yellow sweatshirts filed out of a wave-hollowed cave, dark water stains corrugated around the knees of the boy and girl, and made their way up the sandy path leading to the octagonal parking lot.

The mother alone didn't stop to turn and admire the view, but headed toward the car. From her unsentimental, determined gait I saw that she knew how quickly the world could turn on you, how little provocation it needed to change its mind and leave you to your own devices. She seemed to understand that although the world preferred to do this to the beautiful and talented—to the professional musicians, actors, and athletes who rode high for years, hit one updraft after another and believed in the fiction of perpetual flight, until karma, disguised as chance, melted the wax in their wings—it could do it to regular people, too. It had done it to me.

What made it all so senseless was that my performance at work, as I have said, contrary to Mr. Raven's charge, had not been compromised over the past few months. Danforth was an anomaly and not my fault. And although Chicago had been embarrassing, it was not without precedent in corporate America—or anywhere else, really—and I deserved a stern warning rather than a trip to the gallows. True, I'd also asked out Elizabeth and a few other women in the office over the years, but dating between employees wasn't forbidden so long as one didn't have power over the other, and Elizabeth, working exclusively for Mr. Raven, was leagues outside of my narrow sphere of influence.

There comes a point in most San Francisco days when being outside is like standing in a shower that has run out of hot water, when the cold becomes shockingly immediate. Having reached it, I went home and took a few pills and Teresa's face was inches from mine, imploring, using the bathroom, maybe everyone's not as smart as they think they are. Either check into a sex addiction clinic such as the PASE Wellness Center or be fired. The television news ran a story about a mutant strain of kudzu, a weed that had been strangling trees in the South for twenty years, spreading north and threatening to wipe out half the nation's forests. A serial killer at large in the Bay Area had attracted two copycats. Bus drivers were going on strike. Seattle was blitzkrieged.

I switched channels and while listening to a jingly game show I opened one of my financial magazines to an article about PASE. The author called it an example of America's vulnerability to extremes. In the most vital country on Earth, she wrote, we were inclined to pay for our great freedoms with perverse, self-imposed restrictions. For some of us it was always feast or famine, because a quirk in our collective DNA compelled us to take up and then abandon life's rich rewards—wheat and eggs and cigarettes and alcohol and sugar and civil liberties and lawn irrigation and gambling and love—all in order to feel better. Because generally we didn't feel good. In fact, generally we felt miserable. The author offered a few theories about why this was while suggesting that the real reason was buried in the enigmas of evolution or language or God. If some people were unhappy enough to try celibacy, the rest of us should pity rather than condemn them. Someday they would snap out of it and find themselves on the other side of desirability, where abstinence is a by-product of age rather than a sign of piety, and they would yearn for the opportunities they'd missed.

This further depressed me and I was tempted to pick up one of the Russian novels my parents had made me read as a teenager, the only part of my arts education I had instantly and unequivocally valued, because for insight into the human condition, with its relentless struggle for and against itself in an impassive world, so that every single life, no matter how superficially ordinary, can reveal its most dramatic rise and fall, no one provided more return on my reading investment than the old Russian masters. In less serious times I had tried to carve out a sober hour or two every week for *The Idiot* or *Hadji Murat* or *Fathers and Sons,* and just then the wisdom of those books seemed like the right balm to soothe what I feared was about to explode into a four-dimensional anxiety attack. From my roost on the couch I spied a rare edition of Tolstoy's *Confession* on the brick-and-plywood bookshelf next to the TV, and I thought about retrieving it. In ten seconds it could have been in my hands.

Instead I called Juan to see if he wanted to get drunk. He answered on the first ring and I suggested we meet in a half hour at Rudolfo's Tavern to process, or obliterate, our pain from the Employee Conduct Board's decision against us. Juan, after a pause, said that he and Dexter and Philippe hadn't been given any demerits, that the Board had issued them warnings with travel probationary status. I was stunned. How could they have gotten such a light tap on the wrist when I'd been bludgeoned over the head? Juan didn't know. I asked him to plead my case to the Board and explain that I wasn't any guiltier than him, that in fact I was less guilty because in Chicago I'd suggested we catch "Blind" Willie Johnson perform at the Delta Pyre instead of lose all discretion at the Crazy Horse, but he said he had no influence with the Board—nor could he jeopardize his own and the others' position—and hung up.

The television ran commercials promising cures for male-pattern baldness, erectile dysfunction, heavy menstrual bleeding, and depression. The great maladies of our time. It seemed then, as it had in Mr. Raven's office, although this was the first time I used the word, that something like a conspiracy was in place against me. Yes. I'd been singled out for punishment while others were given token warnings, and like an antenna searching for the strongest signal I gradually tuned in to the Californian question: *Why not sue?* Why not take Couvade to court and win a victory against religious persecution, provided enough could be made of Mr. Raven having told me to check into a PASE-run health clinic, and make a little money at the same time?

Reasons not to quickly occurred to me—the time, the no-guarantees expense, the litigious reputation I would get among the city's financing companies—but that I had to do something was not in question. I turned off the standing lamp behind me as a story began about Montgomery Shoale's donation of fifty million dollars to state-funded cancer research. In a PASE Station conference room that afternoon, surrounded by a phalanx of suited officials and dignitaries that included the San Francisco mayor, two state senators, and the Department of Health Secretary, in front of a crowd of smiling onlookers, Shoale said that science could and would triumph over disease, for which he welcomed a new synergy between the business, political, and medical communities.

I felt tired and was just entering the gauzy preamble to sleep, thinking that PASE's sudden ubiquity in my life was like learning a new word and then hearing it everywhere, when a woman on the television screen behind and to the left of Shoale caught my attention. She was partially obstructed by the mayor's Afro and a senator's shoulder, but her short dirty-blond hair and profile were visible. I knew her from somewhere but couldn't place it. At the PASE seminar, a party, graduate school, a neighborhood bar? My head felt massaged from the inside out by the sedatives, and the couch heated up seductively, but still I struggled to remain conscious and to remember. She took my bus, ate at my favorite taco stand, walked her dog in my neighborhood, dated one of my friends, worked for a Couvade client company, had a cameo in a movie? The memory was just ahead of me, just . . .

I woke up at five A.M. in the same slack position, dehydrated and fully dressed. It was dark outside but for the misty glow around streetlamps and apartment windows behind which no one slept. I drank a cup of thick day-old coffee and dropped my damp clothes into the laundry hamper, feeling the defeat and bone-and-sinew fatigue of yesterday's events, in addition to my standard lumbar pain, wrist trouble, and nausea. I scoured the kitchen for food, showered, and prepared for a day of action.

At nine I got in my car and phoned Elizabeth, who cut me off by saying, "I have nothing against you personally, but you shouldn't call here. Mr. Raven said you lost control in his office."

"I only yelled for a minute."

"Exactly."

"Could I ask you for a favor?"

There was a muffled sound. "What did you say?"

"Half the reason Mr. Raven is firing me is because he claims not to have gotten the Danforth file I sent him on Tuesday, so I wonder if you'd look in his deleted email folder to see if it's there."

"Why would it be?"

"I think he and the Employee Conduct Board are manipulating the case against me."

"Jack."

"If it's not there, I won't bother you again. Please."

"No one's manipulating your case."

"Mr. Raven told me to check into the PASE Wellness Center, which was probably illegal in that he promoted a spiritual agenda in the workplace, and the Board gave me ten demerits for Chicago and none to the rest of my squad. How do you explain those things?"

A pause punctuated her sigh before she said, "This must be a hard time for you and I'm sorry, but you'd do best to accept it and apologize to Mr. Raven so he doesn't ruin your chances of getting another job."

"I've been fired because of false evidence and arbitrary, trumped-up penalties, and there could be wrongdoing going on."

"The world doesn't revolve around you, Jack; bad things can happen without a villain or plot behind them. Move on and forgive everyone, including yourself. Now I'm getting another call. Take care, okay?"

She hung up and I set my phone on the passenger seat. Without having planned to go there, I was driving slowly past the Couvade building on Market Street. I turned on to Post Street and then took a left at the steep ascent of California Avenue. Bad things could happen without plots, villains. Elizabeth was amazingly naïve. Cresting the top of Russian Hill, I looked at the Fairmont Hotel and Rose Cathedral and fog covering pockets of the low-lying city below, then descended the other side of the hill, where I turned on to Union Street, swung down to the Palace of Fine Arts, and then drove along the Marina. This was my favorite route through the city, a succession of epic peaks and valleys and Bay vistas and pastel Spanish villa-style homes that usually filled me with contentment, though I was too preoccupied then to appreciate natural beauty. I stopped on Palatine Hill, where I always did, to stare at the Golden Gate Bridge directly ahead, its massive suspension cables flaring in the sunlight.

Perhaps Elizabeth was not amazingly naïve; perhaps she was right that I had blamed others for problems for which I alone bore responsibility. Sitting in my car at a time of day when I should have been working, when the weight of idleness felt especially heavy, I had to consider that there might have been no machination to discover other than my own bad behavior. That mine was a simple case of harsh yet warranted justice. Certain facts loomed: I'd had an erotically charged night in Chicago at the company's expense, turned in an important project late (I ought to have asked Mr. Raven for receipt confirmation the moment I sent it on Tuesday), and not been fired outright but instead told to get help for what even I in dark moments admitted was a near-fixation on sex. My life had become a cautionary tale for future Shoale lectures.

Maybe, I thought, being painfully open-minded, I *do* have an excessive sexual condition, and the wiring in my body, badly rigged from the beginning, has now shorted any chance I once had for normalcy and happiness. All this time I've preapproved my thoughts and actions without any sense of the moral dangers involved, like floating on a raft toward a waterfall and, when the sound of falling water grows to a distinct roar, singing so as not to hear it.

An oil tanker glided into the Bay and I turned on the radio and summoned every bit of optimism available to me. Because my situation didn't have to be hopeless. It wasn't too late to change. I could, as Elizabeth suggested, put what had happened behind me, move on, and look for a new job; I could even take an antidepressant with libido-diminishing effects. And the sooner the better, for I had sizable debts and couldn't afford not to earn a paycheck for long. Yes, it was just a matter of exchanging a broken outlook for a new one, I thought, deciding to go home and work on my résumé. People who tried radical cures for what ailed them might not be fools, but rather ordinary folks with troubles grown too large for regular treatment.

Back on Market Street, waiting at a stoplight for the tide of crosswalk pedestrians to recede into four corners, listening to a radio talk show enumerate the near-future effects of global carbon dioxide emissions, when the Antarctic and Greenland ice shelves would melt and global sea levels would rise five feet—the millions of displaced people when New York, London, Tokyo, and Bangladesh flooded; the arable land lost to ocean or desert; the freshwater access disputes that alone would destroy the United Nations—I was staring ahead when the woman I'd recognized from Montgomery Shoale's press conference walked in front of my car. Wearing trim pleated trousers, a black two-button coat with a Peter Pan collar, and a matching pillbox hat from which her blond hair skirted out, she glided past me and in an instant I knew she was who'd come to my apartment and kissed me: the femme fatale, Conrad's student, Teresa.

I hastily parked in a bus lane and ran after her. "Hey!" I shouted, threading through oncomers and trying not to crash into the rolled luggage, baby prams, and unattended dollies spaced like track hurdles at regular intervals. "Teresa!" She kept walking. A few seconds later I matched her stride with mine.

"Excuse me," I panted, tapping on her left shoulder.

"Yes?" She slowed her walk and tucked her purse tightly under her right arm.

"It's me, from the other night, your piano teacher's neighbor."

She resumed her normal walking speed and looked straight ahead. "I've never seen you before."

"You were the one wearing a wig."

"If you don't get away from me I'm going to scream for the police."

"I want to know why you asked if I were a Paser and then came on to me. And what were you doing at Montgomery Shoale's press conference yesterday?"

She stopped and pivoted away to yell, "Help! Police! Police! Help!" This happened suddenly and loudly, and a small crowd gathered around us, through which two policewomen with raised guns squeezed their way. Instinctively I held up my hands and folded them behind my head.

Five minutes later the crowd had dispersed and I leaned against a thin poplar tree with the taller policewoman guarding me, as Teresa explained that I had accosted her. At first, she said, she'd thought I mistook her for someone else, but when I mentioned having seen her at a PASE Station press conference she knew that I knew who she was.

The shorter policewoman, cupping a small digital recording device in her hand, said, "What is your name, miss?"

"Mary Shoale. My father is Montgomery Shoale."

"Would you like to press charges?"

"What kind of charges?"

"You say he assaulted you?"

"More like he tapped my shoulder. To get my attention."

"You're welcome to go to the station and fill out a formal complaint and apply for a restraining order against him, if you think he's stalking you."

She bit her lower lip in the same manner she had as Teresa and said, "That's probably not necessary. Pasers like him think they know me or have this intimacy with me because of my father. I try not to acknowledge them, but sometimes I can't help it, like just now."

"So you don't want to press charges?"

"I guess not."

The shorter policewoman signaled for her partner to accompany Ms. Shoale to wherever she was going and when they were out of sight said to me, "You need to leave her alone. Do you hear? You're not to go near her in public or in private, beginning now."

"This was a big misunderstanding," I said.

"You got that right."

I walked back to my car, where an orange parking ticket fluttered under the windshield wipers like a fish trying to flap its way back into the water.

CHAPTER 5

On my second morning at the Wellness Center I woke up without an erection for the first time in recent memory, and my back, instead of aching, was limber and loose. It could have belonged to someone else. My nausea was gone, too, as was the warning of carpal tunnel syndrome. I ran my hands over my arms and torso to see if I'd been given medical treatment during the night, but felt no bandages or tenderness or signs that I'd been tampered with. Except for the asexuality, this was how most adults remembered their teenage bodies, as airbrushed and unblemished, as yardsticks against which to measure the minor and major pains that crept in later and, unless we'd been paying attention all along, were as amazing in their quantity as the number of musicians who contribute to symphonies that begin with a single instrument.

I was so pleased that I willingly, even gladly, took part in morning exercises. With Mr. Israel calling out instructions, I ran laps around Elysian Field, did push-ups and jumping jacks, participated in relay races through obstacle courses of car tires and two-foot hurdles, and played catch football. Not a twinge of discomfort. It was as though instead of spending the last ten years slouched over a desk with my fingers glued to a keyboard, stuffing myself compulsively, I had sat upright with my hands in a relaxed position and eaten like a monk. It recalled the moment following my surgery when I saw in the mirror a slender frame instead of my lifelong large one, as though I'd had a piece of Alice's cake in Wonderland, and I realized that from then on I wouldn't need oversized clothes or specialty chairs. I wouldn't arouse others' disgust or pity or tempered discomfort. I might, at last, not think about my body for whole days at a time, nor feel conspicuous in elevators or on airplanes or in line at grocery stores, nor know exactly what someone was thinking when they said hello to me and forced their eyes not to drop below mine. Coming off the field and heading toward the showers, I started to laugh for no reason.

I stopped laughing, though, when I thought about the change in my sex drive. This concerned me because although thirty-four years old is not seventeen, it isn't yet sixty-eight, so in the bathroom I sat on a toilet with my member tucked between my legs—from Tyrone's experience I gathered that the surveillance was total—and teased myself into a state of excitement. As my erection pressed up against the underside of my thigh, with its blind insistence on climbing higher than it could go, I was reassured that that morning's flaccidity had been an accident. But then, almost immediately, it began to fall, and thirty seconds later it had shrunk to less than its two-inch default setting. I wiggled it some more to no effect. In the next stall over someone asked if I was okay. "Maybe," I thought, "I'm adjusting to this new reduced-calorie diet, and my energy is being temporarily redirected from its normal avenues."

At breakfast I tried to eat more but could barely finish a bowl of unbuttered oatmeal. While Mihir and I were alone he showed me pictures of his wife and daughters, "once and future virgins," but when Eli and Tyrone sat down the conversation turned to and stayed on the Last Day. Then Alastair joined us. Then Rema. When Warren came near Mihir draped a leg over the remaining empty chair's seat. There were questions, unsettling unknowns: When exactly would the day come? Was the environment UR God's only reason for instituting it? What if none of them could become ur-savants in time? What would happen to their non-Paser friends and family? Eventually Mihir tried to muzzle their panic by saying that they would know the date when the time was right, and UR God had reasons they couldn't begin to fathom, and Shoale would find a way to deliver them, and their loved ones would be taken care of somehow.

"We should be focusing on improving," Mihir concluded. "Worry and second-guessing are no better than procrastination, and really we have known from the beginning that we couldn't dawdle forever. UR God is just bringing us to Him faster. If anything, we have cause for celebration!"

Then we got up, bussed our trays, and walked to the ivy-covered library, where all the guests swarmed around three tables stacked high with beautifully bound copies of *The Prescription*. I grabbed one and found an open study carrel with a bright desk lamp, prepared for act one of my Paser transformation. I set the book down and gazed intently at it. Anyone watching was about to see me deliberate over each page, mouthing the words like an adult learning to read, visibly affected by its message. Anyone watching was about to see someone seeing the light.

The cover of *The Prescription* depicted thousands of glowing lines the size of hyphens that seemed, via a design trick, to vibrate when looked at from different angles. The title page read "The Prescription for a Superior Existence, by UR God," and below that was a small Citadel icon and the words "PASE Publishing, Inc." Opening my eyes wide and throwing back my shoulders—this bordered on caricature, but I thought it better to over- rather than underplay it— I turned to the first chapter, which was surprisingly unsurprising. Whereas Montgomery Shoale might have thrown a curve ball to distinguish his religion from the Bible's in both form and substance, he instead began, like the other book, with a description of the universe's origins. The writing, plain and unadorned, had its rival's confidence, as well, though it used pseudojargon that made my mind wander.

For trillions and trillions of years—for nearly an eternity—Ultimate Reality God had composed everything in existence, matter and antimatter and un-matter. This was expressed as a near palindrome: He was all and all was Him. Within that all—that is, within the protoplasm of His being—a soup of living essence called "sourcespirit" floated around made up of individual impulses known as "wands"—the sticklike entities I'd mistaken as hyphens on *The Prescription*'s cover—that collectively supported UR God's will and in return were rewarded with the truth, the awareness that they, as part of Him, lacked for nothing. Fifteen billion years ago, however, a group of these wands decided that there was more to the truth than UR God was telling them, and they decided to break away and exercise their own wills to discover the truth for themselves. UR God asked them not to leave, and He warned them of what would follow, namely estrangement from Him and one another, and then an end to being, called death, but they insisted, so He caused the Big Bang explosion and created a place outside of Him, planet Earth, for them to go.

At first the wands loved their new environment and reveled in being simple life microorganisms—bacteria—but over time they learned nothing and got bored. To challenge themselves many evolved into more complicated animals, and then evolved again when that became dull, and again, and so on. With each new onto-logical advance their satisfaction period shortened—they weren't getting any closer to the truth—so that although they were content as bacteria and blue-green algae for two and a half billion years, they grew tired of being aquatic worms after two hundred million years and couldn't stand being fish for more than a hundred and eighty million years. From the oceans they made their way onto land and after a humdrum hundred and fifty million years as amphibians they took a monotonous hundred-million-year turn as primitive mammals before growing into sophisticated primates. Then the novelty of this too wore off, and they swung through seventy mil-lion years as apes before becoming hominids.

(Yes, *The Prescription* said boldly, revealing its major plot twist, *we* were the wands who'd rebelled against UR God. *We* were the pro-tagonists of this awful and useless biological saga.)

Not all wands evolved this far, though. Some had a greater tol-erance at the beginning for being worms and so stayed that way, others were not strong enough as fish to crawl out of the water, and still others through confusion or molecular accidents morphed into the variety of lowly life-forms extant today. There were gradations within the self-exiled wand community, zoological tendrils going in every direction.

The defining trait of those that evolved quickly and intelligently—that is, us—was restlessness, as well as an increasing sense that things were fundamentally wrong. In our epic journey to discover the truth we were in fact distancing ourselves from it; UR God remained where He'd always been as we got further away from our wand selves. Consequently, we devised ways of changing the world around us with the hope of easing our worries. These ways—these technologies—enhanced our lives, but they also, unexpectedly, diminished them. As *Homo habilis*, for example, we made tools from stone and animal bone and our thick claws were reduced to fingernails. As *Homo erectus* we gained fire and lost the ability to digest raw meat. As Cro-Magnons we shed enough body hair to live in hot climates and so concomitantly were forced to wear clothes at night and during winter. This quid pro quo continued as we became modern humans and invented language and domesticated agriculture and advanced weaponry.

By this point our brains had grown large enough for us to comprehend our vulnerability to the weather and the land's caprices and our own irascible natures, and it dawned on us that life on Earth was difficult, that we would never discover the truth here, and that we needed supernatural help. We had, however, forgotten UR God during the preceding billions of years, as He'd warned would happen, so the poets and philosophers and medicine men among us invented other gods—Zeus, God, Allah, Krishna, etc.—and implored them to save and protect us. Meanwhile we went about our business of battling one another for control of the planet's resources and building cities and trash heaps and hydroelectric dams and arsenals powerful enough to destroy the whole tottering experiment, ourselves included. This would have gone on forever except that, not long ago, without much worry or fanfare, we crossed an ecological threshold and found ourselves sitting on a ticking time bomb.

UR God, who had long wanted to intervene but refrained out of respect for our past wish to be left alone, chose that moment to give us a lifeline in the form of *The Prescription for a Superior Existence,* an instruction manual for rejoining Him and being spared the fate of extinction on this ruined rock. Its message was clear and straightforward. We were to abandon selfishness and pride and dissatisfaction—the qualities that led us to mutiny back when we were quarrelsome wands—and in their place cultivate charity, humility, and self-sufficiency. We were to put others' needs before our own, eliminate our ego, and conquer desire. We were to dislodge the greediness and narcissism that lay deep within the core of each of us, and therein become like the wands who had stayed behind. None of this would be easy, but by following *The Prescription* and attending a PASE Station and visiting a Wellness Center, we could grow more in a short period than we had in our entire residence on Earth. We could remake ourselves in the image of UR God by renouncing the trappings of the flesh and becoming divine, able to enter into Synergy with Him free of the desires that had enslaved us for billions of years and that otherwise would prevent us from knowing eternal happiness.

After finishing the chapter I jotted down a few ready-for-inspection notes: "We got fed up with being fish circa five hundred million years ago. UR God gave us *The Prescription* when the planet was about to die."

Fortunately, a facilitator I didn't know, an attractive young woman with platinum hair and a strong Roman nose, noticed me doing this and came over to the side of my carrel. "I see you've been reading chapter one," she said.

"Yes." I looked up at her.

Despite the loose fit of her navy blue tunic, the bulging of her breasts was visible. I subtly concentrated on them but felt nothing in my loins. "What do you think?" she asked.

"It's very interesting. I didn't know any of that about the wands."

"It can be hard to accept at first."

"Maybe a little." I smiled and thought that she might, beneath a hard crust of belief and commitment, want to sneak off with me, that if I suggested it in a delicate enough way her latent desire might bubble to the surface, and that in a private spot I might respond properly.

She put a hand on her hip. "When I first read it I thought, 'Oh *really?*' but my teacher put it in context by pointing out that not many people believed Galileo when he proposed that the sun was the center of the universe a mere four hundred years ago."

"That's true."

"It's not like there aren't people still today who think Darwinism is a complete myth."

"Also true."

"And Heisenberg's uncertainty principle was such a blow to rational scientific assumptions in the 1920s that he received death threats from angry scientists!" She smiled like a children's television show presenter and I pictured her bent over a bright purple building block with her tunic thrown up around her neck, which inspired only a fraction of the erection the image deserved.

"I hope other religious leaders aren't sending death threats to Montgomery Shoale," I said.

She laughed. "We'd never let that happen."

"No, you probably wouldn't."

"My point is that you should let chapter one simmer in your head for a while. The truth of it will reveal itself."

"I like to watch things reveal themselves."

Her smile faltered for a second and then recovered, like an ice skater coming down badly from a lutz yet determined to carry on, as she left to talk to Shang-lee, who held *The Prescription* six inches from his face, his left foot sliding in and out of his slipper.

At counseling I sat next to Mihir, who, while we waited for Mr. Ramsted to come out of a private conversation with Quenlon and Helmut by the door, said that he'd just been studying the prophecies laid out in chapter nine and found hints about the Last Day. Intimations. Suggestions. We could be sure that UR God was not springing this on us, but had been planning it all along. His eyes were bloodshot. Had I thought about what he'd said the day before, that if he could overcome the sexual bravura expected of men then so could I? Admitting my problem to myself ought to be my five-day goal. After that I would admit it to him and then to everyone in counseling. The life I saved would be my own.

"Before we get started," said Mr. Ramsted, returning to the table, "let's thank Rema again for her presentation yesterday. I'm sure we're all still thinking about it. If there's time at the end of the session maybe we can go over some of its instructional aspects. First, though, I'd like to give Mr. Smith a chance to revise his position, in case he's had any new insights in the last twenty-four hours."

"Please," said Mihir, "if I may be permitted to speak on Jack's behalf, it will take a few days for him to improve enough to contribute to counseling. I ask us to be patient. Perhaps now instead we could tackle the next item on our agenda."

After a deliberative pause, Mr. Ramsted said, "We could."

"Actually," I said, "I've given it some thought and want to say that I do feel bad about some of my past sexual activity. Not all of it, but some."

Mihir looked at me. "You do?"

Mr. Ramsted pinched his goatee and nodded as though, having been told he would never train a bear to juggle, his pet grizzly had just done the Cascade in both directions. "I'm delighted to hear it," he said.

"Yes, and it's interesting because—"

"Stop right there," he said, holding up a hand. "This illustrates a point I've made before that is worth repeating, which is that it's easy to think we can fool others if we can fool ourselves. If someone says, 'Having sex with a stranger is great. So what if they get hurt afterward, or I feel empty, or our potential for friendship is destroyed?', it's a practiced lie that comes out easily. But when they think about it, which they can't help doing, such is the gift and curse of consciousness, they recognize that lie as an affront to the truth, and they must retract it. Just like Jack has. The ease with which people lie means nothing. Sex is so conflicted a topic in our society that they adopt a cavalier attitude toward it in order to smother their guilt. Remember what Jack said yesterday? That he had no qualms with sex? Most adults go to great lengths to accept and approve of what they want to think is a natural, necessary act, though really sex must be renounced not because it's a transgression but because it's an obstacle on our path to UR God."

I was about to make a production of agreeing that I had been wrongly oriented all my life, that I had indeed tried to fool myself into thinking of sex as harmless fun, in the same way that a murderer, to assuage his conscience, will brag about killing—*I shot a man in Reno just to watch him die*—when for a split second I believed this contrived speech. For a heartbeat it was true, and I felt dismay, a fear that I'd played the devil's part in my own deception for years, for decades. This moment passed quickly and my old way of thinking— "the real me," I thought, taking myself firmly in hand and warning me against losing my bearings—returned, but still I was so shaken by my fleeting agreement with Mr. Ramsted that I didn't trust myself to speak.

At lunch I walked past the meat and pasta tables to the salad bar, where I built a colorful plate of spinach, tomatoes, broccoli, red onions, carrots, yellow peppers, and cottage cheese. I selected a sugar-free iced tea from the beverage bar. Sitting at my table, Tonya noticed that the painting I'd done the day before was now hanging on the dining hall wall. I allowed that it might be a portrait of UR God. One man's humble and unwitting attempt to capture His mighty visage. I felt strangely confident—without knowing of what—and tried not to evaluate the motivation or sincerity of what I was saying. Alastair asked if UR God had implanted the knowledge and talent in me, or if I'd been inspired in a dream. I can't say, I said, chewing my salad. But you must have some explanation for it, he said. No, I answered, unsure if I was fooling myself, him, or nobody.

*   *   *

In class Mr. Ortega gave a lecture on renunciation, the necessity of which every religion recognized and extolled and which, outside of *The Prescription,* had been noted by sages from Pythagoras to Julian of Norwich to Kierkegaard to the Dalai Lama—Augustine had written that one must choose "love of God in contempt of one's self"—all of whom believed that giving up something we love, of saying no, was, although disguised as a negative, really the ultimate positive, that only when we deny ourselves pleasure can we attain something greater, such as the eternal and irreducible bounty of UR God's presence.

"But what's wrong with pleasure?" I asked. "We all like it."

"It ends in itself," said Mr. Ortega. "It doesn't point or lead to anything more because it is outside of UR God—that is, it is *here*—and here is not part of ultimate reality."

"It feels like reality to me," I said.

"You used to have insomnia and back pain, didn't you?"

"Yes."

"And now you don't."

"Well, today I don't."

"So what was a real condition isn't real anymore. What you thought was true isn't true anymore."

"That's—I wouldn't put it that way. My insomnia and back pain come and go."

Mr. Ortega turned to the others. "Pay attention, everyone, because this question of reality is crucial to understanding PASE. We were brought up to think about it as the world around us, as everything we can touch, hear, see, taste, and feel, but those things change over time, like the circumstances of life itself. Our hair changes color, our bodies grow and shrink, we are well sometimes and sick at other times. Accordingly, we've been trained to view reality as fluctuating, ebbing and flowing. As Jack said, we think that it comes and goes. *The Prescription,* however, tells us that reality is in fact constant. It is always true. Consequently we are not in it. If we want to see through the illusions of illness and death and unhappiness, we must embrace the permanence of UR God. Only then will we earn—and return to—our place within Him."

"If UR God never changes," I said, "how did we break away from Him in the first place? Wouldn't that have caused a change in His being, just like us fusing back into Him would?"

Mr. Ortega pressed his palms together. "What appears to us to be a paradox is in UR God a consistency. This is a difficult part of PASE doctrine and won't become clear until you reach the master actuated savant stage of learning."

"What about Him wanting us back? Isn't that the same as desiring us?"

"He doesn't want us back. He is complete with or without us."

"But he gave us *The Prescription* so we could return to Him."

"That too is a puzzle you mustn't hope to solve yet."

During the research period I watched a video parable about a woman who changed into a tree to escape a lustful coworker, and whose roots burrowed to the center of the Earth while her trunk grew up into space, and who then allowed people not carrying or wearing anything to climb her "all the way to UR God." It was done in the psychedelic style of sixties art-house cartoons, with loud, garish colors and bubble figure grotesqueries, and a Crumby Yellow Submarine, and when it ended I went to the bathroom to splash water on my face. Returning to my seat I passed Warren at the water fountain.

"What did you think of Synergy?" he asked, straightening as the arc of water died down the drain.

"It was pretty good," I said, stopping to look around. The other guests and facilitators were engrossed in their projects.

"Yeah?" Warren folded a PASE pamphlet in half and ran his fingers along its crease to create a sharp edge. "But not enough to change your mind about getting out of here."

"Excuse me?"

In a low voice he said, leaning toward me, "I've got a plan but it's not a one-person job."

"Is here the place to talk about this?"

"Talk about what?" Mihir, though he'd been across the room staring at a computer tablet just a second before, was standing between us, a manufactured look of innocence on his face. He glanced at a facilitator sitting behind a desk twenty feet away, who with his head lowered was staring at us and organizing stacks of pamphlets.

"I was telling Jack about how hard it is to control my anger sometimes," said Warren, cracking his knuckles, "and how I get the urge to beat up people who annoy me because they're loud or stupid or interfering."

Mihir's upper body tensed and he closed the gap between himself and Warren. "In that case I wonder if the Wellness Center is the right place for you. Maybe you would find the Adjustment Facility more helpful. Maybe we should go right now to Ms. Anderson and tell her that you would like to be transferred."

"What's the Adjustment Facility?" I asked, stepping into and widening the small breach between them.

Mihir said, "It's a more structured place than here, with more hands-on guidance, designed for people who require extra discipline to improve. Not everyone responds best to positive inducement, you know."

"Why don't you let Jack and me finish our conversation?" Warren said. "Doesn't seem like you have much to contribute."

"I have something more edifying to share with my mentee than tales of ignorance and aggression. Jack, please come with me for a moment, if you don't mind, and then you must want to return to your videos."

With a light hand on my back, Mihir steered me to his desk while Warren stayed behind with his arms folded. Once we were seated, Mihir warned me again about the company I kept. What did it take to get me to grasp the gravity of the situation? Then, brightening, he read aloud the op-ed piece he planned to send to newspapers all over the country. Warren was gone when I looked over at the fountain.

"Were you listening closely?" Mihir asked when he finished, studying my face.

"Yes," I said.

"What is most persuasive about it, in your opinion?"

His article was an impassioned defense of UR God's selection of Montgomery Shoale to be His spokesman for the truth. Businessmen, Mihir wrote, were in the same relationship to money that kites were to air, which made them natural enemies of the truth that desire, in whose service money had been created, had to be stamped out. Knowing this, we might find it hard to accept that Mr. Shoale, a venture capitalist, had been chosen to be the prophet for this message. But UR God had an excellent reason for his choice. Mr. Shoale's inappropriateness for the job made him an ideal candidate, because if one of the most desire-oriented people on Earth could change and follow the truth, so could we. Mihir Singh, the author, himself a successful businessman, had discovered this personally and invited readers everywhere to explore the ultimate wisdom of PASE.

I told Mihir that its sincerity was undeniable, its reversal of expectations clever, and its style accessible. Then I went back to my seat, where the facilitator had deposited a stack of pamphlets. I read them all in turn.

During the recreation period I played a board game in which the object was to get one's stand-in piece (mine was a coal miner) past a series of temptations: a lonely housewife, a pyramid scheme to get rich, a double cheeseburger, an interest-free cash loan in Las Vegas. At dinner I had a bunless vegetarian hotdog and a side salad.

The evening's group activity was a film called *PASE in the World* at the Prescription Palace. We were given more juice, another fig bar, the same green seats. It opened on a balding, clean-shaven, tall man in his late thirties—Denver Stevens—standing in midafternoon on the roof of a Chicago skyscraper, with Lake Michigan stretched out behind him and a tripod-mounted globe in front. He removed his hands from his pockets and said he wanted to share some exciting developments with us. We knew about the explosive effect PASE was having on America, but were we aware that it was being embraced in dozens of foreign countries? That people of all creeds and colors found it an inspiring belief system, and that they were joining in staggering numbers?

Stevens spun the globe and stopped it with his right pointer finger. "For instance, the United Kingdom," he said, suddenly standing in London as Big Ben towered over him. "After America, we're growing fastest here. Thousands of new Pasers flock every month to the temporary PASE drop-in center at Covent Garden while a bold new PASE Station is erected near Kew Gardens. We can hardly keep up with the British demand to be part of ultimate reality." He spun the globe again. "China." The Forbidden City was etched behind him against the sky in dusky blues, like an ink drawing on a porcelain teapot. "The President here and his advisers have commissioned a thorough study of *The Prescription* and found a great deal to praise." The President at a factory opening, with subtitles: *PASE has a fascinating approach to zero population growth. We are pleased to consider its methods as we plot our course for continued prosperity for all our people.* Globe spin. An imam from Iran who between his turban and beard was just a pair of gold-framed sunglasses and a nose, standing before a giant mosque: *We greatly esteem PASE's enjoinment to chastity and modesty. PASE recognizes to a degree that few other religions do the hazards of sensuality. If Islam has a moral ally in the world today it is Prescription for a Superior Existence.* Globe spin. "Africa." Near an entryway to Serengeti National Park, with semiwild ungulates roaming in the distance, a dozen men in suits stood with their hands behind their backs. *PASE is potentially a breakthrough in global health development,* said one, *a viable plan that could save millions of lives while promoting peace and personal responsibility. I speak for my colleagues here today, representing seven great nations, when I say that we are very hopeful about what it can do for our people.*

The screen cut back to Stevens, whose keen expression turned thoughtful while the Eiffel Tower sprang up in the background. "Even France is now embracing PASE. Perhaps you've heard that last year Minister of Culture François Pissoud, under the influence of petty xenophobic advisers, attacked PASE and tried to prevent a Wellness Center from being built in Marseilles. That was a dark day for liberty in this freedom-loving country." On-screen a red-nosed man addressed the National Assembly; English subtitles scrolling along the bottom of the screen: *PASE is little more than an American by-product of fast food and television, of a lifestyle so fattening and masturbatory that it has invented an excuse to do away with labor-intensive intercourse; we should not be surprised that it has come in the form of a new religion, for at heart Americans, beneath their incredible gluttony, have always been hysterical Puritans.* Stevens came back on. "More recently, however, after investigating PASE for himself, Monsieur Pissoud had something quite different to say." Pissoud again, calmer, with a paler complexion and a respectful quiver in his lower lip: *My comment several months ago about PASE was itself hysterical, and I am deeply ashamed of it. PASE is a profound and vital religion that I have proudly joined. If France is to escape its sadly divisive ethnic quagmire, if it is to hope for universal improvement, it would do well to embrace the practices set forth by Montgomery Shoale in Prescription for a Superior Existence.* Stevens again. "As you can see, no corner of the planet is blind to the wonder and splendor of PASE."

The screen then segued into a montage of people representing nearly every race, culture, age, gender, class, and physical condition. They wore PASE buttons on T-shirts emblazoned with the PASE logo—*The Prescription* cover, with all its glowing dashes (wands)—and were either seated against a solid white backdrop or engaged in charitable activities. A Japanese schoolgirl pushed an elderly Egyptian man in a wheelchair into a PASE Station. A Dutch businessman read from *The Prescription* to barefooted Mayan Indians in a hilltop Guatemalan schoolroom as an ox stuck his head through the glassless window. Three middle-aged women—black, white, and South Asian—embroidered a giant quilt with the Reality Facts stitched onto it at a PASE Process clothing distribution warehouse. Two men helped a junkie wrap up his crack cocaine paraphernalia and throw it into a Dumpster outside a Wellness Center. A short woman wearing a PASE hat walked down a Jerusalem street holding hands with an Israeli girl on one side and a Palestinian girl on the other, and as the shot faded to gray she stepped back from the middle and linked them together.

The lights went up and I clapped respectfully along with the other guests. Whatever arguments could be made against PASE on rational and theological and scientific and biological grounds, its usefulness in the global struggle against overpopulation could not be denied, nor could the benefit of its philanthropic work combating poverty, drugs, and the neglect of old people. And its actions against sexually transmitted diseases were commendable, even heroic. Mihir and I filed out of our row and said good night to the facilitators closing up the theater. Outside, pools of ground lighting illuminated from below the trees and gardens and path we followed back to the dorm, where, exhausted from a day's activity that was more varied and educational than any in my working career, I brushed my teeth. Also noteworthy was the religion's role in uniting cultures traditionally antagonistic toward one another. Yes, to see so many world leaders endorse PASE across so many political and ideological divides—and to know that it intended good without prompting by government or concerned citizens or greed, sui generis, because its nature was to help those in a position of weakness climb to a position of strength—well, I was impressed.

I fell asleep the second my head touched my pillow.

CHAPTER 6

F riedrich Dürrenmatt, a Swiss dramatist, novelist, and essayist, once wrote, "The worst possible turn can not be programmed. It is caused by coincidence." He wrote this because he knew nothing about how life and the world operated. I wouldn't mention him, for he ought to be forgotten, a crushed carbon flake on the ash heap of history, if his belief in coincidence weren't so widespread. Elizabeth, for example, like Monsieur Dürrenmatt, denied the gravitational forces that cause misfortune because she had never been pinched by their influence, whereas I, who after being fired at Couvade, was being flattened by them, knew immediately after seeing Teresa/Mary on the street that her relation to Montgomery Shoale was no more a coincidence than was the moon's maintaining a constant distance from the Earth, and I knew, as a bus horn trumpeted behind my car and the policewoman eyed me suspiciously, that the sooner I discovered the properties of attraction involved, the better able I would be to cultivate those of repulsion.

At home I printed out a picture of Mary Shoale from the Internet and took it to Conrad, who answered his door wearing a gray bathrobe so loose and rumpled on his round body that it resembled elephant skin. His wiry, untrimmed eyebrows splayed out in every direction like the bristles of a worn paintbrush.

"Is this your student?" I asked, holding up the picture.

With a tobacco-stained forefinger he lightly traced the outline of her face. "No."

"This isn't the woman who was here the other night?"

"It's her, but her hair's different."

I could see behind him into his apartment, the structural layout of which was identical to mine, though its walls were a brownish taupe that gave the place an earthy, underground feel. A baby grand piano stood between two footstools against the side wall, and stacks of music books and blank score sheets were arranged around the square room like chess pieces in midgame. A portrait of J. S. Bach— except for one's powdered wig, the resemblance between the two portly men was uncanny—hung over the piano, framed in a resplendent gold leaf chain of treble clefs and G-bars.

"Why did you say she's not your student?" I tried to slip the picture of Mary into my breast pocket, but it was too big and I had to fold it in half and stuff it into my back pocket. Conrad tracked its movements as though we were playing a shell game.

"She quit taking lessons yesterday."

"Why?"

"She didn't give a reason, but I think it's because you complained."

"Did you know her real name is Mary?"

"Of course."

"She didn't tell you it was Teresa?"

"No."

I turned and ran down the stairwell to the street level where, opening the door that led to the corner of Hayes and Fulton, determined to find answers to questions that weren't entirely clear to me, like a scientist who has found data anomalies that appear natural but must be the result of human error, I slammed into someone coming in. It was a violent collision and we staggered back like gonged bells. My chin and jaw felt wrenched out of place and I sank to the ground in pain, while she covered her forehead with both palms and leaned against the wall. Rising to my feet as the world came back into focus, I checked for my wallet and saw that I had collided with Mary in the Teresa wig.

"You," I croaked, the single syllable gargling out thickly from the back of my throat.

"Are you okay? Let's go inside. I need an ice pack."

"So you know me now?" I touched the lower half of my face gently, applying little or no pressure. Every word was torture.

"Yes. Please, let's go in."

"There must be cops waiting in the hallway to entrap me."

"It's not like that. I'll explain inside. Let's just—please!" Dropping her hands to reveal a round red welt spreading from beneath her bangs to her eyebrows, she took my elbow and slowly climbed the stairs to my apartment, the maimed leading the maimed. I filled two washcloths with ice and wrapped them up, one for her and one for me, and we stared at each other from either end of the kitchen like wounded duelists.

"Thanks," she said, applying the pack to her injury. "Maybe you should sit down."

I shook my head and winced.

"Mind if I do?"

I gestured to a chair.

Wiping away the tears that slowly collected and fell from the corners of her eyes, she said, "Could I have a glass of water?"

"I'll remind you to use the bathroom before you go."

"I feel dizzy." She stared uncertainly at the wall calendar's picture of a moonlit Yosemite Park. "I'm sorry about the police earlier, but I had to call them in case anyone noticed us talking. What I said about my name and father was true. And this isn't my real hair." She tugged on the black wig and a crop of short dirty-blond hair sprouted up in its place. Then she took a long series of gulps from the water I set beside her on the table, draining the glass as a few drops ran down her mouth and onto her sweater. "I don't know how we could have been moving fast enough for that impact. Everything seems so bright—I may need to lie down in a minute—unless there's a light we could turn off? Anyway, what I'm going to say is embarrassing, but I have to say it so let's just act like this is a normal conversation. I didn't randomly sign up for piano lessons from your neighbor. I did it because I wanted to meet you, and I wanted to meet you because I overheard a conversation between my dad and Couvade's CEO, who said there'd been sexual misconduct at your company and mentioned you as one of the offenders. It was just in passing as an example, and he named other people too, but my dad zeroed in on you and asked what kind of worker you were and what else you might have done against company regulations. Then he offered to provide the seminar to Couvade for free. That never happens. Normally PASE charges sixty thousand dollars for that kind of event, and more when my dad speaks."

"Why was your dad interested in me?"

"I don't know."

"Then why did you want to meet me?"

"So we could have sex."

I coughed violently, five seconds of agony. "But you're a Paser."

"No I'm not."

"You're Montgomery Shoale's daughter."

"Do you believe in everything your parents do?"

"Well—"

"My dad and I have a complicated arrangement," Mary said, "but basically I get an allowance in exchange for acting like a Paser and going to his charity events and conferences, for keeping up appearances."

"Having sex is not acting like a Paser."

"I cheat a little."

"But it's the most important thing."

"Not always, and besides he doesn't find out. I wear a disguise and use false names with men. You're the first one who's ever recognized me without the wig."

"I don't understand why overhearing your dad's conversation with Mr. Hofbrau made you want to have sex with me."

"I'm not ready for psychoanalysis right now. My head is killing me. Could I lie down? Just for a few minutes. And maybe I could have another ice pack?"

She stood up, eyes as wide open as if she were trying to see in the dark, the dripping washcloth pressed against her forehead, water drops from the melted ice mixing with her tears, and then, squinting as though floodlights had been thrown on, she fell to the ground.

Fifteen minutes later she regained consciousness on the couch and asked for another glass of water. I fetched it and a muscle relaxant—I'd taken five myself and felt exponentially better—and arranged a pillow behind her so she could sit up. The whole of her forehead had subsided from an intense, iron-oxide red to a dull aubergine, though the bump at its center was still angrily swollen.

"I think you have a concussion," I said. "I called an ambulance, which should be here in a minute."

"What?" she said, trying to sit up. "No! Call it off! If there's a medical record saying I was picked up here, someone will tell someone who will tell someone close to my father that you and I were together."

"And then you won't get your allowance."

"It's not that. What would happen to me is nothing. There'd be a scene and repercussions, but I'd live."

A knock sounded at the door, short but purposeful, followed by, "Hello! Open up! Medic!"

"Get rid of them!" Mary hissed, almost hyperventilating. "You must!"

Reluctantly, I went to the door and apologized to the paramedics and explained that the injured woman had left already, that I hadn't been able to prevent it. One of them asked me twice if I was sure that I was telling the truth. Back in the living room I found Mary's eyes rolled back, her jaw slack, and her breath coming in gasps. I tried to wake her with gentle slaps that grew in strength and volume to something like violence, then poured cold water on her face and sprinkled cayenne pepper into her nostrils. If anything she fell further from consciousness; a faintly aspirated sigh escaped her lips irregularly and her eyelids were motionless and REM-free. I was tempted to call the ambulance again but remembered Mary's words: "but I'd live." Had she placed a stress anywhere? *But* I'd live? But I'd *live*? But *I'd* live? The last variation, impossible and ridiculous, chased the other two out of my mind. *But I'd live and you wouldn't,* it implied. I sat on the edge of the couch beside Mary's supine body—she looked like a floating Ophelia—and told myself,

"I am not in any danger. 'But I'd live' is a figure of speech like 'she killed him with kindness' or 'I'll die if she doesn't call me.' Montgomery Shoale has eccentric ideas that have been codified into a religion, and his power and influence are wide-ranging, but he wouldn't kill someone for being alone in a room with his daughter."

When Mary's eyes opened she put diffident fingers to her cheek and the top of her head. "My face stings. Where's my wig?"

"In the kitchen."

"Did you send the ambulance away?"

"Yes. Were you saying that if your dad found out we were together, something would happen to me? Does he go after guys you've been with—as in, to hurt them?"

She closed her eyes again. "I told you, he doesn't find out about them."

At that moment, even disfigured, with half her face a rash of irritation, she struck me as the most lovely woman I'd ever seen. So that although she might objectively be called attractive, I felt myself to belong to a small subset of the world, perhaps encompassing me alone, that saw in her absolute beauty, the culmination of the female form. This sensation—wherein it's unclear if you were created to admire an object or it was created to be admired by you, and the question is meaningless against the force of your admiration—can either be a passing infatuation or a life-altering election. And even though at first you don't know which it is, the temptation to think, *I know this certainly, without preparation or precondition,* is irresistible. For me, at least, it was, and I know enough to call my behavior human nature when in hindsight it appears to have been foolish.

She opened her eyes and I looked away, prepared to say something to defuse the moment, but then we were kissing, and a second later we were holding each other with the desperation of a last embrace. "We shouldn't do this," I said inaudibly. Then we were on the floor with our hands everywhere, rolling around as though our revolutions would add up to a single, greater Revolution, and cloudlight filled the room like transparent smoke, and the roughness and smoothness of our skin, and the heat along its surface conducting back and forth, and our mindless sensitivity were all sides of a single shape.

At a certain point the silent noise in my head grew deafening and my body convulsed in relaxation and our fingers intertwined so fiercely they turned a bloodless white. Then everything quieted to susurrus and I became calm, as though I'd scaled a sheer cliff and could at last sit on its edge, able to survey the panorama that had been at my back. We were in the bedroom and lay faceup on a Peruvian throw rug my brother, Sid, had given me the year he went to Machu Picchu, our flush, warm bodies trembling.

"I didn't know that would happen," I said.

"Yes you did," said Mary, her temples smudged by black mascara and tears and sweat. A vein running beneath the bump on her forehead pulsed softly. She took my left hand between hers and traced my lifeline with a hooked forefinger.

"How often do you have sex with strangers?" I asked.

"Look at this pigmentation." She pointed to a tiny brown spot on my palm just below my thumb. "Chiromancers—palmists—in the seventeenth century would have said it means you've made a deal with the devil."

The room brightened and then darkened as a cloud break opened and closed before the sun. "What does your mother think about you pretending to be a Paser?"

She dropped my hand. "She died when I was a baby, before my father wrote *The Prescription*. He says she'd have been a Paser if she'd lived, though, because she believed he'd become the greatest prophet since Muhammad."

"Do you believe that?"

"Let's not talk about him anymore. I'm sick of the subject. Tell me about you."

"What about me?"

"Anything."

"I'm thirty-four years old and between jobs at the moment because of your—just because. My brother, Sid, is a graduate student in theater arts studying to be a director. He's African-American."

"Is he adopted or are you?"

"We both are."

"Are your parents still alive?"

"Yeah." I rolled up a shirt lying on the ground behind me and put it under Mary's head as a pillow. "They live in Fairfax."

"What about your real parents?"

"They are my real parents."

"I mean the ones responsible for your birth."

"I've never met them."

She pushed away the shirt underneath her head and replaced it with my right arm, a pose we held for a time. Then she stood up and padded down the hallway collecting her panties, skirt, bra, blouse, socks, and shoes. I watched her dress and desired her all over again, wanted to remove her clothes as soon as she put them on. "I've got to go," she said, standing in the doorway.

"Can I see you again?"

"No."

"Why not?"

"I don't see anyone twice."

"Never?"

She shook her head.

"So you haven't ever had a long-term relationship?"

"Not a romantic one."

"But don't you want love and intimacy?"

"I love a lot of people. And I have intimacy. I was just intimate with you."

"But you can't commit to someone and build a life together. That's—You're a prisoner, like Rappaccini's daughter."

"Who's that?"

"A character in a Nathaniel Hawthorne short story whose evil scientist father fills her with poison."

"What happens to her?"

"A young man falls in love with her."

"And then?"

"I don't remember."

She turned to go.

"So you're leaving now and we'll never see each other again?"

"I'm sorry."

Again.

And then again she was gone.

With my vast experience of being denied and left by women, I shouldn't have taken any more notice of her exit than does a scarecrow of a departing bird. I should have shaken off my budding attachment and told myself that there would be other fleeting encounters in the future, that I had many disappointments to go before I could rest, and that compared to Supritha and Camilla, Mary could not have meant anything to me by then. Instead I felt the loss sharply. It was as though I'd arrived at the place where I would have liked to live forever—after years of finding every settlement inhospitable—only to be told that its governor had ordered its evacuation, that he'd decreed it too beautiful for mortals to inhabit. I ached everywhere but in my jaw, which the memory of Mary's kisses numbed into wellness. She had never seen me fat or known what a poor figure I cut in the world, didn't know what an untouchable I was in the realm of love. In her mind I could be anyone. I could be the One. To her I didn't have problems with drugs and alcohol and insomnia; I could have a glorious professional future; I could be my parents' favorite child.

But it wasn't the opportunity to reinvent myself that excited and filled me with regret at its disappearance; it was the comfort I felt with her—quite opposite of my apprehension when she'd been Teresa—the way she and I simultaneously anticipated and were surprised by what the other had done during sex. The way every action complemented the ones before and after. I thought that in another situation this could have turned into love, that if not for a certain third party, we could have worked toward and fashioned the most meaningful bond imaginable. I decided while lying there on the ground at eye level with my shoes and socks and crumpled pants that the third party, Montgomery Shoale, had come to occupy too central a place in my life, and I wanted him gone. He didn't belong in it. Nor, really, did he belong in Mary's life if his influence was going to be so detrimental. Her behavior, except for during clandestine meetings like the one we'd just had, simulated a Paser's, so it almost didn't matter if in her heart she didn't subscribe to its tenets. She was forced, on the surface at least, where it's so easy to get stuck, to act as though she did. We had no chance to save each other.

This was especially upsetting because it seemed that if allowed to be together, we might even go beyond saving to reach a level where our compulsions—mine toward food and alcohol, for example, and hers toward transgressive sex—would slow down or shut off, leaving us free to do as much good as our defects had formerly led us to do bad. It seemed that there was nothing wrong with us that love, meaning-maker and pain-absolver, couldn't fix, just as there was no reason why with luck, with Mary, with some adjustment, I would remain broken.

After showering and working through a half-tray of lasagna that Imelda-Maria had left in the fridge that morning, I sat down to watch television. One of the climatologists I'd heard on the radio was discussing the steps people could take to lessen pandemonium in the future; by totally changing their lives right now, by making personal sacrifices on a hitherto undreamed-of scale, the planet would be less devastated in a hundred years. She had a hard time maintaining professional composure, like a teacher lining up her students for a fire drill evacuation after learning that flames have engulfed the floor below them.

Some time later I woke up from a partial nap to answer my doorbell. Conrad, angrily tapping his cane on the carpet, said that he could hear every word of the game show blaring out of my television. While agreeing to turn it down I spied a piece of paper on the ground that had been slipped under my door. I picked it up. A photocopied, typed note, it read: *Your recent association with "Teresa" must end now and should not have begun in the first place. Maybe you acted out of ignorance? Have no further contact with her and tell no one what happened between you. If you disregard this warning retaliation will be swift and severe.*

Conrad, annoyed that I was ignoring him, said he wouldn't hesitate to complain to the Tenant Committee if I didn't do what I'd promised. I shut the door and went to the kitchen and worked through a quart of ice cream. The note had a terrible vagueness and familiarity. I cut a block of salami into six thick wedges and chased them down with a glass of milk. Was it serious or just the bluster of a man whose messianic complex, informed by a deep and irrational hatred of sex, led him to bully and intimidate people who'd accidentally, although, in retrospect, gratefully, been intimate with his daughter, like me? The darkness outside was total and my afternoon had evaporated without my doing anything more to find a job. How had Montgomery Shoale found out about us? Perhaps Mary lied that he knew nothing. Or perhaps she was unaware of what he knew. Whatever the explanation, it was an ugly, disturbing message.

I searched online for her phone number, hoping to learn that she'd written the note herself as a prank so that I would call and she could laugh at how easily I spooked. However juvenile and sadistic and unlikely, it was preferable to any other explanation. But there was no Mary Shoale listed. Or Teresa Shoale. I called the PASE Station and in an unnaturally low voice asked for her number and was told it was private.

On television the news ran a story about the still immeasurable destruction in Seattle as rescue workers hunted for bodies and neutralized downed power lines. The president pledged his support for the Pacific Northwest and called for more religious tolerance among the American people, touting bipartisan support in Congress for a planned Have Faith in Faith Day the following month. Another story came on about the sickly oceans, with an inevitable wipeout of the world's seafood supply, dangerous tidal irregularities, catalyzed water warming, polar glacier liquefaction, and rock destabilization in newly submerged islands. My problems seemed trifling in comparison to the planet's impending death from a dozen causes at once, as though it were a victim on the Orient Express, and for a moment I felt nothing.

But then, upon changing the channel to a soft-core Western, I felt something. I felt arousal. It was all-at-once and all-consuming, so I grabbed some lotion and a hand towel, adjusted the room's lighting, massaged my wrist, and reclined on the couch for a private moment. A car commercial without sexual undertones interrupted the movie. While waiting for it to end a knock came at my door that I ignored because the television had returned to a pert young squaw slapping the cowboy who was creeping into her teepee. She fought off his advances—protesting too much, the movie implied—before giving in enthusiastically. Forty-five seconds later, frozen in ecstasy, I heard the knocking grow louder and more insistent. Toweling myself off and muting the television, I tiptoed to the door and looked through the peephole. It was Conrad.

"I know you're in there," he said.

"Yes?" I answered, opening the door a crack.

"I told you that I'd complain to the Tenant Committee the next time you played your television too loud. Is it cable or something from your own private collection?"

Just then a sound, soft but distinctive, came from my kitchen window, which opened onto the fire escape. "Wait," I said, putting a finger to my mouth and molding my body to its most receptive, radarlike shape, trying to catch every datum of information the next sound would convey. The kitchen window in question was locked, but I knew that with skill and dedication, with the requisite tools and patience, it could be opened. A creak. "Did you hear something?" I asked and then ran to the hallway utility closet to root through the clutter of a vacuum cleaner, dust mop, and window squeegee. Conrad hobbled along behind me.

"What's the broom for?" he asked, peering over my shoulder.

"Someone's breaking into my kitchen from the fire escape." I pulled out my phone and called the police and was put on hold.

"Go in there and they'll get scared and leave."

"They're not thieves; they've come to kill me."

"Do you owe them money? Is it the Mafia?"

"No."

"Because the Mafia have guns and a broom will be useless against them."

"It could get dangerous here; you should go back to your apartment."

"Why would they break in through a window instead of busting down the door?"

I didn't answer and he left. Then, tucking my phone between my shoulder and ear, I held the broom in a defensive horizontal posture and went to peek into the kitchen, where a man in a purple ski mask was hoisting himself through the window. He was a giant, perhaps six foot ten and built like a longshoreman. The Goliath of Pasers. I retreated to the bedroom and locked the door behind me and prayed for the police to pick up my call. This was my chance for them to catch PASE in the act and then protect me as I clearly needed to be protected. Otherwise, alone and defenseless, I didn't have much hope. PASE had apparently decided to snuff me out in a brutal and violent way, despite my being no more guilty than a cockroach for the revulsion it inspired in people to whom it had done nothing. I deserved to live on in darkness.

There were footsteps in the hall. I grabbed a pair of pajama bottoms bunched nearby on the floor and draped them over me as camouflage. They didn't cover much, so I added a jacket and two T-shirts to complete the cocoon, then like a moth I lay immobile, my call still on hold.

The door rattled and I whispered into the phone for an officer to pick it up. The door rattled some more and then popped open. Light flooded in and a pair of cut-out eyes rested on me. Dropping my phone just as a voice asked what the emergency was, I jumped up and waved the broom in front of me.

"Put that down," said the giant in a low, serrated voice.

"I'm at 549 Birch Street, apartment 8-A!" I shouted. "Send help it's murder!" A fuzzy response crackled out of the phone, which the giant smashed with an enormous steel-toed boot. *Like a cockroach,* I thought.

When I windmilled the broom around, as I had seen done in kung fu films, he charged at me, seized and disposed of the broom, and slammed me against the wall, knocking the wind out of me and renewing the pain in my jaw tenfold. I lifted my arms but he clamped them together with one viselike hand and then stepped back to deliver what would have been a first and final blow to my head had not Conrad entered the room with a gun and said, "Stop it! Let go of him. That's right. Step away and take off the head mitten."

The giant was at once calm and collected, at complete variance with the whimpering, shivering wreck I'd become, as he peeled off the mask to reveal the mongoloid arrangement of his oversized nose, mouth, forehead, and ears. He rubbed his scalp and ran his hands over his face to wipe away sweat.

"What are you doing here?" asked Conrad, holding the gun in his right hand and leaning on his cane at a Little Tramp angle.

"I came to rob the place."

"That's not true," I said, slipping past him, rubbing my wrists.

"Why did you attack Jack?"

"I heard the guy who lived here was on vacation. I wasn't going to hurt him, just tie him up so I could do the job."

"Who told you I was away?" I asked.

"Some guy I met."

"You're not with the Mafia?" Conrad asked.

"He's with Prescription for a Superior Existence," I said.

"I'm not with anybody," said the giant. "Why don't I leave and I'll never bother you again? I've got fifty bucks and you could have it."

"Why would PASE send this man to harm you?" Conrad asked.

"There are reasons."

"So it's not the Mafia you're afraid of?"

"No. I need to tie him up till the police can get here. Let me use your phone."

I called the police again, fixed a triple whiskey, and then with extension cords bound the giant's hands and feet together, so that he sat in a Lotus position.

While I lit and concentrated on a cigarette, he said, "These are tight."

"Shut up," said Conrad, who landed a solid blow on the middle of his back with the tip of his cane. The giant winced but said nothing; a bead of sweat rolled down the side of his wide glossy face.

"Don't use excessive force," I said.

"He came to kill you."

"I didn't!" cried the giant with a trace of panic that pushed his voice up past the adult register to land in a child's. Before he could say anything more Conrad rapped him on the head and he slumped over, his mouth drooling, his drawn eyelids a dark crimson.

"I need to talk to him," I said, taking the cane from Conrad's hands. "You can't knock him out like that, or kill him, or whatever you did."

"He's not dead." Conrad gently took back his cane.

I kneeled down and placed a hand on the giant's neck to determine that he was still alive. "You're lucky."

"He's an intruder. If I killed him it'd be self-defense; every court in the country would rule in my favor."

"This is my apartment, and I don't want him dead. Please just stand here and be supportive."

When the giant stirred, Conrad, looking very excited, prodded him with his cane.

I said, "What are your orders?"

"I told you I was trying to score. Maybe someone else is coming here too, but I don't know anything about it."

"You're a Paser and you're going to tell the police that. You came because you're a sexophobe with a mindless vendetta against me. I want to know exactly what your plan was from the beginning up until my death."

"I never wanted to hurt you!"

Conrad raised his cane in the air but I put up a hand to stop him from lowering it. Then I went to the kitchen and pulled the fire extinguisher from its wall hook beneath the sink. It was cherry red and compactly heavy, like a bundle of dynamite.

"It's up to you whether I use this," I said, bringing its nozzle close to the giant's face.

A pitiable sound escaped his throat. "I'd tell you if I knew!"

I unlatched the extinguisher's safety valve and he tried to move away and I pulled the trigger. The sodium bicarbonate exploded onto his face, its hiss creating a demented harmony with his cries while I held the canister steady. Conrad sat on the couch and smiled with a combination of bloodlust and awe, his good leg bouncing up and down.

When I released the trigger the giant, who'd twisted his head around in a futile effort to escape the blast, shut his mouth and moaned through his nose. Where his skin was visible a great red rash puffed up and in places showed that epidermal layers were sheared off. I could see glazed patches of pus and exposed capillaries. The rest of his head dripped white goo.

"Jesus," said Conrad. "You got him."

"Admit that you're a Paser and want me dead."

The giant opened his eyes cautiously, like someone peeking in a game of hide-and-seek, and said, "I swear—"

I cut him off with another discharge, this one longer and trained on his nose and his left ear and his chin. He gagged and coughed and seemed beyond expressing pain in sound, was just a massive writhing body of snorts and convulsions, until eventually, tiring, I turned it off again. Minutes passed before he moved without twitching.

"Shouldn't the police be here by now?" I asked Conrad.

"It's Friday, the busiest night of the week."

"You'd think they'd put more officers on duty."

Conrad shrugged.

Turning my attention back to the giant, I said, "Which Paser are you reporting back to? Denver Stevens?"

After a moment, looking like a body that has washed ashore after a storm at sea, he whispered, "Yes." Orange gelatinous matter trickled out of his mouth. His eyelids were swollen shut, his nose was slanted to the right and bruised blue.

"You don't believe that, do you?" asked Conrad, whose fascination with the spectacle on the ground was now total. "He's just saying what you want to hear."

It is true that at a certain point in interrogations involving torture, you can't trust a confession. Enough pain has been administered to either addle the victim's brain or make them say whatever will bring respite. I'd reached an impasse with the giant where the truth could no more distinguish itself than a future president could be selected from a nursery, which made me wonder if the police would believe my story, especially if, as was possible, the giant was a paid mercenary without any demonstrable links to PASE.

"Well?" said Conrad.

"I'm thinking."

"Please take me to a hospital," the giant murmured. "I could get an infection."

"Don't be a baby," said my neighbor, swatting him on the back of the thigh before I could prevent it.

As I considered what to do, and as Conrad stared at the wounded man, the front door crashed open and four armed men took up positions around us. *The police!* I thought, overjoyed, until a woman strode through the formation to the middle of the room, pointed a gun at the giant, and fired. Then she turned it to me. I dropped the extinguisher.

"Sorry about this," she said, her gun going *bang*.

CHAPTER 7

On my third morning at the Wellness Center I again woke up erectionless and pain-free. This time I neither lamented the first condition nor exulted over the second, for the trade-off was at present unimportant, since I had no outlet for my sexuality anyway. There would be time later to resuscitate my libido; now I had to concentrate on my performance.

It was a sunny morning, the sort that makes San Franciscans think theirs is the most temperate, interesting, blessed city in the world, impervious to the point made by New Yorkers that small people get drunk easily. The fresh air during exercises had a soft merino warmth and a sweet citrus fragrance and an almost mythic texture, like an updraft from the Aegean Sea to the top of Mount Olympus. I jumped and ran and caught and crouched and climbed. Although he hadn't the day before, Mr. Israel, unlike a drill instructor or coach, worked out alongside us, so that we all moved in tandem, a clutch of people exerting ourselves for health and heartiness, fortifying and raising our metabolisms like a public works project, a barn or civic center or bridge that would carry us to safety.

Apparently my reserve and caution against the Wellness Center was weakening. In a moment of reflection I scolded myself for the Aegean Sea/Mount Olympus fantasy—such a stupid comparison—but while running laps around Elysian Field I lost sight of whether I was pretending or actually enjoying myself. This worried me until endorphins flooded my brain and I reached the finish line, where Mihir and Tyrone were mock-kickboxing. After catching my breath, I joined the sparring—a few air jabs at Mihir's ear, a couple of roundhouse swipes at Tyrone's legs—and the three of us rolled about on the grass, wrestling and putting one another in choke holds. We ended up in a Möbius strip with Mihir's head stuck between my right arm and chest, Tyrone's neck clamped between Mihir's pronged calves, and my left leg held taut by Tyrone's feet. On the count of 1–2–3 we all let go and I fell on my back, laughing so hard tears streamed down my face. Something—yes, something significant—was going wrong with me.

Because the weather was so fair, after a breakfast of papaya, mango, and muesli, the reading period was held in the courtyard instead of the library. I found an empty bench and sat down with my copy of *The Prescription,* staring for a moment at the bodies lounging on the grass, alone or in clusters, as they would on a college quad. The difference, though, was that they were not arranged in sectarian cliques; I might have sat with any of them and been welcomed. The self-consciousness around my peers I'd had growing up, a condition that went into remission once I began my career and formed the sort of work-related bonds with people like Max and Juan that in adulthood replace youth's more cutthroat and idealistic friendships, yet that never fully disappeared, responded to this scene as to penicillin. Rema caught me looking at her and erupted into a great uncomplicated smile. I smiled back, realizing that for the first time since I was a child there were no sexual undertones in my smiling at her or her smiling at me, that although we were a man and woman we could regard each other in strictly platonic terms, without either of us wanting more or feeling imposed upon or questioning our own or the other's intentions. I felt that throughout my adult life the world had been tilted but now it was level. I didn't have to compensate anymore for my tendency to list in one direction or the other, a victim of sexual magnetism. I could walk in a straight line.

Chapter two of *The Prescription* began with UR God's forgiveness: "I forgive you any lies you've told to protect yourself or others, for although each was an abomination, you had not yet looked at the truth." It went on to apply the same formula to hitting, cheating, ignoring someone in distress, stealing, and a slew of other misdeeds. UR God wanted us to know that everything prior to the moment we began reading *The Prescription* didn't count. It was all preseason. Before then we had had a number of fine moral traditions to choose from—almost any religion, as well as secular humanism dating back to Socrates—but none that had prepared us properly or introduced us to the truth. *The Prescription* promised that if we kept our eyes open now, we would see it and never again be unsure of how to act.

I liked not being asked to go back and enumerate each of my past sins and apologize for them, as I had neither the memory nor the patience for so large an undertaking. Chapter two was a dry baptism. Although meaningless in the sense that Montgomery Shoale had no more authority writing under the pseudonym UR God than he did under his own to forgive my and others' moral lapses, it was a nice sentiment, an act of compassion so different from what had happened to me lately—those occasions when I was accused of things I hadn't done—that I felt an invisible cord draw tight between me and the author of *The Prescription* and everyone else currently reading the same thing. It was a fable, yes, a flight of fancy by a peculiar venture capitalist who may have been—probably was—non compos mentis, but I was finding things in it to like. Laudable qualities. There were worse vanity projects out there, political and cultural platforms designed to divide and conquer the world, whereas Shoale's sought to improve it. Given its role in my recent troubles, I ought to have kept my approval to a minimum— or to nothing at all—but there was no way to fight it just then, and I was tired of full-bore resistance, and I was feeling magnanimous. But only for a moment, I told myself. Only for now.

During counseling Mr. Ramsted asked if I was ready to share my story. I could, he said, in a more conciliatory mood than on my first

day, start out slow by describing my past sexual encounters without condemning them, as I would instances of any other activity,
like job-hunting or housecleaning. I could do a short warm-up.
Mihir didn't interject and I began tentatively to list the times I'd
bought drinks for women in bars and exaggerated my salary, intelligence, penis size, and endurance, which, when exposed as decep-
tions, led to more and less terrible scenes. Then I recounted the
occasions on which this approach had not succeeded, a chronicle of
failure depressing in its length and repetitiveness, so that if I'd been
a lab rat my handler would have put away the cheese long before my
hundredth or thousandth electric shock. I discussed the problems
sex had caused in my few long-term relationships, stemming from
my badly executed cunnilingus to my too-dirty dirty talk to my
partners' reluctance to role-play or film ourselves. I described my
porn collection—the boxes of magazines and videos, the terabytes
of computer files—and the hours I'd lodged at strip clubs downing
tequila shots and stuffing dollar bills into feline women's G-strings.
I told them about the half-dozen prostitutes I'd picked up in the
inner Mission district when barred from bars or alone at four A.M.
or on long lunch breaks. I told them about Chicago. It was an orgy
of disclosure, and the longer it went on the freer I felt, released from
a pressure I hadn't known weighed on me.

At one point I blurted out that my pursuit of sex was largely
directed by advertisements, bar counter conversations, and expectations placed on adult males. Although an obvious, outlandish lie on
its face, it seemed true on a deep unexplored level. After all, I
thought, setting aside my regular rationality, how did I know that I
would've worked so hard all my life to procure sex if it weren't an
obsession in society? How did I know what was natural when
everything had been altered by mankind, from bodies to brain
chemistry?

Although I didn't go so far as to agree that sex ought to be eliminated in order for us to leave the Earth for UR God, when the
counseling session ended and I was walking with Mihir and Tyrone
to lunch, in a dull trampled mood akin to sobering up after a three-

day bender, I wondered what had moved me to say so much more than a few general remarks, why I had instead gone on for two hours about the guilt and evil and sad redundancy of sex. It was an award performance and I was not an actor. Why? What had I been thinking? Early in my story I had stopped consciously faking it and spoken as earnestly as if I were drunk with a friend.

It occurred to me, because nothing else explained it, that I was being brainwashed by the PASE facilitators, and perhaps even by my fellow guests, or that I had developed Stockholm syndrome or one of its variants. This was a dark thought. I'd always considered mind control tricks like brainwashing and hypnosis scams on the order of faith healing and levitation, and now I had possibly become a victim of them. True, I'd only been there two days and no one had threatened me with pendulous stopwatches or violence, and I'd successfully reasoned away my gratitude for Ms. Anderson's professional help. Could the facilitators have changed my mind via honest legitimate means in so short a time? Was I that mentally weak? That suggestible?

No, something else had to account for my slippage. As we neared the dining hall I decided that my newfound sympathy for PASE was a correction for past erroneous thinking. Having been considered unattractive and largely ignored by women since the dawn of my sexuality, no doubt because of my weight and other factors, I had viewed sex, when it came my way, as an unmitigated good, an all-too-rare and wonderful occasion on which I was desired. I'd ignored its drawbacks and defects, the underside of the act that so plainly existed, because it made me feel better about myself. The blistering critique I had just laid out in counseling was thus a long-overdue swing of my judgment in the opposite direction, and I'd soon come to rest in a middle position.

But what about the porn, prostitutes, and strippers? How did they fit into my poor-fat-man-feeling-okay-about-himself revisionist theory? Easily. I'd been drawn to the seedy world of sex commerce as a temporary substitute for true human connection, when and where it wasn't available to me, which was almost always and almost everywhere. There was mixed into my murky pathology some self-loathing, a feeling that as a person who couldn't control his appetite I deserved the humiliation and abasement that redounds upon patrons of adult video stores and burlesque clubs and low-watt red-light districts. At the Wellness Center I was simply developing a fuller understanding that sex could be both magnificent and hateful—that it was shot through with ambiguity—neither all this nor all that. I would leave the place wiser but essentially unchanged.

After a lunch of squash risotto, a whole-grain roll, and an orange wedge more rind than flesh, I walked out of the dining hall by myself and ran into Paul. A recovering heroin addict, he was a scrawny young man with a close-shaven head and fidgety hands moving about in his pockets like mice looking for a way out. We descended a flight of stairs and he used the handrail for support, a little unsteady with each step. I offered him an arm and he accepted it.

"You okay?" I asked.

"Better than when I first got out of the Seclusion Ward," he said. "I had to use the electric rail chair to get up and down steps."

I opened the door leading outside after his light push failed to budge it.

"My muscles are pretty atrophied. It's why I sit on the sidelines during morning exercises instead of joining."

"I wondered about that."

"I hate not being able to do anything."

"It'll come back to you."

"You think?"

"When I had a weight problem I thought my days of exercise were over, but here I've been running two miles and doing the relays. You know what might help? Positive visualization. While you're sitting there in the mornings, imagine your body doing the same things everyone else is doing."

"We did that in Seclusion. Visualizing a life without heroin."

"Exactly."

He licked his chapped lips and stopped when a bee flew in front of him, lingering by his feet on its way from one flower patch to another. "You have any plans for recreation?" he asked.

"No."

"Because some of us are forming a discussion group to talk about our recovery without an instructor or facilitator or anybody to give official opinions, and I was wondering if you want to sit in."

"I talked a lot during counseling this morning. I don't know how much more I can say."

"Ms. Anderson said that these independent groups usually help guests become savants quicker."

"Did she?"

"Yeah. You'd be a good fifth, because you came as an involuntary admission and at first had a contrary vibe, but then right away you painted that portrait of UR God and it seems like you understand the idea of improving."

"Let me think about it."

I was a minute late to class and found Mr. Ortega asking for responses to the previous evening's film, *PASE in the World*. Not waiting for an answer and rubbing his enormous hands together, he said it had bothered him. He detested seeing Monsieur Pissoud's rabid attack on the truth again, even if it was juxtaposed with more recent, educated footage of the statesman, because it was so typical and provincial and infuriating. Mr. Ortega was sick of the bullying and hatemongering that went on in supposedly tolerant, democratic societies. Without the right to pursue the truth in whatever form it takes—and yes he did mean the infinite expanse of Ultimate Reality God—was anyone free? Was our world civilized?

"I'm not just talking about a few loose cannons in France," he said. "There are people in our own country, enemies of PASE who have forgotten that the Pilgrims came here to escape persecution from officials accusing them of bad faith. They conveniently ignore that Jesus and his disciples were considered a cult first by the Pharisees and then by the Romans. These people are outraged at how their own martyrs were treated but don't see that their actions parallel the Pharisees' and the Romans' and the Church of England's. The fact is that every established religion in the world has gone through a period of demonization and ridicule."

Mr. Ortega spoke as though each word burned his tongue, and his face turned a cochineal red. No one responded, presumably, like me, because they were unsure of what to make of his changed demeanor. Gone were his normal flat affect and daycare mien, and in their place was high dudgeon, almost fury.

"But it's not just the PASE critics' disregard for history or their efforts to destroy us that upsets me, it's the condescension they use in talking about us. People on the outside will say they don't understand why anyone would join a hierarchy that demands belief and fidelity and conformity with certain shared beliefs. They call us automatons and sheep and mindless followers, as if to subscribe to PASE is proof that we haven't the sense to take care of ourselves. That we've renounced our free will. You may not know this, but there are frightened, reactionary people out there who think that the lifestyle practiced here at the Wellness Center constitutes grounds for shutting down PASE."

This elicited gasps from two of the guests and solemn expressions from the others. I myself was bothered. Someone out there felt so much vitriol and hatred that they wanted to forcibly stop people from worshipping freely? Monsieur Pissoud's first speech had suggested this to me, but I hadn't extrapolated from it to the idea that PASE had active opponents working toward its demise. Why? Even I, who understood as well as anyone how unethical PASE could be—I was Exhibit A—thought that destroying the whole religion because of a few judgment lapses was excessive. If I were a real Paser I'd have considered it discriminatory.

Mr. Ortega's face returned slowly to a sandy brown. "The United States military expects just as much behavioral conformity from its members as PASE does—more, actually, given that recruits have to sign up for years and be willing to kill and injure people. And governments and corporations make their citizens and employees look and act a certain way. If you work for a private business, for instance, you wear a suit, just like at a fast-food chain you wear a uniform. And you memorize your company's bylaws and sign on to its mission statements. And promote it over and above rival companies. And spend the majority of your time thinking about and acting on behalf of it. And bend your free will in the service of an organization the priorities and dictates of which you had no hand in crafting."

Put this way, the movement against PASE seemed even smaller-minded and more troubling. Were people really so hypocritical? So ready to condemn others for normal behavior? What had happened to live and let live?

"This raises an interesting question," Mr. Ortega said, "which is this: Why do our attackers themselves live so subserviently? Rather than to improve as human beings, they conform in order to pay their mortgage and go to Disneyworld once a year, and save up for the medical bills that are going to weigh heavier than a coffin lid on their corpse. And to have something to do with their time that prevents their feeling like deadbeats or social pariahs. And to scrape together status in their community so they can someday sit on the board of this company and the steering committee of that social club. To me, this is far more objectionable than what we're doing.

"I'm sorry, I don't mean to rant, but Monsieur Pissoud's speech gets me mad in a hundred ways. By now, seventeen years after PASE first unveiled its message of truth and improvement and synergy with UR God, you'd think that he and those who share his tired prejudices would have learned that there is nothing puritan about PASE. We don't talk about sex more than any other desire. And even if we did I'd have to ask whether that would be so extraordinary. The Shakers banned sex just because it was sex. Catholic and Buddhist monks and nuns are abstinent, as are priests and holy people of nearly every major religion. Millions of Christians believe sex is good only for reproduction, and they'll often resist admitting even that.

"If you want to apply logic to it, as certain Frenchmen and other unimaginative rationalists do, why not ask if PASE's prohibition of sex is any more senseless and arbitrary than that against eating pork in Islam or Judaism? Or against eating beef in Hinduism? For that matter, why are women prohibited from baring their breasts in public? Why can't someone be married to more than one person? Why can't two homosexuals be married, period? Why is alcohol legal and marijuana not? I don't ask these rhetorical legal questions for an answer but to point out, as I did yesterday, that every belief system incorporates taboos and sets aside words and objects and actions that it deems off-limits. PASE, as the ultimate true belief system, is no different, and I am losing patience with people who criticize it on those or any other grounds. It's time for the religious chauvinists to end their campaign against us."

Mr. Ortega stared through the window as though a mob were about to collect on the lawn and demand that we all come out for a reckoning. Although I would have liked to pose a challenging question to him, as I had on previous days, so that he would compliment me on my inquisitive nature, none came to mind. I looked at him and felt an equal indignation toward Monsieur Pissoud and the other PASE naysayers. I saw the parallels between how corporate citizens and Pasers behaved, and I knew that to condemn one and not the other was bigotry. I thought about the accident of time that caused people in the dominant Christian tradition to consider their own idiosyncratic rituals to be normal and safe and noble, whereas, had the clock been turned back nineteen hundred years, these same people would have been imprisoned or murdered for their beliefs.

I said, "Besides Monsieur Pissoud, who is working against PASE?"

Alastair blew his nose and said, "I met people at home who were anti-PASE. A woman said to me just before I came over that I may as well commit myself to Bedlam as check into the Center. She laughed at me and this was after I'd given her my seat on the tube."

"That's how they return kindnesses," averred Mr. Ortega. "The mellower ones are likely to try having you declared mentally incompetent so they can remove your children from your care. It happened to my friend Salvatore. His ex-wife filed a court order to obtain full custody of their twin girls when he converted to PASE. She failed because the judge was a wise man, but that's the sort of thing we're up against. And people like Salvatore's ex are, as I said, the mellower ones. The more militant anti-PASE activists, members of what we call the religious gestapo, are determined to wipe out PASE altogether. These people, and may you never come into contact with them, aren't above anything: character assassination, evidence planting, terrorist bombing. In the past they've spread lies about Montgomery Shoale, left caches of weapons at PASE buildings and then sent anonymous tips to the police, and hidden explosives at facilitators' homes."

"Why do they do it?" I asked.

"The short answer is that they're sick. Maybe their mothers didn't love them. Maybe they haven't got any friends. I personally suspect it's because they recognize the truth of PASE and haven't the strength or the willpower to do what it takes to become an ur-savant; they figure that if they can't fuse into UR God, no one else should be able to, either."

"It's like the kid whose ice-cream cone falls to the ground and so he tries to knock yours down," said Tonya.

Mr. Ortega leaned forward and signaled for us all to do the same. "But don't worry. No one can erase the truth or make it not the truth by slandering it or blowing things up. It's inside you. Make no mistake: By following Prescription for a Superior Existence you will become a part of UR God, and all the gestapo operatives in the world won't be able to stop you. I know this is an unusual class period. We're supposed to be discussing *The Prescription* and instead I've railed against faceless enemies, but it's important that you understand the challenges we face as Pasers, that you see how we will meet and overcome them. Life is always hardest for people with convictions. Those who are weak hate the strong."

He leaned back in his chair and everyone rose and I fought off the adenoidal tug of tears.

During the research period, without thinking about its political value or scoring points with Ms. Anderson and the other facilitators, I joined the discussion group with Paul, Daytona, Shang-lee, and Rema. We arranged our chairs in a circle and Paul suggested that anyone who wanted should begin.

After a cursory pause, Daytona, a twenty-two-year-old doe-eyed alcoholic from Daytona Beach—when choosing her name her parents "were not imaginary"—said she may as well go first. Becoming a savant was so hard. Giving up booze would alienate her from her best friends, make meeting new people impossible, deprive her of a stress reliever, and leave her to fry in the anxiety that sometimes heated up within her. She understood and respected the PASE mission, but she wasn't sure she could achieve it.

"Drinking is what I do," she said, fingercombing her long blond hair. "I can't be around other people without it. Not to mention that no one likes the sober person in the room."

Paul said, "It's the same with heroin."

"You're around us now and you're doing fine," I said.

"That's because we're all here for the same reason. We have the same goal to become a savant."

"When you go home, find other Pasers to be around," I said, remembering a talk show that had given this advice to a similarly whingy young man trying to escape the party scene. "At least for a while, don't spend time with your old friends."

"Yeah."

"Don't worry if they interpret your change as a negative commentary on their lives, because they'll still be the same and they'll want you to be like you used to be."

"Yeah."

"Remaining the same forever is not in the nature of the order of things."

"Yeah."

"And forgive yourself."

"What?"

I couldn't think of what else the talk show had said, so I switched to *The Prescription*. "I won't guess all your reasons for drinking, but I'll bet the primary one was to overcome insecurity. Forgive yourself, because now you know the truth of PASE, that insecurity is as irrelevant and superannuated as teenage acne. You're courting the favor of UR God, not some group of lost boys and gaga girls."

She buffed her fingernails on her knees. "I'm fine with that now since I'm three thousand miles away, but back at home everything might get confusing."

"It won't, because your determination to stay sober and become an ur-savant is stronger than any situational difficulty you'll face. Just remember what we learned in class—our body isn't real or lasting or true; it changes. Even in the best of circumstances it will be gone in eighty years. Our spirit, on the other hand, is forever, and if we continue to improve it'll fuse into the permanence of UR God."

Shang-lee said, "Don't think of your future behavior based on the past. The whole point of improvement is that you become superior to your old self."

"That's right," I said. "A PASE pamphlet I read says it's like driving along the highway. You might sing or clip your nails or root around for something in the backseat, but when you come to a bridge and the road narrows you need to forget your distractions and concentrate on where you're going. The same thing is happening to us now as a species and as individuals; we've just crossed onto a bridge and have to get to the other side."

When the research period ended I told Paul how helpful I'd found the meeting and how oftentimes we discover our thoughts by listening to ourselves speak. He agreed and I felt a pang of guilt, because I saw in his face the purpose and intention to find and apply PASE's meaning to his own back-alley life. I saw that for him improvement was not a choice; it was an imperative. He had to turn around and go back to the highway he'd left a long time ago for heroin. I felt bad about being a pretender, a posturer, for the stakes were high here, and these people deserved to be around fellow travelers who supported them and their beliefs. I had no right to talk as though I were one of them. Unless—and this was just an idea—unless I decided to be a Paser for as long as I was at the Wellness Center. It might quell whatever inner chord of uneasiness the other guests heard in my presence. Yes, if I was going to be there and do everything a Paser did, there was no reason not to accept the beliefs that go along with it for the time being. I could—*would*—simply drop them once back on the outside, which was bound to happen even sooner if I took this step. My behavior, no longer a performance, would be a fast track to freedom. Yes.

For recreation we were given a lump of clay, a bowl of water, a throwing wheel, and a paring knife. Ms. Bentham, who'd first recognized UR God as the subject of my painting, made frequent passes by my work, each time with a pixieish grin. I built a little house that in some ways resembled a barn, with great swinging doors, shuttered windows, a gabled roof, and a water pump. I enjoyed working with the cold thick clay; the grainy residue that collected on my hands was like a slippery cousin to the sand I'd pushed into castles when I was a child and my parents had taken me and Sid to the beach in Bolinas, evidence that building something left its mark physically as well as psychologically. When I finished my clay house, Ms. Bentham noted that it was an exact scale rendering of Montgomery Shoale's childhood home in Wisconsin. I betrayed no surprise. It was, I seemed to say by saying nothing, part of my design.

From there I went to dinner, an eight-bean soup and nonfat plain yogurt, with Mihir, Tyrone, Shang-lee, and Tonya. Everyone seemed in better spirits than they had that morning, except for Mihir, who, holding a cheese quesadilla, was preoccupied. When Tyrone asked what was the matter, he said he was, with the Last Day approaching, increasingly concerned about how his wife would handle giving up their home and comfortable middle-class luxuries when he became a functioning savant. Of course he would press PASE on her as soon as he got home and pray to UR God for her conversion, but you could lead a horse to water and not make it drink, and there was Reality Fact #32, which he'd quoted to Warren to consider (not everyone will embrace the truth). What should he do if she took legal action to prevent his giving away their house and fortune to charity?

The question wasn't addressed to anyone specifically, but I felt moved, as a newly self-declared Paser, to answer. "Our greatest contribution to others' salvation is the example we set." I took a bite of soup. "If you follow PASE your wife will be moved by the power of your sacrifice and share in it. Moral truth is unassailable and in the end irresistible. Think of your countryman Gandhi, who was told that nonviolent resistance would do nothing to expel the British occupying army. Ultimately the English left without a war because in the face of Gandhi's actions and influence, they could no longer believe in the rightness of their colonial mission. The truth is stronger than any sophistry we invent to justify our own greed. By the time you've become a functioning savant your wife won't be able to resist joining your cause, because you are a Paser and in possession of the truth, marching straight toward UR God."

Mihir, his glasses riding low on his nose, said, "I would hate to have to divorce her in order to fulfill His prescription."

"You won't need to."

"I can tell you certainly that she loves our house with such intensity it's as though she built it herself. And the furniture and art she has spent our entire marriage selecting and arranging until it's all just so. She can be very headstrong, very inflexible."

"We're conformist animals," I said. "As a result we can be moved to good or bad based on the actions of those closest to us. People are said to resemble their pets for the same reason that they resemble their longtime spouses, because when we are in sympathy with a creature we mimic their facial expressions. When they are sad we reflect that sadness, when they're happy or consternated or intrigued we become their mirror images because that is how we show and convey love." I took another bite of soup. "My point is that we wield influence on people who care about us and vice versa, and by modeling your best—that is, Paser—self, you will win your wife's backing." I scraped the bottom of my soup bowl. "My younger brother, Sid, and I are both named in our parents' will, which doesn't amount to much in terms of money or property, but still, when they die, if the Last Day hasn't yet come, I'll donate my half to the PASE Process. I won't tell Sid that I'm doing it—I'll just write a check and have some movers take the things to 1152 Market Street—but once he finds out about it I expect that my donation will be doubled."

While speaking I'd kept perfectly still, as though in imitation of a Tibetan lama, but now I scratched my stomach and rubbed my face like someone who, after disturbing a hornet's nest, has inched free to safety. Safety? Was that the state I'd entered? My speech to Mihir, unlike the ready-made confession I'd made in counseling, had come from somewhere beyond me—from *somewhere else*—and I could not say just then if the reception would soothe or scorch me. It was as though after years of imagining myself to be real, I felt a tug on my arms and discovered wires extending from my elbows to the sky, and as though my voice, which I'd also thought my own, really belonged to a ventriloquist.

For the group activity we returned to the Prescription Palace to hear a concert. The musical director prefaced a performance of Shostakovich's first string quartet by saying that enjoyment of music was almost as difficult to break as appreciation of food and water, for which reason it was allowed Pasers until they became ur-savants, and that we shouldn't upbraid ourselves if, hearing a melody, we felt a frisson of pleasure, but that we ought to work on diminishing our response to it by actively disengaging from the music.

Afterward I slept for eight uninterrupted hours and felt no pain, and thoughts of sex were as scarce in my mind as in a newborn's.

The next morning I sprinted like a gazelle—Mr. Israel's comparison—across Elysian Field, outperforming my teammates in the relay competition and doing three push-ups for the others' two. Again the weather was ideal. I ran in several races, the first against Mihir and the last against a long-legged Kenyan who at home had wrested provincial power from his best friend, a two-term governor, by murdering him, and I beat all but the Kenyan. Mr. Israel said that my natural athleticism with training could develop into "something truly sensational." When Tonya dragged a hose over and used her thumb to create a vertical spray, I took turns with the others running through the multihued rainbow that sprang to life.

The reading period was again held outside. I took up my spot on the bench and read chapter three, a scathing indictment of desire that named and defined each of its main varieties and then gave capsule biographies of historical personages who had responded differently to them. Gourmands like Henry VIII and Ariel Sharon sought but did not find happiness through their stomachs; consider the enlightened fasts of César Chávez and Lanza del Vasto. Captains of industry like J. P. Morgan and William Randolph Hearst discovered sorrow at the bottom of their bank accounts, as opposed to the succoring poverty of Jesus and Mother Teresa. Philanderers like Martin Luther King Jr. and John F. Kennedy were afflicted by their sexuality, unlike the abstemious Pope John Paul II and Moses. Julius Caesar and Napoleon were undone by their lust for power; not so Benjamin Franklin and Marcus Aurelius.

After finishing chapter three, I tried but could not find fault in its argument. Having read a number of presidential biographies lately, I knew that its point about power being a Faustian bargain for those who attained it was absolutely true. Could there be a more broken man in the end than Lyndon B. Johnson? One as depressed as Abraham Lincoln? Or anyone, president or civilian, as disgraced as Richard Nixon? The other desires, the ones for which I personally had a weakness—sex, alcohol, food, drugs, money—I thought about just long enough to bemoan their abuse. It was clear that I'd been as reckless in their pursuit as a small child trying to get cookies down from the top shelf, and that I'd been lucky not to be too badly injured.

Although I should have spent the remaining reading period time taking notes and looking contemplative, instead I read chapter four, "Fables and Parables." It included the story I'd seen on video of the woman turning into a tree, as well as one about a man wearing sackcloth to work; a queen bequeathing her empire to a blind three-legged dog; a beggar refusing to live in a mansion; two turtles debating the best recipe for turtle soup; a lonely star waiting to supernova; a tree asking a woodsman to cut him down; and a group of children who lose their sense of smell, sight, touch, taste, and hearing, and who discover, when they are completely senseless, the meaning of life. There were other affecting tales, but something about the children made my throat and eyes burn. I closed the book and my vision blurred, and after counting to ten I opened it again but didn't get any further before it was time for counseling.

Mr. Ramsted had to tell me twice when I entered the room—I was so distracted—that I had been transferred from sex to food counseling. Because of my speech the day before, he had suggested to Ms. Anderson and the food counselor, Mr. Martinez, that I was ready to move on from sensuality to my other problems. He shook my hand and congratulated me on improving.

Up one flight of stairs, on the third floor of Celestial Commons, Mr. Martinez invited me to sit at a table with LaTeesha, Samantha, Dmitri, Brianne, Olive, and Tiberius. The room's walls were decorated with posters of the food pyramid, nutrition charts, and exercising contests (one, of the 2003 San Francisco Marathon, I recognized from Mr. Raven's office). In a corner sat three treadmills that we were allowed to use at any time.

Mr. Martinez, whose thick neck and plump cheeks sat incongruously on a thin body, showed me a picture of himself from five years before, when he'd weighed 302 pounds, and, convening the session, asked me to tell my story.

In a repetition of the day before, I meant to tell a few short anecdotes about my dependence on food but then spoke for an hour and a half. Beginning with a general description of the external and internal conditions that drove me to overeat as a child, I gave specifics about my lonely, disappointment-laden days at elementary school, where my grades and social conquests were mediocre, after which, to reach a baseline of contentment, I ate massive midafternoon bowls of cereal with vanilla ice cream, chunks of salami, and raw cookie dough. Following that I indulged in high school cafeteria binges and Friday night party snacks. I recalled with eidetic precision the all-you-can-eat buffets within a mile radius of my college dormitory. And the whole rotisserie chickens sold at the deli near my apartment in Hayes Valley. And the three-for-two candy bar deals, family-sized calzones, and prepackaged French dinners "specially made for epicures." All this, I said, ending a narrative I'd told in a kind of trance, had continued for years despite my having a self-image comparable to the Elephant Man's—I would hate myself and then feast and then hate myself much more—until finally, just recently, I had had liposuction surgery. My subsequent thinness would have been only temporary, though, if I hadn't then come to the Wellness Center. It was no exaggeration to say that PASE had stopped an avalanche in progress.

My entire speech was, I thought, upon finishing, even for someone who'd decided to be a Paser, too much. Way, way too much. Without any editing or careful elisions, it could have been the centerpiece of a PASE promotional video. There was a certain disturbing forfeiture of dignity in it, an unsavory exhibitionist element, and I was about to register self-disgust and rein things in, when I felt how powerful the Center's gift to me was. Since arriving three days earlier I had not wanted the high-fat, high-carbohydrate, high-cholesterol, high-calorie foods that were permanent fixtures in my refrigerator at home. I had not loaded so much onto my trays at mealtimes that they sagged in the middle, nor had I cleaned up others' plates or snuck into the bathroom with contraband snacks in between meals, or daydreamed painfully about food when it wasn't in front of me. I had even felt some repulsion that morning when I saw a warming container of bacon beside the fruit bowl.

Realizing this in the hushed counseling room where the other guests and Mr. Martinez had watched me tear off my cloak of respectability like some modern-day St. Francis of Assisi, and then proceed to rend it into a million useless scraps, I began to cry. Not so that my breathing was hindered or my face turned blotchy, but tears pooled together on my chin until I wiped them off with my shirt.

"I'm sorry," I said. "I don't know what's come over me." Except that I did know. I was either a very emotional Paser or suffering from a delayed reaction to the events of the previous week or in awe of PASE's ability to curb a hunger that had been with me for so many years. I felt completely and heroically transformed, the man I'd always wanted to be, triumphant over the cause of a problem that my surgery had merely covered up.

"You may sit down now," said Mr. Martinez. "Thank you for sharing."

I didn't know I'd been standing.

After lunch, which I willed myself to eat with the same force of mind that impels an exhausted man to keep walking when in sight of his home, I was told by Mr. Ortega that, as in counseling, I'd been moved up to class Introductory Level B with Ms. Webley in the room next door. The other students were Ang, Quenlon, Tyrone, Helmut, Paul, and Aranzanzu, whom I knew either through conversation or by sight. Taking a seat between Quenlon and Helmut, I noticed that the teacher was, as Mihir had said to me once, ethereally beautiful, which no more affected me than did the volume of her speaking voice or the shade of her tunic, as external, irrelevant facts.

"Does anyone have a question about the reading for today?" Ms. Webley said.

Ang, a woman with searching green eyes and long fingers woven together on the table in front of her, said, "I'm wondering how UR God can say the Last Day is coming up, when some of the prophecies in chapter nine haven't happened yet."

"Which ones are you referring to?"

"All of them."

"But they all in fact have occurred."

"When?"

"The assassination of Nigerian president Ben Membawa two weeks ago, for one. In the 'Following the Leaders' section it says, on page 376, 'Those who are raised up with one hand will be torn down with the other, for hearts of darkness will admit no light. Where order is destroyed, chaos will reign, and a million widows and orphans will go unheeded by those beyond the valley of their tears.' The Midwestern water shortage is mentioned in the 'Nothing to Spill' section, page 402: 'The land like old skin will crack and no moisture will provide relief.' The earthquake in Seattle and the hurricanes in the Gulf of Mexico were written about in the 'Final Rumblings' section, page 414: 'When earth turns fluid and mountains exhale and clouds touch ground, the clock will tick faster.' The slackening of America's economy, which has led to a recession that will become a depression, is written about at length in the 'Wanting More When There Is Less' section, page 433: 'The big, heavy engines will run out of fuel and those on the bus will be forced to get out and walk to nowhere.'"

While Ms. Webley spoke I flipped to the passages she mentioned. She was right. They predicted disasters going on at that very moment. A fool might say they were too cryptic or figurative to refer to any specific political turmoil or weather event, but the truth was there for everyone else to see.

"Is there any chance," I asked, using my thumb as a bookmark and closing *The Prescription,* "of the world ending before the Last Day? Say some catastrophic thing happens tomorrow. We're not ur-savants yet. Most of us guests aren't even savants and we need time to climb through the ranks."

"There is a way to expedite Paser growth in case of an emergency," she said. "But we don't think it will come to that for people here."

"What is the emergency growth way?"

"Let's not worry about that now."

"I've never understood why the planet has to be destroyed in the first place," said Helmut.

"It won't be destroyed, but it will die like everything outside of UR God. There's no why for this; it simply is."

"Can't He let the Earth keep going, as a favor to people who don't become ur-savants in time?" I asked.

Ms. Webley said, "With the way we human beings are acting, that would not be kind to those who remain."

During research—Paul's discussion group had decided to meet every other day—I watched a video on meditation that demonstrated the proper sitting position, breathing technique, and panegyric to achieve Synergy without a Synergy device. It was important not to meditate on a full stomach or in anger or without a goal, such as sublimating a desire. When I put down the video screen, a guest who'd arrived the day before, whom I hadn't yet spoken to, came over and stood beside me.

"I know about you," he said.

"Excuse me?"

"You're an involuntary admission, just like me."

"I was, yes."

"My name is Chaim."

"Jack."

Chaim had a blow-dried pompadour and wore the sleeves of his Center outfit rolled up to his elbows. "I heard that a couple days ago you said you didn't want to improve."

"Yes."

"So you're acting like the facilitators want so you can get out early."

"Actually—"

He squatted and rested his elbows on his knees. In a soft voice he said, "You know that the inmates are in charge of the asylum, and this joke about quitting desire has got about ten more minutes before it quits being funny. Warren sent me to talk to you about his plan—the Indian guy won't let him do it himself—to get out tonight. We want you to come with us. For a very fair price, one of the night watchmen has agreed to leave a door unlocked and look the other way. You pay a third of his fee, about three hundred bucks, and by tomorrow we'll all be on the outside, able to go back to our regularly scheduled lives."

A facilitator walked by holding a phone, with her head tucked into her shoulder like a sleeping bird's into its wing. When she was out of hearing range, I said, "That's not a good idea."

"We won't get caught, and even if we did, life can't get worse for us than it already is."

"I feel differently than I did a couple of days ago."

"They kidnapped you, like me."

"I can't do it."

"You think they're going to let you go just because you run around during exercise like a spastic? They'll keep you here for a month at least and then make you sign away your rights to ever say anything bad about PASE. I think they're practicing brainwashing techniques we're not even aware of."

I put on my video headphones and cranked up the volume as loud as it would go. The proper response to stress was to press your hands together with equal pressure over the surface of your palms and fingers, while thinking of UR God. Conflict was a trick of unreality, a legacy of the billions of years during which we'd forgotten Him, and it wilted next to the truth like a flower brought close to fire. I felt Chaim's eyes on me for a moment before he stood up. He and Warren had no idea what they were doing, rejecting discipline for the illusory charms of the outside, like children desperate to avoid vegetables in favor of desserts. Wait for the rotted mouth. Wait to go blind from staring too long at the sun of their own pleasure. The meditation video ended. Perhaps I had an obligation to inform Ms. Anderson of their plan. Perhaps it would spare them ulcerated gums and sightless eyes. What would hurt them in the short term would save them in the long.

These thoughts did not go away during recreation—I wrote a song on composition software, "Give PASE a Chance," that Ms. Bentham passed around to the other facilitators, one of whom thought it should become the religion's anthem—and grew more persistent during dinner. Chaim and Warren sat together at a table by themselves, talking privately. I got up to refill my water glass and then stopped at their table.

"Hi," I said.

"On your way back from Damascus?" asked Chaim.

"I think you should reconsider about tonight. There's no need to get hurt by making a hasty decision. The Center has your best interests at heart and you don't want to treat it this way. It's legally responsible for you; your sneaking out could be a big liability for it."

"What do you mean we'll get hurt by a hasty decision?" asked Warren, his eyes dulled to an overcast gray.

"Your chances of improvement would go down," I said.

"Because if you're planning to tell on us," said Chaim, "that wouldn't be friendly."

"I'm not threatening you. I'm saying that running away from here would be a mistake."

"Thanks for the warning," said Warren.

"Appreciate it," said Chaim.

"I want to help you," I said.

"Didn't we just say thanks?"

I turned and looked at my table, then at Ms. Anderson seated at a table of guests not far away. Warren and Chaim went back to eating. I sat down.

"Your buddies are waiting for you over there," said Chaim.

"I need to say a few things to you first."

They didn't answer, so I explained in great detail the reasons why they should stay, the rewards both immediate and eventual. I knew their mindset, having had it just days before, and anticipated and described and undermined it. They went on eating with their eyes fixed on their plates, as though nothing mattered but the next bite. I didn't care if they wanted me to leave. I would win them over. If I could paint UR God and make a clay replica of Shoale's Wisconsin home, if I could write a PASE anthem and be an elder statesman to Pasers who knew the religion better than I did, I could with all my rhetorical power, which seemed to have entered its zenith, prevent these men from leaving. Mihir came over when dinner ended and I sent him away. Walking to the Prescription Palace with Warren and Chaim for the group activity I continued my argument even while accepting the juice, fig bar, and chair. Onstage a panel of PASE officials talked about how membership was up by a thousand percent over the year before. Land had just been purchased in Los Angeles for a celebrity PASE Station to accommodate new interest from movie and music industry people. An interfaith program with the Roman Catholic church had inoculated a million South Americans against AIDS during the past year. The birth rate among Pasers was one per five hundred, and in every case pregnancy predated the female Paser's induction into PASE.

"If you had a terminal illness," I whispered to them, "and a doctor said there was a new procedure to cure it that involved, say, giving up red meat, would you refuse it just to keep eating steaks?"

Chaim said, "Yes, if no one thought I was sick but that one doctor."

"A doctor whose credentials were better than everyone else's combined."

I kept it up on the way back to the dormitory, and then in the bathroom while we brushed our teeth. Finally, just before going to sleep, they said they'd give the Wellness Center another week.

"You've convinced us," Warren said.

"Really?"

"You're very persuasive," said Chaim.

Part of me knew that they were lying, but another part of me knew otherwise. I had made powerful ethical, logical, and emotional appeals, spelling out in detail the advantages to staying and the disadvantages to leaving. I had begun, sustained, and concluded the argument. As the wall lamps beside everyone's beds shut off one by one, it seemed possible, however unlikely, that I had succeeded.

When I woke up at six A.M. the next morning and their beds were empty, I was disappointed but not entirely surprised, as though a pair of feral cats I'd hoped to entice through care and affection to stay indoors had stolen back to the city streets, where their prized freedom was in fact a license for savagery and a shortcut to death. Dressing quickly, I decided to tell Ms. Anderson and on the way met two escorts who had been sent by her to fetch me. In the Red Room, she was rooting through her desk, and all of my teachers, counselors, and facilitators stood in a row behind her like witnesses to some grand Oval Office legislation-signing—Mr. Ramsted, Mr. Ortega, Mr. Martinez, Ms. Bentham, Ms. Webley, Mr. Israel—beaming as though UR God Himself had called them there.

"Good morning," I said.

If they knew about Chaim and Warren, which I assumed was the reason I'd been summoned there, they didn't display any anxiety or worry. Just the opposite. "Good morning!" they said.

Ms. Anderson said, "You got here fast."

"I was on my way already to talk to you about something."

"What a nice coincidence. Did you sleep well?"

"Yes, thank you."

"I sent for you in order to say that the affinity you've shown for PASE customs over the last few days has been remarkable and extremely gratifying, further proof that PASE can turn resistance into inspiration. Your recreation work—for example, your painting of UR God and clay representation of Montgomery Shoale's childhood home and your original song—have given hope and clarity to facilitators and guests alike, as have your sophisticated engagement with PASE ideas in class and your recognition in counseling of the dangers of sexuality and food. These wonderful developments have made us all very proud."

"I'm glad."

She waved her hand and the lineup behind her copied the move so that it rippled across them from Mr. Ramsted to Mr. Israel. "Your eating habits haven't escaped notice, either. We're aware that before your liposuction surgery in November you were obese, and that just before coming here you were on track to gain back everything you'd lost, but that in the past week you've taken on your own to salads and low-fat vegetable dishes."

"I feel much better."

"Tell us something. Do you consider yourself a Paser?"

"Yes." I said this with as much confidence as I would have admitted to being a man.

"You see the truth of *The Prescription* and believe in the revelation of Montgomery Shoale?"

"I do."

"Then you will understand how unfortunate it is that last night two of our guests, Warren Axelrod and Chaim Singer, attempted to leave the Wellness Center without authorization. Perhaps you saw that their beds were empty when you woke up this morning?"

I swallowed and felt cold all over, as though a snowflake had fallen on the back of my neck. "Yes."

"They made arrangements to escape two days ago with one of the night watchmen, who told us about it beforehand so we could take preventive measures."

"That's terrible," I said. "I mean, it's good that you stopped them but terrible that they tried to leave."

"Even more terrible is that during questioning they said you had planned to go with them up until the very end, but then, complaining of stomach cramps, you backed out and said you'd go another night."

"They said that?"

"Warren claimed that you originated the idea, and that your actions since then have been a ploy to get out early, as though for good behavior. He said you've been pretending to go along with PASE teachings while secretly compiling information to use against us on the outside."

"That's—I'm not doing that." Although this was true, I felt as nervous as if it weren't.

No one was smiling anymore and a pall hung over the room. Warren and Chaim were treacherous individuals and I was to suffer for trying to help them. An inversion of justice. I should have gone to a facilitator right away.

Ms. Anderson, perched on the edge of her desk, said, "Of course your teachers and counselors and I recognized that Mr. Axelrod and Mr. Singer were incriminating you for some personal reason, and that we shouldn't credit a word of theirs. They had no evidence other than that you ate dinner and attended the group activity talk with them last night, which is not evidence at all. They probably spoke from jealousy of your conversion to PASE, because it has been so inspirational to the other guests and to us. Their actions were taken right from our enemies' playbook. They envy your conviction and strength. I wouldn't be surprised if you spent last night talking them out of running away."

"That's exactly right," I said, with a flood of relief that drained away quickly and was replaced by the alarm of before.

"I thought so." Ms. Anderson leaned back and Ms. Bentham reached over the desk to squeeze her shoulder. "It's what I told Montgomery Shoale this morning."

"You spoke to Mr. Shoale about me?"

"The attempted breakout of two guests warranted Montgomery Shoale's notice. He quickly decided on a course of action to take— even in the middle of the night his mind is a steel trap—and I thought that that was the end of the matter, but an hour later he called to say that his advisers were concerned about the charges made against you."

"Why?"

"Some of them think that your turnaround from opponent to proponent of PASE has been too fast and complete. They suspect it's a subterfuge, and early this morning they advised Mr. Shoale to sentence you to the same treatment as Mr. Axelrod and Mr. Singer received, believing, unlike everyone in this room, that the two guilty parties were right about you in spirit, if not in detail. I assured Montgomery Shoale that that was not so, that you were as devoted and sincere a Paser as exists in the world, and I told him how many defenders you have among the staff of the Wellness Center, as well as among the other guests. He is, as you know, in a weakened state, being almost an ur-savant, but that didn't stop him from requesting that I and your teachers and counselors go to the PASE Station to make our argument in person. So at four-thirty A.M. we went and testified on your behalf while several PASE administrators spoke against you. In the end Mr. Shoale applied his immeasurable wisdom and stated the issue clearly. 'If,' he said, 'Jack Smith is playacting in order to harm PASE, he will have to be stopped. But if his belief and actions are genuine, we must welcome him to UR God.' This I thought was perfectly fair, perfectly typical of his reasoning powers."

"Yes," I said faintly. The men and women behind Ms. Anderson appeared excited again, and my mind was an exquisite blank.

"Obviously," said Ms. Anderson, her feather earrings dangling from her hair as though caught in a spiderweb, "no one knows what's in your heart but you, and this morning's proceedings were based on suppositions and speculation. How could they not have been? Someone suggested giving you a polygraph test, but Mr. Ramsted, one of your great champions at the trial, pointed out that those are unreliable, and that with someone's life hanging in the balance we shouldn't take any chances. Then Mr. Shoale announced the perfect solution. We were all amazed at its ingenuity. He said that you are to go on a Synergy device and receive a dose of Synergy approximately ten thousand times stronger than what is normally administered."

I swallowed and looked at all the expectant faces. "What will that do?"

"If you are a Paser it will elevate you instantly to the status of ursavant. If you aren't a Paser its electrical charge will kill you."

I was unable to respond, though this news seemed to release whatever had held the teachers and counselors in check, and they rushed forward to crowd around me, smiling and pumping my hand in congratulations.

"I know you'd like to say good-bye in person to your friends and family on the outside, but under the circumstances that is impossible. Non-Pasers would object to Mr. Shoale's solution, and we're in no mood to fight that battle or deal with legal interference from people who don't comprehend the first thing about PASE. You may write letters, though, which we will mail for you, explaining why you can't see your loved ones again and that your mental faculties

are sound. If you'd prefer, we may be able to arrange a video recording session. Your relatives might appreciate the opportunity to see
and hear you one final time."

"When is this set to take place?"

"Today," Ms. Anderson said, "at one o'clock."

With that the meeting ended. I got up and thanked everyone for
their efforts on my behalf. The following hour was dreamlike. I
went back to the dorm room and bundled my things so they could
be disposed of easily, then went to Elysian Field. Paul, who had
jogged a lap and was clutching his chest, said he would miss my
contributions to the research group. Rema asked me to save her a
good spot in UR God. Shang-lee gave me a complicated East Bay
handshake and said he had known some trailblazers in his time, but
none who could touch me; I was so far ahead of the pack that he
wasn't even jealous. Mr. Israel and I did twenty jumping jacks
together, two Vitruvian Men in sync, and although neither of us
spoke we had an understanding. Mihir said good-bye last and gave
me a big hug. He was sorry I wouldn't get to meet his family on
Earth, but I was right about the infectious power of PASE and so
would meet them when we were all wands together, ecstatic vibra-
tions side by side forever.

"What you are doing is the ultimate form of bravery," he said.
"Leaving the known for the unknown is at the heart of every great
story and the story of every great man. I am honored to have met
you. Bear in mind that your journey will provide strength to countless others."

We clasped arms and then I followed my escorts to a room in
Celestial Commons outfitted with a chair and desk, on which were
a pen, paper, and video camera. At first I couldn't write much
because facilitators kept stopping by to wish me well and share their
excitement that I would be the first—before Montgomery Shoale,
even—to return to UR God, a goal toward which they would work
for the rest of their lives. Mr. Ramsted, who stayed a long time talking about Synergy and how we would be treated by the wands
who'd stayed behind, finally asked me in a lowered voice to inter-

cede for him with UR God because, without admitting anything, he might have fallen short of his best self once or twice—or maybe more, he wasn't sure—since he'd joined PASE. He would never do it again, and those exceptional occasions on which he had done it in the past were revolting to him, and I had to understand that he was stronger now, an immovable pillar of commitment, and by asking UR God to forgive him I would embody PASE values. I told him that it sounded as if he'd chastised himself enough, but that I would do what I could. This cheered him up until he grew more despondent and wondered if he should join me for ur-Synergy, for that was, realistically, given his terrible weakness and the possibility of his falling short of his best self again, his only hope for achieving ur-savant status. I told him that wouldn't be a good idea, and he got up and went away.

From the room's single window I saw a female guest I didn't recognize down below in the garden, bending over the only rose in bloom among a bush's thorns. It was a lovely vision, like something remembered. There would be no distinct bodies, no individual flowers where I was going, for UR God was a great multicolored spiral in which everything bled together to form a more perfect union. There would be no me/you and I/thou. No separation. No remove. I looked at the letter-writing paper in front of me and pushed it away; I didn't reach out to switch on the video equipment. What could I say to my parents or friends to make them understand what I did? Some would be saved and some would not. The woman in the garden might take a misstep and never enter ultimate reality. What would death be like without any future possibility of fusing into UR God? Was it a version of purgatory? Could one change there and someday be culled from it by UR God?

Waiting for my escorts to take me to the Synergy Station, where a small assembly of guests and teachers and facilitators and Ms. Anderson would bear witness to my departure, I quit thinking about PASE eschatology and the transitory connections I'd made on planet Earth, the great rocky falsehood beneath my feet. There comes a point where answers, always provisional when the questions are meaningful enough, must no longer be sought, where you must walk headlong into a light too bright to see by, and accept it as illumination.

A small bird hopped into the garden like a toy, poking its head here and there into the ground, grubbing with stop-motion quickness. Very soon they would come for me. When the bird flew away I randomly opened a copy of *The Prescription* to the middle of chapter six, called "Reflections and Refractions of Ultimate Reality," and read: "The impulse that drives man to desire—that is, the impulse to stay alive and pass on his genetic material—makes up the fabric of his cosmic blindfold and blocks from his sight the myriad signs of truth in the universe. He must rip it off and undergo the rigors of returning to what he knew in the beginning— first chill, then stupor, then the letting go—of UR God. At that moment happiness will cease being an idea and a pursuit and become the foundation of being. Man as wand will wave about within a commotion that is in fact serenity." I closed the book.

At twenty minutes before one P.M., two new escorts arrived, men in their early twenties, one a foot taller and a shade darker than the other, and led me from the room down to the courtyard—the woman was gone and the bird had returned to pull a worm from the dirt. For a second I had the sensation that I was the bird and my entire body was tensed and engaged in a pursuit that would prolong my life—not forever or even indefinitely, but for a matter of hours— not questioning whether this was what I should be doing, but knowing that it was so. It was a strange hallucination that I forgot as soon as the bird got its prey and flew off to be alone, thinking that to have what others want is to be vulnerable.

When we passed the now-empty Elysian Field and Synergy Station and reached the front gate, I asked my escorts where we were going. "There's been a slight change of plans," the darker one said, signaling to the gate attendant to let us through. "Montgomery Shoale's orders."

CHAPTER 8

The gates swung open and a white van with the PASE logo on its side started its engine. I climbed into the back with the lighter escort; the darker one sat in the passenger seat beside a driver wearing sunglasses and a gray fedora and a mossy green pinstriped suit. "Buckle up, sir," the driver said, raising two fingers to wave good-bye to the gate attendant, who closed his hands together as the electronically controlled doors swung shut, as though magically commanding them to do so. A minute later the lighter escort handed me a red bandanna and told me to tie it around my eyes. This made no sense and when he said that this too was Mr. Shoale's orders I almost asked why. Instead I tied it on and he checked it in the back and front to make sure it covered enough and was securely tied.

No one said anything for the duration of a thirty-minute drive that included many turns and two freeways, a route that couldn't have ended at the PASE Station or any other PASE-affiliated building I knew of in the Bay Area. When we parked I was taken still blindfolded out of the van and into a warm humid building, where we passed through a few doors before I was allowed to remove the bandanna. It took a moment for my eyes to adjust to the brightness of what appeared to be an office reception room, with fluorescent lights and a deodorized smell and a knee-high coffee table in one corner, atop which issues of *Psychology Today* and *The Journal of Cognitive Science* were fanned out like blackjack hands. A statuesque blonde rested her arms Sphinxlike on a crescent desk directly in front of us, a computer screen at her left. She said hello, accepted the keys from the darker escort, and pushed a bowl of chocolate mints toward us. A tortoiseshell fountain burbled on the floor to her right.

"What is this place?" I asked.

"The Cult Opposition Network," said the lighter escort, who with the driver then made a little bow and left the way we'd come in. The receptionist began typing on the keyboard with an open file next to her that had a picture of me paper-clipped to it. The darker escort led me down a long corridor with lush burgundy carpet, past a dozen unpainted doors, some without handles. We turned a corner and came to an emergency exit at the end. There he knocked on a door with a "Director" plate nailed to its center. The escort pushed it ajar and said, "Tomas? We got him."

A wiry man in his midforties with curly red hair foaming out of his head got up from his desk and ushered me in.

"Excellent," he said to the escort. "Would you mind closing the door on your way out?"

Turning his attention to me, he sat and indicated the chair facing his desk. I lowered myself into it.

"After everything that's happened to you," he said, twisting his wedding ring nervously, "I imagine you're upset, discombobulated. We know all about the scheduled electrocution and couldn't feel sicker or angrier. What barbarism! Would you like some tea? We have herbals, chamomile, green. I think Katie out front has that Mongolian red everyone's drinking now. Unless you only drink coffee?"

"Nothing, thanks."

He returned to his desk drawer a handful of small tasseled bags and unplugged a teakettle hissing behind him. "You probably think you're stuck in a nightmare, the first person ever to suffer like this. I would think that in your place, too, but if it's any comfort to you, yours is an old story. Americans have been caught up in quack religions since before they thought to call themselves Americans. These days it can be hard to keep that in mind; most people think that just because they and their relatives don't personally belong to a cult, and because they don't see many media stories about them, cults must have gone away or stopped destroying innocent lives. You may have thought that yourself until recently. We at the Cult Opposition Network, however, are better informed. We appreciate the continuing seriousness of the situation because we've all been there ourselves or lost friends and relatives to it. This is a war. Lives are lost and casualties sustained. An unmistakable line separates good from evil."

"I'm not sure what's going on here."

Tomas folded his hands. "You've never heard of us because we don't advertise our services. In fact we don't officially exist and in a way are unknown even to ourselves. If the FBI were to storm the building or infiltrate our computer system, they wouldn't find any biographical information on our personnel or business affiliates. Likewise if someone from a target cult broke in or talked to a former CON employee who's decided to inform against us, they'd learn nothing because we don't keep centralized records and we work in autonomous cells that have little contact with one another." He lit a cigarette and spoke while exhaling smoke through his nose. "Do you know what deprogramming is?"

"No."

"Also known as exit counseling, it's the act of rescuing cult victims from captivity and talking to them until they recognize the false nature of their inculcated belief system. It's like an exorcism, except that we cast out both gods and devils. It's one of our primary activities at the CON, and even though it's benign—not to mention necessary, if you ask the families ripped apart by cults and the ex-members we've treated—for political reasons it's been outlawed in this country. There used to be several professional deprogramming organizations, but then a coalition formed between the American Civil Liberties Union and the cults themselves that closed down all the greats: Operation Free Thought, Religious Truth Now, the Liberation Project. It was a terrible clampdown, a kind of pogrom. People fighting the tyranny of cults were jailed on charges of abduction and attempted brainwashing. As if abduction and brainwashing weren't the very crimes deprogrammers are against! We at the CON were lucky in that we had just started out and no one knew about us yet; since then we've worked hard to stay underground, hidden from the First Amendment fanatics and cult mercenaries."

"I think a mistake has been made. Why am I here?"

"I'll get to that, but first I want to say that we aim to do more than just save individuals; we want to strike at the root of the problem by wholly eliminating the most insidious cults. While administering a pound of cure we'd like to produce an ounce of prevention. So far we've had some difficulties—no cults have shut down as a result of our efforts—but that's because we've focused on organizations that are too well established, like Reverend Moon's Unification Church and the Transcendental Meditation movement and Scientology. You see, the longer a cult survives, the better able it is to portray itself as a legitimate religion and gain mainstream acceptance. There's an old saying that the only difference between a cult and a religion is the amount of real estate it owns." Tomas put out his cigarette and I saw a series of scarred tattoo erasures on his right fingers. "In spite of that, and in part because of you, we've decided to go after a cult that has grown very large in the seventeen years it's existed but is vulnerable nonetheless: Prescription for a Superior Existence."

We stared at each other for an uncomfortably long time, and I said, "You think PASE is a cult?"

"When we're done it's going to be a distant, embarrassing memory, but right now we *know* it's a cult. You know it, too, even if they've done their best to convince you otherwise over the past week. We wish we'd gotten to you sooner, but it took a while after your parents contacted us to verify that they were legitimate clients, and then requisitioning a PASE van and rigging a phone so that its ID showed up as a call from Montgomery Shoale slowed things down as well. Looks like we rescued you just in time."

There were no windows in the room or even functional touches like a wall clock or calendar or thermostat. The air had a cryptlike quality, moribund and mortuary, and I felt fatigued and weak, as though my limbs were weighed down under an X-ray apron. My parents were involved in my being here. Ms. Anderson and the others were waiting for me at the Synergy Station. I'd been warned about people like this. Mr. Ortega may have had this very man in mind. "You want to take down PASE?" I asked tremulously.

"We have attorney friends outside the CON infrastructure who've agreed to file a pro bono class action lawsuit against it ostensibly on behalf of ex-Pasers, but who will really be acting as our legal agents. PASE has built up some goodwill in the community through its charity work, but we've compiled lots of anecdotal evidence against it, and with your help we're optimistic. If the suit goes well we'll be vindicated and strike a major blow against thought control."

"Why do you say it's thought control?" I had no idea where we were in relation to the city or the Wellness Center but I knew I had to do something, go somewhere. Thoughts danced and evaporated in my head like water droplets on a frying pan.

"Do you know the definition of a cult? It is—I'm quoting from a 1985 paper by West and Langone here—'A group or movement exhibiting a great or excessive devotion or dedication to some person, idea, or thing and employing unethically manipulative techniques of persuasion and control (e.g., isolation from former friends and family, debilitation, use of special methods to heighten suggestibility and subservience, powerful group pressures, information management, suspension of individuality or critical judgment, promotion of total dependency on the group, fear of leaving it, etc.) designed to advance the goals of the group's leaders, to the actual or possible detriment of members, their families, or the community.' We got a call from a woman the other day whose son joined PASE and then left his pregnant wife, quit his job at a cable TV service because it ran 'salacious' programs, and now won't talk to anyone he used to be close to who isn't also a Paser. Another woman, a Paser of five years' standing, told us that at PASE meetings if you make a sexual reference that isn't negative—if you say, 'I once had sex in a water closet,' or if you make a Freudian slip like, 'Put a cock in it' instead of 'Put a sock in it'—you're sent to something called the Adjustment Facility to be deprived of food, kept awake all night, and forced to watch acts of rape until you're sick. It's right out of *A Clockwork Orange*. And consider how PASE makes money. To remain in good standing with the so-called church, every Paser has to subscribe to its weekly magazine, *World PASE,* which costs three hundred dollars a year; go on a weeklong three-thousand-dollar retreat every six months; tithe ten percent of his income; and make regular charitable contributions to the PASE Process and its International Educational Fund, which sends Paser missionaries to thirty-four countries on six continents. It's an enormous conspiracy that we are going to stop."

"You're missing the point," I said, completely unnerved and unable to have this conversation any longer. The room's oxygen was as thin as turpentine vapor. I pulled at the neck of my shirt for air and felt more enclosed and needed first of all to breathe. "It's about overcoming desire, the source of all human suffering."

Tomas raised his eyebrows as he stared at me for a minute. Then he lifted his phone, pressed a button, said "Code one," and hung up. "I'm sorry," he said. "I didn't realize you were so far advanced. I'm usually more observant. We'll talk again soon." The door opened then and I turned around to see two men enter, one carrying a syringe that found its way into my neck while the other held me still; they didn't know that I couldn't have moved if I'd wanted to, not in that oxygen-depleted vault. Then the darkness.

CHAPTER 9

I woke up without any sense of how long I'd been out, on a padded examination table under the blue ceiling of a spacious honeysuckle room, in a pair of jeans and a sweatshirt I'd bought just after my surgery. I sat up and a current of pain ran through my back. The room was decorated with daisy-link trim around its walls, eight-by-ten photographs of children playing on the beach, and a giant Monet print of a lily-strewn pond. A marble-framed vanity and two Viennese music boxes shaped like Gothic cathedrals sat on top of a butternut country dresser, and a pillow-backed wood rocking chair rested beside an overstuffed red couch with pink arm sleeves, in the purview of a small video camera nailed above the door. There was a television, a computer, a stack of books and magazines, two packing boxes, and my Couvade duffel bag zippered shut on a folding card table in a corner.

A man in his late fifties entered the room wearing a white coat and rimless spectacles, with a computer tablet tucked into the crook of his arm. His beard was trimmed so close to his face it might have been a few days' oversight.

"Hello, Jack," he said in a soothing bedside manner, standing a foot away from the exam table where I rubbed my back. "My name is Dr. Cantor. How are you feeling?"

"Not well."

"I expected as much, considering that you've come directly from a PASE Wellness Center, which in its short history has contaminated scores of adults with deep-seated neurological disorders geared toward suicide. From what Tomas tells me, I gather that its operators had some degree of success with you, and that you consider the people there to be your friends. You may even have found value in some of their teachings. That would be understandable, since they're not wrong about everything. As the saying goes, even a stopped clock is right twice a day. And yet the goal of all their actions and teachings was not to help you, but rather to exercise power over you."

I folded my arms and the room's bed-and-breakfast décor was creepy in its strained effort to appear pleasant, in its Norman Rockwell adornments, as though put together by aliens hoping to calm skittish human abductees.

Dr. Cantor said, "You may not want to do this at first, but over time light will be shed on every inch of the crime committed against you and other captives at the Wellness Center, and you'll thank us for this intervention."

"I want a lawyer."

"You're not under arrest and you have nothing to fear from us. We aren't going to hurt you; we're going to save you."

I didn't guffaw because it was all too depressing and tiring. "Why did you take me? There are two guys there now who want to leave and they'd have been perfect for this place."

"On the contrary, anyone wishing to leave the Wellness Center has no need of our services."

"I don't either."

"Tomas may have mentioned that your parents hired us to get you out. They've been very worried since your disappearance last week."

"Then this is a misunderstanding. I'll talk to them and clear it up."

"They plan to visit when the time is right. It can be dangerous to try to rush your recovery."

My jeans and sweatshirt felt binding and constrictive and vainglorious, the symbolic and spiritual opposite of my powder blue tunic. "So what's supposed to happen now? You're going to try to deprogram me?"

"The process is not as mechanistic or clinical as its name suggests. We're just going to discuss things in a warm, comfortable place, with music if you like and plenty of good food and whatever else will be conducive to an honest exchange of ideas. You have a bag here full of your clothes and two boxes of your personal effects. You are free to watch television, access the Internet, read—anything you want."

"I want a copy of *The Prescription for a Superior Existence* and the clothes I came here in."

"Those particular items aren't allowed."

"Then I'll take the PASE pamphlet series A to Z and you can remove the other stuff, unless there are any videos of Montgomery Shoale talks. And I'd like to speak to Ms. Anderson at the Wellness Center."

"It's seven o'clock at night, so I should make something clear, though I think you know it and are being facetious: You will not be exposed to anything related to PASE. You won't read its literature or listen to its party line or talk to its adherents, nor will you visit its buildings or write to its leader or promote it to anyone else. PASE had its day in court with you and now it's our turn."

He left and might never have been there. I lay down and thought of UR God and meditated and after great effort felt a touch of Synergy. For three minutes or so I conjured that magnificent feeling until slowly, as though I'd held up a heavy object for too long, my strength gave out and I lost contact with it. I stood up and walked around the room and poked through the boxes full of miscellany from my apartment. I saw the edge of an adult-video case and then the front cover—two candy stripers pushing a football player down a hospital corridor—and my penis moved of its own accord. The feeling, so sudden and unwelcome, was as startling as if a snake had slithered nearby.

I sat on the couch, which, perhaps because it was too soft, turned up the heat of my back pain. And a distant throb in my wrist drew closer. Without warning, with awful predictability, my old symptoms were converging on me from everywhere at once, like some prearranged ambush. Pain, arousal, anxiety. I felt like an encephalitis lethargica patient who, after a miraculous L-dopa awakening, was beginning to relapse into catatonia. Or someone in the early stages of Alzheimer's aware that soon he would forget a lifetime of memories, that one by one his mind would erase them like a computer infected by a rogue virus. So quickly, so finally.

"But I was well," I said, the words evaporating on my lips like soap bubbles. Then louder, looking directly at the camera, "I was well!"

In an instant of overwhelming force, as when you return after a flood to the washed-out frame of what had been your house, and ruin blankets the world around you, a cleanup task so large you don't know where to begin and so turn away to do nothing, defeated at the outset, I sensed the enormity of what had been taken from me when I was taken from the Wellness Center. The room's lighting seemed to come in pulses with a strobe effect, and I tore off my sweatshirt and jeans and tried overturning the examination table that was bolted to the floor. The doorknob also wouldn't budge and I couldn't reach the camera or jump to knock it away. I beat on the thick Plexiglas window through which I could see only the beige of the hallway wall. I beat on the door with my fists and palms and screamed that I had been well and that I'd been promised eternal synergy with UR God. I was as naked as when I came into the world and I'd been promised and they couldn't take it away from me for they had no right! I would return to the Wellness Center! CON was full of poison and they delighted in infecting others, but I would be well again! Like scorpions, I screamed, you are like scorpions! And all the while I threw myself against the door like a wave, and like a rocky promontory it would not be moved.

At the Wellness Center I'd heard stories about its Seclusion Ward, where people with physical dependencies—drug addicts and alcoholics, as well as those who elected, as Tyrone had considered doing, to stay there—went to get clean and dry out under locked, careful supervision. The accounts were of the guests' desperate pleading and cold sweats and violent nausea, of love so tough it was indistinguishable from cruelty, of men and women miserable enough to consider dashing their brains out on their bed frame, anything to escape the misery of who they were and what they lacked. Several Seclusion Warders told me after their release that no experience was as unbearable. They'd rather have their eyes poked out than go through it again. Hobble or impale them, cut off their hands, set them afire.

I had tried to empathize by remembering my own feeling of withdrawal when I'd first been cut off from alcohol and painkillers and muscle relaxants and sleeping aids at the Center, but really I'd had no idea of what it was like until my first night in that honeysuckle room at the Cult Opposition Network. It was beyond awful. Although they didn't have an active physical component, my claustrophobia and distress splintered into countless dimensions, so that when I concentrated and quelled one aspect of my misery, ten more rose to take its place, like brooms in *The Sorcerer's Apprentice*. I'd been robbed of the ultimate treasure and if the world were to end in the night I would die a mere savant. Paradise now was to be paradise never. I curled into a ball on the table and shook.

According to legend, Fyodor Dostoevsky, after having been arrested in Russia for treason in 1849 and sentenced to die, stood before a firing squad listening to the countdown, and time slowed for him until he experienced an eternity in an instant, a mystical rapture and premonition of God that shocked and elated a man who had moved far away from the Russian Orthodox Church and from belief itself. But just before the attendant military man called out *Fire!—СТРЕПЯТЬ!* in Russian—a word to be synchronous with his mortality, a messenger arrived on horseback from the governor's office with a note commuting Dostoevsky's sentence from death to four years in a hard-labor camp. A reprieve, a reversal's reversal. Although devoutly Christian from then on, he never got over the disappointment of being pulled back to Earth just when he expected to transcend it forever.

When at some hour of the night the door opened and Tomas entered with a stranger and said something, I was too weak to expel the pill he pushed through my lips and between my teeth. In a hiccup of grief I swallowed and he said something else and then the two men left and I stared into the abyss of the here and now, which was soon replaced by another, fuzzier one.

Morning came and I woke up as body-slammed as I used to feel after a night of kamikaze raids on my liquor shelf and medicine cabinet and dessert pantry, as if instead of sleeping I had just won a pyrrhic victory for the rights to my head. It was seven-fifteen and I had a full-blown erection and my lower back crackled with pain. Again I was dressed in my old casual clothes, which chafed like wool trousers and a hair shirt, and again I thought of consciousness as a punishment too heinous to fit the crime.

In the past, before I became a Paser, my partial recovery from this condition would have involved ten minutes of dry-heaving over the toilet, three or four cups of coffee, and a scorching shower followed by five bicep repetitions with twenty-pound hand barbells. Now I would do none of those things. Just because I was physically removed from the Wellness Center didn't mean I had to forfeit the gains I'd made there. I would follow my old regimen as best I could and, like Sir Thomas More studying the catechism in his Tower of London prison, retain what I'd learned of the truth and build on it inside me.

Yes, I decided, feeling better in anticipation of feeling better, it didn't matter that I wouldn't effortlessly fuse into UR God via a Synergy device. No one else had, and this was a chance for me to reach ur-savant status through diligence alone. I would cleave ever more to PASE. My erection and backache and other troubles were temporary insignificant setbacks that would, like tropical depressions in the ocean predicted to turn into hurricanes that then dissipate of their own accord, fall away while I prevailed.

An hour later I sat in a different room with Dr. Cantor at a table set with a cup of coffee, plate of pancakes, eggs, a sour cream muffin, and a portable air purifier. He lit a cigarette—he smoked the brand I once had—and turned on the purifier, so that only a hint of smoke reached me. I began to meditate and think about UR God and the unreality of this situation. I imagined a better place.

"Please go ahead and eat," said Dr. Cantor. "We understand you love this particular breakfast."

"Loved. In the past tense."

"So you don't want it?"

"I know what you're trying to do and it won't work."

Dr. Cantor wrote that down on a pad of paper. "Your parents didn't make you go to church or give you a religious upbringing, and before being taken hostage by Pasers you weren't much interested in religions or cults or spirituality of any kind. Is that correct?"

"Yes."

"But now you are committed to PASE."

"Correct."

"Would you say you're a savant?"

"Yes."

He scribbled something and underlined it twice. He didn't touch the cigarette except to push its ashtray, in which it rested, out of the way to make room for his pad of paper; its smoke, freed from the purifier's draft, wafted more fully in my direction. "What has changed about you in the last week? I ask because you're thirty-four years old. Most people's identities are fixed by that age."

"What most people do is not my concern. I can't save them. I can only attend to my own conduct and make sure it accords with UR God's teachings in *The Prescription*." My meditation technique, geared toward Him and our ultimate union, wasn't working just then—I couldn't get airborne in my thoughts or lose sight of the temptations in front of me—so I switched my focus to how I was separate from the cigarette and food. If I couldn't get into Him I could at least stay away from them.

Dr. Cantor rested his left hand on his right, like paws, and there was something canine about him, an unsettling soulfulness in his expression, as though I might by being uncooperative break his heart. "My question is, why make such a radical break with your former life and join what you might have described as a crazy religion just one week ago?"

"When I was a child, I spoke like a child, I thought like a child, I reasoned like a child; when I became a man, I gave up childish ways."

"That's from a different religion."

"A week ago I didn't know anything about PASE except some bogus reports in the media." Sour cream muffins had always been irresistible to me. The eggs on the table were scrambled with cheese and liberally peppered, as I'd once liked them. The pancakes were a perfect golden brown.

"And now you know better."

"Now I know best."

"Could you tell me specifically what that best is?"

Fixing my eyes on Dr. Cantor's, I said, "I know how to break out of the cycle of desire that has fed me false hope ever since I was born and prevented my being satisfied with what I have. I know that an alternative exists, Prescription for a Superior Existence, and that I can follow it until I fuse into UR God."

"What would you say to the idea that you believe these things because of the major disruptions you've experienced lately, such as losing your job, breaking up with your girlfriend, and undergoing a transformative surgery?"

"I'd say that you probably have a lot invested in finding any cause but the real one for my spiritual growth."

"Do you think your heavy reliance on alcohol and sleeping pills played a part in your conversion?"

"No, but I think your heavy reliance on rationalistic thinking and traditional psychiatric treatment methods limits your ability to comprehend what has happened to me."

Dr. Cantor took a final drag on his cigarette, exhaled, and then stubbed it out slowly and ineffectually, so that it continued to burn, like a sloppily extinguished campfire from which scouts and posses would deduce that their quarry wasn't far away. "Are you afraid of losing your faith?" he asked.

"That's not possible."

"Yesterday you shouted for a long time, while doing considerable harm to your hands, that you had been well and that you would be well again. What did you mean by that?"

"There's no point in telling you."

"Can't you explain it?"

In my agitation—which I couldn't for the moment master—I tore off the overhanging edge of the muffin and put it in my mouth. Dr. Cantor gave no indication that my eating pleased him, though I knew it did. He and Tomas and the others thought they could wear down my defenses, whereas really—I turned the muffin's torn side away from me, and it was okay that I'd had that one bite because until I became an ur-savant I would have to eat a few calories here and there—they hadn't the power. I told Dr. Cantor that my nausea, backache, extreme hunger, and wrist pain had gone away at the Wellness Center, along with my tormentuous erections.

"Tormentuous?" he said. "Strong word, if it is one. What I wonder is why sex, which I assume you found pleasurable before your exposure to PASE, so disgusts you now?"

"It doesn't disgust me. I just want no more part of it. It's a distraction."

"From what?"

"UR God."

"Yes, Ultimate Reality God. I've studied the PASE cosmology—in fact I've read the entire *Prescription* and most of the supplementary tracts Montgomery Shoale has published, the pamphlets you asked for last night—and I'm curious about what you make of its being a hodgepodge of other religions, with a soupçon of science thrown in for good measure."

"It isn't one, a hodgepodge."

"PASE features an entity similar to the Judeo-Christian God—an omnipotent creator—as well as separatist wands similar to Milton's fallen angels but modeled physically on what string theory suggests are the smallest units of matter, and it is based on the Christian Scientist idea, which is actually borrowed from Gnostic and other traditions, that the corporeal body isn't real and therefore can be controlled and transcended, itself a philosophical outgrowth of the Buddhist belief that attachment, or 'desire' if you'd prefer, is the ultimate evil. These to me seem like plagiarisms."

"This conversation is a waste of our time. Will you please just call my parents and I'll talk to them and then we can go home?"

"Why is it a waste of time?"

"Because you don't know anything."

"What don't I know?"

"That before Montgomery Shoale was given *The Prescription,* some people who'd forgotten the truth about UR God had intimations of Him that they spun into religions because the compulsion toward Him was so strong. PASE isn't copying them; it's correcting them."

"Then we're extremely lucky to be living at this time."

"Yes we are."

"People who came before us were at a disadvantage."

"If you read *The Prescription* you would know that wands have been reincarnated through all the evolutionary stages beginning when we were bacteria."

Dr. Cantor flipped through pages of his notebook until coming to one he studied. "Prior to your arrival here I talked to your parents about your childhood, which they said wasn't easy. You often rebelled against them, flying into rages and screaming that you didn't have to do what they said because they weren't your real mother and father."

"That's— All kids do that. Rebel, I mean."

"Apparently you didn't have many friends, you struggled in school, and you suffered from a weight problem that contributed to your social difficulties. Perhaps compounding these issues, your brother was something of a golden child, gifted in academics and popular with his classmates and a brilliant artist. For years you two fought over everything and you attacked him for being a suck-up and a Goody Two-Shoes."

"This is ancient history. Sid and I are best friends now and we have been for a long time."

"I'm not saying, and your parents didn't say, that you were a lost cause or incorrigible. You went on to finish college and get a job and have a couple of girlfriends. The point I'm making is that while on the surface you turned out okay, underneath your wounds have been festering a long time. Most people's view of themselves, their self-conception, is to a large degree established by the age of nine."

"Where did you hear that?" I leaned toward the partially burning cigarette as though a rope tied around my neck were being pulled. More than a third was left and I could reach out and grab it. To be able to freeze time for five short minutes! Dr. Cantor need not know, nor Ms. Anderson, nor UR God, nor even myself. The right hand keeps things from the left.

"How fawningly did they behave toward you?" Dr. Cantor crossed his legs at the knee the way old men did when sharing expired wisdom. He was part Labrador, part basset hound, part pit bull: watchful, lugubrious, impassive.

"Excuse me?"

"A common practice among cults is to praise new members in everything they do and make them feel wanted and special, as though recognizing beauty and value in them that has gone unacknowledged by the outside world. It's called 'love bombing.' People who feel neglected or down about themselves are prime targets for it."

"I assume you mean me."

"In your time at the PASE Wellness Center they must have treated you as if you were wonderful and unique and gifted. Perhaps they praised you excessively for something you did, or just for being who you are."

"And if they did that means I was love bombed."

"I don't know. I wasn't there. I'm just saying that cults use an arsenal of tricks to lower people's guard and win them over. Because of your history of self-esteem issues—which grew and hardened over time, turning into something of a petrified forest in your head—they might have employed certain methods that we can establish as insincere."

There was a maddening reasonableness to his tone, as though what he said was so incontrovertible that he needn't add emotion or emphasis to carry his point, that anyone with a brain would upon using it concede victory to him.

"Love bombing sounds more effective than what you're doing now, hate bombing or whatever this is. I'd rather be praised than insulted."

"How did they do it? By calling you handsome or reassuring you of your physical attractiveness?"

"You can't really be a doctor."

"I imagine they laughed at your jokes and complimented you on your intelligence."

"Everything you're saying is wrong. It's incredible how wrong you are. Nobody said I was good-looking or funny or smart."

"Then they must have called attention to something you did. Your performance in a sport, perhaps? Or on a musical instrument? Maybe you painted a picture they said they really liked?"

I scooted my chair back and arched my back and straightened my shoulders. "You're basically saying that I'm a witless, untalented moron whom nobody would acclaim without ulterior motives."

Dr. Cantor said, "What was the painting of?"

"I'm not saying there was one."

"A landscape? A portrait?"

"You're a cynical, pathetic man."

"A portrait."

I tore off another piece of the muffin and swallowed it whole. "It was of UR God, and the facilitators and everyone said it was a revelation. They said I painted Him just as they'd always imagined but had never been able to express in words or images. They said it was a masterpiece."

"Your adoptive parents are artists." Dr. Cantor relit his cigarette without turning on the purifier, set it back down in the ashtray, and stood up. I stood up also, ready to be anywhere but in that room.

"I've got to go now," he said, shuffling into his coat, "but I'll see you again soon."

"I hope not."

He glanced at the plate of food and then left. I rested my hands on the tabletop, a foot away from the food and cigarette, and did not sit down for fear that my back, which had been heating up during that unhappy interview, would begin to burn. The muffin was really quite small and lean-tasting, probably less than three hundred calories altogether. I looked at it and a minute later it was gone and the fluffy pancakes and eggs seemed like smaller portions than they had appeared at first. I picked up the fork and with a groan dug its tines into the tabletop.

When the door opened I threw down the fork and saw Tomas's oppressive red quiff. "Here you are," he said. Standing behind him, the driver from the day before smiled and his two front teeth were gold. "What do you say we get out of here for a bit? After being cooped up for so long, you could probably use some fresh air."

I felt sandblasted with tiredness and asked, without energy or curiosity, "Do I have a choice?"

"No."

We passed into the office, where I was given another bandanna for my eyes, and was guided outside and into the backseat of a car whose doors, like a police vehicle's, didn't open from the inside. Tomas sat beside me and the driver up front. After a thirty-minute drive, I took off the bandanna and saw that we were in San Francisco's Mission District. It was a little after noon, and Tomas told me to look at all the hard work and initiative going on: the graffiti art and wild celebratory clothes and succulent Mexican food. This is the real world, he said, full of real people creating real, meaningful lives. And all of it is fueled by desire. Desire is what makes us who we are. It gives us direction and motivation; it causes us to act, to make a difference, to improve ourselves in tangible, real ways recognized by people other than billionaire crackpots and the dupes who follow them. The temptation is strong to look at the negative extreme of any action—of eating or doing drugs or sex—and condemn it, but that is no reason for us then to neglect its positives. Would it be right to outlaw bicycles because a few people crash on them, or aspirin because an overdose can kill? Tomas looked at me but I was concentrating on meditation, on conjuring the feeling of Synergy. It was close but not quite there.

From the Mission we drove across town—there's so much ingenuity and cause to be optimistic, Tomas said—to Fisherman's Wharf, where tourists ate clam chowder out of sourdough bread bowls and street magicians bent bars of steel and the Bay drew gulls by the thousands. The sailboats formed an armada of white playthings shuttling across the water's whitecap apostrophes. Of a teenage couple walking hand in hand, Tomas said, "Makes you feel good, doesn't it? See how the girl adjusted her step to match his? And how he unscrewed the water cap so she could drink and then screwed it back on? That's true selflessness, the kind born of genuine affection. There's nothing sterilized or contrived about it." I did not respond. "You have to ask yourself what PASE is doing when it says that charity and putting others first should be your top priorities, but it sequesters you away from people and has you think about yourself constantly."

Like suppressing a sneeze, I again didn't speak, though a rejoinder burned my throat the way a sneeze does one's nose. I was not able to enter Synergy. It lay behind a bricked-up entryway and I had nothing but my fingers to dig through to it. The sights and sounds of San Francisco were a vivid, convincing daydream. Tomas took two candy bars from his knapsack, ate one, and placed the other on the seat between us so that it pointed at me. In front of us were the Marin Headlands and Alcatraz and Vallejo and El Cerrito and Oakland and a hundred other communities I'd spent my life wandering through as comfortably as I had my own house.

Then we crossed the Golden Gate Bridge and the pearl of Sebastopol glinted down below as we headed up Highway 101 to the Richmond Bridge. Various landmasses and cities solemnized out of the water, their permanence like the solid and fixed and illusory images on celluloid. I twisted the bandanna around my thumb and wanted to put it back over my eyes. On the 580 North we turned off at University Avenue and entered Berkeley, an upward slant of Indian restaurants and hatha yoga centers and discount import shops. We drove along Telegraph Avenue while Tomas went over the macro- and microcosmic details of this living, breathing, mutable, growing, accommodating, studying, dirty, clean, searching, discovering modern city. Did I really want to opt out of all this vitality just because someone said desire was bad?

Cutting over toward Oakland we passed an outdoor market full of Middle Eastern basketry and ceramics and burning spires of incense, a quasi-Bedouin operation that seemed to be run by a single man wearing a Nehru jacket and a fez. I said I was feeling carsick and asked the driver to roll down my window. He pressed a button and it lowered halfway as we stopped at a red light. Tomas told him in a clipped voice to raise it back up, that it was too low, but before the driver could comply I punched Tomas in the testicles, reached through the window, opened my door from the outside, and jumped out. We were at the corner of Telegraph and Fifty-second Street, and cars were lining up on either side of the stoplight. I ran toward the UC Berkeley campus, whose Campanile building resembled the Citadel, and so at that moment was a beacon.

The CON car made a screeching 180-degree turn. Being used to running at the Wellness Center, I flew along the sidewalk past the Bedouin market, where the man in the fez arranging goods on a table shouted huzzas at me and clapped, though right away I felt winded. When I heard Tomas, abreast of me in the car on the other side of a traffic lane, call out to passersby that I was an escaped patient and should be apprehended, so that a couple of pedestrians looked at me hesitantly, I answered that I was being held prisoner and needed protection. This made up the pedestrians' mind to do nothing. I abruptly turned off the sidewalk and ran along a gravel driveway separating two creamy houses, hoping for a clear passage to Stuart Street, from which I could get to Shattuck Street and jump into a taxi or BART station, but instead I came to a tall chain-link fence connecting the two buildings. I had half scaled it when the flat side of a metal rake slapped me on the back, stunning me to the ground like a flyswatter. I got up and confronted the woman holding it; she was yelling that she lived in one of the houses and wouldn't let me cause mischief in her backyard. I stuttered an explanation and dodged another swipe, getting around her and back to the sidewalk, where the CON car had pulled up at a forty-five-degree angle. Tomas and the driver jumped out and stood on either side of me, their bodies hunched like dogcatchers. They thanked the woman and I begged her to call the police and not let these people take me, for they wanted to kill me, but she didn't seem to believe or care what I said, and ten seconds later I was alone in the backseat of the car. Tomas and the driver sat in front.

For several minutes the three of us didn't move. I panted and rubbed my face and felt for the most tender spots on my back. Had I been taller I might have made it. Had I had taller birth parents. Had I not started smoking when I was thirteen. Had I practiced jumping like those small men who could slam-dunk basketballs, their size no match for their ambition. But no, it was to end in defeat, in my inability to get over what would keep me down.

That evening, in my room, I was given a steak dinner, a glass of water, and a mixed bottle of sleeping pills and muscle relaxants. I went through my Couvade duffel bag, which contained most of my smaller-sized clothes and a few bigger sweatshirts, and then through the boxes of things from my apartment: photo albums, books, music compilations, old concert ticket stubs, my MBA diploma, and porn videos. Tomas and the other CON employees didn't bother to disguise the intended effect of these mementos; I was to see them and incrementally or, better yet, immediately feel nostalgia for my old life. The cumulative weight of those thirty-four years was supposed to snap my hastily erected Paser identity and restore the Jack of all craves.

To show my captors that I was immune to these things, that I regarded them as Constantine and his apostatical empire did the pagan deities that had long ruled Pax Romana, I spent the next several hours staring at the photographs and watching the pornography and listening to the music that had once driven and provided substance to my life. I lazily flipped through snapshots of proms and graduations and parties and girlfriends and vacations and barbecues and restaurants, each shot a colorful, spiraling association of memories, a mnemonic fractal by which formerly I'd been as comforted as a mathematician by a familiar algorithm. The first and only weekend Supritha and I spent in Mendocino, partially smitten as we sat on benches between short walks to and from the Sea Castle Bed and Breakfast Inn. My parents cutting me a small piece of cake when I finished junior high school, a shiny new digital watch programmed with two basic games adorning my chubby wrist. Closing the photo albums, I put on a few videos and yawned at the uncut footage of unlikely encounters between historical and futuristic personages who, no matter how exalted or lowly their station, no matter how pressing their need to prosecute or escape justice, no matter how flimsy or outrageous the premise of their world and character, found the time and opportunity and equipment to have sex in every conceivable location. Duchesses scolding their priapic gardeners on lush botanical grounds. Solar-powered cyborgs and the Earth girls who'd tried everything else. I responded as a child does to an ant colony, mildly amused by the hard work on display but ready on a whim to ignore or knock it down. When the movies ended I played music and feigned a nap during the second song of my favorite CD, a sublime four-minute ditty that had, throughout my ungainly adulthood, inspired me to move, if not dance, with comparative grace and coordination. The most successful of my one-night stands—that is, the one that was consummated—had followed my spinning a young businesswoman from Dubuque across the slippery dance floor of the Up and Down Club to its whirling melody. What had been a burst of sonic serotonin was now, to judge by the face I displayed, no better than an elevator banality.

All of this required huge effort on my behalf, a watchfulness against pleasure and sympathy with my old self in constant danger of slackening. I was like a policeman in his childhood neighborhood listening to the clemency appeals of his onetime best friends caught for drunk driving or minor drug possession. It demanded a hardening of the heart. I couldn't tell if my performance impressed the CON, because no one came to take away my undisturbed dinner plate or check on me. I was alone with the pain and frustration and fear that my PASE improvements were eroding in a feedback loop and would soon disappear altogether. I still couldn't reenter Synergy; like an oar that has slipped overboard and into the water, it drifted farther away the more I splashed to retrieve it. My vertebrae were hot iron spikes that pinched and scalded the attached nerve clusters. I flexed my groin muscles to keep an erection from forming with the desperation of a child holding his breath underwater, frantically hoping for help that couldn't come from without. Things might get worse rather than better, despite my intentions and exertions and protestations.

At ten P.M. I shut off the light and got into bed and lay on my side and sleep was light-years away. I inhaled and exhaled adrenaline. The room's silence was too loud. The bed was too soft. I was too alone. What if, after my time at the CON, PASE would no more take me back than a mother bear would accept a cub that had been touched and therefore contaminated by human hands? What if I had become damaged goods, spoiled, an unreclaimable outcast? Some questions, framed negatively enough—as mine were then— produce only one answer. At one A.M. I turned on the light and tried the locked door and examined the sleeping pills. They were brand name, high quality, the sort I kept at home in regular quantities. Small enough to fit in a dollhouse bathroom. Like the eggs of some mythically tiny bird. Lightweight and perfectly rounded and buffed. I peered at them and they arranged themselves along my hand's lifeline like the tail end of a fantastic constellation.

With my hand lightly shaking I flipped a coin to determine if I would take one: tails no, heads yes. It was tails. No. I flipped again, going for two out of three. Tails again. I turned the quarter over and rubbed George Washington's shy regal head. He was telling me not to take the easy road to sleep and to the breakdown of my resolve. He was saying, *Don't give in. Don't remove your finger from the dam; don't scream near fragile glass. If drugs put you under now, you will be less able to do it on your own later. There are processes that once set in motion are difficult to stop. Just because you did so once doesn't mean you can do it again.* Like any good father—of a family or nation—Washington cautioned against a gamble that he wouldn't have hesitated to take when younger.

And yet without the pills, I thought, answering him apologetically and with what might have been cheap casuistry, though it seemed like calculated wisdom, I won't sleep at all, and my defenses will be weak against the CONslaught awaiting me in the morning. Shouldn't I preserve my energy by getting some restorative rest, allow a minor front to fall so that I can send reinforcements to the other, more important battle site? A sacrifice must be made somewhere. This is about damage control, not damage prevention.

I flipped the coin again and it was heads and, lifting two blue tablets to my mouth, I avoided the dead man's steely gaze.

In the morning, following seven hours of unconsciousness, I was not restored or in control or noticeably stronger. If anything, I felt worse and thicker-headed than on the day before, like a boxer regaining consciousness after being knocked out for the second fight in a row. A full cup of fragrant black coffee rested on a warming pad beside my bed. My back and stomach were the physical equivalent of pounding on the deep end of a piano.

When I entered the interrogation room to talk again to Dr. Cantor, he pulled out my chair in front of a steaming plate of eggs Benedict with a tall orange juice and another cup of coffee. A fresh pack of cigarettes lay in front of him. No air purifier. Cool jazz played, a saxophone and clarinet duet in which neither instrument had the upper hand. I sat down and looked at him coolly. He was powerless and I knew the truth. For thinking makes it so.

"How did you sleep?" he asked, removing the protective wrapping around the cigarettes and tapping one out. An extra landed on the table and rolled toward me; a third jutted halfway from the pack like a cannon barrel.

"Fine."

"You look like you could have used a few more hours."

"Couldn't everyone?"

"I suppose we should get started, in that case." He lit his cigarette and the smoke dance started up again. It was all sickeningly familiar, with the second cigarette calling for me to help it up as though I were a passing good Samaritan. "Do you know anything about Eros and Thanatos?"

When looking out from inside a heavy fog, mental or meteorological, you notice that objects and events lack precision. Dr. Cantor and this room, for example, had for me soft rather than sharp edges, as though someone had drawn them in charcoal and then with a thumb smudged their outlines. I wanted a pair of glasses for my mind.

"They are the Greek gods of sexual love and death, respectively. In Freudian terms, Eros represents the life instinct and Thanatos the death instinct. Some people believe that the two vie for primacy in every individual and in society as a whole, that our urge for life, as enacted in sex and desire, moves in lockstep with our attraction to death, which is manifested in war and self-destruction. To be healthy therefore is to maintain an equilibrium between the two. Devoting yourself to either god, or instinct, is like living with only the right or left half of your body, like flying with one wing. It is, in short, an impossibility, because too much Eros or too much Thanatos overloads the body and mind and creates a kind of ontological black hole from which nothing can escape, not even light, and ends in either overintoxication or asceticism." He transferred the cigarette from his right to left hand. "I won't spell out the obvious application of this theory to what happens to a Paser, but I will ask you to ponder it later on your own."

"I won't," I said, struggling not to ponder it already.

"Well, I can't make you think of pink elephants." He laughed. "That's a joke."

I sighed and watched the smoke.

"How about we go back to what we talked about yesterday, about why you decided to join PASE?"

I didn't answer.

"I've thought a lot about it and have a theory. Mind if I share it with you? It has to do with the 'bowling alone' thesis concerning contemporary America, which you might already know of. The gist of it is that we in this country feel less connected to one another than past generations did, which has created a kind of vacuum in our lives. Sociologists call it a decline in social capital. In the 1960s, for example, eight percent of Americans belonged to a bowling league—they would get together once or twice a week in a friendly, social environment to bowl and interact with one another—whereas now fewer than one percent do. Add to that the fact that in the 1950s people got married on average six years younger than we do now, so that the mean age of a man and woman marrying were twenty-two and twenty, compared to twenty-eight and twenty-six now, meaning they had children at an earlier age and developed closer coupled friends, and of course the divorce rate was lower then, too. All this is to say that whereas in the past we were part of various groups that met regularly to socialize and act as extensions of the families we already had at home, giving us a rich and vibrant sense of community, an emotional network that we'd cultivated in different forms since our time as hunters and gatherers, these days we have nothing—"

"How sad for us."

He paused to show that he didn't mind my interruption and would welcome more of my thoughts, then said, "These days we have nothing to meet those needs but work and religion. Man is a social animal by nature. Living as isolated as we do now is affecting us in ways we can't yet understand fully, but that are almost certainly unhealthy. It breeds extremism and desperation. Look at you, for instance. You live alone and apparently have no hobbies or activities outside of your job, which, when you lost it, turned out to have been the only bulwark between you and the first community and belief system that came along." Although animated while speaking, he went back to his expectant dogface when he fell silent, like a mime after performing his dollar routine.

"Maybe your other patients like being reduced to a statistic and belittled," I said, "but I don't. In fact I find it annoying."

"I don't mean to annoy you."

"Too late."

"Okay, then let's talk about something else."

The pack of cigarettes between us on the table was a perfect rectangular object, without nicks or scratches, fresh and clean and promising, the ratio of its size to its effects like a stick of dynamite to its explosion.

"Have you had a nocturnal emission since you became a savant?" asked Dr. Cantor, sticking his pen behind his ear.

"Excuse me?"

"While sleeping, have you had an orgasm? And if so, were you upset by it?"

"That is a stupid question."

"Men who don't have sex or masturbate, a category I presume includes you, often have nocturnal emissions."

"Savants don't. We control our bodies at all times, even when we're asleep."

"Very interesting. How do you manage it?"

"As *The Prescription* says: 'Desire is a by-product of ignorance, of the idea that human beings are limited by their bodies and in need of a corrective in order to survive and be well. Once ignorance and superstition are vanquished by wisdom, by the full personal revelation that we are part of a greater truth, of ultimate reality, desire will lose its strength and have no more influence over us than a witch doctor's spell. The truth is the antidote to desire. The truth is all-powerful. The truth works during the day and night, before and after, always and always.'"

"An impressive recital."

"How much longer do we have to talk to each other?"

"About an hour."

"No, I mean in general when do you plan to admit to my parents that deprogramming won't work with me? Because they're not rich. While we're here chatting so amiably, you're bankrupting a retired couple on a fixed income. Not that I think your conscience could be tweaked by anything short of murder."

"We're not charging them a fee."

"But they hired you."

"Our hope is that when you understand the secret nature of PASE, your testimony against it will help us bring it down. That will more than offset the cost of your stay here."

"So you're doing this for free?"

"Yes."

I grew sullen and didn't answer Dr. Cantor's next few questions. Soon he stopped asking them and circled back to the ground he had covered earlier about how troubled I was. He was sorry if it annoyed me but I needed to hear it. I had a death fixation. I was lonely. Did I know about the followers of another Bay Area guru, Jim Jones, who in the 1970s mixed together a potent blend of apostolic socialism and liberation theology in a cult called the Peoples Temple, which to escape scrutiny fled to Guyana, where, in 1978, increasingly despotic and given to sexually and psychologically abusing his acolytes, Jones forced all of its members to drink cyanide-laced fruit punch after a California congressman came to see how they were doing? More than nine hundred people died, including women and children, and the congressman was murdered along with his traveling companions. I had a death fixation and was lonely. And surely I remembered David Koresh, who converted his Branch Davidian ministry into a heavily armed compound in Texas and burned it down, killing eighty people? I was a lonely, death-fixated man who'd accidentally entered the orbit of a ruthless cult whose destructive powers were as yet unknown, but which umpteen historical examples suggested would be horrible. In the battle between Eros and Thanatos for dominion over me I'd given everything to Thanatos and become a bitter foe of Eros and why was this? Many people were lonely but they didn't have to be death-fixated. If I felt the absence of community I could seek it out.

I could join an intramural basketball team or take an adult education class or start a book club. There were a million things I could do to reconnect with people around me, to feel a part of something.

Dr. Cantor used preacherly cadences that in a church context might have zigzagged between the River Jordan and Mount Sinai until, too weary to make another pass, they would have finally bid a congregation to go forth and sin no more. You got the sense that he hated charismatic leaders because they reminded him too much of himself. While listening to him it occurred to me that all we really had was our decision to go one way or another, and where we went helped settle the dust of this or that path, and the people further along for whom the decision was already irreversible would do anything to make the rest of us settle the same dust they had, because otherwise the dust might rise and blind and choke them. It was all a wild gambit to keep the ground from swallowing us up.

Eventually he asked what I thought.

"About what?" I said.

"About anything I've been saying. For example, what do you think of not having any nonwork interests?"

"I think it's beside the point."

"What point?"

"The Earth is in such critical condition that it doesn't matter whether I join a bowling league or start a book club."

"How is that?"

"We've done so much damage to the planet that talking about our future here is like fantasizing about what to do with a lottery jackpot. Look at the political problems in the Middle East and Africa. Look at the extreme weather and the natural disasters, the earthquakes and hurricanes and volcanic activity, plaguing our cities and countryside. Look at violent crime. Look at the outbreaks of war. Look at the spread and increasing virulence of animal and vegetable diseases. Look at drug addiction and the collapsing global economy. And if that doesn't finish us all off, some bellicose country will start a worldwide nuclear war sooner than later. We can no longer fix what's gone wrong here. It's over."

"You believe that?"

"Yes."

He wrote in his notebook for five minutes, occasionally stopping to look up and stare into space. I regarded the eggs Benedict, the hollandaise sauce of which had congealed and glistened as though wrapped in cellophane, and my stomach felt as empty as a well when there's nothing left to wish for.

That afternoon I went online and found all the PASE and PASE-affiliated websites blocked, along with email capabilities. I hadn't seen or heard any news in ten days and was surprised to find so little about Ben Membawa or the war or the country's rising unemployment rate. Those things were either resolved or in a holding pattern. Now it was a dockworkers' strike, illegal gerrymandering, underperforming public schools, and academic disparities between boys and girls in middle school. I decided to meditate again and tried not to think about my previous failures—one had to do, not reflect—but for the third time in a row Synergy eluded me, like fire to someone striking a used match. I wondered, like Warren and Chaim, whom I could bribe at the CON to alert the police of my whereabouts, because if my captivity didn't depend on my parents' money, a finite resource, it might go on indefinitely.

I lay down and my back pain cooled off. I told myself again, though with less conviction than before, that I would not be broken by the CON. It was bound to find better witnesses out there to help prosecute its hopeless case against PASE, and then it would let me go. If this was a war, as Tomas claimed, it would discharge anyone unwilling to fight on its side, for, although not wise, it was not dumb. I lay there and my regression was only temporary and I had to keep this in mind. It was a test. A proving ground. My belief in PASE would not waver.

Then I was being shaken awake and taken to Tomas's office by the two escorts who'd tricked me away from the Wellness Center; each kept a step ahead of me. My life had become an unending series of office visits. I sat across from Tomas, who smiled warmly and dipped a tea bag in and out of a football-shaped 49ers mug.

"First of all," he said, picking a wiry red hair from his mouth, "I'm sorry that you're not enjoying your time with Dr. Cantor, that he's exasperated more than helped you. I know what it's like at the beginning; I went through a whole deprogramming treatment with him myself. He means well, of course, and would prefer it to go happily and smoothly, but the nature of his job is to find our most sensitive spots and press on them to drive out the pain, like rubbing a knotted muscle until it's healed. Hurts like hell. I was in deprogramming for a full week before I was fixed."

"So you weren't always a criminal?"

He laughed. "I used to be like you, in that I too was seduced into a fringe religious organization. In the mid-1980s I joined the Om Federation, a kind of Hindu sect, when swami Sanharatha gave a talk on the Berkeley campus. I was studying Indian history at the time, and I went to hear him more for academic than personal reasons, but while leaving his talk I met some people who invited me to a weekend of learning in Napa. A month later I dropped out of school and joined the Om Federation's living quarters in Elmwood, and then I took vows to uphold the Way. Sanharatha seemed like a wonderful teacher, the other members were supportive and loving, and we did what I considered to be important work promoting Sanharatha's message and collecting donations."

"Then why did you turn your back on it?"

"My girlfriend and my parents hired Religious Freedom Now to liberate me. Like you, I was resistant at first and wanted to get back to the cult, but they helped me to recognize the insular, suspicious underbelly of Sanharatha's teachings. I had, like the Paser I told you about, been instructed to break off ties with my old friends and family. I'd been told that anyone who wasn't for the Om Federation was against it, and that people hostile to Sanharatha were in fact hostile to everyone in the group, and that I had to keep myself pure by avoiding contact with any criticism or dissent from orthodox Om Federation beliefs. There was a lot of paranoia involved, a lot of mistrust and denial of the very things that had first attracted me to the group, namely love and human interconnectedness."

"You were following the wrong leader."

Tomas sipped his tea. "Do you see an element of paranoia in PASE?"

"No."

"Dr. Cantor says you believe the world is going to end."

"I don't want to talk about that with you." It was cold in the room and I sat on my hands. This test of my faith was difficult but not impossible. My back pain and erections were perhaps even blessings insofar as they made me hate my body and drove me toward ur-savant status.

Tomas said, seeming to grow larger in his seat as he bent toward me, "You know when it made sense to think that the world was ending? Ninety years ago. Before 1914 there was a consensus amongst most people that mankind was getting better, that we had moved past war and were on a teleological path forward, that we'd learned from our mistakes. Then World War I came along and shattered that idea. Millions died in combat and millions more died of influenza—Europe, not to mention parts of North Africa and Turkey around the Dardanelles, was laid to waste—and by 1919 every other person you met thought they were living at the end of times. But nearly a century later we're still here; only now we have commercial airplane flights and space travel and the capacity to feed everyone alive. There hasn't been a major conflict in Europe in sixty years."

"I'm not going to argue with you."

"The Taborites believed the world would end in 1420, and for twenty years prior to it they waged a war in Bohemia that did nothing but establish a reactionary church in Prague. During the Interregnum in England, from 1649 to 1661, the Fifth Monarchy Men thought that 1666, with its numerical significance, would mark the end. In 1844, Adventist founder William Miller convinced fifty thousand people that the apocalypse would begin on October 22, which led to what's called the Great Disappointment. Tens of millions of evangelical Christians today think the Rapture is coming and are buying *Left Behind* books by the truckload to prepare for it. The Mayan calendar says that time will end in the year 2012, when predictions have been made that the sun's magnetic poles will shift, major astrological signs will collide, the Hopi Indians' 'Fifth World' will commence, two worlds in Maori legend will mesh, and the Earth will be in perfect alignment with the center of the Milky Way."

I massaged my back and breathed in and out deeply. PASE would want me to keep my calm, to suffer fools gladly, to not get angry. I said, "I don't think it's going to happen on any particular day at any particular hour; I know that the sun will last for four billion more years, and that the Earth could last as long. I'm only saying what PASE says, which is that UR God will rescind His offer for us to fuse into Him."

"Why would he do that?"

"Because a major environmental crisis is going to strike soon, and He wants to save as many of us as possible beforehand. And because He'd like us to choose Him for His sake, while we still appear to have an alternative."

A trilling sound came from Tomas's computer; he typed something and then turned the screen away from him; it had a race car screen saver. "You're right to worry about the environment, because much of what's going on in it is genuinely alarming. You're right to resent your body's imperfections, the backache and what have you, because getting older steals a lot of what we take for granted. But to think that the world should be perfect, or that because it's sick it's going to die, and to think that we should be perfect, is childish. Everything is not fair and everyone will not live happily ever after."

"I agree with you completely."

"We've got to keep carrying on, though; keep trying. That's what'll save us, if anything. Killing ourselves is not a solution to anything but our own private problems."

"I'll say this one last time: Becoming an ur-savant is not dying. It is, in the only true sense of the word, living."

Tomas folded his hands and looked down at the hard plastic cover over his desktop calendar. "But what if you're wrong? What if things are as they appear, and death really is death and life really is life? Doesn't the emptiness of one and the plenitude of the other give you pause? Don't you think, deep down, that this is all too important to be simply a game we're playing?"

Back in my room I read an encyclopedia entry about Wisconsin (Montgomery Shoale's home state) and ignored a superfluous erection and did jumping jacks. I didn't attempt and therefore didn't fail to achieve Synergy. My outlook swung between confidence and despair, so that at one moment I thought this CON episode was just a blip on my journey to UR God, and at the next it was the journey's cancellation. I didn't know whom to believe, the optimistic or the pessimistic Jack, and whether my doubts signified that true faith was beyond my reach or deep within me.

When a knock came at my door I hoped it might be Tomas coming to send me away, to admit that I couldn't help him or the CON. Instead Elizabeth, dressed in the two-piece gray business suit I'd seen her wearing on the day everything began to go wrong, the one that went with her charcoal eyes, entered.

"Elizabeth," I said, wiping my nose and mouth and sitting up, uncramping my legs.

She smiled and looked about nervously, as though she'd been waiting in the wings of a talk show and was scared to be in front of an audience. "Hi, Jack. It's good to see you again."

"What are you doing here?"

She sat in the rocker and set down her purse. "I want to apologize for the last time we talked on the phone, when I didn't believe you about the conspiracy at Couvade. I'll never forgive myself for being so dense. Last week I asked someone in accounts how much we'd billed for Danforth, and she said that Danforth had withdrawn its contract with us three weeks earlier. Before the PASE seminar."

"I see."

"That means you weren't late getting Danforth in because they weren't our client anymore, which means that Mr. Raven dismissed you illegally. It's just like you suspected. I'm so sorry I didn't look into it right away. I blame myself for what's happened to you since then and I hope you can forgive me."

"Done."

She waited, as though being a good host I should ask her a question or say something to fill the dead air. After a few seconds she said, "I heard from your parents that you were sent to the PASE Wellness Center."

"Oh?"

"When I couldn't get ahold of you, I tracked them down. That's how I found out you were here."

"You put yourself to all kinds of trouble."

She folded her hands loosely and I remembered too clearly why I'd asked her out, the direct and slightly worried way she looked at you before something caught her attention off to the right or left. She wasn't wearing earrings and had a slender, graceful neck, and I fought down my attraction to her. "I talked to Mr. Raven on Thursday night after work—I confronted him, basically—and he admitted to setting you up. He said that the CEO and some other higher-ups had converted to PASE and insisted that someone with a record of sexual misconduct be made an example of, and you were chosen randomly. He started crying while telling me this, begging me not to tell anyone. But it's a major scandal; it's illegal what they did to you and possibly to others. The world needs to know about it so workplace persecution stops before it spreads."

"You don't have to say all this."

"I want to help and support you. When you get out of here we'll collate the evidence of corporate malfeasance at Couvade and prosecute the company. I'm not sure you'll get your job back—not that you'd want it after all this—but there should be a big settlement package, a kind of reparations. I've talked with Mr. Kowinski and Dr. Cantor here, who say we could link the suit with their case against PASE. Or we could file it on its own. Either way, I want to reassure you that you're not alone in this."

Elizabeth seemed almost to believe what she was saying, an

actress who, once warmed up to the studio audience, could rely on whatever skill had brought her to this point in her career.

"I'm not taking Couvade to court, so tell them that you tried but it's a no-go. I don't imagine they're paying you."

"Who?"

"The Cult Opposition Network."

"Paying me for what?"

"For coming here. You wouldn't give this performance for free."

"No one's putting me up to this. I want to help you expose what's going on at Couvade. Everything you told me last week was true: PASE was responsible for you receiving ten demerits while Juan and Dexter and Philippe got none, and for you being let go unfairly. It all really happened."

"PASE did what it had to do, as did Mr. Raven. I'm much better off for their actions."

"But they're working against you. You can't not see that. And if you don't do something to stop them, more people will suffer."

"I have nothing against you personally, but I don't believe a word you're saying."

Getting up and pulling her chair around the table in front of mine so that our knees touched, Elizabeth said, "When you asked me out on a date I said no because of an office romance I had at my last job that didn't go well. It ruined a year of my life and I swore I would never go out with anyone I worked with again. In other circumstances I would have said yes."

I didn't answer.

"You ran off too quickly at the time for me to tell you that. Then you acted like it was no big deal and I thought maybe you asked out everyone and didn't care why I'd turned you down or what my real feelings might have been. I'm not trying to trick you and I'm not lying and you should think about what PASE has done to you."

"I don't think about anything else."

Elizabeth looked at me for a long time and then closed her eyes and tilted her head to the left at a pre-kiss angle. Her knees parted by two inches. She reached out to touch my hand as one would a cat stuck in a tree, a tentative move that reflected the idea of the action as much as any desire to rescue. Just before she made contact I stood up and went to the door and said, "It's time for me to rest now."

Night fell and I went with it into a deep hole where everything was shrouded and darkly ominous, where a step in any direction would send me plummeting farther down. I'd had to work hard to maintain a hard-boiled response to Elizabeth's tacit sexual invitation. My mind was determined to keep me in one state—though already fissures veined its surface—and my body the other. As a savant I was supposed to be beyond this disintegration, this disagreement; I'd made a stand on it with Dr. Cantor. I sat with my hands folded, perfectly still, thinking of a temptation so great it assumed a shape and solidity and color, as when a cirrus cloud turns into a nacreous cumulus, and I didn't try to prove anything to the CON by examining my belongings. That strategy hadn't worked the first time and might actually have harmed more than helped my cause. Minutes passed like hours, devoid of interest or meaning, and I began to think that like a fish kept too long out of water I would not survive.

This reverie of self-pity ended abruptly with the sound of a door closing and a woman walking over to my bag and boxes. I rubbed my eyes and cleared my throat and looked at this stranger bending down in low-riding tan jeans that hugged her hips and flared out at the ankles. Her T-shirt rode up to reveal an Ouroboros tattoo on her lower back while she zipped the bag closed.

"Hey," I said, sliding off the table, my back as silent as a prisoner who stops shouting when an officer arrives with a crowded set of keys, "what are you doing here?"

Mary Shoale stood up and turned around with my bag slung over her shoulder, her dirty-blond hair in a bedhead tussle. With a finger to her lips she said, "Shhh."

In a lowered voice I asked, "Are you taking me back to the Wellness Center?"

"You haven't figured it out yet?"

"Figured what out?"

Her shoulders relaxed and my bag almost slipped to the ground. "You never left."

CHAPTER 10

M ost of us try and manage for long stretches to bury the doubts we harbor about ourselves, the flock of neuroses that would otherwise feed on our self-confidence like eagles at Prometheus's liver. Because if we think we are at core unlikable, it is best, so that we may get ahead, win friends, and influence people, to inter that thought in an airless tomb to which we don't have ready access, to stow it away in the catacombs of our unconscious. The same is true of any suspicion that we are unintelligent, slow-witted, ugly, socially inept, overbearing, useless, scary, or in any other way repellent. Deny, repress, conceal. Submerge. People who've felt the incisive tear of self-doubt's beak know that it ought to rest far belowground, with flowers growing over its burial site and worms decomposing it.

Some of us, however, have a hard time with this. We can't dig a deep enough hole using only our willpower for a spade, and from its shallow grave self-doubt rises to haunt us for hours or days or years. And while there are self-credentialed ghostbusters and demonslayers out there, therapists and other soldiers armed with silver bullets and wooden stakes, they're often too late or ineffectual or wounded by their own problems to take care of ours.

As a child, as I've suggested, I had many worries. They centered on my weight, height, physical coordination, attractiveness, future earning potential, and lovability, all of which lay beneath a thin layer of topsoil made light and porous by the reagent of my adoption. Had Dr. Cantor approached the subject with greater finesse, he might have learned that the phrase "I was unwanted" used to enter my head unbidden fifty times a day: waking up, walking to the school bus, in recess, taking tests, playing with a friend, getting taunted by bullies, fighting with Sid, watching my parents get drunk, doing my homework, and lying in bed. These three words evoked, in graphic detail, the sequence in which my biological mother had given birth to me and seen me with her own eyes and then overcome what by all accounts is the greatest bond a woman can form, with her child, in order to hand me over to strangers to rear and mold. I was unwanted after having done nothing but come into existence. Like being born with original sin. Like being guilty of being guilty.

I think that my obsession with what I considered to be an almost primal injury derived not from inevitability but from a haywire self-pity that others in the same situation didn't share. Sid, for example, who had been equally unwanted by his birth parents, and was in addition African-American, wasn't bothered by the fact of his adoption, which may have had something to do with his being our parents' favorite, in the same way that my not being their favorite may have compounded my sense of rejection—even my adoptive parents, whose early care for me was meant to compensate for my biological parents' absence, didn't seem to love me enough—though my feelings were too severe for that explanation. In either case, I knew I needed to get over it. I couldn't change the circumstances of my birth, and every minute I spent wishing otherwise was a minute subtracted from my store of potential happiness. Life is very short, however much it may seem otherwise to the young.

Therefore at age eleven I decided to confront my biological parents about why they'd gotten rid of me—in my preadolescent way I thought that the answer would provide closure and carry me cathartically into puberty—so I asked Rick and Ann for their names and phone numbers. This neither surprised nor upset my adoptive parents, who said that the child placement agency had kept identity matters private and that there was no way to find out now. They were sorry. Three years later I asked again and got the same story. Which is perhaps where I should have left it. History and mythology abound with warnings against knowing too much about one's parentage. It's impossible to forget Oedipus poking out his eyes and wandering away from Thebes. But on my eighteenth birthday, at a party in our backyard full of Sid's drama student friends and two of my regular ones, as an a cappella group performed Sid's avant-garde reworking of "Happy Birthday" and I reduced a dollar sign cake to its vertical bar, I told my parents, in recognition of my legally becoming a man, to tell me. I had a right to know. Instead of denying everything, this time they said that I wouldn't like what I heard and that my birth mother had asked never to be contacted by me or hear anything about my whereabouts and goings-on. Please, I said, assuring them that I wouldn't call or write if those were her wishes, but that just knowing her name would help me in indescribable ways. The more I could invent details, the more I suffered psychologically and found myself unable to be fully comfortable in life. Her name, however unrevealing in itself, would improve my understanding of and facility with others and myself. They looked at me curiously, as though I might have dimensions they hadn't suspected, as though by admitting to a lack of self-knowledge I was already on my way to restoring it and deserving of assistance.

After talking in private for a few minutes they told me that my birth mother, Pamela, had been raped at age sixteen by an unknown assailant; when the adoption process was complete she had returned to her hometown in Massachusetts. They didn't have her phone number or address, nor were they even sure if she was still alive. The whole transaction had been so emotionally difficult—she'd cried throughout their single meeting—that they'd never before considered contravening her request. They understood, however, that I was going through a difficult time, that nothing is a greater mystery to an eighteen-year-old than him- or herself, and they hoped that knowing was better than not knowing.

I asked why she'd been in California. They said she'd come to attend a youth group or camp—they weren't exactly sure what it was—near Monterey Bay. My dad went inside to root around his office, and upon returning he gave me a picture of her from the adoption packet; it showed a young girl sitting in what looked like a park, writing in a journal, a wreath of cornflowers crowning her head. She had a round face like mine, with the same spattering of pimples on her chin and forehead, the same narrow shoulders and thin mouth. My birth mother.

Following that birthday I framed and hung the picture in my college dorm room, and later in my graduate school apartment. When I got my place in Hayes Valley, though, I put it in a desk drawer, thinking that at age twenty-five I could finally bury the feeling of not being wanted so deep that it wouldn't escape without a massive excavation effort.

Nine years later that excavation began on a cold November day when I received an email that said: "Dear Jack, I am going to be in San Francisco in December and wonder if you would like to meet your real mother, Pamela." I stared at the computer screen for an hour before replying with a torrent of questions and exclamations and hopes. Her answer didn't address my concerns or elaborate on her life or even say why she was coming to the Bay Area, but it did agree to meet me for dinner at Firestick, a pan-Asian restaurant on Guerrero Street. The next month at the appointed time I waited for three hours and drank so much sake that a team of Malaysian busboys had to carry me outside. Pamela, my mother, never showed. I emailed her the next day and the day after that, and every day of the following week. If it was possible to be heartbroken by someone who had once broken my heart for many consecutive years, I was. The great lengths to which I'd gone in preparation—from my liposuction and laser eye surgery to the professional manicure and electrolysis on my back—were for naught; she had not seen me at my reconfigured best. In early January I tracked her down on the Internet and discovered that she was employed by Boston's First International Bank, that neither death nor a terrible accident had prevented her from meeting me or answering my emails. She'd simply stood me up. End of a story that had already ended.

*   *   *

Except that nothing really ended, because I got it all wrong, because all was misrepresented to me at the time. I should be clearer so that you don't think I can't admit my mistakes. I can and I would admit them, if not happily then at least audibly, but to a degree unmatched by anyone of my personal acquaintance, and perhaps by anyone of theirs, I was willfully deceived again and again, and so should be forgiven my errors of understanding. Mountains were moved like chess pieces to keep me misinformed. Consider when Mary zipped up my bag and said that I was not, as I'd been led to believe, in a maximum security deprogramming center, but rather in the very place I'd longed to be, the PASE Wellness Center, Daly City.

I told her to be serious and she said that I'd find out for myself in about two minutes. She slid on my shoes and tied their laces and said we had to get out right away, because the surveillance crew assigned to monitor my room had probably already seen her there and dispatched facilitators. I asked what was happening and was told to trust her. Once off the Center grounds we'd be partially safe, and then in her car with the engine running and with road disappearing under our tires we'd be mostly safe. She had someplace for us to go. But, I said, if we were truly at the Wellness Center then I didn't want to leave, for that was precisely where I'd been angling to return for days. She answered that if after hearing her explanation—which would have to wait until we were out of there—I wanted to return, she would bring me back herself, that I had her word as Montgomery Shoale's daughter.

It was eleven-thirty at night. The hallway outside my room, which I hadn't ever seen without a guard, was empty, and we ran down it with our heads ducked low, Mary just ahead of me, as though keeping our faces hidden was as good as wearing a cloak of invisibility. I tripped on a wave in the carpet and she put a steadying hand back for me to grab on to. We turned a corner and a ceiling light ahead of us died. Then another and another and within a second we came to a standstill in pitch darkness. Mary's hand tightened around mine. "Shhh," she said again. The darkness was immediate and impenetrable and seemed to billow out, like black smoke. I heard Mary digging through her handbag. "Shhh."

A door at the end of the hallway creaked open and then an industrial-grade LED flashlight blinded us, accompanied by the tromping of several pairs of footsteps. Mary yanked me toward them in a charge, and a second later we collided with people we saw only in snippets of limb and torso. Strong arms clasped around me, pinning my hands to my side. There was a loud spray bottle whoosh, followed by yelling. I couldn't see anything but the jerking light and struggled to get out of the bear hug. More spray, more yelling. The flashlight fell to the floor and I saw two kneeling bodies with their hands clutching their faces, grunting in pain. The hug tightened and I was losing my breath until a third spray sounded and the arms around me loosened and I slipped away as easily as if my assailant were a coat being removed by a butler. Then Mary's hand took mine again and we sprinted down a chiaroscuro hallway framed by the beams of unattended lights.

We burst through a heavy exit door using our shoulders and stood outside on the grated metal landing of a flight of stairs corkscrewing down to the ground. Seventy feet away the Wellness Center's wall, in the daytime a batter white, was tinted green by a swollen moon. Mary ran down the stairs, pulling me toward it. The wall didn't have any visible doors and I wondered if she hoped we could hoist each other over its fifteen-foot height. When we got nearer, though, I saw a small control panel, like a home security system, embedded into it at eye level. Mary punched a few numbers and a section of the wall swiveled open like a trick panel in horror story libraries.

On the other side we forced passage through a thick shrubbery and came to the street, where Mary's two-door hatchback was parked. My face and arms stung from the shrubbery's branches and my chest felt constricted, but sitting in the passenger seat I felt better. A minute later we were on Nineteenth Street racing north, with the Pacific Ocean lapping at the shore to our left, low-resolution cars on their nocturnal rounds, and the sound of her engine revving up and down as we put a dozen stoplights between us and the Wellness Center. My heart beat at slower intervals and the air vents dried out my eyes.

"Can we talk now?" I asked.

"Yes."

We turned on to Lincoln Way, and the Sunset District was entombed in stillness, its extended families and narcoleptic medical students put down for the night. Gas stations glowed among the surrounding unlit buildings, turning the city blocks into jack-o'-lantern smiles. Mary smelled of aloe and pine, and she held her breath while shifting gears, breathing out when we were safely in second, third, fourth. As with Elizabeth, I tamped down an attraction to her that rose within me without permission or approval. She was a mistake and I had been a fool to think that I was elected to love her. The old Jack might have been so anointed, true, but not me. Not now. Whatever reason explained my sitting beside her after that mad scramble, it wasn't love. She looked at her rearview mirror every two seconds, like a driving student trying to appear conscientious in front of her instructor.

"Are we being followed?" I asked.

"No. Those people back there were just extra night staff at the Center, the dumbest of the dumb. They can barely operate a phone on their own. Plus I Maced the hell out of them."

"Why did you do that?"

"They seemed to be attacking us."

We drove past the entrance to Golden Gate Park and turned left at Stanyan before arcing on to Haight Street. As the adrenaline seeped out of my system, the aloe reminded me of a hiking trip to Lake Trinity my parents had taken me and Sid on when I was thirteen; I got a fourth-degree sunburn on the first day and when my arms and legs sprouted colonies of heat blisters, as though my skin were the surface of a boiling liquid, I applied an aloe cream and knew relief that was close to euphoria.

"Why is the Cult Opposition Network at the Wellness Center?"

Mary said, "It's not. The CON doesn't exist. PASE administrators wanted you to think you were in it."

I waited a second, to give the appearance of being unfazed. "Why?"

"To test your belief."

"But Ms. Anderson said I would undergo ur-Synergy."

"That was a ruse. My father wanted you to go through deprogramming, so he had one of the Center buildings converted into a mock underground cult-fighting operation. You were meant to think it was in a South San Francisco or Emeryville warehouse, and that it was a serious resistance group. The guys you thought ran it are actors from Los Angeles training to become actuated savants."

"So there's no such thing as the Cult Opposition Network."

"There are a few operating cult watchdog groups, but none with that name."

"I don't see how deprogramming was a test of my belief; for the last two days I was given every reason not to be a Paser."

"And if tomorrow you still believed, my father would know it was real."

"Why does he care?"

"I don't know." We parked outside 549 Birch Street. "Now go inside and get some clothes. You might not be back here for a while."

I found it difficult to move. "I need to know why my belief is so important to him."

"Hurry!"

In my apartment everything looked unfamiliar, as though the past ten days had been as many years, and I stood for a moment on the edge of the living room in shell-shock. Because home is more than a collection of electronics, worn furniture, clothes, trip souvenirs, pornography, dirty dishes, and empty bottles of top-shelf whiskey, because it is a state of mind, I ought to have been as comforted by it as Ulysses was by Ithaca, a haven after my long strange sojourn. Instead it was chaotic and meaningless.

I packed two bags and unplugged the appliances and turned off the heat and brushed crumbs off the counter. I grabbed my checkbook and extra credit cards and a fur-lined gabardine coat. After closing and locking the door I pressed the down button on the elevator, which began a slow and creaky ascent from the bowels of its shaft, and then I remembered my mother's photograph. I went back inside to retrieve it, and once in the hallway again I saw Conrad standing in his doorway wearing his gray elephant-skin robe and rubbing his head.

"Jack," he said, frowning. "Where have you been? What happened?"

"It's a long story. The woman used a stun gun."

"That's what it sounded like. The police came over and dusted inside but there weren't any usable fingerprints, so they couldn't get a warrant for you. I told them everything I knew."

"Thanks."

"Geraldine on the fourth floor has been particularly worried about you, but I told her you were probably all right."

I pressed the elevator button again.

"I've got excellent news," said Conrad, yawning. "Do you remember my student you asked about, Mary Shoale, the one who quit? She's referred seven new students to me in the past week. In a year I'll have enough money saved up for a surgery on my leg that the doctor says will fix my limp entirely, correct it so it's gone."

"That's great."

"Modern medical science is full of miracles. As you know from your own procedures."

"True."

"We'll go running together when I'm better. Do you play basketball? I used to be everywhere on the court. We could put an intramural team together with some of the other guys from the building, have uniforms made. I'll lose weight first. I started a vegetable and tofu diet a couple of days ago. Maybe in two years I'll be able to get the stomach surgery you did."

"That'd be something."

"Why do you have those bags?"

"I'm going away for a while."

He approached me and touched my elbow. "Fortune's a funny

thing. I was just thinking I'd never get another student again. Now I have more than I can handle. Maybe I'll be entirely well by the next time we see each other."

Outside, Mary's car was gone. I looked up and down the empty street and the poplars rustled in the Hayes Valley breeze, a soft tinkling sound that softened what was otherwise a hard urban scene of shuttered buildings and trash grilled into gutters and a middle-aged guy bicycling around the corner, waiting to give or receive or take. I was cold and pulled on a sweater. Then a pair of headlights bent on to Birch Street from Fulton and Mary pulled up.

"I went to get a pack of cigarettes," she said, lowering the passenger side window. "Want one?"

"No." I climbed in and the blast of warm air from the vent made me shiver.

She lit two and handed me one and I held it over the floor between my legs.

"There's something we need to talk about, so I'm taking us to a friend's place in North Beach."

We passed bars and nightclubs closing for the evening; streams of people poured out to whirlpool on the sidewalk before cabs and friends' cars siphoned them away. I tried not to look at Mary, because when I did I couldn't breathe well and my confusion about PASE was eclipsed by a warm unthinking orb that was many colors and resembled UR God but was not Him. We got to North Beach and parked four blocks away from a small one-bedroom apartment that belonged to Alyosha, a friend of Mary's from high school who was away for a month doing an internship in St. Petersburg.

Mary unlocked the door to let us in. "Want a drink?"

"Water, please."

"There's scotch, gin, rum, whiskey, and beer. I'm making a margarita if you'd like one."

"I don't drink alcohol."

"You're keeping that up?"

"Yes."

She dumped tequila, lime juice, and triple sec into a blender and sloughed off her shoes in the kitchen that doubled as a wall of the apartment, moving sideways to and from the wet bar. "The thermostat's on the wall if you're cold. And you can sit anywhere; the futon's comfortable."

"Maybe," I said, "you're really working for the Cult Opposition Network."

"Hold that shrewd and ingenious thought." She ran the blender and during its grinding I looked at the Nijinsky posters on the wall and the books stacked in a corner, in the middle of which was the new Roosevelt biography's blue spine. The room filled with the sweet aroma of tequila. A stack of music next to the stereo was topped with Prokofiev's *Lieutenant Kijé* Suite. When the noise died down she turned on the radio, lit a cigarette, emptied the blender into a tall glass, filled a cup with water, walked over to kneel on the floor in front of the couch where I sat, and placed an ashtray from her pocket by her knee. A radio DJ said it was 2:22 in the morning, the witching hour.

"Your father doesn't need to doubt my loyalty," I said. "I am a Paser."

"Then you have to stop being one right now."

"That won't happen."

She squinted and I squinted back at her, and when she scratched her ankle I did the same, and only when we both returned our hands to our laps did I catch myself. As she exhaled smoke I coughed and leaned back into the futon. We were not in harmony or sympathy or empathy. I had less in common with her than with thousands of Pasers I'd never met, because she was, despite her lineage and firsthand knowledge of the subject, an enemy of PASE. I should not have come with her to a place where I felt so simultaneously weak and energized, so tired and alert, so susceptible to changes in the magnetic pole.

"I'm going to tell you about my father," she said, taking a sip and crunching the ice of her margarita, "and you're not going to like it, so reserve judgment until you've heard the whole thing."

"I already know everything about him."

"You know an official, bowdlerized version of his life story that will soon—but not soon enough—be totally discredited." She put out her cigarette. Her margarita glass frosted over and the salt crystals along its lip resembled an ice crown. She rubbed her nose vigorously. "First of all, his real name—the one his parents gave him—is not Montgomery Shoale. It's Dale Wilkins, and he was born to an oil-rich family in Oklahoma in 1942. He went to college and business school in Tulsa, and his first job was for a venture capitalist in New York in the late sixties. After two years he quit and moved to a Buddhist priory in northern California. Six months later he joined the Children of God, which was a nomadic Christian sect; then the Om Federation, a kind of Hindu group; then the Staff & Wheat Tribe, who were Druids; and then the Perpetual Light Society, which was a mystical Christian Islamic Jewish hybrid. When he left them in 1976 he changed his name to Montgomery Shoale and got plastic surgery on his nose, chin, forehead, cheekbones, and jaw. These are before and after pictures from the hospital where he had the procedures done." She handed me two glossy photographs and turned on the lamp on the table beside me. One showed a buttery young man with thin sideburns and a mane of wiry brown hair, and the other was of Montgomery Shoale from the same time period, against the same gray background. "Look specifically at the eyes and ears and you'll start to recognize one in the other."

The two men were completely dissimilar. Where the pudgy Dale Wilkins had heavy jowls that thickened the sides of his mouth, which was just a slit above his pointy chin, Montgomery Shoale's face was gaunt except for his mouth, a warm and welcoming orifice from which wisdom was as inevitable as breath. Wilkins had a low hairline and bulbous nose; Shoale was balding with a thin aquiline nose. Cosmetic surgery might have produced these discrepancies, but I no more accepted that than I did the possibility that man invented UR God.

"I've seen pictures of Montgomery Shoale from before 1976," I said.

"They're forgeries doctored with imaging software."

I set down the pictures. The radio was describing a triangle of forest fires incinerating San Bernardino county in southern California. Two men on the street outside Alyosha's apartment trumped each other in insults until one folded and ran away. Mary looked at me with absolute focus and I kneaded a throw pillow on my lap.

"Your dad was born in Racine, Wisconsin, on October 12, 1947," I said. "When he was six, his mother left him in the care of an uncle who five years later got run over by a tractor combine. An aunt in Idaho then adopted him and he lived near Sand Point until she died from a snakebite, after which he became a ward of the state. At eighteen he worked for an Arizona firefighting unit, then in an Alaskan cannery, and then on the Long Beach docks before majoring in agribusiness at a small college in Idaho. Between 1971 and 1979 he traveled the world and spent time volunteering at a medical clinic in India. Then he moved to Silicon Valley and became a venture capitalist; in 1983 he met your mother and a year later she died of tuberculosis after giving birth to you. While raising you as a single father he continued to build up his business, and in 1991 he completed transcribing *The Prescription for a Superior Existence* from UR God's dictation."

Mary finished her drink and switched her position to lie front-down on the floor, propped up on her elbows. "There really was a man named Montgomery Shoale who was born in Wisconsin and lived in Idaho, but he died in 1970. My dad stole his identity."

"That is exactly the sort of thing the Cult Opposition Network would say."

"Quit thinking about the CON. It was a hoax. Its acronym says as much. I wish you hadn't had to go through the whole charade, but your stint as a Paser is over. Everyone's is and you need to deal with it."

"I disagree."

"It isn't a question of your agreeing or not."

"I want you to take me back now, like you promised."

"My father plans to kill all of his followers." She ran a forefinger through the carpet threads in front of her. The radio announcer said that in Japan a physicist had conducted a laboratory experiment expected to lead to cold fusion in the next decade, an energy source that would obviate the need for fossil fuels and radically reduce the amount of atmospheric carbon dioxide. "In a week he is going to order everyone to climb aboard a Synergy device and electrocute themselves."

The central heating system started up with a muffled clanging and a breath of preliminary cold air hit us.

"That's—" I said, unable suddenly to understand what the radio announcer was saying, as though the transmission were being scrambled, "then UR God told him when the Last Day will be. At last. This is wonderful news." My voice caught on the last word and I didn't want to know why. I didn't want to know anything, in fact, and wished to go to sleep or to the Center or to my own apartment. Listening to Mary talk about PASE, like watching a sandcastle on the beach, I had a foreboding of an imminent and destructive ending I no more wished to witness than I did the collapse of a day's work sculpting sand. And from the beginning there was so much longing. I wanted to stand up and walk away. To leave. She couldn't have prevented my going; I could have kept unsullied what I knew to be sacred.

Mary, her legs entwined behind her, licked all the salt from her glass and said, "For a long time I've known that my dad has delusions of grandeur, such as thinking God talks to him, which I've accepted for a few reasons. The first is that he raised me after my mom died, and I love him like a father. Another is that he supports me financially, which I know isn't the most noble reason, but I figured that since his beliefs didn't hurt anyone there was no point in openly contradicting them. A few times I was tempted to do it anyway, like when I got sick of having to pretend to be a Paser and the privations and compromises seemed too hard." She stared at her glass and fell silent.

"None of this will matter after the Last Day," I said. "All of us Pasers will be gone and you won't have to fake it anymore. Not everyone will embrace the truth."

She had the expression of a woman whose child has been sent to jail for doing something she knows is wrong, when caring is complicated by distress. "A year ago I was going through my mother's old boxes looking for a brooch I'd seen on her in a photograph, and I found some letters he wrote to her. Because I was alone, I read them. In the earliest one he said that he wanted to legally adopt her baby when she had it, which means she had been pregnant with me before they got together, which means he's not my real father. I was shocked and almost went right to him to ask about it, but instead I kept reading and during the course of seven or eight letters I learned the life story I just told you. At first I was disturbed that he had lied to me and to thousands of other people, that he had passed off a fabricated history as real, but still I didn't do anything about it. I convinced myself that it didn't change much in essence, and that besides violating my trust, the name he used to promote his made-up religion was irrelevant. I thought that maybe he was just embarrassed for having at one time been such a promiscuous spiritual seeker. Or that maybe he thought UR God told him to do it."

I didn't feel well.

She bowed her head to the floor and rubbed her neck and then looked back up. "Have you ever heard of the Faces of PASE campaign?"

I shook my head.

"It's an operation that gathers damaging information about celebrities and people in power, which it then uses to blackmail and manipulate them. It forces famous people to come out publicly in favor of PASE, to lend their star power and credibility to it. If they refuse, the operation threatens to give the media a full scoop on their homosexuality or drug addiction or infidelities or tax fraud or pedophilia or involvement in some past hushed-up crime. Obviously these people aren't angels, but to submit them to that kind of treatment, to turn them into PASE puppets, is execrable. In a way it's worse than what I've had to go through. I found out about it six months ago, and ever since I've wanted to go public."

"I don't believe it."

She reached over to her handbag and pulled a parcel of envelopes and a newspaper from it. "Here're copies of my dad's letters, and here's a story in yesterday's *New York Times* about the French Cultural Minister, François Pissoud. About nine months ago PASE told him they would leak evidence to the press about his visits to prostitutes unless he withdrew opposition to a planned Wellness Center in Marseilles and stated that he'd become a Paser. He went along with it for a while out of fear for his career and marriage, but he left his job yesterday and has now decided to make a stand. This is huge. It'll inspire others to come out as well and describe how they've been strong-armed and coerced."

The letters rested under the newspaper, which was a blur of two-toned pictures and words, a tableau of lies that history would reverse someday, like the *Chicago Tribune*'s headline about Dewey beating Truman in the 1948 presidential election. I held the documents in my lap and tried to discern the cant and propaganda and blasphemy driving Mary to say and do this, but unlike when I first met her, and unlike with Tomas and Dr. Cantor, I knew she was telling the truth.

"I don't believe it," I repeated, but softer, less forcefully. I read the article. As Mary had said, it explained that Minister Pissoud, citing irreconcilable differences with the French President, had resigned his post and was being divorced by his wife, also because of irreconcilable differences. Consequently he "no longer saw the point of jumping through hoops so an obscure and vindictive California cult could make inroads into France." Yes, he had hired prostitutes, but that was no one's business but his own and he would not be anyone's stooge. It was better to be an honest nobody than a dishonest minister, and he didn't care how grandstanding that sounded. The picture next to the article showed him marching away from the National Assembly Building in Paris, loosening his necktie. Next I read portions of the letters corroborating what Mary had said.

"You're just upset that you can't openly have sex," I said weakly. "You probably wrote these letters yourself to slander your father so you can act on your desires." The ink from the newspaper stained my fingertips and I rubbed them together, mixing ink and dirt from my skin into little eyelashes that fell to the ground.

"My dad's plan to put Pasers through ur-Synergy is tantamount to mass murder."

"This could all be a misunderstanding."

"The Faces of PASE is about to be exposed; my dad's health is terrible; there are at most ten thousand Pasers worldwide, probably fewer. The whole thing is falling apart and he's decided to die and take everyone with him."

"I'm really tired."

"Maybe every religion begins this way," Mary said, "with someone going crazy and thinking they've been chosen for a higher purpose, and certainly most religions have blood on their hands, but those crimes are in the past and we can't do anything about them. Now, though, we know that my dad aspires to kill thousands of people." She sat up straight and grabbed the pillow I'd been mangling and smoothed and fluffed it on her lap. The letters and newspaper were on the floor, congruent damnations, artifacts of artifice. And although nothing could have been more disruptive or horrible to me personally than what she'd just said, and although it suggested that I give up the progress I'd made as a Paser, come down from a peak untouchable by desire and pain and uncertainty, when Mary scooted forward and I looked at her and our faces were two feet away from each other, I felt, commingled with sadness and disappointment, Synergy. It was part of a range of emotions but still distinguishable, still unmistakably itself, and I thought that instead of the analogies and approximations I'd once used to describe it, Synergy was in fact nothing greater or sweeter or more exalted and transfiguring than—nothing else but a kind of shorthand for, in a language that predates ours and our ancestors'—what all profound philosophies and religions and lives strove to embody and enact, the feeling that inspired and rewarded every higher quest, that had been drained and replenished a million times before the first poem was written, so that it ceased to be a cliché whenever it materialized: love.

Mary said, "You have to stop him."

"What?"

"You have to stop him from telling his followers to undergo ur-Synergy."

Like looking from the watery reflection of an object to its solid original, I saw her face assume a permanence it hadn't had before.

"I would do it myself but his advisers won't let me near him, supposedly because he's almost an ur-savant, but really it's because they know I'm not a Paser and they don't want me to use my influence with him. What little I have. You'll be able to see him, though."

"That's crazy."

"No it isn't."

"I can't get an audience with Montgomery Shoale."

"Yes you can."

"What makes you say that?"

"The reality of the situation."

I set down my water glass and looked at Mary, whose face was a blank of determination. "And if I tell him to cancel his plan to put all the Pasers through ur-Synergy, he'll do it?"

"No," she said, laying aside the pillow and placing her palms flat on the floor, "he won't. Unfortunately we have no other option but to forcibly prevent him from going through with it, and the only way to do that is for you to kill him."

CHAPTER 11

While Mary slept soundly—or at least soundlessly—in the bedroom, I lay on the edge of the futon sweating. The heating system had shut off and I was cold, though my worry generated a compensatory warmth. I read through the letters chronologically, recognizing the handwriting as Shoale's from a facsimile of the original *Prescription* I'd studied at the Wellness Center, and thought about the conflicting biographies, the charges of blackmailing, the disputed spiritual authenticity. If PASE weren't true there was no reason not to get up and drain all of the liquor bottles lining the kitchen counter, to hide behind a wall of inebriation. There was no reason not to eat everything in the refrigerator or climb into bed with Mary. If PASE were untrue, if there were no injunction from UR God, if ultimate reality were the ultimate illusion, I would have to ask why, in the absence of a higher authority than biological dictates, I shouldn't satisfy my urges and desires and compulsions and wants and needs and cravings. And if one way of life was intrinsically better than or even preferable to another, how without a god or gods were we to discover it? I had spent my entire life either uninterested or unable to answer these questions, as unimaginative as a mannequin dumbly posed for this or that seasonal fashion. I had never known restraint or seen where it led; I had always thought that the capsizes of excess were as necessary as falling while learning to walk. What, though, had I learned from them? Anything as useful as the ability to move myself from one place to another? Anything at all? No other animal but human beings denied themselves pleasure, our past and present abuse of which had become too costly to pursue at the old amounts—we who prioritized growth above all things—and if the supreme generative force in the universe were ever needed it was now.

Of course there were philosophical grounds for temperance and conservatism, earthbound arguments against profligacy and unchecked self-gratification, which perhaps now, holding on to the tatters of my faith as they grew less and less substantial, I needed to adopt. The fire of PASE was about to be extinguished by scandal, and something else had to take its place as a provider of light and heat.

First, though, if I were to follow Mary's plan, there would be a period of cold darkness.

Hours passed and I went over the details and implications of killing Montgomery Shoale. The act, the aftermath, the price it would exact on all parties. The question wasn't just should I do it, but could I. Gung-ho soldiers required months of psychological conditioning to kill enemies their government told them had to die. People who committed crimes of passion were left passionless. Murderers motivated by greed—dimestore Raskolnikovs and ladies Macbeth—went mad from their own company. Political and religious assassins were full of a fervor that was in fact mania, the John Wilkes Booths and Lee Harvey Oswalds and Sirhan Sirhans. Cain struck down Abel and in an instant expanded the arc of evil beyond what their parents, the hapless Adam and Eve, had brought about in their primordial garden; he made possible Caesarean patricides and bloody Inquisitions and civil wars and genocides and every manner of human wickedness. To end another's life was in a way to end one's own, and however excusable suicide was to those whose souls were besotted with the anguish of here and now and then and there, I shrank from the possibility.

At six o'clock I went to the bathroom and stayed for an hour.

At nine o'clock an alarm rang, an air-raid drone that dropped a precision headache on me. Then the preprogrammed coffeemaker started to hiss and sputter, and I sat leadenly at a card table stacked with Russian-language magazines, my eyes smarting from lack of sleep. Ten minutes later Mary, her hands clasped behind her back in a stretch that pressed her breasts into view, padded into the kitchen area and dragged two clinking cups from a shelf to the counter. The glass pot slid out of its groove.

"I can't do it," I said. She poured coffee into each cup as carefully as if at a fund-raising dinner. "Maybe Montgomery Shoale is guilty of everything you say, but I don't have it in me to kill anyone, especially someone who hasn't attacked me, especially him."

She added soy milk to one and paused to examine the resultant brown before adding a splash more, and the gesture, nothing in itself, despite what we were talking about and my resolution not to go along with her and to feel nothing for her, made me smile.

She sipped her coffee down from the brim and crossed the room to sit across from me at the card table, placing my cup handle-side to the right. "Do you know about the Berlin students who plotted to assassinate Hitler in 1943? They called themselves the White Rose movement, and they were pacifists and so opposed to murder, but they knew that sparing Hitler's life would condemn millions of innocent people to die, and that a single act of violence against him would prevent a much larger one against others. Everyone now agrees that if they'd succeeded they would have deserved a thousand Nobel Peace prizes. I'm sorry it has to be you now, but that's the way it goes."

"Let's call the media and the FBI and the police, and they'll stop him from putting everyone through ur-Synergy."

"The police commissioner is a thumbscrew Paser. The Faces of PASE has proof that he's made money from heroin seizures over the last ten years."

"Then he must want PASE exposed and made powerless."

"No, when it goes down it'll take everyone else, including him, with it. Besides, the police and the FBI and others can't arrest someone before they commit a crime unless there's evidence of a plot, which we don't have."

"Tell the newspapers and television news programs; have them get the message out. It's sensational enough that word would spread everywhere in a couple of days."

"There, too, a lot of prominent national editors are afraid to broadcast anything negative about PASE for fear of what would surface about them. And if I were somehow able to get a big national forum for the announcement—or even just post it on the Internet—PASE would deny it and say that I was bitter because my father cut me off financially when he heard that I violated PASE principles. Some people would believe me, but Pasers wouldn't. Like you did last night, they'd say I'm not a credible witness."

I was about to raise another important objection when a knock came at the door. Mary slapped her hand over my mouth and shook her head. Then, removing her hand, she rose and slipped to the door and looked through the keyhole, her left arm stretched back as though to restrain onlookers at a crime scene, her left toes planted and heel up on point position.

"Alyosha!" came a voice from the other side. "It's me, Cheryl! Sorry to bother you so early, but I need my crepe pan. I have guests in from out of town and I've been promising them my *crepe Andalouse*; it's practically the only reason they're visiting."

Mary turned around and signaled for me to get up quietly, put on my shoes, grab my things, and go to the fire escape. As I did this and she gathered her own belongings, spending a frenzied ten seconds scouring the living room floor for her car keys, the knocking continued interspersed with a woman's voice: "Come on! If you're naked I'll keep my eyes shut while you hand me the pan. Please, this is important!"

As Mary pulled her last foot through the window the front door splintered open and three men flowed in with a woman I recognized as the facilitator who'd asked me what I thought of chapter one of *The Prescription,* for whom I'd been unable to get an erection. They ran toward us and I bounded down the rusty ladder, banging my knees violently against the iron rungs and tearing my left hand on a protruding squiggle of metal, until I reached the bottom and geronimo'ed six feet to the ground below, leaving a palm print of blood on the alley sidewalk as I pushed myself up and staggered beneath the ladder, my arms outstretched to catch Mary.

"The car!" she said, disentangling herself from my messy reception. We ran and my hand gushed blood with each footfall, each heartbeat, a pulsing stigmata, and I didn't think but rather moved unconsciously beside her, on an autopilot mission to stay near. There was no indecision. No sawtoothed debate about the truth and its doppelgangers. With Mary at that moment I simply was.

"Where are we going?" I asked after we got in her car and lit out onto the road, into a brakeless momentum. I imagined soon being faint with blood loss.

"I don't know yet."

"You said that place was safe."

"Apparently I was wrong."

From Post Street we turned on to California Avenue and climbed to the top of Russian Hill, the world aslant in our side mirrors, where we leveled off at the flag-waving Fairmont Hotel and the Gallic glory of Rose Cathedral. Fog covered pockets of the low-lying city below, like polyurethane foam insulating the ground against hoarfrost, and to the northwest, directly over the Golden Gate Bridge, which was hidden on the far side of the Presidio, a sharply defined cone of sunlight connected the land and sky. I finished bandaging my hand with a T-shirt from the back floor of the car, and when I elevated it, my elbow resting on my knee, Mary touched one finger tentatively and asked how I was doing. Before I could answer we reached the edge of the hill's plateau and began our descent. "Okay," I said, my body straining forward against the seat belt. Which was true. I felt, as on the night before and during our run, an element of Synergy—of love—that tempered but did not erase my physical pains and fatigue, a sustainable state. We turned on to Union Street and then passed the Palace of Fine Arts, followed by a drive along the Marina. A flash of déjà vu hit me.

I said, "If your father is on the offensive like this, I don't see how I'll be able to get to him."

"He's not on the offensive."

"What do you call that invasion back there?"

"They weren't acting on his orders."

"Of course they were."

"I recognized one of them, a guy named Abner, who's Denver Stevens's personal assistant."

"And Denver Stevens is your dad's adviser."

"Mostly, yes." She waved for a pedestrian to cross in front of us before carefully turning right. "But he's also secretly working against him."

"He is? Then let's go back and join forces with him."

"It's not like that. Denver isn't opposed to PASE or the Last Day, and at heart he really does revere my father; he just wants to thwart the plans concerning you. He sent that guy to your apartment on the night you were taken to the Wellness Center, for example."

"I was told that that guy acted alone as a renegade."

The route we were following through the city, without, as far as I could tell, anyone following us, was one I'd taken a hundred times, and looking at Mary I saw that it involved no forethought or deliberation.

Mary said, "Denver also argued for you to be put through ur-Synergy after those two guys escaped from the Center. He was furious when you were sent to the CON instead."

"What's the plan involving me?"

"I told you I don't know."

"You seem to know everything else."

"This is different. I only know that my dad is committed to it and Denver isn't."

A few minutes later we parked at the top of Palatine Hill, from which the sheets of fog spread over sections of the city were again visible; the Golden Gate Bridge loomed directly ahead of us now, its massive suspension cables flaring in the sunlight.

"Why are we stopped here?" I asked.

"To figure out where to wait until you can get inside my dad's house. During the day he's surrounded by people, but in the middle of the night he's alone except for two attendants. You won't have any problem then."

"I didn't say I'd do it."

After a pause, she said, "No?"

I looked at her for what seemed like a long time, perhaps minutes, and she gave no sign of impatience or frustration. "Tell me if we're at this exact spot by accident."

"What do you mean?"

"When we started driving did you have it in mind that we would take the route we did to come to Palatine Hill?"

She shook her head. "Why?"

"I was thinking about coincidences. And sympathy."

The insignia on the steering wheel of the car was a series of dots that made a bear shape, like Orion. Steam bellowed out from the basement window of a building across the street. I lowered my hand and the blood rushed back like a river that has pierced its dam to again run along its immemorial channel. A vintage Cadillac with burnt-yellow fins nosed up to parallel park in front of us, and then a pair of children scrambled out of the back while its elderly driver heaved herself from the front, holding a clear plastic bag of multi-sized marbles, a thick gold chain necklace spelunking between her bosom.

"Give me the gun," I said.

"But . . ." Mary said, her voice trailing off. I nodded. She withdrew a small object wrapped in a sequined handkerchief from her purse and gently laid it in my lap, as though it were a wounded bird or sacred talisman. "It's loaded."

I pulled back the soft fleur-de-lis cloth and looked at a shiny black gun; it smelled like shoe polish and candle wax, a dark antique odor. I lifted it with my good hand and squinted to look at it through one eye, as though this were a barter. It felt solid and sure of its design; form followed function. I rewrapped it and wanted to hand the package back to Mary. I wanted to disclaim responsibility and repeat my arguments against killing Shoale while retreating from the car and her and this situation.

I said, "Do you think you're strange?"

She looked at me blankly.

"I mean, what do you think about never having been in love?"

"Where did that come from?" she asked.

"I'm wondering if you think it separates you fundamentally from other people."

"Not everyone has been in love."

"Most have."

"Have you?"

I paused. "No."

"Then you're a hypocrite," she said, poking me hard on the chest and then brushing my shirt free of her finger's indentation. "You told me I was depriving myself because of PASE, like you knew from personal experience what a great robbery that was, when you've never been in love yourself!"

"But I've always wanted to be."

"That doesn't make you any better."

"I agree."

She was silent for a second. "So why haven't you been in love, if you've always wanted to?"

A pickup truck pulled into the parking space behind us. My lowered fingers had regained their color and were a row of pink appendages jutting out from a strip of cotton dyed red over the inside of my hand. The bleeding had stopped. With my good hand I shoved the wrapped gun into my pants pocket. "It's not easy for people like me," I said.

"And what are people like you like?"

"Unattractive."

The word came out automatically, as though we were playing a word association game in which a quick and honest response was the only rule and the filter that prevents our being radically direct— ergo reviled—had been shut off. I didn't say it in order for her to protest, though I realized that she had to. That everything depended on her denial. This conversation and our sitting there needed to be, in its roundabout way, an overture to her saying that I was no longer as I'd always seen myself, that I was remade and refashioned in love, which had eluded us both but would now, with loops crossed and bows tied, with million-to-one odds beaten, hold us tightly. I needed her in my arms agreeing that this was what we'd been waiting for our whole lives.

"Get out!" she shouted, stretching across my lap to shove open the passenger door and push me roughly through it, so that I fell back on my elbows and smacked my head against a hard patch of dirt bordering the sidewalk.

On the other side of her car a plain white van had pulled to a screeching halt and its door was sliding back. The vehicles in front and behind us were parked within a few inches of our bumpers, making escape impossible. I stood up to help Mary out, her legs swinging to the ground with a gymnast's agility, and then backed away from the four men jumping from the van. Sucking in air and turning, she indicated that I go in the opposite direction. "I'll find you later!"

I hesitated for a second and then ran to Lombard Street and cut down its serpentine block through flower beds and half driveways, never looking back to see if the men from the van were there. When I got to Juniper Street and bolted right and flung myself in front of a passing cab, which braked with a banshee screech a foot away and let me in, no one was behind me. I told the driver, a small Bulgarian man with a black quarter-sized scab on his bald crown like a shrunken yarmulke, blaring a Spanish radio station and eating a ham sandwich the size of his face, to drive and drive fast. He looked at me skeptically in his mirror, on which was pasted a sequence of Looney Toons stickers, but then, perhaps noticing the expensive make of my coat—the fur-lined gabardine—he obliged, and three minutes later we were on Columbus Avenue in the stacked traffic headed toward downtown. If not far away already from Palatine Hill, we were at least a single anonymous vehicle among thousands in the city's mid-morning gridlock. I slouched down and lowered my head.

"You have street address?" he asked, bringing a soda cup up to his mouth and rattling its ice.

"No."

"Name of business or hotel?"

"Just keep driving."

The fare meter ticked upward as we crawled past the Trans-America Pyramid and the Embarcadero complex, along avenues shaded by skyscrapers with scale and sea vessel and globe statues adorning their entrances, monuments to the banking and shipping and Internet commerce inside. I didn't have a phone or Mary's number or any hope of arranging an appointment with her before nightfall. The gun anchored me to my seat and a mariachi band crooned from speakers at my shoulders. Your true love was out there, waiting in a room where the teakettle never blew, ready to take you back without question, without demand. I had heard the song performed live at a mambo festival in Marysville I'd attended in January, hoping but failing to run into Mr. Raven, when like all the other empty meaningless promises art made to people who didn't know better, it hadn't meant anything. My cab turned right on to Market Street and the Couvade building was a few hundred feet ahead. Several pedestrians on the street resembled my old coworkers—Max coming out of a deli, Juan running to catch a bus, Mr. Raven making a phone call—though on closer inspection they became strangers.

"You want for me still to just keep driving?" the Bulgarian asked.

"Yes."

We sat at a traffic light next to 595 Market Street for ten seconds and the song ended. I felt neither the rage of being fired nor the thrill of being promoted nor the solidarity/disillusionment of knowing it was run by Pasers. The building was just a place I'd gone for so many years. Like a comet returning to its perihelion after the sun has died, I was no longer affected by the proximity.

Then we passed midtown's tourist knots waiting to get on or off a trolley, and the U.S. Mint and Van Ness bottleneck, and the adult shops selling live views of paradise for a dollar a minute. A billboard on our right advertised a floral exhibition at the Golden Gate Park greenhouse, which I read uncomprehendingly before understanding that it promised a series of gardens duplicated from famous literary works. I thought of the conversation I'd had with Mary about a story by Hawthorne, and how there were no coincidences. As we crossed Haight Street, I told the driver to get over to Fell Street and drive by the Panhandle's eucalyptus processional and stop at the park entrance, where a sign pointed to the box office that sold tickets to the floral exhibition. I paid the cabbie and got out.

Inside the giant greenhouse I came to the first display of *Les Fleurs de la Littérature,* a replica of Don Pedro's garden in *Much Ado About Nothing.* Behind it was the Garden of Eden from *Paradise Lost.* I couldn't see a directory of the individual exhibits and the ticket lady hadn't given me a map or guide, so I went down the nearest path, which led to the staging ground for the tropical plants in *Suddenly, Last Summer* and the carnivorous Venus flytraps of *Little Shop of Horrors* and the perfect rosebushes of *Beauty and the Beast.* I seemed to be the only person there until from across a bed of *The Sound and the Fury* honeysuckle the back of someone's head moved toward the mushroom garden in *Alice's Adventures in Wonderland.* I kept walking and on one side was the *Pride and Prejudice* garden where Lady Catherine de Burgh rebukes Elizabeth's impudence, on the other a rendering of Charles Kinbote's sidehouse plot in *Pale Fire.* I began to think that the display I hoped to find had, due to space or the curators' literary limitations, been omitted, that my hopes of meeting Mary would be dashed. I turned completely around, like someone who has lost his child in the middle of a crowded beach, trying not to panic.

I stopped. There, on a rectangular patch of ground twenty feet away, I saw it: the vibrant Mediterranean flora of "Rappaccini's Daughter." I sat on a bench beside it and waited for Mary to arrive, for she and I were in sync and harmony and jeopardy, and the force majeure sweeping us along would not lose its momentum. There was no such thing as coincidence, only sympathy.

The hours passed with prehistoric slowness, every minute a Pleistocene, and when late that afternoon a loudspeaker announced that the exhibition was closing, I stood up as though just thawed from a cryogenic freeze, and fleetingly saw the back of someone's head, the only person I'd seen since morning. I walked creakily past the flower collections famous to so few people as hardly to deserve the name, and outside, parked in front of the greenhouse like Hades' charioteer, I got in a checkered cab driven by the same Bulgarian from earlier. He acted surprised to see me and said, with wonder spiking his phlegmy accent, that only in a city as small as San Francisco would it be possible for someone to get in his cab twice in one day; I told him to take me to a bar on Lower Haight Street, where I drank two beers in seven hours.

After midnight I got into a cab that was again driven by the Bulgarian, and he joked that he should work on a monopoly of the city's customers, that at this rate he might become the only cab-driver in all of San Francisco, able to give rides to everyone all day and night with the same miraculous efficiency as Santa Claus. He laughed jollily. I got out on Pacific Heights, a block away from the mansion Montgomery Shoale had vacated for what had formerly been the groundskeeper's residence on the same property. Walking uphill I grew warm and the grass and the stone parapet beside me glistened with evening dew and the only lights burning in the apparition-like mansions were over front doors and walkways and planted security signs, lollipops of caution. In the distance a dog barked and was abruptly quieted. I did not think about Mary. Between some of the buildings I caught glimpses of the moonlight glittering off the Bay, which borrowed traffic sounds to produce a gentle oceanic murmur, as though despite the mechanisms of civilization girding the world at that moment those of nature were stronger. The gun in my coat pocket produced serenity. PASE would dissolve and I, who the day before had believed in it entirely, was to be the agent of that dissolution. And I was lonely and death-fixated and ugly and unlovable and secretly fat and dependent on drugs and unemployed and doomed to a spot on the Earth big enough for all this self-awareness. Not such an untenable or even unusual fate, really. I stopped walking when Shoale's house came into view. Palming a concealed weapon outside one of the largest private residences in San Francisco, as blind as Samson preparing to knock down the columns that supported the roof over his head—that is, possessed of improbable sight—I saw a shooting star and envisioned Mary's face and if you didn't know the constellations then any picture could be drawn in the night sky.

At the gate in front of Shoale's house, as craggy and blackened as an abandoned castle, I found a video call center and followed its instructions—announcing my name and intent—and a second later the gate swung open soundlessly. Motion detector lights flooded the area with brightness. Although now overrun and neglected, the front lawn had evidently once been extravagant, with echoes of Xanadu in the topiary sculpture and mermaid pool and Japanese rock garden, replete with torii and quartzite boulder radiating half-inch ripples.

A moment after I stepped on to the stone path leading to the front door of the house, two women wearing blue tunics approached and greeted me. Their hair was cropped into matching Joan of Arc cuts and they stood in an identical posture, hands cupped together beneath their diaphragms, shoulders pressed back, faces washed clean of expression. Without any interview or exchange, they took me behind the house through knee-high grass to a small building with one glowing window. There they stopped and told me to go in alone. The lateness of the hour, my being unannounced, the fact that I'd lately broken out of PASE custody: none of that mattered. I hesitated but they nodded encouragement, so I opened the door and entered a room colder than outside; a candle flickered on an end table, beside which a small figure rose from a rocking chair and came toward me tentatively, as though the earth were moving unpredictably beneath his feet.

"Hello," said Montgomery Shoale hoarsely, a hand moving slowly over his lizardlike throat. Even in this bad light I could see that his face was an ashen gray strawberried with blood vessels, and that the downy wisps of hair around his ears were translucent. Either he'd deteriorated rapidly over the last few days or he benefited from a makeup artist—a makeup magician—before giving speeches. I released the gun in my pocket to shake his hand but he stepped close and hugged me with great frailty, his arms dried twigs and his body an antique wood box. "Please sit down." He shuffled back to his seat, where two cups of green tea rested on a stand-up tray. Another rocker, with arms covered in blue corduroy, was stationed at a forty-five-degree angle to his own.

He stirred his drink with a miniature spoon that might have come from a child's tea party set and said, "I hope Mary is well."

"I do too."

"I would like to be able to say good-bye to her, but as you know she is not in sympathy with PASE, and so our meeting is impossible. I'm afraid that all her years of acting like a Paser exhausted her patience rather than whetted her spiritual appetite. Still, she humored me for a long time. That's more than many daughters do for their old fathers."

"I'm here to tell you not to have your followers commit ur-Synergy."

His head swayed slightly, too much for the stem of his neck, an old sunflower that from the gust of a passing creature would fall off. "Is that right?"

"Yes."

He sipped from his cup and then pushed his tongue through closed lips. "Drink your tea. It's very healthy, you know, full of antioxidants. I maintain that a cup of green tea a day will do more to rid your system of toxins than any number of enemas and diuretics. There's no reason to poison the bodies we have for so short a time."

He smiled and his face cracked into a thousand shards, like a broken mirror. I gagged on my tea, which tasted as though it had been skimmed from the surface of a pond.

"I gather that your crash course in all things PASE and anti-PASE during the past two weeks has been educational. Maybe not what you signed up for, but then so much of what befalls us is out of our control."

I said, dropping my voice to a commanding baritone, with great sangfroid, "I will not let you kill anyone on the Last Day. Do you understand?"

"If it's out of our control, you might ask, in whose control is it?" His smile was gone and his face returned to its glassy smoothness, as though the mirror had reconstituted itself. "This question used to obsess me. Mary no doubt told you about my youthful wanderings in search of an answer. I was what they called a circulating saint, someone who turned from religion to religion trying on different faiths, always looking and always failing to find the perfect fit. Although you and I are similar in any number of ways, we differ in that important aspect. You seem not to have thought much about God. When I first learned of you this grieved and perplexed me. Why, I wondered, has he been so incurious? How is such indifference possible?" He picked a scrap of tea leaf from his tongue and wiped it on his chair as a child would something unmentionable. "But when I learned more about you, I realized that the need for an answer was always inside of you, however dormant, like a talent for a sport from which you had been kept your whole life. You were Sleeping Beauty waiting for a kiss. I knew that when exposed to Him you would have an awakening."

I was wrong to let him go on like this. I had told myself to shoot at the first opportunity, before he pacified or weakened my resolve. I had promised not to look at the Medusa's head even through a reflection, or listen to the Sirens' song even tied fast to a mizzen, but instead get in and out quickly and not tarry beyond a courtesy announcement that he was to die so that others would live. I hadn't the time or luxury or stamina for questions.

"Why did you care whether I thought about God?"

He smiled again and was all shards. "Your generation is in such a rush to get to the end of everything. This impetuosity used to bother me too, until I learned that it is the result of an evolutionary process begun long ago. I no longer blame individuals for giving in to forces larger and more insistent than their own wills. Their exclusion from UR God will be punishment enough."

I felt an ache of curiosity in my gut, a harpoon wedged in deep, and really he was so small and vulnerable, so clearly limited by his physical condition that I began to consider the threat he posed more phantom than real. No one of his stature could do much harm. Natural laws acted as insurance against it. Shoale was a kind of Wizard of Oz, a faux bogeyman to be easily and peremptorily exposed somehow, not requiring the drastic measures Mary had rushed to deem necessary.

"Maybe," I said, "we can work something out. You could come with me now and be on house arrest for a few weeks; I'd make sure you were comfortable but unable to communicate with the outside world. Like what you did to me."

"You were asking why I care about your relationship with God. That is a very important question and bears considerable weight for this conversation. Did Mary mention that when I was your age exactly, thirty-four, I joined a group called the Perpetual Light Society?"

Grudgingly I said, since he had either ignored or not registered what I'd said, strangling in its cradle my hope to save us both, "Yes."

Shoale coughed so delicately I barely heard him. "Six months after I moved to its ranch near Monterey, God spoke to me for the first time. He said that my life thus far, three decades during which I had vainly looked for Him, was no longer my own. He needed it for a special task, the nature of which would be revealed to me at the right time. Until then, I was not to tell anyone about His contacting me. As you can imagine, I was both ecstatic and frustrated, as though I'd been given a million dollars but told not to spend it.

"A week later God spoke to me again and commanded me to mate with a young woman new to the Perpetual Light Society. She was a lovely girl to whom I was already attracted, so the next time she and I were alone, looking for mushrooms on a hillside overlooking the ocean, as sublime a spot as any on Earth, I told her of my strong feelings for her. At first she laughed and kept her eyes on the ground, but after a minute she said she didn't feel the same about me. Although she was kind about it, her manner left no room for me to mistake her seriousness. I said that it was too soon for her to decide how she felt about me, and that I was happy to wait until she consented to be mine. She repeated, less kindly this time and more firmly, that she didn't love me and never could. I mentioned that God Himself intended us to be together. At this she got angry and abused me in very heated terms, very incensed language. People can be cruel when discouraging a love for which they have no use. They can exaggerate things and go on too forcefully about the other's deficiencies. I tried not to take offense, and I patiently explained that it was not our decision to make, that we were destined to mate and the sooner she accepted this the better it would be for both of us. She yelled for me to stay away from her and then ran back to the ranch house.

"Afterward she wouldn't talk to me, and within a week she began sleeping with a young man I detested. This filled me with rage and jealousy and pain, as well as indignation that she would reject the will of God. One night, therefore, I went to her room asking to apologize, and when she let me in I overpowered her."

He crossed his scrawny legs and held his tiny tea cup in both hands, as though one would not have been sufficient support.

"What are you saying?" I asked. The candle was no bigger than a thumb, with an hour left before it melted away.

"Everyone at the Perpetual Light Society was upset, as you'd expect. More than upset. They were enraged. Horrified. Within fifteen minutes of the event three men locked me in a room and with a butcher's knife made sure I could never do such a thing again. They might then have killed me if others hadn't intervened and commenced a dialogue and finally decided that I should be banished instead of executed."

I set down the tea and stared transfixed at this shriveled old man confessing what scarcely seemed possible. I wanted him to continue talking only slightly more than I wanted him to stop, for his story, the second to damn him (and more completely than the first) in twenty-four hours, had a rehearsed quality, an emotional divestment from its content—which required either unfathomable contrition and self-censure if he were good, or sadistic glee and self-glorification if he were evil—that, rather than cast doubt on its veracity, strengthened my need to know its conclusion.

"After going home to recuperate in Oklahoma, I asked God why He had led me to commit a crime and then let me suffer for it, and He answered that by flouting His command to not reveal our pact to anyone, I had forfeited His protection and interest, and He had no more use for me. I begged Him for another chance, promising never to repeat my mistake and always to place obedience to His will above all else. He did not answer. I was distraught, and over the next few months I kept entreating Him to tell me how I could win back His favor; I prayed constantly for forgiveness; and all the while He maintained silence. Finally it occurred to me that if He wouldn't give me instructions, I would have to figure them out on my own. After all, what God considered valuable work was no secret. One did not have to be an initiate or holy man to know that He encouraged care and consideration of others, respect for nature, thrift, temperance, and humility. All of these I could put into effect right away.

"But before beginning a new life of piety and penitence, I changed my name and had facial reconstruction surgery to remove every trace of my former self, so that I appeared to be a new person when, a month later, I volunteered with an international charity organization that sent me to India, where I remained for several years working with the sick and elderly at a free clinic in Benares. During that time I grew less concerned with proving my worth to God than with helping people, and I gradually emerged from the torture of thinking constantly about what I'd done and lost. I made such progress, in fact, that I befriended and fell in love with a pregnant American woman. When she then died in childbirth, since the father was a stranger she'd met once and didn't know how to contact, I adopted her daughter, Mary.

"With a child to raise, I returned to America and told myself—without lying—that I was content with a regular life, and that I no longer needed or sought divine distinction. I could never fully atone for the violence I'd done the young woman at the Perpetual Light Society, and I should not expect to be treated as if it were possible.

A certain calm settled on me then, the peace of no longer desiring what could not be had.

"At that moment, like the return of a parent you'd thought gone forever, his or her affections transferred to new, worthier children, God spoke to me again. In a dream, with the same voice and demeanor I had last encountered ten years before, He explained that His real name was Ultimate Reality God, and that the time had come for me to announce the truth about Prescription for a Superior Existence to the world. I wept so copiously that when I awoke hours later to transcribe the opening of *The Prescription,* which He had recited to me, my pillow was soaked through. This process continued for the next six months, dreamtime recitations and morning transcriptions, until the book was finished. I then published and promoted it myself, and gave talks and handed out copies at ecumenical religious gatherings, self-help seminars, political rallies, business meetings, and entertainment functions. My contacts were extensive, and in a short time I got the book to thousands of people and invited them to the first PASE Station, where they took classes and had one-on-one tutorials. They also tried a prototype of the Synergy device I had commissioned a Stanford engineer to produce, which I had tested along its developmental path until it reproduced the feeling I'd had in UR God's presence. Some argued at the time that the device was a cynical invention—if the experience of Him was real, why did it need to be manufactured with a machine?—though really its purpose was to give people an incentive to learn more about the religion, after which they could develop the techniques for unaided Synergy.

"Slowly at first but then more quickly, word spread and PASE found a growing corps of dedicated followers. As its success mounted, I came to believe that my past mistakes had been forgiven, and that the rest of my life would be spent in advocacy of the truth with which He had charged me. I believed I would never again know worry or loneliness or disappointment, which even caused me in a way to bemoan the loss of my old afflictions, as one does the passing of an ailment the longevity of which links your current and past selves.

"But generally I was happy and content until, for no discernible reason, my happiness and contentment were replaced by doubts. About everything. Overnight I began to suspect that *The Prescription* was not actually the word of UR God, and that what I'd heard in my sleep was simply my own projection of His voice. It occurred to me that my belief in His authorship of PASE was just wishful thinking or megalomania, and that I was a false prophet, perhaps the worst who had ever lived because rather than admit my uncertainty about PASE, I continued to act as though the religion were true. These thoughts came to a head one morning and I fell into a totalizing and debilitating despair.

"I then stayed in bed for nearly a year, morbidly thinking it would be better to kill myself than go on living a lie. At a particularly self-critical moment, unable to stand the dissemblance anymore, I called a conference of my closest PASE advisers and gave them the full and truthful account of my life, hoping they would take it upon themselves to put an end to the religion. Instead they assured me that my revelation was genuine and swore not to reveal my doubts or secrets. They pointed out that all great men suffer from like apprehensions, that Tolstoy himself, after writing *War and Peace* and *Anna Karenina,* felt like an abject failure as a human being and artist. He carried rope with him in case the urge to commit suicide became too great to withstand, and he subjected every minute of his past to severe self-castigating scrutiny. Like his doubts, my advisers claimed, mine were evidence of my essential goodness. Would a madman or charlatan admit to such thoughts? No, therefore they were groundless.

"The logic of my advisers was deeply flawed, of course; to suspect that something isn't true is not proof of its truth, and I was more convinced than ever that PASE was an elaborate lie I'd told myself and others. UR God never spoke to me when I was awake, for example, and I reread *The Prescription* with an icy certainty that I had made up every word. I slept little at night—my insomnia was stronger than it had ever been—thinking that when Samuel Taylor Coleridge wrote 'Kubla Khan' in an opium slumber he at least had

had the sense to credit his own powers of creativity rather than a higher power's. Sometimes I squeezed an ounce of calm out of the idea that all invention is traceable to UR God, being the source of all creation in the universe, but then my misery would return with redoubled ferocity. Making matters worse, my back pain, which I have known all my adult life, grew appreciably worse, as did my chronic nausea and myopia."

I took another sip of my tea and found it palatable this time, even nice in its aftertaste, as though my initial dislike stemmed from prejudice rather than honest assessment. Shoale had not taken his eyes off me the entire time he'd spoken. The candle rolled a drop of clear wax down its side, the windowpane groaned in the wind, and the odor of potting soil, though it must have been there the entire time, seemed suddenly powerful. I was tempted to reach over and hold Shoale's hand. It is rare to hear people discuss their fears and self-disgust and pains with such candidness, such fearlessness. It changed nothing—I had to kill him—but I knew at least a mitigating kind of love just then, as I would for a dog I needed to shoot because it had, innocently in its fashion, contracted rabies and so become a threat to others. Killing with compassion, I thought, might answer the objections that had plagued me the night before. It might elevate this encounter to the realm of unquestionable good—or at least necessity—at the micro as well as the macro level, strip the act of its savagery.

Shoale held his teacup in his left hand like an offering. "While this was going on, though, a strange thing happened. I began to receive a number of reports charting the improvement being made by Pasers all over the state: of their saved marriages and conquered addictions and anger control. Testimonials piled up on my desk from people amazed by the positive changes in their lives PASE had inspired them to make. They told in minute detail stories of how they'd nearly given up on life when PASE found and nurtured and saved them. They described being empowered for the first time to look beyond themselves to help others in need. After reading enough of these, I concluded that whatever its source—my dreams or UR God—PASE had a beneficent effect on its followers. Practically, it worked.

"My despair soon abated and I felt an inkling of hope. Not that PASE was true, but that a lie with such results might be worth promoting. Ten years ago, then, I returned to helm PASE and embarked on an extensive international speaking tour. The public restoration of my faith was greeted joyfully and enthusiastically by my advisers, particularly Denver Stevens and Gloria Anderson, who launched a recruitment effort at the same time that boosted the membership rolls impressively and garnered a great deal of media attention for PASE. I am sorry to say that they kept some of their effort's unsavory aspects from me, such as the Faces of PASE campaign, which I forbade once I found out about it, and I am even sorrier to say that they then publicly obeyed while privately defying my order. Zeal led them to mistake the wrong course of action for the right one, a too-common phenomenon in the history of religion.

"Years passed and I accepted the idea that PASE was a benign self-help program whose supernatural shape did not reflect a spiritual reality. I appreciated whatever good had come from my delusion and considered the bad its regrettable but necessary waste product.

"Then, with the same triumphal surprise as when He'd first told me about PASE, UR God appeared to me one afternoon while I was awake. It was in this very room where we're sitting now. I was hungry, as one gets as an actuated savant—I advanced through the savant stages to provide an example for others—when the giant spectral circle of UR God materialized in the air. A miraculous vision. When I conquered my surprise and awe—when I rose from the ground—He told me that the young woman I'd violated in the Perpetual Light Society had had a child nine months later, and that this child, my son, had grown into the man who would execute the final stage of PASE. I was astonished by both the fact and the content of this communication. PASE was in fact true! And I had a son! What's more, a son who had been chosen for the most important task of all time! After UR God left I discovered my son's identity and where-abouts, which turned out to be here in San Francisco, where he worked at a company whose board of directors included some of the first converts to PASE."

I wished to trade in my tea for a shot of whiskey. The candle flame flickered and a moment later the window rattled and I wondered if the two were correlated like thunder and lightning, and if measuring the time lapse between them might determine the remaining lifespan of the building's weatherproofing or the difference in indoor and outdoor air pressure. A heaviness settled over my chest then and my intakes of breath were confined to short puffs. I squeezed my kneecaps and thought of the description Mr. Raven had once given me of his heart attack, in a conversation whose intimacy had filled me with hope at the time, but I couldn't recall if he'd said the pain came at sharp intervals or was dull and persistent.

I said, releasing my knees, "You sent me that email from my mother."

"Yes."

"You're my father."

"Yes."

The miniature grandfather clock tolled the three o'clock hour. "Because you raped her."

"I haven't eaten in twenty-three days, and besides tea I have ingested no liquids. My doctor tells me that at most I can live another few days, which is not long enough to conduct the world's Pasers in the ritual of ur-Synergy and so into the splendor of UR God. But this is as it should be, because He has selected you to preside over the great migration of those who know best from this world to the next. On Sunday at eleven forty-five P.M., you will stand before a hologram transmitter and deliver a final benediction to every Paser around the world who will be connected to a Synergy device. Then following your signal you all will simultaneously and instantaneously become ur-savants."

I didn't realize I was sweating until a bead slipped from my forehead into my eye and I had to blink away the muddle of half my visual field. The pain around my heart alternated between sharp, dull, and imperceptible. "I will not allow you to kill innocent people."

He straightened up in his chair. "You must listen now very carefully. After UR God's appearance, I told my advisers about you. Most were excited by the news and agreed to treat you with as much deference as myself, but some, including my closest adviser—Denver Stevens—reacted badly. They did not want you to be allowed to do what I know you must do. Thinking that I was as mistaken as when I'd doubted PASE's truth, they argued that you were not my real son and explained away my encounter with UR God as the effect of a hunger pain. When I persisted, they finally pretended, as they had with my Faces of PASE directive, to accept it; in private, however, reflecting an independence and partial distrust of my leadership that might someday have led to a schism in PASE, they made contrary plans to eliminate you. Although you are divinely appointed and so have not been in any real danger, this afternoon I had them rounded up and put through ur-Synergy early so that you could have free rein to prepare for Sunday without any petty intrigue and futile power politics. Unfortunately, this has upset some people in the PASE organization. They will be even more upset when they learn about this evening, and they will try to prevent you from assuming your rightful place on the Last Day."

I stood up and took the gun from my pocket and pointed it at Montgomery Shoale. "My only place in connection to the Last Day is to stop it from happening. That is why I'm here."

He smiled at the gun as though I'd produced it at his request. "I know exactly why you are here, and so do you even if you're still clinging to the illusion that it's to prevent a crime from taking place. That will fade shortly and be replaced by the awesome sensation, not altogether unfamiliar to you, that you are the medium by which many people will be saved, that you will deliver unto them a priceless gift."

I said with much less outward conviction than I intended, "Mary told me about the threats to PASE and how it's about to fall apart. That's why you want to go through with this now."

"You must forget these small machinations and concentrate on what matters."

"PASE is about to end and you're desperate to take as many people with you as possible." I sounded like a child repeating the Pledge of Allegiance, memorized words the meaning of which had been forgotten even though their necessity had not. "Mary told me it's all over."

"With great but misguided powers of deduction, Mary has let her skepticism color the mixture of fact and fiction she's uncovered over the last year, but I assure you that although Monsieur Pissoud and other victims of the Faces of PASE campaign are justified in walking away, they no more represent the end of the religion than a stray drip does the end of a faucet."

I felt curiously disembodied, as though the gun were the only thing anchoring me to the floor. I struggled to stay centered, focused, strong. "But PASE isn't real. You were right when you thought you'd made it up."

Montgomery Shoale was perfectly still. "You are living proof of PASE. I never had a tenth of your native ability or wisdom. Even before my doubts I was unable to reduce my appetite and so had to take diet pills. I couldn't get to sleep naturally and relied on sedatives for my every moment of rest. I haven't known respite from my back pain or nausea or wrist pain in forty years. I required months to improve my oratory and counseling skills, whereas yours developed within two days of entering the Wellness Center. And just think of how happy you were when you were there, how powerful your belief was! I needed miracles to see the truth and you saw it through faith alone."

"That's—" I said.

"You are the spitting image of me at your age, when UR God first told me to do His bidding, and now it is your turn."

I lowered the gun halfway and felt anger and resonance and a terrible conviction that I was on ice and one step in any direction would cause me to slip and fall. "Because of you I was rejected by my birth mother and grew up in a family that disapproved of me. My whole life has been a mistake."

Shoale held out his free hand palm up and said, "Because of me you are here today. I am only a man, like you—more like you, in fact, than anyone else who has ever lived—and I have erred and asked for forgiveness, and now you must grant it, as every son must, because bitterness and delusion are the only alternatives, and those are unendurable. Because everyone's life feels like a mistake. I understand your conflicted feelings, but UR God told me you would come tonight and you drank the tea I poured for you in anticipation. Everything has been preordained."

I pulled the trigger halfway and reached a pressure beyond which I knew there would be explosive sound and discharge. Montgomery Shoale smiled and closed his eyes and his face was a smooth pure adamantine glass in which I saw, with a violent telescoping depth, my own expression relaxed into a profound readiness.

"I can't let you do it," I said, though my voice was so small I couldn't hear it. Louder, I said, "It doesn't matter if we're related and you have this vivid continuous dream. I have an obligation to help others even if they can't help themselves. Everyone has to do all in their power to rescue everyone else. That's why we evolved as social animals. Do you see? I can't let you do it. I have an obligation."

"Yes," he said with a look of equanimity that so terrorized me as I pulled the trigger and the gun fired that I fell to the ground—I slipped and was caught—while Shoale's body slammed against his seat, his head whipping back and forth with a loud snap. His teacup tumbled forward to dribble between his legs, forming a puddle two feet away. I turned around after a few seconds to see the two blue-tunic women standing there. One came forward to help me to my feet while the other picked up the teacup, dabbed at the spilled liquid with a washcloth, and laid a dark blanket over Shoale's face and torso. My helper took the gun from my hand and wiped its handle and barrel with her sleeve before depositing it in a plastic bag that she held open for the other's tea-stained rag.

"What are you doing?" I asked, now holding a plane ticket and passport.

"You have travel reservations to Spitsbergen, an island in the Svalbard archipelago, where you'll be safe. Nobody besides us and the advisers Mr. Shoale handpicked to accompany you there will know where you are when on the Last Day you deliver us to UR God." She covered my hands with hers and smiled worshipfully; the other stood by the cloaked body watching me with similar adoration.

"I just killed him."

"A cab is waiting out front and there's no more time to spare. Please, you must hurry."

I needn't mention who drove me to the airport, where I boarded a plane to London and then Oslo before a boat ferried me to the farthest north settlement in the world. The three men and one woman assigned to come with me slept the whole way. I stayed awake and stared out plane windows at the darkness and light that alternated across continents and oceans, divisions that have been useful for too long.

CHAPTER 12

Religious texts are full of stories about people trying to evade what they have been told is their duty: Jonah setting sail for Tarshish because God commanded him to preach in Nineveh, the Prodigal Son running away from his father's house to drink and whore his way across the land, Atlas attempting to trick Heracles into taking his place as the heavens' eternal support. They also include stories of those eager to comply: Siddhārtha leaving his palace to sit beneath a ficus tree and become enlightened, Moses guiding his people to the Promised Land, Krishna infringing his ethic of nonviolence by killing Jarasandha to save the world. Coming from different traditions, these stories might be expected to provide different lessons, but really they offer only one: Disobedience is futile (Jonah was cast into a leviathan's belly and Atlas outwitted) and acceptance rewarded (Siddhārtha became the Buddha and Moses delivered his tribe to Canaan). They teach that destiny is real and ineluctable, that saddled with one you must ride until you and it merge into the same substance.

I spent my life repudiating my parents' artistic plans for me, a course I defended with amateur theories about character and temperament. This required so much effort, such a windstorm of rationalization and counterfeit self-confidence, that I came to believe that my life, like everyone's, was just a single act of carelessness away from slipping into the void, and that survival meant pitting my will against all challengers. I know now that I was no more called to be a senior capital growth assessment manager than I was a painter, and that I might with more purpose, not to mention filial integrity, have gone to art school and repaid my parents for their trouble and heartache. I might not have been seduced by the idea that I could live according to whatever gratified my ego—that hothouse flower I tended so heedfully, so disastrously—and that by doing so I could be delivered from the thousand protracted pains that accompany a dance across this planet. I might not have thought I knew best when it was plain to everyone, not least to me, that I knew nothing. Because everything that can form the daily foundation of a life, whether curing cancer or teaching children or polishing brass or digging ice cores, is fraught with repetition and stress and setbacks and progress and boredom and spells of satisfaction, and in the end I was a fool to think that choosing this over that in order to be true to myself meant anything. I repeat it now with the pride of humility (of which I am not yet ashamed enough): I was a fool.

Today is the Last Day and tonight I will stand before the hologram transmitter installed in my bungalow and address all the world's Pasers for the first and last time. I will tell them what is common knowledge, that the world is going to end, and what isn't, that at midnight UR God will lift up the drawbridge of PASE, thus stranding everyone who doesn't perform ur-Synergy on the other side of a rising, deadly moat that will someday flood our poor beleaguered planet.

I haven't eaten or drunk much since I got to this village. I have given away my money and discounted my vanity and resisted desire. I have recited long passages of *The Prescription* and meditated and prepared to fuse forever into UR God. But not because I have regained the conviction I had before Mary revealed the Wellness Center's con. My preparations have nothing to do with that. I don't know if I was once a dissolute wand who demanded a space outside of UR God and now needs to become worthy of rejoining Him. The Reality Facts may be as arbitrary as the rules of a board game. Montgomery Shoale, my father, may have been driven by his desire for divine election from the crime of sexual assault to the larger, exponentially worse decision to kill thousands of people who trusted him with their souls and would ultimately have done so with their bodies. PASE could be nothing but a salmagundi of other beliefs, a patchwork as carefully worked out and sown with symbolic truth as a piece of fiction, and as a result admirable and edifying only if not taken too seriously. It is possible that Pasers are, as I once thought them with implicit condescension—me, who stood for nothing and so could fall for anything!—a collection of the lost who found, rather than what they were looking for, only one another.

Tonight I will corral them through the electroshock gates of a Synergy device because outside it is so bright that if I didn't know better I'd think it always was and always will be so, that this is the constant state of the universe. Though I do know better. I had nothing and then everything and then nothing again, and to be aware of what I'm missing is too awful. Or I had everything and then nothing and finally everything again, and I cannot live with that kind of instability. This is my last day.

I am standing at the corner of Christiansand and Erikson roads. The Pasers assigned to protect me—my advisers—are at the bungalow. Thirty minutes ago I met Bjorn Bjornson in front of the bait and tackle shop. He had just made arrangements for his trip to the United States in November. He will begin in New York, drive down to Florida, and conclude his vacation in San Francisco. Perhaps, he said, we might walk together across the Golden Gate Bridge. When I told him I wouldn't be around this fall in a way that implied an absence on Earth as much as in San Francisco, he said, "I see. Well. It is always foolish to depend on the future being what we predict. But it is good to be foolish about some things, yes?"

The news, when I read it, is alarming. Global warming is set to a boil. Species are dying out at the rate of seventy-four per day. Sectarian violence continues in Northern Europe, the United States, the Middle East, and Indonesia. Deadly viruses are pouring out of the Amazon and Southeast Asia. Small nations run by fanatics continue to rattle the saber of their nuclear warheads at trembling giants who soon will stomp on them, and poison will seep out everywhere.

These are the facts, and even though I will be gone when they reach their unimaginably horrible conclusions—their disaster movie premises—I feel sad about them. I wish they did not have to happen. My father was right that we are hardwired to believe in happy endings. I and all the Pasers will go to ours while the world slouches toward their opposite.

You might wonder, given the attention I've paid to it, how my body is doing. I can't honestly say. I use the Synergy device in my bungalow so regularly that I haven't felt any discomfort since I got here. This is an abuse and only excusable to me because I am poised to escape the dilemma of pain management forever, when the very concepts of agony and loneliness and ignorance and sadness will become meaningless.

The village I'm in is built low to the ground; no structure is higher than two stories. The waves that wash up to it are so cold I can't walk barefoot along its beach, where there are never any girls making sandcastles. Desire may have marked the beginning of my life, but it has no place at its end.

All around me is a barren, white-chapped land with hills of gray earth capped by dirtying snow, as though at this latitude color can't take root. Sites that look dull from a distance are even more so up close. When the ocean levels rise, this village will be among the first to drown, but for now it seems a preview of what the rest of the world will be like when its death moves into the next phase.

I can see the small outline of my unremarkable bungalow against the cobalt sky striated with cloud remnants. It occurs to me that—

"I'm sorry," she says.

There's a stinging in my nose and the back of my head feels like an excavation site and I reach up to feel for the damp of blood.

"I figured you'd have your muscle relaxants and painkillers, like you did the time we bumped into each other, but I've looked everywhere and unless they're hidden somewhere clever, they're not here."

"What time is it?"

"I made an ice pack. Lift your head up."

"Mary."

"I'm not mad that you ran away. I knew something like that might happen. You change your mind a lot. I did not expect this town, though. Not at all. When my source at PASE told me about it I thought she was lying, but I had nothing else to go on."

Whatever she hit me with has affected my vision and I can't see her distinctly, though I can make out that she's sitting on a chair a few feet away in my bungalow's living room. The blinds are drawn, but planes of sunlight come through the slats. "Is it nighttime?"

"It's a little after eleven."

"What are you doing here?"

She scooted her chair closer. "I need to tell you something." Her face is easier to comprehend up close.

"Where are my advisers?"

"Locked in the laundry room. Whatever my father said, I'm sure he was sincere, but it's not a reason to go through with this. I was at the Golden Gate Park floral exhibition, and I saw you talking to yourself on that bench. You made little hand gestures on your lap and it looked as if you were waiting for me. A couple of times you got up and counted individual flowers' petals, like you were playing she-loves-me she-loves-me-not."

"That's—" I say. "Why didn't you come to me?"

"I wanted you to think something bad had happened, so that whatever hesitation you felt would disappear."

My visual field corrects itself and her face seems to expand. I could jump up and away and she would be no match for me.

"Did you know," she says, "that after you asked me if I regretted not being in a loving intimate relationship—the day we talked about it in your apartment—I cried all the way home? It's funny, because the first time I saw you, when you asked your neighbor to end the piano lesson and he snowed you, I was put off. I'd always thought that forceful guys were the only ones worth pursuing. I felt safe seeing and knowing that their self-prepossession was possible. But I'd picked you out for a conquest, so I went back the next night and you didn't drop everything to fall into bed with me, which made you an army of one in my experience. I was annoyed then, which is probably an emotional synonym for feeling hurt, until I decided that you had refused me out of strength, and for a tenth of a second I respected the part of PASE that finds nobility in saying no. The 'negative is really positive' line. When that went away, though, I wrote you off again and hoped we'd never run into each other, so when you recognized me on the street I was flustered and angry. And then suddenly I didn't know how I felt anymore. The cop asked if I wanted to press charges—I should've said yes to keep up appearances, but I couldn't because I wanted to see you later. Maybe I was just amazed to be recognized as myself. But maybe it was more than that. More than surprise. More than gratitude. What I want to say is that Prescription for a Superior Existence removes love from the human sphere, the one we're all part of and can contribute to, and directs a simulation of it outward to a cold distant god. PASE demands respect and awe but can't value us as we are or provide real empathy for anyone. UR God and ur-savants are perfect and so know only perfection. If there is any validity to the story of those mutinous wands who opted out of UR God, it is that they needed to see and know and love one another in their own right, with all the force and compulsion of desire. Like staring at the sun, being part of Him would make you blind. Really blind. Not the abstract warning *The Prescription* gives about how our bodies are an eyecover preventing us from seeing ultimate reality. Everything Pasers do that is positive—and it's a lot, an incalculable amount of good—falls short of love between men and women and parents and children and strangers who outgrow that categorization. That's what PASE can't provide through its anesthetics and regimented march toward a state of disconnection."

"You could just kill me if you want to stop ur-Synergy."

She looks at me with dark worry, though the sunlight behind her produces a corona around her face.

"Or is someone else lined up to officiate in my place if I don't show up? Maybe you're here to get me to tell everyone that this isn't the Last Day and there never will be one."

"I'm here because I love you."

There is a long silence. Unlike the other times we've been together, I cannot tell if she is lying. It's possible that part of what she said is true and part false, or that all of it is one or the other. I have no idea. I get up and grab the corner of a table to steady myself. The hologram transmitter is a few feet away, and as I walk toward it I see Mary standing at the counter beside a block of knives. The femmes fatales I picture in my head are cartoons, drawn from the imaginations of small men trying to scare other small men. The transmitter is very simple. Via an instant satellite upload it is set to broadcast my image to the PASE Station and Wellness Centers and makeshift locations set up all over the world to house Synergy devices, where people, full of faith and commitment and trust, are gathering so that they might be released, and in this strangely lit room with Mary and me and a choice to be made I ask myself: *From what?* And think: *From themselves.* And think: *From characters and destinies that, like stones skipping across water, must not be scooped up by any human hand.*

So much comes down to choosing this path or that, and the selection we make disturbs or gratifies people whose decisions are already made because they would have us tamp down the dirt behind them, because they don't want to be swallowed up. Montgomery Shoale, father, Father. Absolute laws to be followed or broken absolutely. After I shut off the hologram transmitter at five minutes past midnight, having just announced my father's final communication from UR God before dying—that the Last Day had, through His infinite mercy, been postponed forever, and that becoming a master actuated savant was now the highest achievable status—I went with Mary to ask Bjorn Bjornson to open the laundry room door of my bungalow in the morning. Before leaving I gave him my phone number and said I'd gladly meet him on the pedestrian walkway of the Golden Gate Bridge in December.

Mary has said very little since we arrived at the ferry station that will take us to the mainland, from which we can get a flight home. I still cannot tell if her love is real or not. Maybe she's planning to stay with me just long enough to establish my defense in the Montgomery Shoale murder trial, some noblesse oblige that stems from her good heart. Maybe she'll slip away when we reach Oslo. Maybe, though, just possibly, she and I are the point of what's led up to this moment. Is it so incredible to imagine that every coincidence and existential echo has served not to advance the cause of another supreme deity, but rather to bring two people together for the purpose that unites all of mankind, from prophets to troubadours? I remembered the complete plot of "Rappaccini's Daughter" an hour ago. The hero, a romantic youth named Giovanni, falls in love with his beautiful neighbor, Beatrice, and then discovers that her father, Rappaccini, has reared her as a scientific experiment to be full of poison, with the result that every living thing she touches or breathes on dies. As the two lovers lament the barrier between them, Rappaccini takes pity on his daughter's solitude and so works the same dark magic on Giovanni, rendering them biological equals who can be together safely. At this moment, however, Giovanni's friend gives him an antidote, which Beatrice drinks first. She dies then, so integral has the poison become to her being, and the story ends with Giovanni and Rappaccini bereft of the thing both loved more than any other. In our story, the father has died first, and we must wait to see what will happen to us.

The restaurant here serves excellent coffee. Mary and I each add a dash of milk and a half packet of sugar to our cups, and this is synergy, sympathy, solidarity, sodality. Or it is none of those things. It has been a long day and I'm pleasantly tired, as after a vigorous swim when your limbs are heavy and you lie on a blanket to be dried by the breeze and sun, the sound of others' laughter like great outdoor wind chimes, at peace. I take her hand or she takes mine and the sun, after a seeming age, is beginning to set, as we've long known it would, and in this climactic twilight I consider that we may regret for the rest of our lives and beyond the possibility that we are acting not for us or them or me or her, but instead, despite our proud declensions and piteous exaltations, despite the caveats of a hundred false positives, for the love of God.

There's a chance, however, if we're lucky, if accidents and coincidences happen for no greater or lesser reason than life itself, that we will be wise enough to take solace in the hope—in the infinite complexity of our glorious averring desire—that this is all there was, is, and ever will be.

ACKNOWLEDGMENTS

I am deeply grateful to everyone whose support and guidance made this book possible: Katie Ford, Susan Golomb, Reza Aslan, Bret Anthony Johnston, Fred Tangeman, Rich Green, Samantha Martin, and Nan Graham.

ABOUT THE AUTHOR

MMONS is the author of *The Loss of Leon Meed*. He grew up
lifornia and currently lives in Philadelphia.

ANY RICH MAN WILL DO

~ Francis Ray ~

 St. Martin's Griffin ✿ New York

ISBN 0-7394-5815-9

To my sister, Velma Lee Radford, a woman of substance, courage, and an unending capacity for love. I miss you still.

To three uncompromising women of faith and fortitude, Mrs. Vernon Radford, my mother; Mrs. Mattie Edgar, my mother-in-law; and Mrs. Robbie T. Byrd, past Director of Women's Ministry of Concord Missionary Baptist Church. These three amazing women look at the hearts of men and women and leave judgment to a higher power.

Special Thanks

Dr. Karen Hollie, noted Dallas psychologist, radio hostess, and columnist, who answered numerous questions as I worked on this book. My utmost thanks.

The Linen Gallery, Peacock Alley, and Hotel ZaZa for helping me research the sublime pleasure of sleeping on luxe linen. The experience was awesome.

1

Jana Franklin was out of luck and running out of time. She'd always believed she had more than her share of both. She'd been wrong. She had less than ninety-seven cents in her evening clutch and if she didn't come up with the rent for her motel room tonight she'd be out in the streets tomorrow.

What she needed was what she'd always used—an accommodating and generous man. She'd crashed a charity gala in a three-story Georgian mansion in the most exclusive area of Dallas to find one. But this time desperation, not greed or the allure of being in control, drove her.

Even as the frightening thought materialized, Jana fought to deny it. Desperation was not a word she had ever associated with herself. Why should she? She'd lived a privileged life and was accustomed to having whatever she wanted, whenever she wanted, and she'd always wanted the best.

As for need, by the time she was twelve her parents' disinterest had taught her never to need anyone. Her mother had taken the lesson one step further and drilled into the head of her only child to need men least of all.

Jana had learned that lesson well.

Since she was fifteen she'd carelessly used men as the whim struck, then moved on to the next gullible fool. If life had taught her anything it was that need made you weak and love was a joke for those stupid enough to believe in happily-ever-after. People who thought otherwise were asking for their hearts to be trampled on. Jana had always prided herself on being too smart for that, but somehow she'd taken a wrong turn and no matter what she did she couldn't seem to get her life back on track.

Tonight was her last chance.

Life was no longer an amusing game where she made the rules, then bent them for her own satisfaction and enjoyment. Her safe comfortable world was gone, perhaps forever.

Her trembling fingers clenched the stem of the champagne flute as she glanced around the formal living room of the palatial mansion. For the first time in her thirty-two years, she had no place to go and no one to turn to. Her black clutch held loose change, lipstick, and the key to a bug-infested motel room. Friends and family might be an option for some, but not for her. She'd never bothered to have friends and her parents had never bothered with her.

Another cursory glance around the elegant room filled with the wealthy and elite, and those who desperately wanted to be, increased the jittery feeling in Jana's stomach. She'd been here for twenty-five minutes, and although she'd shared good times and a bed with a couple of men in the room, neither had approached her nor spoken.

She felt uncomfortable in her own skin, restless, too keyed up to even enjoy her favorite drink. She was too aware of what would happen to her if she didn't accomplish her goal tonight.

Hope surged as she caught the eye of Dan Jefferies, a wealthy restaurateur and one of several men in the room who had once pursued her relentlessly. She'd rebuffed him and chosen a man ten years his senior and twenty times as wealthy. She hadn't been subtle in her rejection. Dan's sixty-foot craft couldn't compare to a luxurious yacht with its own helipad. As if remembering her very public put-down, he turned away, just as the other men in the room had done that evening.

A hint of color bloomed in Jana's pale cheeks. Her hand fluttered to the plunging neckline of her ill-fitting purple gown. It was a hideous dress, but it was the only appropriate attire she had left. If she had on one of her Armani or Valentino couture gowns, her nails and hair done at Neiman's salon . . . her thoughts trailed off. Somehow she knew those superficial trappings wouldn't help. Nothing had gone right since she'd fled Charleston in disgrace almost a year ago. Corrine Livingston had made sure of that.

"How the mighty have fallen."

"And it couldn't happen to a more deserving bitch."

Jana heard the snide comments of the nearby women as she was meant to and barely kept from tucking her head and leaving. Once they wouldn't have dared cross her and if they had, she'd have given it back to them in spades. What kept the harsh words locked behind her teeth was the vision of the small, cramped space that was now her home . . . at least for now. She could stand their abuse. What she couldn't stand was the possibility of never regaining her position in society.

A rich man would change that. But what if . . .

Her fingers tightened on the stem of the flute. She refused to let herself think about not succeeding. With an unsteady hand she tilted the crystal flute and drained the glass. The vintage wine tasted flat and left her feeling the same way. Once the thought of the chase, of seducing any man to her will, would have made her feel alive. Now it made her stomach roll.

She hadn't eaten all day. The women standing nearby laughed as Jana's stomach grumbled. She flushed with embarrassment.

Apparently tired of their little game, Priscilla Haynes, the hostess who had been standing with the two other women, confronted Jana. "I didn't know you were in town."

Priscilla was flawless in a black silk Armani gown that hugged her trim figure. A million dollars' worth of pure pink sapphires surrounded by oval-cut diamonds hung from her ears and circled her throat. The matching bracelet on her right wrist completed the one-of-a-kind suite. The diamond wedding ring was ten carats and flawless, as was the ten-carat diamond tennis bracelet on her other wrist.

Priscilla was a class-A snob and bitch. The slow drawling words were a none-too-subtle swipe that that knowledge would have precluded Jana being invited to the charity ball, since Priscilla was chair, in her home.

Unable to think of a quick comeback, Jana waved the empty flute in a dismissive gesture, then watched the other woman's hazel eyes narrow and grow even colder. Jana remembered, though now too late, making the same careless gesture shortly before leaving a party in Vail several years ago with Priscilla's fiancé.

Jana hadn't wanted the rich oilman. She'd simply wanted to show Priscilla, who thought she was all that, that she could. She'd sent him back to Priscilla the next day. Apparently his wealth far outweighed her humiliation because they had married six months later as scheduled.

"I . . ." Jana began, but couldn't quite come up with a witty remark. Smart comebacks had once been her staple and trade, that and getting any man she wanted. Saying she was sorry to Priscilla would have been a lie, but then when had Jana ever been bothered with the truth? Her prime objective was self-gratification, but look what that had gotten her.

Mitsy and Sherilyn, the two women who had spoken earlier, flanked Priscilla, bolstering her. A show of strength that said Priscilla had friends and Jana had nothing and no one. She never had. She hadn't thought she'd ever need them.

"Jana, you must have missed your salon appointment. I've seen better hair and nails on my cleaning woman," Mitsy said gleefully.

"We hear you're missing a lot these days." Sherilyn dared to flick the limp, ruffled sleeve of Jana's out-of-season gown. The bright purple design clashed garishly with her cinnamon-hued completion. "Where did you get this? The Salvation Army?"

"She earned it on her back like she has everything else," Mitsy answered.

"Not anymore," Sherilyn said. "Payback's a bitch."

Jana could have stood laughter better than the malicious glee in their eyes, the knowledge that Jana Louise Carpenter Livingston Murphy Franklin, the thrice-married woman who had once ruled those around her, especially men, was almost destitute with no friends, no family, and no place to go.

And it was her own fault.

Jana's brain urged her to leave, but the thought of what would happen to her if she left without accomplishing her mission kept her rooted on the Oriental rug. Without finding a wealthy man to support her she'd be out on the street tomorrow. The motel manager had already said she could "work it off." That she had been scared and desperate enough to momentarily consider his offer made her ill. There had to be one man here who still wanted her.

"I lost weight and didn't have time to shop." Jana carefully set the glass on a nearby table. "Excuse me. I see someone I know."

"We all know you, Jana. That's the problem," said Priscilla.

Jana flinched at the undisguised contempt in the woman's voice, then she continued past the hostile stares of the other people in the room. Most of them as gleeful as the women she had left. It wasn't difficult to read their thoughts: bitchy, man-stealing Jana was finally getting what was coming to her.

Jana's hand trembled as she grasped the brass knob of the powder room down the hallway. Thankfully it opened. Entering, she shut the door, then slid down until her bottom hit the cool black marble floor.

She'd called her mother for help, but she had said that she was having problems of her own. Jana's father had hung up on her. Neither had ever been there for her. Her mother has always been busy with the current lover: her father with his telecommunication firm. Why should now be any different?

Yet she couldn't help hoping that one day things would change.

She'd never worked a real job in her life. First there had been her wealthy father, who gave her money instead of his time, and her mother, who gave her lessons on handling men instead of handling the ups and downs of life, then a succession of men, each one wealthier than the last one. Five months ago that had stopped. Now she had to fend for herself, and had absolutely no idea how to do so.

It seemed that a beautiful face and a shapely body only worked for so long. She had been reduced to selling her clothes and jewelry, even her shoes, and moving to less and less expensive places to live until she had ended up in a dump that, a few months ago, she wouldn't have recommended a dog sleep in.

She lifted her head and leaned it back against the door. She'd read about the charity event tonight in the newspaper at the McDonald's where she had been able to con the young man behind the counter into letting her have breakfast while she only paid for coffee. But this week he was on vacation and the woman behind the counter wanted cash, not flirtatious smiles and a glimpse of cleavage.

With the elite in attendance—brown, black, white—she had been sure she'd find a man. She'd lived abroad long enough to have crossed the color line before, and saw no reason not to take the opportunity if it presented itself. Dallas was in the South, but the city had a cosmopolitan attitude about relationships.

But the opportunity hadn't presented itself. She wasn't five feet inside the great room where everyone was gathered before the buzz of whispers began to follow her like a bad scent. Her reputation and downfall had preceded her. Women who once cowered before her now smirked. Men who had once begged to be with her now barely looked at her.

No man wanted a woman no one else wanted.

That was the first lesson her mother had taught her when she was fifteen. They'd bonded as much as possible over discussions of men and sex when they had nothing in common to link them but blood. Her mother had taught her how to get a man, but she hadn't bothered to teach her daughter how to keep one. Jana had been taught that there wasn't a man she couldn't get. She found out too late that not all men were ruled by their zippers and now she was paying the high price, and so was her mother.

The brisk knock on the door made Jana jump. "I need to get in."

No please, no excuse me. Whoever was knocking knew Jana was inside, knew she was hiding.

The knock, more demanding, came again.

Jana struggled to her feet and swayed. Two glasses of champagne shouldn't have made her tipsy. She'd been drinking since she was fourteen. First in hiding, then after her mother had finally started to pay attention to her, they'd drink champagne and cosmopolitans when her father wasn't around. They'd done a great deal behind her father's back.

None of it good.

Jana made herself look in the mirror. She winced at the dark smudges beneath her eyes, the gaunt face, and the dull shoulder-length hair she'd tried to cut into a semblance of style with a pair of scissors she'd borrowed from the hotel manager. Her eyes looked old and defeated. She'd lost weight and the gown she'd bought on a wild shopping spree last year sagged on her. Not eating tended to do that to a person. She couldn't remember a day in the past three months when she hadn't gone to sleep hungry.

"Jana, open this door!" Priscilla demanded.

Jana flinched, swallowed, then rubbed her damp palms on her dress and opened the door. She wasn't surprised to see several women crowded into the hallway. They presented a united front against one. Once she would have been included, if only superficially, but that was before Charleston, before her life began its descent into hell.

"I don't want you in my house. A cab is waiting for you," Priscilla said.

Jana almost laughed. She had come by bus. Million-dollar residences needed a barrage of people, preferably at minimum wages, to keep them maintained and the occupants happy. The bus line was essential in bringing much of that help.

If only Jana could say her car was waiting or name a man who wanted to take her home. *Home.* Had she ever really had one?

"What's the matter with you? Are you so dense that you'd stay where you're not wanted?" Priscilla walked closer. "Get out of my house. Your presence offends me and every decent person here."

The verbal thrust made Jana cringe and come out fighting. "Since I know of your affair with a certain doctor in New York last year, and the rest of the women standing around you are just as bad, except Mitsy who prefers women, I'd say I'm in good company."

The slap across Jana's face snapped her head back and caused her to stumble against the wall. Stunned, she rubbed her stinging cheek. The attack was so unexpected that Jana simply stared at Priscilla as the verbal hatred poured from her mouth. Then, the male guests and a servant were there.

"Get this trash out of my house," Priscilla said, her voice and body trembling with rage. Everett, her husband, his face as closed as that of the other men with him—as if he'd never begged Jana to run off and marry him—put his arm around Priscilla and curtly nodded his head in Jana's direction. The stiff-backed butler stepped forward and grabbed Jana none too gently by the bare arm and led her past the watchful crowd.

It was all Jana could do not to hang her head in shame. By tomorrow news of her humiliation would have reached from one end of the country to another. Her fall from grace was complete. Opening the door, the servant kept walking until they were on the sidewalk. The garbage disposed of, he reentered the house.

For a long time Jana simply stared at the closed, recessed door, the light spilling from the many windows of the three-story home. The poorest to the wealthiest person inside had a home, maybe family and friends, waiting for them. What wouldn't she give to have as much? She'd never realized how desperately she wanted both until it was too late.

Trembling, Jana swallowed the knot in her throat, then turned, looked up and down the wide street bordered by million-dollar homes and flawlessly manicured lawns. Luxury cars and the Texas elite's newest darling, Hummers, lined both sides of the exclusive address, but there was no taxi. Jana glanced at her wrist, then felt a tear slide down her cheek. The 18-carat white gold Rolex with a mother-of-pearl face surrounded by two rows of diamonds, given to her by a very generous lover, had been sold weeks ago at a grocery parking lot to a man who had given her a tenth of what it was worth, but more than a pawn shop would have.

Opening her small clutch purse, she pulled out a wad of toilet tissue and dabbed her eyes. Pay-by-the-day motels didn't have Kleenex. But crying wouldn't change things. If it would have, she'd be back inside snubbing the hostess and selecting the lucky man to take her home. In the morning she'd have breakfast—mimosa, freshly baked flaky croissants, and waffles piled high with plump, juicy strawberries and fresh whipped cream.

Her stomach growled again. She should have eaten at the party when she had the chance, but she had been afraid that once she started she couldn't have stopped. Or worse, she might have thrown up the rich food. She was learning that hunger was manageable if you kept starving it. Feed it and your body wanted more.

She turned toward the bus stop, thinking as her steps quickened on the deserted street that she should have checked to see when it stopped running. The wealthy might want help during the day, but at night the servants went home unless they were working.

"Hey, beautiful, need a lift?"

Jana almost stumbled, then jerked around and saw Douglas Gregory in a $75,000 Mercedes. Salvation! She felt almost light-headed. Douglas was a second-string player for a Dallas sports team that was last in their division. At the party he'd been loud and obviously out-of-place and trying to fit in. He had probably been invited because of his connection to the team, but he wasn't accepted into the upper ranks. Each time he had joined a group, it splintered off.

"I'll take you anyplace you want to go." He glanced over his shoulder and behind him, then shoved open the passenger's side door.

Where he planned to take her was to bed. She hesitated. She hadn't been with a man in five months and frankly, for the first time in memory, she wasn't looking forward to it.

"Come on," he urged.

She took a step closer. In the dim light coming from the car she saw his angular, clean-shaven face. He wasn't much to look at, but she'd been with unattractive men before. Money, not looks, was important. Another lesson her mother had taught her.

Douglas glanced over his shoulder again. "Come on, get in."

Jana quickly understood what was going on. He didn't want anyone at the party to know he had picked her up. That was all right with her. He wasn't the type of man she usually chose either. The men she allowed her favors were charming, sophisticated, connected, and very wealthy. They had to be to be able to afford her. If she woke up at three in the morning and was hungry, there had better be a chef in residence or a hotel with twenty-four-hour room service to accommodate her.

"You coming or not?" he asked, impatience in his voice.

Jana quickly stuffed the tissue back in her purse then rounded the hood of the gleaming black car and got inside. She had barely closed the door before the vehicle took off. The smell of the new leather mingled unpleasantly with his heavy, woodsy cologne, causing Jana to feel queasy.

"I'm Douglas."

"Jana." First names meant sex for a night and good-bye in the morning. She'd played the game before, but this time she needed more than a night.

Bringing a smile to her face she turned toward him, thankful that the dimness of the car's interior showed only profile and cleavage as they passed the street lights, not the ravages of the past five months. "Thanks."

He chuckled. "I aim to please."

I just bet you do, Jana thought. Another man who thought he had the right moves to bring any woman ecstasy—which usually meant he didn't. But that was all right. Jana was a pro at faking it. Sex was a device to control men. Occasionally she found pleasure in the act, but she wasn't bothered if she didn't.

What she cared about was his paycheck. Since he'd been invited to the gala, it must be substantial which meant he could afford to keep her in the style she'd grown accustomed to.

"I just flew in for the charity event. I'm supposed to fly back out in the morning, but who knows. . . ." She let her voice trail off seductively.

He gave her a quick grin, then let his beefy hand fall heavily on her thigh. She wanted to shove his hand off. Instead she chatted, her edgy feeling returning as time passed. He didn't ask for her address.

A short time later she frowned as he pulled into the darkened theater parking lot of Highland Park Village. The upscale shopping center strip had single-level shops that rivaled those on Rodeo Drive.

Parking in a dark corner of the lot, Douglas cut the motor and reached for her. Jana inched back against the door. She didn't want a quickie, she wanted someone to take care of her. Someone to fix things and make her life right again.

"Why are we parked here?"

"My wife is home and I can't risk going to a hotel where I might be recognized," he told her impatiently.

Jana almost felt cheap and ashamed. "You could give me the money and I could rent the room, then call you on your cell," she suggested.

"I'm not going to risk it. From what I heard about you, this can't be your first time in a car," he said snidely.

It wasn't, but it had never been in these circumstances and never so crudely initiated. Jana stared at the disgruntled man and realized she had finally hit rock bottom.

All these years she'd told herself that she was using men. With startling clarity she realized they'd been using her. Her mother had been wrong. The man glaring at her wouldn't mind taking her in the front seat of his car, but he wouldn't want any of his friends to know, except the few he'd later brag to. He'd probably already bragged to at least one man at the party that he was going to score with her.

How could she have been so blind?

With a quick turn, she opened the door and got out. She heard the curse behind her and deftly evaded the hand grabbing for her. The chiffon ruffle on the back of her dress wasn't so fortunate. Her curse joined his at the sound of the fragile material tearing, but she didn't dare pause. Some men didn't take no. Her heels clicked loudly on the pavement as she headed toward the beckoning light of the shopping center.

"Get back in this damn car!" he yelled.

Although she felt light-headed, she increased her pace, fearing any moment she'd feel his rough hand on her arm. Instead she heard the slam of a door, then another. She dared glance over her shoulder to see the big car back up, then roar out of the parking lot. Panting, she slowed to fight off another wave of dizziness, unsure if it was from not eating a full meal in the last week or the intense heat. Even at night, the temperature in Dallas hung in the low nineties at this time of the year.

Catching her breath, her steps measured, Jana emerged from the parking lot and started toward the street at the other end of the shopping center. She was too wary to even glance into the store widows as she passed St. Johns, Gucci, and Cartier. Her focus was the street ahead. Hopefully a bus would be there, but the way her luck had been going, she doubted it.

A few steps later another wave of dizziness forced her to stop and press her hand against a plate glass window to steady herself. Eyes closed, she waited for her head to clear, painfully aware that each time the dizziness came it was more difficult to fight.

What wouldn't she give to be able to lie down on cool, clean sheets or for a cool glass of water. She didn't think she'd ever been as tired as she was now. If she didn't rest and get something to drink, she was afraid she wouldn't make it to the bus stop. Worse, she might pass out on the bus. And if she sat down on the sidewalk, she wasn't sure she'd be able to get back up.

Opening her eyes, she lifted her head and stared into the store. Directly in front of her was a king-sized brass bed piled high with luxurious linens and pillows. On the chrome nightstand was a silver pitcher, two silver flutes, and a small bouquet of fresh-cut flowers. Some might see the humor in the situation, but humor had never been Jana's strong suit.

As her gaze tracked around the store filled with colorful linens and bath products, she saw a tall, well-built man sitting behind a French country desk, his long legs, encased in jeans, stretched out in front of him. He wore a white shirt with the cuffs rolled back. His long-fingered hand slowly turned the pages in front of him.

As if suddenly aware he was being watched, he looked up and their gazes met. His dark eyes narrowed behind wire-rimmed glasses. For some odd reason his direct gaze made her want to step back into the shadows. She attributed the pounding of her heart to fear that he might recognize her. Priscilla and her friends would have a good laugh on hearing that Jana had passed out on the sidewalk.

Jana glanced toward the busy street that was a block away. She'd never make it if she didn't rest for a moment. There was only one choice left.

Before she lost her nerve, she reached for the crystal doorknob.

2

Tyler Maxwell was at the end of another long day. He'd just flown in from Chicago and had been up for the past twenty hours to ensure the updated computer system his team had installed to link Sterling Bank's 1,500 branches across the country was error free. The company before them had flubbed the job when the system overloaded, leaving thousands of tellers across the country with the very unpleasant task of telling their customers they were unable to access their accounts.

By attempting to save money the bank had lost millions *and* the goodwill of customers. Stockholders weren't happy. Tyler hadn't minded stepping in and correcting the problem. His success only served to further his reputation as a system analyst engineer and the owner of Prime Objective. His team was one of the best in the country.

On the way home from the airport, he'd called his sister Olivia, to let her know he had landed. He'd learned she had returned to her linen boutique, Midnight Dreams, to meet a couple whose special order had come in.

Instead of going home, he'd stopped at her store. Security was excellent during regular store hours in the upscale shopping complex, but scattered afterwards. Crime didn't have any borders. Since Olivia prided herself on customer satisfaction and service, she wouldn't have dreamed of telling the customers to wait until morning.

He'd arrived at the same time the anxious couple had. They were smiling broadly as Olivia led them to her office in the back. Grabbing a bottle of water from the refrigerator in the lounge, he'd made himself comfortable at the desk on the sales floor. His mouth twisted wryly at the seductive woman in a black negligee on the cover of the lingerie catalog in front of him.

It had been a long time between women and it wasn't likely to change anytime soon. Olivia thought he was still hung up on Courtney, but he'd simply decided he didn't have time to cater to another woman who wanted to make him over to suit her needs. He liked the way he was. Sliding the catalog aside, he began to look through the papers he'd removed from his attaché case.

Then something made him look up. A woman was staring back at him. He couldn't tell much about her except that she wore an evening gown. People often window-shopped after the movie or other events, so he wasn't particularly surprised. That changed when she opened the door and came in. He chastised himself for not making sure the door was locked.

His eyes narrowed as he got a better look at her. She appeared tired and had dark smudges beneath her eyes. Her shoulder-length black hair was uneven and looked as if someone had cut it blindfolded. Her movements were slow and deliberate.

He wasn't into fashion, but the evening gown looked outdated and worn. Most of the women who shopped the stores in the complex had money to burn, but he'd learned long ago not to judge people's financial status or their character from the way they looked. Many times he had been on the receiving end from Courtney about his shortcomings.

"I'm sorry, miss, but the store is closed."

Jana stopped at the sound of the deep Texas drawl. She stood a few feet inside the store as the man rose easily and stepped around the desk. His chest was broad, his legs long and muscular. He wasn't handsome in the traditional sense, but he had a kind of potent maleness that probably had women falling over themselves for him. For once, Jana was more interested in the cool air and sitting down for a moment.

Frowning he took a step closer. "Are you all right?"

"I . . ." was all Jana was able to say before her legs gave out. She felt herself falling. She thought she whimpered in protest, but wasn't sure. In the next instant she was lifted and gently held against a wide chest. Opening her eyes she stared up into a pair of intense black eyes and shivered.

"Tyler, what happened?"

Out of the corner of her eye, Jana saw an attractive petite woman rushing toward them. In her late twenties, she was wearing a pale yellow linen suit. Her arms were full of bedding. Behind the woman was a stylishly dressed couple of about the same age. They carried bed linens as well. Unlike the woman, they made no move to come closer.

"She fainted," Tyler answered calmly, as if it was an everyday occurrence. He never took his eyes from Jana. "Can you stand?" he asked her.

Jana managed a nod and readied herself to be dumped back on her feet. She hoped she wouldn't keel over.

"Put her here, Tyler," the woman instructed, then proceeded to move a stack of sample books from a Queen Anne chair in front of the desk where Tyler has been sitting.

Tyler placed her in the rose silk-covered chair, then turned away only to return with her scuffed and worn olive suede Manolo Blahnik mules. His carefully assessing gaze ran over her again. Jana's bare toes curled beneath the gown. Thank goodness her feet were hidden. It was all she could do to not shrink back in the chair.

Her mother had always maintained that a fashion faux pas was as bad as any other transgression. She'd been able to hide the fact that she was down to her last two pairs of Manolo Blahniks, neither of which were evening shoes, with her floor-length gown. It was too hot to wear hose even if she had a pair, which she didn't. Wordlessly, she reached for her shoes.

He gave them to her, then plucked a bottle of water from the desk, broke the seal and handed it to her. "Take a few sips of this."

Gratefully, Jana's hands closed around the cold bottle of water and lifted it to her lips. She would have guzzled it if he hadn't taken it from her.

"Not too much," he said, then allowed her another couple of swallows. Jana thought of snatching the bottle, but didn't think she had the strength. She swallowed convulsively. *Please don't let me throw up.*

"It's probably the heat," said the woman who had spoken earlier. "Can I get you anything or call anyone?"

With them watching her, Jana knew she had to say something. She couldn't decide what she wanted more, to slink away in shame or to close her eyes and rest. "If I could use the restroom?"

"Of course," the woman said. "I'll show you the way."

"She'll need her shoes, Olivia." Before Jana could protest, Tyler plucked the shoes from her lap, hunkered down, then held out his hand expectantly for her foot.

She moved her feet back further beneath her gown. "I—I can do it."

He stared at her a few minutes longer as if he might challenge her, then came easily to his feet. Envying him his easy strength, Jana slipped on one shoe, then the other, grateful that the dizziness cleared when she lifted her head.

As soon as she straightened, Olivia reached for her, but it was Tyler whose calloused hand curled around Jana's arm and helped her to her feet. He didn't let go, she was sure, until he was satisfied she could stand by herself. "Thank you."

"Bathroom is this way," Olivia said, taking slow steps as they moved toward the back of the store. "Are you sure there's no one I can call?"

"No." *No one who cared.*

"Here we are." In the back of the store Olivia opened the door to the surprisingly large bathroom. "Feel free to use the towels to freshen up. I'll be back shortly to check on you."

"Thank you," Jana said, then walked inside the spotless white and chrome bathroom, closing the door behind her. She hadn't said thank you so many times in such a short span of time in longer than she could remember.

The crowd she used to run with thought only of themselves first and always, just as she had. She'd lived a selfish, worthless life and it had finally caught up with her. If she died tonight no one would mourn her or care. Her head fell forward as misery swept through her.

She was alone.

This time when the dizziness came she didn't try to fight it. She embraced the peaceful oblivion that she had never been able to find when awake.

"I hope she's all right," Olivia said as she reentered the showroom.

"That awful dress she wore was torn in the back," Cynthia Ingram said, her green eyes rounded in shock and excitement. "And those shoes! Even if they were Manolo Blahnik. Suede in the summer! And so scuffed and worn. Perhaps you should call the police."

"Police?" Olivia's brows bunched in puzzlement as she took a seat at the desk.

Cynthia's brunette head nodded emphatically. "My guess is a man ripped her gown. He might come looking for her."

Olivia's worried gaze sought her brother. He leaned casually against the door jam separating the shop from the back room. "Tyler?"

He smiled in reassurance. He'd noticed the rip as well, but he didn't think anyone was coming after her. As weak as she was they could have easily caught her if they'd wanted. "Mr. Ingram and I can handle him if he does."

Dennis Ingram, Cynthia's husband of three months, laughed and slung his arm around his wife's slim shoulders. "Tyler is right, honey. Don't you worry. Besides, she could have just as easily caught it on something."

"I suppose." Cynthia appeared somewhat disappointed. "Our speaker at the Junior League luncheon today was a woman from a local women's shelter. Guess all the horror stories are still with me." She wrinkled her pretty mouth. "Although I must admit I can't see how any woman would stand to let a man use her as a punching bag. The things women put up with and the lies they tell themselves just to have a man, it's pitiful."

"I'll get your receipt," Olivia said, then began writing up the sale.

Tyler kept his attention on the door of the bathroom. He didn't want to worry Olivia or alarm her customers, but he'd worked in enough hot spots around the world to be able to sense when something was off. The woman looked as if she was on her last leg. It might have been a coincidence that she just happened to come into Olivia's store or it could have been planned. Once she came out of the restroom she could leave or try to run a scam. He wasn't taking any chances. Olivia, with her trusting nature, would instinctively reach out to help in any way possible.

Olivia was the most trusting and unassuming person he knew. Her ex-husband had used her naïveté to ensnare her in a marriage that was doomed from the beginning. The heart-wrenching ordeal of her divorce a year later had almost destroyed the laughing, generous girl he had grown up with.

Tyler had been out of the country most of the time during her sham of a marriage and hadn't known the full extent of the problem until the divorce was almost final.

He'd kept his anger hidden and concentrated on helping Olivia rebuild her life instead of going after her manipulating and underhanded husband. With the help of her family, she'd survived and flourished. If humanly possible, he planned on making sure no one ever took advantage of her again.

Olivia finished writing the sale receipt and handed it to the Ingrams. "Thank you and enjoy."

"We will," Dennis Ingram shoved the slip of paper into the inside pocket of his tailored sports jacket. "We fell in love with Frette sheets when we stayed at the Ritz in Paris on our honeymoon. When we got your call this afternoon that our order had come in, we couldn't wait until tomorrow. Thank you for staying open."

Olivia smiled. "My pleasure. Your bed linens are the ultimate in luxury. I understand completely how anxious you must be to try them out."

The couple looked at each other and grinned.

Tyler noticed that his sister grinned back. Her smile was for a different reason. The set cost close to $4,500. He'd rather invest that kind of money, but others saw the purchase of luxe linens as an investment in itself, either for sheer indulgence or as heirlooms. Either way, they had made his little sister a wealthy woman in her own right. That she'd done it almost single-handedly, establishing her independence and bolstering her self-esteem, was priceless.

"Remember, if you need laundry service you have only to call for pickup and delivery. I included a pamphlet on caring for them if you wish to do it yourself."

"You think of everything."

"I try." Olivia came around the desk. "I'll show you out."

The couple didn't budge. "We'll wait until she comes out. If you hadn't waited on us, you wouldn't have had to let her in," Mr. Ingram said.

"I'm glad we were open," Olivia said, her brow creased in concern. "She looked worn out."

"She looked unsavory to me," commented Mrs. Ingram. "I wonder what she was doing in this neighborhood."

"You can bet it wasn't shopping, the way she was dressed," her husband answered.

Tyler noticed Olivia barely kept the smile on her face. Neither of them liked narrow-minded, snobbish people. Unfortunately, on occasion, their work demanded they associate with them. "Olivia, maybe you better go check on her."

"Please, excuse me." Olivia started walking to the back with Tyler close behind. She knocked gently on the restroom door, realizing as she did that she didn't know the woman's name. "Miss? Miss? Are you all right?" No answer. She knocked again. "Miss?"

Tyler stepped around her, his hand going to the doorknob.

"Tyler, wait." Olivia placed her hand on his.

"If she's not answering, she might have fainted again." Jana's worn, out-of-season shoes had a designer label and the torn gown had fit poorly, but her voice had been educated. Perhaps she had hit on hard times. But that didn't explain why she was wandering the shopping village when the stores were closed.

Olivia withdrew her hand and stepped aside. "Do what you think is best."

Tyler didn't take her unwavering trust lightly. He pushed the door open a few inches before it stopped. He cursed beneath his breath when he saw the woman's slim arm, her palm down. Slowly, not sure of what he'd find, he eased the door open a little more. There hadn't been any track marks on her arm, her pupils hadn't been dilated, but there had been a wild desperation in her face when she asked to use the restroom that had made him uneasy.

When the opening was wide enough, he slipped inside. Olivia was right behind him. By the time he'd done a cursory examination, his sister was kneeling by his side with a damp washcloth. Lifting the woman up, he took the cloth and ran it lightly over her pale face. Despite the obvious ravages, she was beautiful, her features delicate.

"Should we call an ambulance?" Olivia asked.

Tyler shook his dark head. "No. There are no broken bones or bumps."

"You better make sure. If she's hurt, you're liable," Cynthia said from the doorway.

"She could be running a scam," added her husband.

Olivia shook her head. "I don't think so."

Tyler agreed, and kept running the cloth over her face. She felt so light, his arm gently tightened around her as he tenderly bathed her fine-boned face.

The woman's lids fluttered, then opened. "W-what happened?"

"You fainted again," Tyler told her, helping her to sit upright. "Do you have any medical problems?"

She started to shake her head, then paused when the dizziness returned and said, "No."

"You better have her checked out just to make sure," Mr. Ingram said from the doorway. "People say that then sue later."

"Dennis is right, Olivia, I'd have her checked out," his wife commented. "You don't want any surprises down the road."

Tyler watched the woman lower her head and was afraid she was going to pass out again. "Miss?"

"I won't sue," came the soft whisper.

"If I had a dollar for every client that was told that, I could retire tomorrow," Dennis said.

Tyler didn't have to think long to recall the recent newspaper article touting the success of Midnight Dreams. "Perhaps it's best that we have a doctor check you out."

"I don't want to go to the hospital, and you can't make me." She closed her eyes for a moment, then reopened them. "I'll be on my way."

Tyler came to his feet bringing her with him, then released her. Almost immediately her legs buckled. His hand closed around her forearm. "I don't think so."

She glared at him. "You—you did that on purpose."

"It's either the hospital or the police. Your choice."

Her eyes widened. She paled even more. "I haven't done anything."

"That may be, but you're in no condition to go anyplace by yourself."

"I'm not your responsibility."

"I'd say that was true until you came into the store and fainted, which made my sister's store liable if you suffered any injuries. Or did you already know that?" Tyler asked, watching her closely.

She held his gaze. "Believe what you want, but you can't make me go to the hospital."

Tyler's eyes narrowed. All that bravado, yet she was trembling like a leaf. He admired courage, but not stupidity. Releasing her arm, he stepped back. "You know the way to the door, but this time, instead of reviving you, I'll notify the police. They'll take you to the hospital whether you want to go or not."

Her reaction was swift. "You bastard."

"I've been called worse." He nodded toward the door.

Jana took a step and the room swirled. She felt the soft hands of a woman and knew it was Olivia.

"Perhaps you should go to the hospital," Olivia suggested gently.

Jana decided to stop this nonsense in one surefire way. "I'm not paying."

"I don't recall asking you to." Tyler took her by the other arm and gazed at his anxious sister. "I suppose you want to go?"

"I'd like to make sure that she's all right."

Jana snorted, then turned her head away. "If you're so worried then you could call me a cab and pay him to take me to my place. Because if you think you'll stick me with the bill, you're in for a surprise."

Olivia's expression saddened. "I'll be responsible for the bill. Do you think you might be pregnant?" Shock raced across the woman's face. Olivia glanced at the woman's left hand. There were no rings. "I'm sorry if I insulted you."

"Save the apology. The only reason you care is because you don't want me to sue." No one had ever cared about her except her first ex-husband and she had blindly killed that love.

"The way you look, you can hardly blame her," Mrs. Ingram said from the doorway, looking down her nose at Jana.

Tyler felt the woman flinch. "Mr. and Mrs. Ingram, thanks for staying and for the advice. I'll see you out." He turned to Olivia. "Lock up. I'll wait for you outside, follow you home, then you can ride with me to the hospital."

"You just got back. I'll take her," Olivia protested.

Tyler was shaking his head before she even finished. Olivia was too easy a target. He was ninety-nine percent sure the woman wasn't running a scam, but the one percent bothered him. "We do it my way."

Olivia stared at him a few moments, then nodded. Tyler wasn't the type to change his mind once it was made up. "I'll just go inside to check on Griffin, then I'll come back downstairs."

"Let's go." His steps slow, Tyler started for the front door, his hand still around Jana's slim upper arm. His hand easily circled her arm. He wondered if she was fashionably thin on purpose.

Outside, he bid the Ingrams goodnight, then started for his truck. He felt Jana's resistance when he neared the vehicle. He glanced down and read the apprehension in her strained features. "You have nothing to fear from me."

"I'm not scared of any man," Jana told him. As if to underscore that point, she moved closer, letting her breasts brush against him, her free hand gliding suggestively down his chest. She should have thought of this sooner. "Why don't we go someplace quiet and I'll show you."

"Tyler?" came Olivia's hesitant voice.

Jana jumped, snatching her hand back, stumbling in her haste. Tyler caught her before she fell, his hand like a vise around her arm. "It seems your patient is recovering."

Jana felt heat surface to her face, but she held her head high. They were going home to a clean bed where they didn't have to prop a chair against the rickety door or listen to roaches, and heaven only knew what else, scuttle across the floor and fear they might get into the bed.

"Then I guess introductions are in order." Smiling, Olivia stuck out her hand. "I'm Olivia Sanders, and this is my brother, Tyler Maxwell."

Jana glanced from the extended hand to the small woman in front of her. *Play this for all it's worth,* a voice told her. She might get enough out of this to change hotels at least for a few days. She clasped the woman's small hand. But wasn't taking a chance in case they knew anyone in Priscilla's crowd. "Janet."

"What's your last name?" Tyler asked.

"Street," she replied.

"You live near here?"

"No."

"You ever fainted before?"

"No. Look, you're so anxious to go, let's go."

"Of course," Olivia said, pulling her car keys from her purse. "I'm sorry, introductions could have waited until later."

"A few minutes won't hurt, Olivia," Tyler said, his annoyance at Jana plain.

His sister nodded, then hurried to a white Lexus SUV parked a few spaces away and got in. Tyler waited until his sister backed out, then led Jana to his truck and opened the door. She started to get inside, then glanced back over her shoulder when he didn't release her.

"If I were you, I'd try to remember that Olivia is on your side. Lose the attitude."

He wasn't going to bully her. "I told you, men don't scare me."

"Maybe you haven't met the right man." None too gently he helped her into the cab of the truck, then slammed the door.

Twenty minutes later they entered the emergency room of Presbyterian Hospital. People spilled from the waiting room to outside on the sidewalk. The wails of small children and the moans of adults created an edgy cornucopia of sounds, and attested to the reason the clerk had said Jana might have to wait up to six hours to be seen. Jana had no intention of waiting that long.

As soon as they put her in a room and the nurse left, she planned to be right behind her. The only reason Tyler and Olivia were playing the Good Samaritans was fear of being sued. They needn't have worried.

Lawsuits took time, and in her case, she'd have to find a lawyer who'd work pro bono, which wasn't likely to happen. She was more concerned with returning to the motel and trying to get an extension on her rent. She'd seen a bus, but didn't know if any still ran to her side of town.

Somehow Jana's scheme didn't work out as planned. An hour after she was finally admitted and placed in a small cubical, her two watchdogs were still with her. At least her head had stopped swimming as she sat on the side of the gurney in an ugly hospital gown.

She was pretty sure she could have gotten rid of Olivia without any problem or talked her into a "loan," but Tyler was another story. He stared at her with those cold assessing eyes of his, giving away nothing. She stared right back. Not for anything would she reveal how his rejection had made her want to crawl under the covers.

"What's taking them so long?" Olivia glanced at her watch. "We've been here almost two hours. It's been over an hour since they put us in here."

"Why don't you two go get some coffee or something?" Jana suggested.

Tyler merely lifted an eyebrow and continued to lean against the wall on the far side of the room, a position he had assumed when they entered. He had a capacity for stillness that was unnerving, whereas Olivia was almost always in motion.

"I'm sorry, Janet. Would you like some coffee?"

What she'd like was food and for them to leave. "No."

Olivia glanced at her watch again. "I'm going to see if I can find out what's keeping them."

The door had barely closed before Jana said, "On second thought, I would like that coffee."

"Is that right?" Tyler said, not moving an inch.

Her mouth tightened. "Yes, it is."

"Olivia would never forgive me if I left and you ended up on the floor again." He kicked up the brim of his Stetson. "I'll wait."

Gritting her teeth Jana turned around too quickly. A wave of dizziness hit her and she had to jerk back to keep from falling on the floor. It was too much to hope he hadn't noticed. Taking it slower, she lay down and turned her back to him. Her bad luck was holding steady.

3

Julian Cortez strode through the crowded emergency room corridor of Presbyterian Hospital, his long-fingered hands stuffed in the pockets of his white lab coat, his gaze locked on the revolving door leading outside to freedom. That morning he'd been awakened from a sound sleep shortly before six by a phone call from a doctor in the emergency room saying that he was needed. The call had come more than sixteen exhaustive hours ago.

Julian was used to those calls. Even during his internship in surgery at Parkland Hospital, renowned for its trauma center, it had been clear that he had been gifted with the skill, dexterity, instincts, and sheer nerve to operate on mangled bodies and save lives.

He'd barely finished that case before there had been another. That time an idiotic young man who had learned the hard way that speed and alcohol don't mix. Julian had fought with death many times in his thirteen years as a doctor, first as a surgical resident, then in private practice. Today he had won. Tomorrow, who knew. He'd learned to take victories where he could.

He didn't notice the stares and wishful looks of the women, both employees and visitors, any more than he took note of the beating of his heart. Since medical school he'd been teased by classmates because woman were drawn to his dark, sensual looks.

Julian wasn't conceited, but he knew women found him attractive. There weren't many days that he didn't find at least one phone number stuffed in his lab coat pocket or on the windshield of his car.

If only they knew he thanked God that he bore a striking resemblance to his Cuban-born grandfather and not his father. Julian couldn't have stood looking daily into the mirror and seeing the face of the man who had made the lives of his family hell, the man who had let Julian's mother die needlessly.

Julian's hands clenched. He fought to push the old, bitter memory away. Velma Radford Cortez wouldn't have wanted him to blame or to hate. Her love had been boundless. Too bad she had loved a man who couldn't love her or his children the way they deserved. His mother was the reason he had gone into medicine, the reason it would always be his first passion.

He saw the petite woman in the middle of the hallway, turning around as if she was lost or looking for someone. Perhaps he noticed because she was wearing yellow and looked so fresh. When he neared she turned and saw him . . . and went still.

Then she started toward him. He'd been boldly approached before. He was too tired to even think about a woman, but tomorrow was another day. He was trying to decide what his response would be when she came to a stop in front of him.

"Dr. Cortez?" she said, her gaze going from the name written in black cursive on his lab coat to his face.

"Yes?" She had a sweet, almost breathless voice that was intriguing. Perhaps he wasn't as tired as he had first thought.

"I know you probably have a lot of emergency cases, but could you please take a moment to see Janet?" The woman bit her lip. "She walked off the street and fainted in my store's restroom. She's still unsteady. It's probably the heat, but I'm not sure."

For a moment Julian just stared. "You want me to see a patient?"

Her large brown eyes sparkled. "Could you, please? She's just down the hall."

Julian didn't know whether to laugh or be affronted. "Miss—"

"Dr. Cortez isn't on the ER staff, Mrs. Sanders. He's in private practice," said the charge nurse, a willowy brunette. "I've already told you that you have to wait. There are more pressing cases."

"How do you know Janet isn't one of those pressing cases? No one has even taken her blood pressure," Mrs. Sanders replied.

The nurse's eyes narrowed. "Be glad that she got a room."

Mrs. Sanders's mouth tightened, then she turned to Julian. "If you're in private practice, then you can see patients, can't you?"

Before Julian could answer, the charge nurse spoke again. "He's a trauma surgeon."

"Oh," Mrs. Sanders said, her shoulders drooping. "Forgive me."

Julian watched the woman turn away, her gaze searching the hallway again. She wasn't giving up. He admired her spunk. If there was a Mr. Sanders he was a lucky man.

"Sorry, Dr. Cortez. Have a good evening," the nurse said.

The nurse's eyes said she'd like to be going with him. His face expressionless, Julian nodded and continued on. Just as he passed Mrs. Sanders, she looked at him again. Worry shone in her eyes. His steps slowed. "Your friend is probably fine," he told her.

Mrs. Sanders crossed her arms over her soft, rounded breasts and shook her head of short auburn curls. "Neither Tyler nor I had seen her before she came into the store tonight. Two of my clients cautioned me to have her checked out to ensure she didn't claim she was injured when she passed out, but I just want to make sure she's all right."

Julian wondered who Tyler was. "Not many people would be that considerate."

She sighed, causing her breasts to rise again. Julian's interest peaked. "I learned long ago to live by my own standards and not other people's."

Julian's hand was lifting out of his pocket before he realized it. He balled it instead of brushing it across her face in reassurance. What was the matter with him? Too many long days were finally getting the best of him. "She'll be seen soon."

"I just have this feeling that she's had a difficult time," the woman said softly.

Julian didn't know what to say. He healed their bodies. Their minds were not his problem.

Her hands dropped to her sides. "Excuse me." She started to walk away.

"On the hunt for another doctor?" he asked impulsively, wondering why he didn't just leave.

"I may have better luck this time."

Her compassion moved him. The unspoken plea in her eyes, the unmistakable sadness tugged at him as few things in life ever had.

After his mother's needless death, he'd sworn he'd be the best doctor possible. He'd succeeded. His skills were almost legendary. So was his bedside manner. It was abominable. He was impatient, curt. Some said driven, and he was. His job was to heal their bodies, not be their bosom buddy. Yet, for some reason, he couldn't turn away from the woman in front of him.

"Perhaps you hit pay dirt the first time."

Her eyes widened as she realized he was going to help. "Thank you." Grabbing his arm, she pulled him down the hall and into the room. "I'm Olivia Sanders and this is Tyler Maxwell. Tyler, this is Dr. Cortez, a trauma surgeon, but he's agreed to see Janet."

Tyler came away from the wall and extended his hand, a half-smile on his lips. "Thank you, Dr. Cortez."

"I haven't done anything yet." He walked to the gurney with Olivia beside him. There was no reason for him to be upset that a man was with her, but he was.

Reaching out, Olivia gently touched Janet's arm. She lay on her side with her back to them. "Janet? Janet? Dr. Cortez is here."

Jana glanced over her shoulder. Her eyes widened with interest. The man was gorgeous. He had the face of a fallen angel with jet black hair, and the most beautiful golden eyes she had ever seen. She reacted automatically, her lashes dipped flirtatiously, her voice took on a seductive tone. "Aren't I the lucky one?"

"That remains to be seen," Dr. Cortez said, his voice clipped.

Jana's smile froze. She'd done it again. Even half starved and bone weary, she still reverted to type. Unerringly her gaze went to Tyler. His face was expressionless, yet she felt his disapproval as though he'd spoken it aloud. She made herself smile despite wanting to slink back under the covers.

"I'll get a nurse to assist me." Dr. Cortez went to the door and called. "Nurse." A pert brunette wearing scrubs appeared almost instantly. "Take her vitals."

"Yes, sir." The nurse removed the blood pressure cuff from a wall unit and placed it on Jana's right arm.

"Please excuse us," Dr. Cortez said to Olivia and Tyler.

Jana kept the smile on her face with an effort. She didn't care what any of them thought of her, she told herself as her nails bit into her clenched hands.

"Just relax," the nurse instructed.

"My sister and I will wait outside." Tyler curved his arm around a frowning Olivia and ushered her outside.

Sister. Ridiculously pleased, Julian turned to the patient.

Dr. Cortez's examination was quick but thorough. Five minutes later he lifted his head and draped the stethoscope around his neck. Finished with the nurse, he walked her to the door, then beckoned to Olivia and Tyler who waited just outside. "You can come in now."

Olivia saw Dr. Cortez's angry expression and rushed into the room. She hadn't missed Janet's attempt to flirt. Perhaps she had tried it again. Olivia couldn't blame her. The doctor was gorgeous. But he was the type of man she'd never look at twice. She never wanted another pretty man. "What is it?"

"There's nothing wrong with her that eating won't cure," Dr. Cortez snapped. "Next time you're on a crazy diet don't waste my time or the staff's," he said to Jana. "At least be woman enough to admit the problem."

"Must have slipped my mind," Jana said, but her voice wobbled.

"Don't be flippant!" he snapped, nearing the bed.

Olivia deliberately stepped between them. "I thank you for your help, but that's no way to talk to a patient."

"What?" Dr. Cortez's dark gaze zeroed in on her. "She knew why she fainted and kept this farce going in spite of seeing how concerned you were."

"Perhaps." Olivia stuck out her hand. "Thank you. I signed the admit papers to be responsible for the bill. If you'll let the admitting office know you saw Janet, I'll send you your fee."

Dr. Cortez was dumbfounded. He shook her hand as if in a daze. "Don't you understand she deliberately misled you?"

"Dieting is a very personal matter to some people," Olivia said. "Thank you for helping. As soon as Janet is dressed, we'll be leaving."

"You're taking her with you?" With each of Olivia's statements, his disbelief grew.

"Yes," Olivia said. Her ex-husband had taught her that things weren't always what they seemed. "Thank you again, Dr. Cortez. If you're ever in Highland Park Village, stop by Midnight Dreams."

His brows bunched. "What?"

She smiled. "It's a luxe linen shop."

Julian's frown only cleared marginally as he looked at Tyler. "You approve of this?"

"Against my better judgment."

"You sister is too naïve."

"Compassion doesn't mean I'm naïve," Olivia said, her mouth pouting becomingly.

Julian spoke to Tyler instead of addressing Olivia. "Is she always like this?"

"Always," Tyler answered easily.

Dr. Cortez glanced at Jana in irritation for taking advantage of Olivia, irrationally annoyed at Olivia for allowing it. "Mrs. Sanders, I hope you never trust the wrong person."

Pain shone briefly in Olivia's chocolate brown eyes, then it was gone. Instinctively, Julian knew a man was the cause. Inexplicably he wished he could take that memory away and replace it with . . . what?

Not understanding his protectiveness toward a woman who had decided to make herself the champion and guardian all rolled into one of a woman she'd just met, he decided it was time to leave. "Good-bye."

Tyler caught the door before it swung shut behind Julian. "I'll wait in the hall while she gets dressed, then we can take her home."

Olivia picked up the evening gown. "Are you comfortable with me helping you?"

Jana stared at her. First Olivia had helped, then defended her. Neither made any sense to Jana. No one did anything without hoping to get something in return. There had to be a reason Olivia was helping her. Jana just hadn't figured it out yet.

"Janet?"

Janet, not Jana. Now she understood. Olivia didn't know about her past. No one would help Jana. Pulling off the hospital gown, she reached for her dress.

Tyler didn't say anything as Olivia and Janet, arm in arm, emerged from the room. After a brief stop at the business office, they went to his truck. This time Tyler helped Janet into the seat in the back. Starting the truck, he pulled out of the parking lot. "Where to?"

"Any bus stop." Arms folded, Janet stared out the window.

His gaze caught hers in the rear view mirror. "It's late. Where to?"

Shrugging her shoulders she glanced out the window. "Interstate Motel on 1–35 at Kiest."

Tyler exchanged a look with Olivia and headed toward the freeway. He was familiar with the moderate- to low-income area. The woman sitting in the backseat didn't strike him as a resident of a motel for transients, but it was also used for clandestine meetings. She'd tried to come on to him *and* the doctor. Maybe she was meeting a man there. It was her life and none of his business. Once he got her home she was no longer his or Olivia's responsibility.

Jana wanted time to stand still. If that happened she wouldn't have to get out of the comfort and safety of the truck.

"Which unit?"

When had any of her wishes come true? "Number eight."

Tyler parked directly in front of the unit. The strong beams of the headlight clearly showed the paint-chipped door, dingy windows, and dying shrubs. It was the last stop for those on a road to nowhere.

Jana saw Tyler and his sister trade glances. They probably wanted to get away from there as fast as they could. Jana had felt the same way when she'd walked from the bus stop to the cheapest place to stay she'd been able to find. Some kind of crazy pride reared its ugly head. She didn't want them to know how much she hated this place. "Can't say it hasn't been interesting."

Jana reached for the door handle. By the time she was out of the car, Tyler was standing beside her.

Without a word he handed her the take-out bag of food. The aromas made her mouth water, her stomach growl. Her hands closed tightly around the sack. She'd been surprised when he'd stopped to pick up take-out and included her without Olivia prompting him to do so. "Guess I can always restart the diet tomorrow."

His eyes said he knew she lied. She told herself she didn't care. Looping three fingers through the plastic handle, she walked to the door and took the key from her clutch. Sticking it into the slot she waited for the green light to appear. It blinked red the third, then the fourth time she reinserted the key.

Her eyes closed. This couldn't be happening to her. Her head fell for a moment, then she turned and almosted bump into Tyler. Olivia was beside him.

"Problem?" he asked.

Although Jana's knees were shaking with fear, pride made her smile. "This happens all the time. I'll just go have them make another key."

"We'll just wait," Olivia said, her gaze going to the unit across the way where the music blared and three men lounged outside the door.

Clutching the key and her purse, Jana went to the office. Tyler held open the unpainted door for her and Olivia. The area was cramped with cheap furniture and pots of plastic plants covered with layers of dust. A few steps inside Jana saw her Gucci case by the waist-high counter. Her throat dried. "My key won't work."

The night clerk, a balding man with a beer belly and tobacco-stained teeth, grinned. "Rent was due at twelve. Maid packed your stuff."

She refused to look behind her to see their reaction. "I'll have it tomorrow. I promise."

His eyes roamed her body like greedy, silent fingers. He licked his dry, chapped lips. "Let me take care of the people behind you and then we can discuss it."

"Let's discuss it now." Tyler moved to stand beside Jana.

The man pulled his dropping pants back up over his stomach. "Just because you're anxious to get between the sheets, ain't no need to go off." His gaze cut to Jana. "Can't say I blame you though. After you leave I plan to have a little fun myself. Some women you can tell by lookin' at them that they're gonna give you a good time."

A sound like a growl came from Tyler. The grin slid from the manager's beefy face. He took one, then another cautious step backwards, as if fearing any sudden move would make Tyler come over the counter.

Tyler snatched up the suitcase. "Let's get out of here."

Olivia took Jana's arm and led her back to Tyler's truck. "Is there someone you want us to call?"

Jana looked away. "No. No one."

Olivia squeezed Jana's trembling hand in reassurance. "There is now."

Jana came to an abrupt halt. "What?"

"You have us." Steering Jana to the truck, Olivia opened the back door and ushered her inside. She quickly went to Tyler. "Janet needs a place to stay. Can she come home with us for a few days."

Tyler had known it was coming. "You know nothing about the woman."

"She'll be homeless if we don't help," Olivia reasoned.

"I'll get her another hotel room."

"I think she needs someone who cares just as much as she needs a place to stay."

Tyler stared at his tender-hearted sister. Olivia should have had a dozen kids to love and spoil instead of just Griffin. She had played the mother to her dolls from the time she could walk. Her nurturing instinct was strong. She'd just chosen the wrong man.

"I couldn't sleep at night if I turned my back on her," Olivia said softly.

Neither could he.

Tyler yanked the Stetson down on his head. He had been afraid of this, but he didn't voice his objections. Once Olivia got something into her head it was almost impossible to get out. "Just for the night."

Laughing, Olivia rushed to the truck and got inside. "Janet, you're going home with us."

Jana had already pegged Olivia as a do-gooder, the type of woman who picked up strays and tried to heal the wounds of those around her. Her brother was a different story. He'd immediately sized Jana up as someone he didn't want to know better. He was a good judge of character.

Her wary gaze followed Tyler as he put her luggage in the bed of the truck. "Does he know?"

"Of course." Olivia smiled brightly. "We live together. It's his house as well."

Fear of a lawsuit might have Olivia ensuring herself that Jana was all right, but it wouldn't extend to offering her a place to stay. There had been no mention of a husband nor was there a ring on her finger. She'd given no sign that she wanted anything from Jana except friendship. Jana couldn't remember a time that she was wanted simply for herself.

"You want me to come home with you?" Jana repeated, still disbelieving.

"Yes. It's about time the redecorated guest bedroom was used."

Jana's throat clogged. Relief swept through her. She didn't know what to say. Finally it came to her. "Thank you."

The Greek Revival–style home near Highland Park was beautiful and comfortably decorated. A skylight with intricate decorative plaster surround illuminated the entry. Olivia chatted gaily as she led Jana up the circular wrought-iron and marble staircase that extended upward two floors from the patterned wood flooring in the entry hall. "An elevator offers access to all three floors, but we seldom take it. Tyler thought of including it into the building plans so our parents won't have to take the stairs unless they want to when they visit."

On the second floor, she stopped and opened the last door on the east wing. "You should have everything you need."

Jana stepped cautiously inside and almost sighed with pleasure and relief. All the way there, she'd been afraid Olivia would change her mind.

The walls in the high-ceilinged room were buttery gold with deeply carved crown molding. A wood-burning fireplace with an oak mantel was directly across from the king-sized bed that was covered with a pale gold damask duvet with soft pastel undertones. On top of the bed were mounds of decorative pillows with lace accents and gold velvet strips. Coordinating draperies arches and swayed over tall, narrow windows.

Crossing the polished hardwood floor, Olivia removed the decorative pillows and placed them on the striped velvet bench at the end of the bed, then turned the duvet back to reveal hand-embroidered ivory sheeting with golden embroidery. The last time Jana had been this close to such luxury was five months ago in Seattle, the last stop on her downward slide into hell.

"Janet, are you all right? I asked if you needed anything else."

Jana stared at Olivia and realized she had been talking to her. "I'm sorry. No."

Olivia plumped the already fluffy pillows. "Here I am babbling and you need to eat and rest. I'll bring up a pot of tea, but please don't wait to eat." Straightening, she crossed the room and opened a door. "Bathroom complete with toiletries and the most luxurious towels made."

Jana didn't know what to say, what was expected of her. No one had ever given without expecting something in return.

Olivia crossed back to Jana and pressed her hand against her arm. "Eat and I'll bring the tea."

Jana's gaze followed Olivia and saw Tyler standing in the doorway. Her hands tightened on the plastic bag of food. He unnerved her. It was as if he could see right through her and what he saw he didn't like. He had helped her, but no one had to tell her he did so because of his sister.

Crossing the room, he put her suitcase on the edge of the bed. "I know you don't want me here, but . . . thank you," Jana said.

"I'm sorry for your problems, but know this, I won't have my sister hurt or taken for a ride because she expects everyone to be as open and honest as she is. We both know that that isn't the case."

What was there for her to say? He was right.

"You're here for tonight only," Tyler continued, "and then you're gone. I'll help you get a place."

In spite of herself thinking of the insect-infested motel room she'd just left made her shudder. She couldn't prevent the shiver that raced over her body.

"Someplace you won't be propositioned to pay the rent even if you're willing."

Jana flushed. Again, what could she say? She had been desperate, but she was so used to doing what came so easy to her, what had gotten her what she wanted since she was fifteen until five months ago when everything started to unravel.

"Here you are." Entering the room, Olivia sat the porcelain tea service on a small table by the French doors. "I didn't know what type you preferred with your meals so I brought several."

Jana preferred champagne. She could almost feel Tyler's condemning gaze boring into her. "I'm sure it's fine."

"Well, good night." Olivia affectionately looped her arm through Tyler's. "If you're an early riser or get hungry during the night the kitchen is to the left of the stairs. Griffin can attest that Wanda keeps it well stocked."

"Is Griffin your husband?" Jana asked and watched a shadow cross Olivia's face, and Tyler's lips thin.

"My son, and the most important person in the world to me. Good night."

"Good night," Jana said.

Tyler looked over his shoulder just before closing the door after him. There was a promise in those riveting black eyes of his: *Mess with my family at your own risk.*

Jana wished she could call his bluff, but she'd read another man wrong and it had cost her dearly. Licking her lips, she sat in the Queen Anne chair in front of the table and opened the containers. Picking up a fork she practically shoved the chicken parmesan, salad, and bread sticks into her mouth.

She'd eaten in the most exclusive restaurants in the world, but no food had ever tasted better. Even the English tea was good. She didn't stop eating until only fragments were left. Wiping her hands on the linen napkin, she looked around for a phone. Seeing one on the nightstand she walked over, glad the dizziness was gone.

Her hand hovered over the phone for a long moment before she picked it up and dialed. As the phone rang for a third, then a fourth time she bit her lips. It was almost midnight here and close to ten in San Francisco. Her mother didn't go to bed early, but she might be out on a Saturday night.

"Hello."

Jana sank onto the bed in relief. "Mother, it's me."

"I thought it was Raymond. He's out again with that woman. I know he is."

"Mother, I need your help." Jana's hand clenched on the receiver. "Please. I was locked out of my motel room because I couldn't pay the rent."

"Jana, I taught you to handle men to get what you want."

Sex was always the answer with her mother. Once Jana had thought the same way. "Mother, if you could just send me enough money to come home—"

"No."

"Mother, I fainted tonight—"

"You weren't stupid enough to get pregnant, were you?"

"No, I hadn't eaten because I didn't have any money," Jana said, shame washing over her.

"That's nonsense," her mother scoffed. "Men fall all over themselves for you. I should know, I taught you."

Jana sighed. "Ever since I left Charleston last year, things haven't been going well for me. I told you Gray's grandmother turned everyone against me."

"It's your own fault for trying to win your ex-husband back. He couldn't stand the sight of you after what you did to him." Jana's mother tsked. "You shouldn't have gotten caught."

Jana dropped her forehead into the palm of her hand. "Mother, I need your help."

"Jana, you're thirty-two years old. You can take care of yourself. Raymond and I need to be alone to work out our little differences."

"I wouldn't have to live there. I cou—"

"I think he's back. I have to go."

"Mo—" she began, then heard the dial tone. Her mother had hung up on her. Jana swallowed repeatedly until the lump disappeared from her throat. Slowly she replaced the receiver, then picked it up again and quickly dialed.

The phone was answered on the second ring by a drowsy male voice. "Hello."

"Father, I need—"

"I told you not to call me ever again."

"I don't have a place to stay."

"Call one of your men." The phone crashed down.

Her hand clutching the phone, Jana felt tears prick her eyes. "I called my father and my mother. Why can't you forgive me and she love me?"

She hung up the phone and glanced around the room. She had a place to stay for the night, but what about tomorrow? There was nothing left to pawn. Except for a few pieces, her couture wardrobe and all of her jewelry was strewn from Seattle to Texas. Dallas had not been a random choice. She was here because her father was less than thirty miles away . . . with his new wife and stepdaughter.

Jana had seen them once in Richmond when she'd gone home three years ago after her scandalous divorce from Gray. She hadn't been welcomed. Her mother had been with husband number three in Milan and hadn't wanted to be bothered. Jana, true to form, had crashed a dinner party her father was having for his wife and had left with her stepmother's sister's husband. Jana had foolishly done it out of spite, but it had proven to be another bridge burned. Neither her father nor his wife would ever forgive her.

She hadn't thought she cared until she'd faced death only months ago and realized there would be no one to mourn her if she died.

Getting up from the bed, she went to the window and brushed the heavy damask drapery aside. She was in the heart of a big city, people surrounded her, yet she was alone as she'd always been. She hadn't realized how friendless she was until five months ago when she'd almost died in an electrical fire in a night club.

Peter Wilson, her lover at the time, had shoved her aside trying to save himself. She'd fallen and bumped her head. Dazed, she'd laid there as the posh night club filled with smoke and the frantic screams of people trying to flee the greedy flames. If a man hadn't rescued her and carried her to safety, she almost certainly would have died. As it was, she was kept overnight in the hospital for smoke inhalation.

When she was released the next morning she went back to the hotel to find that Peter and the crowd she'd been partying with for the past month had flown to New York. No one had called to check on her nor had Peter left a plane ticket. He had paid for the hotel room for the balance of the week. Two days.

Angry and irate, she'd called people who ran with them, expecting them to be incensed on her behalf. In each instance they were on Peter's side. They all believed his lie that she had gone off with another man at the club and that Peter thought she was safe. Her pattern of leaving one man for another as the whim struck was well known. As always, the story told by the person with the most money and influence was deemed to be the truth.

Peter's family was very wealthy. On the other hand, Jana's father had disowned her. In a matter of days she learned she had badly miscalculated her appeal. Peter's lies coupled with the threat of her ex-husband's grandmother made Jana persona non grata.

Slipping off her shoes, Jana lay on the bed and curled into a tight knot. How was she going to survive? She'd thought she was so smart. She'd tossed away her life with both hands and had no idea how to get it back.

Her gaze fell on a distinctive figure on the beside table. A Fabergé Egg, intricately crafted with 24-carat gold, Austrian crystals, and hand-enameled guilloche. Slowly she sat up. With unsteady hands she carefully lifted the top to reveal a removable silver swan swimming on an aquamarine lake with water lilies.

She'd seen enough of the pieces to have a good idea of their worth. This particular egg probably cost close to three thousand dollars. Even a tenth of that would give her some breathing room. The thought that formed in her head made her tremble. *Take the egg.*

She hesitated. She'd never stolen anything in her life. But she'd never been this desperate either.

With the money from the sale of the egg she could possibly catch a redeye flight to San Francisco. Her mother would help her once she saw how badly Jana needed her. Her mother was just so worried about Raymond and her marriage that she couldn't think straight.

Getting up, Jana went to her suitcase and knelt down. Even as she unlocked the case and carefully wrapped the Fabergé Egg in a blouse, she felt her throat sting with tears of regret. Angrily she dashed the useless tears away and closed the case.

Olivia was stupid to let a stranger in her house. It was as much her fault as Jana's. Suddenly Jana recalled the promise of retribution in Tyler's eyes if she played Olivia. He'd show no mercy.

Jana got to her feet. She just had to make sure he never found out. After all, she was very good at games.

4

Tyler awoke early as usual. Almost instantly he recalled the woman sleeping a few doors down, which wasn't odd since he had spent a restless night thinking of her. She was oddly familiar, but he couldn't place her. He would. He never forgot a face, and hers was beautiful.

With a snort of disgust, Tyler tossed back the covers and headed for the shower. Janet was hiding something. And he'd bet his portfolio that she hadn't given them her real name. Pointing that out to Olivia wouldn't have mattered. Her only concern would be that Janet needed help.

Turning the shower on full blast, Tyler stepped beneath the six pulsating jets, his thoughts still on Janet. Not for an instance had she let the food go once he'd given it to her. She'd been half starved, but she hadn't bartered her body for food or the rent. Her fear and shame had been obvious at the motel. He had wanted to ram his fist in the clerk's smirking face.

Shutting off the water, he dried himself, then shaved. Her come-on to him and Dr. Cortez had been smooth and practiced, which was at odds with the shame and embarrassment he'd glimpsed in her eyes when they'd rebuffed her. He didn't like puzzles and Janet was certainly one.

Dressed and determined to put the woman out of his mind, he left his room for the kitchen and a cup of coffee. His time would be better spent working out the specifications for his next client.

Entering the gourmet kitchen with its barrel-vaulted ceiling, he came to an abrupt halt when he saw Janet, her back to him, standing in front of the large island. This morning she wore a straight, sleeveless sundress with faded pink flowers sprinkled over a dingy white background. The dress stopped several enticing inches above her knees and fit better than the gown she had worn last night, but it too showed she was having a rough time of it.

Again, he wondered what had brought her to this low point. And who was the real woman? The vulnerable one he caught glimpses of or the hard, manipulative woman who seduced with practiced ease?

He took a step closer, then halted when he saw Janet put something in the open suitcase in front of her. He stiffened with anger. "You didn't listen, I see."

Janet slammed the suitcase shut and spun around. He easily saw the fear in her large brown eyes.

He didn't hit women, but he was too furious to tell her that. "It takes a pretty low person to steal from someone who kept them from sleeping on the streets."

"It's just a couple of apples."

He quickly closed the distance between them. "So you're a liar *and* a thief."

She swallowed, glancing around the kitchen as if searching for an escape route. "I'm not a thief."

"Then you won't mind if I see what's inside." He reached for the case, just as she started to drag it down. The struggle was over almost before it began. He easily overpowered her, taking the case.

"Give that back to me!" she shouted. "You have no right."

Tyler fended her off with his hand on her chest careful not to touch her breasts, but it was becoming increasingly difficult with her trying to regain control of the case. "Stop it before you get hurt."

"Like you care."

She made the statement with such aching loneliness he almost felt sorry for her. "You don't make it easy to care."

Suddenly she stopped, crossed her arms and looked away. "Go ahead and look."

There it was again, the vulnerable woman. He placed the suitcase back on the island, but made no move to open it. Perhaps he should let it go. Whatever she'd taken from the house could be replaced. They were insured. He might steal too if he was faced with sleeping in the streets.

"What are you waiting for?"

He opened the case. On top was a nearly empty bottle of Joy, a neatly folded set of bath towels, toiletries from the guest bath, granola bars Olivia kept in the cookie jar for Griffin, two apples and an orange from the fruit bowl on the counter. He stared at her.

She flushed, then stalked over and reached for the items. Tyler brushed her hands aside and snapped the suitcase shut. "I've stayed in a few places where I wanted a towel that wasn't so rough it tore off a layer of skin or so stained I didn't want to use it." He placed the case of the floor and went to the refrigerator. "How about bacon and eggs for breakfast?"

Now it was she who stared at him.

His head tilted to one side. "Don't believe I can cook?"

"That you'd offer me breakfast," she answered frankly.

"Consider it my way of apologizing." He took out eggs, milk, butter and bacon. "Cups are in the cabinet above, if you want coffee. It's on an automatic timer." Pulling out a skillet, he placed the bacon inside. "You sleep all right?"

Jana eyed him a bit warily. She couldn't understand why he was being so cordial this morning. "No."

With his back to her, he began cracking eggs in a bowl. "You'll get there. Juice and yogurt in the fridge if you want something before I finish."

"I already had a yogurt." She couldn't very well carry that in her case, she thought as she poured coffee into a pretty rose-patterned cup. Passing up a meal would be stupid.

"Good, then have a seat."

Jana sat at the round oak table for six and and watched him cook on the six-burner cook top while she sipped her coffee. She'd thought she had him figured out. She'd been sure he'd get angry about her stealing the towels and the toilet articles. Instead he was cooking her breakfast. It would have been a different story if she'd taken the Fabergé Egg. But somehow she couldn't. She would have sworn she didn't have a conscience. Perhaps there was hope for her yet.

"Where are you from?"

Her hand jerked on the handle of the cup. "No place in particular."

He stopped tending the bacon and looked at her. "Everybody starts out someplace."

But few had probably started as high as she had and fallen so low. "Richmond."

"Do you still have family there?"

"I have no one," she said, trying to be blasé about her announcement, but from the slight catch in her voice she knew she hadn't been able to quite pull it off.

"By their choice or yours?"

Her head came up. No wonder she was uneasy around Tyler. He was too perceptive. "It doesn't matter. Is the food ready?"

"Almost." He turned back to the skillet and lifted out the meat, then grabbed another skillet and forked in butter. "Scrambled all right?"

"However I can get them," she answered, then tensed. She hadn't intended for her answer to be so revealing.

"Can you handle the toast?"

Her eyes widened. "You want me to make toast?"

He turned. "It won't make itself."

"All I did was ask," she said, getting to her feet. He could irritate her faster than anyone she could remember. "Where's the bread?"

Tyler went back to his eggs. "In the bread box."

Jana felt foolish. Of course it was in the bread box, but she'd never bothered with cooking. She'd taken pride in always having someone to do the most menial tasks for her. And look where that had gotten her.

"You all right?" He was frowning at her.

"Of course." She quickly popped bread in the four-slice toaster, then seeing that the eggs were almost ready, reached into the cabinets and got two plates.

"Thanks." Tyler finished dividing the eggs just as the toast popped up. "I'll take care of this. You have a seat."

Jana looked at Tyler busily buttering the toast and realized he must have thought she was getting dizzy again. Every time she thought she had him pegged, he'd change. "I feel fine." She put their plates on the table and sat down.

Just as Tyler joined Jana at the table Olivia and a young boy entered the kitchen. Olivia had her arm around the boy's shoulder and she was smiling down at him. He grinned up at her. The love between them was glaringly obvious. Jana couldn't remember a time either of her parents had put an arm around her.

"Good morning," Olivia said. "Janet, this handsome young man is my son, Griffin. Griffin, this is Janet Street."

The young man, clad in dress pants and a blue oxford shirt, stuck out his hand. "Pleased to meet you, Ms. Street."

Jana hadn't had much dealing with children so she followed Griffin's lead. "Pleased to meet you, Griffin."

Olivia brushed her hand affectionately across Griffin's neatly cut hair. "Come on, help me make French toast. You two want any?"

"None for me," Tyler said. "Janet?"

She did, but didn't have the courage to say so. "This is fine."

"My mama makes the best French toast in the whole wide world. She lets me put strawberries and whipped cream on top," Griffin said enthusiastically to Jana.

Olivia laughed. "We both love breakfast so I let us indulge every now and then. You might as well join us, Janet, so I won't feel like a glutton by myself."

"I want two slices," Griffin piped up as he got the whipped cream and strawberries from the refrigerator.

"Janet?" Olivia paused with the bread in her hand.

Temptation won. "I'll have a slice if it's not too much trouble."

"We have a system, don't we, Griffin?"

"Yes, ma'am." Griffin removed the cutting board and whisk from the drawer.

"Go ahead and eat," Olivia said, opening the refrigerator.

Jana reached for her fork just as Tyler lowered his head and blessed their food. She snatched her hand away, not knowing if she was to say anything or not. Her family had never bothered with saying grace, but then they seldom ate together either. Her father was always at some meeting and her mother had her friends, her clubs and her men.

Lifting his head, Tyler picked up his fork. "Dig in."

Jana didn't need to be told twice. It might have been because she was hungry, but the food was delicious. By the time she'd finished, Griffin personally served her French toast liberally sprinkled with powdered sugar and topped with strawberries and whipped cream. "Thank you."

"My mom said you didn't feel well last night. Grandmother says food always make a person feel better," he offered.

Jana's hand tightened on the fork. She wondered what else Olivia had said. "Your grandmother was right."

Griffin went back to help his mother, but Jana's appetite was gone.

"Do you really think Olivia would have discussed what happened last night with a seven-year-old boy?" Tyler asked quietly.

She didn't know what to think. Everything about Olivia was foreign to Jana so she chose to say nothing. It shouldn't have mattered that a child knew she hadn't been able to pay the rent in a seedy motel and had fainted from hunger, yet somehow it did.

Olivia frowned on seeing Janet's untouched French toast. "If you aren't feeling well I could fix you a tray."

"If you're getting hot like Grandmother I know where she keeps her little fan," Griffin announced, then cut into his toast.

Tyler stifled a laugh as did Olivia. "Griffin, I don't think your grandmother would like for you to mention to others about her need for a fan."

He swallowed a mouthful of food before speaking. "All right, but I'm glad I don't get too hot. I'd miss all the fun in the pool and the games with my friends. We're going to Water World this afternoon."

Olivia smiled indulgently at her son. "Have SUV, will travel."

Jana realized two things at once: Olivia hadn't discussed her, and Griffin was a lucky boy to have her for his mother. What might her life have been like if her mother had taught her about love and compassion instead of deceit and sexual prowess.

"Janet, if you're finished eating, we can go."

Jana froze. Her head whipped around to find Tyler standing. She didn't want to leave. "I . . ." She swallowed and tried to think of a reason to prolong her stay.

"I won't leave you stranded," he told her. "I'll put you up in a reputable

hotel suite where you can cook and I'll give you enough money to buy groceries for a couple of weeks. By that time you should have found a job."

Doing what? she almost asked. She had no skills . . . at least not any
you'd admit to on a resume. Jana slowly rose from the table. For a little
while she'd felt hope. Now there was nothing except a deep yearning in her
gut. "Goodbye, Olivia. Thank you."

Olivia came to her feet as well. "Goodbye, Janet and good luck."

Luck hadn't been on her side for some time now. She tried to smile, but
her facial muscles felt stiff.

Tyler grabbed her suitcase and headed for the front door, his strides long
and purposeful. He didn't look back. Another man who didn't want her
around. She couldn't blame him. Jana had no choice but to follow. Olivia and
Griffin trailed behind them.

Outside the sun was shining. There was a gentle breeze in the morning air,
bringing with it the scent of roses in the well-tended beds on either side of the
house. It was going to be a beautiful summer day. Jana stepped off the curved
steps and started toward Tyler's truck parked on the circular driveway. He
stood a bit impatiently with the passenger's door open.

"Mom, why is Ms. Street so sad?" Griffin asked.

"Because she's alone in the world," Olivia answered, her grip on her son
just a little bit tighter as she said a prayer that he would always have family
and friends who cared about him.

"No mother or uncle or grandparents or friends?"

"No one."

"I wouldn't like that."

She resisted the urge to kiss the top of his head. He was getting to that age
where he didn't want public displays of affection. "Neither would I," she said,
but she recalled a time when she had felt so very alone and isolated. She'd
been a young bride and so much in love. Then her world had shattered into
a thousand tiny pieces and she'd felt the same way. There'd been no one to
turn to, no one to tell her shameful secret to.

She'd been so gullible, so stupid to have been duped by her ex-husband.
Those had been the worst days of her life. She hadn't started to pull her life
back together until she'd felt the first flutter of life in her stomach. The life

growing inside her had pulled her out of her depression and self-pity and given her the courage to confide in Tyler the real degrading reason she had filed for divorce.

Instead of anger at her stupidity, he'd held her. Everyone needed someone sometimes. Yet Janet had said she had no one. From the dire circumstances of where she lived, she was right. No one should have to go through difficult times alone.

"Wait!" Olivia came off the porch and rushed to Janet.

The relief in Janet's face was obvious and made what Olivia had to say easier. Olivia wasn't a gambler, she'd tried once with disastrous consequences, but somehow she felt what she was about to do was right. "My regular sales person is quitting in a week. I was going to hire someone in any case because business at my linen boutique is growing. If you're interested in the job you can stay in the apartment over the garage for as long as you want. How about it?"

"It's already settled, Olivia. Get in, Janet."

"A woman can always change her mind," Olivia said, keeping her gaze fixed on Janet.

"If you don't want to live in a suite, I can take you to a hotel downtown and pay the rent in advance for a month," Tyler said.

Jana faced him. A month. It was a generous offer. Too generous. He wanted to make sure she left. She couldn't blame him for that. She didn't like herself very much either.

But if she took his offer what would happen to her when the month was up? Men weren't lining up at her door as they once had. Her mother was right about one thing. No man wanted a woman no one else wanted. Besides, with the amount of time she'd spent in beds, she knew bedding at least. Her life wasn't working the way she had been living it. Perhaps it was time to change it.

But could she trust someone when she herself had never been able to be trusted? "You're not just saying that? You'd really give me a job?"

"I'm a woman of my word."

"Olivia. Think about what you're doing," Tyler said ominously.

Olivia's gaze flickered to her brother, then back to Janet. "I am. All I ask is that you be honest, dependable, and courteous."

Jana was none of those things. Never had been. Didn't know if she could be.

"You can start Tuesday."

"Why not tomorrow?" Jana heard herself ask. Everyone had to start sometime.

"You'll need that time to get the garage apartment in order," Olivia explained. "No one has lived there since the gardener retired two years ago."

Olivia was offering a place to stay and a job. More than that, she was offering Jana a chance to get her life together. Perhaps it *was* possible to start over. "My name isn't Janet Street."

Tyler rolled his eyes. "We already figured that out."

Jana looked from one to the other. She'd thought she was so smart. Another reality she had to face. They'd known she was lying, yet they had still opened their wallets and their home to care for her. Her so-called friends hadn't done the same. In fact, they'd rejoiced at her fall from grace.

Yet this step was frightening. But even more frightening was the prospect of where she'd end up if she didn't turn her life around. She was at rock bottom. If she wanted to climb out of the pit she'd dug for herself, she had to start fresh. "My name is Jana Franklin."

There was no flash of recognition in their eyes, no stepping back in distaste.

Olivia extended her hand. "Pleased to meet you, Jana. Now, we have to get to Sunday school. Unpack, relax and make yourself at home. There's a pool in back. We'll be back around six." Smiling, Olivia returned to where Griffin waited and they entered the house and closed the door.

Jana wasn't looking forward to facing Tyler. He didn't want her here. Why that should hurt her she didn't know. She turned in spite of her trepidation. "I want this chance."

Tyler picked up her hand, held it despite her attempt to pull it back. He studied her palm. "Soft, not a callous anywhere despite the chipped nails." His dark eyes captured hers. "What's your story, Jana? You probably never worked a day in your life. That gown didn't go with your coloring, but the shoes fit and the few clothes in your suitcase have designer labels. What happened to you, and will it harm Olivia?"

She opened her mouth to lie, but moistened her lips instead as she gave herself time to think. If she wanted to change it had to be complete. "I don't know. I only know that this may be my last chance and I have to take it." She pulled her hand free and for a moment felt a wave of loneliness.

Once she had prided herself on not needing anyone because they always let her down. That was one lesson she wasn't going to forget. At best this was temporary. Taking the suitcase from Tyler, she reentered the house.

Eyes narrowed, Tyler watched her. There was buoyancy in her steps that generated a sway of her hips. It hadn't been there last night.

She was a strikingly beautiful woman with an innate sensuality that was almost palpable. She was trouble. He'd known that from the first moment he'd seen her. He'd been able to remain unmoved by her attempt at seduction because he'd known she was using it to distract him. If it had been real, he wasn't sure how he would have responded. He'd just have to watch himself.

Jana woke from her nap to hear someone knocking on her door. For a frightening moment she was afraid she was still in the motel and had only dreamed she had a job and a place to stay. She sprang upright in bed, then relaxed when she saw the tastefully decorated bedroom. Relief swept through her. Standing, she crossed to the door. Olivia stood there, her brow puckered in a frown.

Fear leaped into Jana's heart again. "You've changed your mind."

"No," Olivia quickly assured her. "I should have guessed you might be sleeping when you didn't answer the door. I'm sorry."

Jana tunneled a shaky hand through her hair. "It's all right."

Olivia's smile returned. "I just wanted to show you the apartment over the garage. Griffin is going to Water World with a friend and I'm joining them later. I thought we'd take a look together and see what's needed to make it habitable. I hope it's not in too bad a shape. Keats was a character."

"It's better than where I was sleeping."

Olivia scrunched up her face. "You haven't seen it yet."

"You didn't see my room," Jana returned and barely kept from shuddering.

"You have a point." Olivia held up an elongated key on a brass key ring. "You might want to change into something that you don't mind getting dirty."

"There isn't much else," Jana confessed, swiping her hand self-consciously over the Prada sundress she'd picked up on Rodeo Drive while on a shopping spree with one of the many men in her life. He was rich enough not to miss the several thousand dollars she'd spent that day. All the while, she'd kept telling herself she didn't care that her father was getting married that day and she hadn't been invited. That night, when her father was honeymooning in Hawaii with his new bride, she'd made sure her generous benefactor had gotten his money's worth.

Thinking how stupidly she'd behaved, Jana briefly shut her eyes.

Olivia mistook the reaction as embarrassment. "Don't worry. I have an idea." Taking Jana's arm, she headed down the wide hallway. "I should have thought of it right away. We're pretty casual at the shop." She glanced at the Manolos on Jana's feet. "We stand on our feet a lot."

"I can stay in these shoes for hours." In fact, she had last winter in Rome while shopping at the Spanish Steps. She'd frittered away her life in pursuit of pleasure and ended up with misery and despair.

Halfway down the hall Olivia stopped in front of a door and knocked. "You decent?"

Jana stiffened and stepped back instinctively knowing this was Tyler's bedroom. "Why are we here?"

"To get you a shirt," Olivia said just as the door opened. "None of my clothes would fit."

Tyler filled the doorway. His white shirt was open, revealing rock hard muscles and a flat stomach. "Yes?"

"Do you have a shirt Jana can put over her clothes while we get the apartment in order?"

His gaze tracked from Jana's face to her feet. She barely kept from squirming. "Sure." Turning, he went to the chest of drawers in the large room and came back with a folded light blue cotton shirt and handed it to Jana.

"Thank you."

He nodded. "Thought you were going to Water World?" he asked Olivia.

"I'm meeting them there, but I wanted to help Jana get settled," she said, taking the other woman's arm.

"Couldn't Wanda tackle the apartment?" he asked.

"Her arthritis has been bothering her lately. I hate to ask her to take on extra duty," Olivia explained. "I'd hire someone to help her if it wouldn't hurt her feelings."

He tapped his sister's pert nose. "You softie."

"She said you told her not to bother with your room," his sister told him, a smile on her lips.

He shifted uncomfortably. "Well."

Laughing, Olivia pulled Jana down the hall. "See you later."

Jana risked a peek over her shoulder. Tyler had walked into the hall, his hand propped on the door. Damn he had a body on him, hard with muscles that made a woman yearn. With all that intensity she bet he could drive a woman wild in bed. She tripped over her feet and flushed in embarrassment.

"You all right?" Olivia asked.

A man was the last thing she needed to be thinking about. "Better than I've been in months."

"Good, then let's go see your new home."

The Jana Franklin of three months ago, even three weeks ago, might have turned her nose up at the two-room apartment. The Jana Franklin who'd suffered degradation, humiliation, hunger, and eviction the night before stared at the room with hope shining in her eyes.

"The walls need a fresh coat of paint. The green tweed sofa has to go and so does the matching side chair," Olivia said. "Mother is a pack rat so you can look through the things in the attic for whatever pieces you need. We might even be able to find a replacement for the sofa and chair."

"Perhaps I'll just keep a dust cloth over it," Jana said, heartened that she could joke.

Olivia laughed. "Let's see about the bedroom. At least we know you'll have sheets."

The bedroom was considerably better, with a wide window and a full-sized sturdy oak bed, dresser, and nightstand. The bedspread was a nondescript plaid. The lamp was Tiffany. The area rug was Oriental.

"This has possibilities. There's linen in the house." Olivia put her hands on her hips. "You want to start in the kitchen?"

"You have to meet Griffin," Jana reminded Olivia.

Olivia glanced at her watch. "I have an hour to give you. Let's get the cleaning supplies out of the closet."

Jana touched Olivia's arm as they passed though the large, open area that served at the living area and connected to the kitchen. "I have a confession to make."

She stopped with her hand on the knob of the broom closet. Jana breathed a little easier to see patience not weariness. "Yes?"

"I've never cleaned a room in my life."

"Well." Olivia opened the door and pulled a broom, bucket and a mop and set them aside to reach for a package of sponges from beneath the sink. "That's going to change as of today. You game?"

Jana didn't hesitate to reach for the boom. All she had to do was remember the seedy motel room. "I can learn."

"I know you can." Olivia put the pail under the faucet and turned on the water. The cell phone clipped to her pants rang. Shutting off the water, Olivia pulled the phone from her pocket, saw the number and smiled.

"They're probably calling to tell me to hurry. Hello." The smile slid from her face. "You're sure he's all right?" She plopped down in a chair at the kitchen table only to quickly stand again. "Griffin, yes, baby, I'm on my way."

"Is he all right?" Jana asked, unsure why her heart rate had sped up.

"Yes. Thank God. But he sounded so frightened." Olivia swallowed hard, bit her lip, then started for the door. "He was horseplaying with his friends in the water and went under. It scared him enough that he wants me to come."

"Then you should go."

"I'll help you when I get back." Olivia raced out the door, and hurried down the stairs.

"Maybe you should get Tyler so he can drive," Jana called from the top of the stairs.

"I'm fine." Jumping into the SUV, Olivia backed out and took off.

Jana debated only for a moment before she raced down the stairs and into the house. She started up the stairs without slowing her pace.

"What's the rush?"

She whirled. Tyler was lounging against the door, his arms folded. Her stomach got that crazy feeling again. "It's Griffin."

Unfolding his arms, he quickly crossed to her. "What is it?"

"He's fine," she quickly told him. "He went under while horseplaying in the water. He wanted his mother and Olivia took off. She said she was fine, but she was shaky. I'm worried about her."

He whipped out his cell phone on the way to the front door and punched in a number. "Where are you?" he asked as he went down the steps toward his truck. "Pull over and I'll be there in five. I can make better time and I won't have to worry about you and Griffin."

Jana chewed on her lower lip and followed on his heels.

"All right, then we'll play it the hard way." He hung up the phone and jumped in the truck.

"She's not going to wait?" she asked, already knowing the answer. Olivia wanted to get to her son as soon as possible.

"You got it." Starting the motor, he backed up and took off.

Jana watched the truck disappear, then went back to the apartment. Griffin was lucky to have a mother like Olivia and an uncle who loved him just as much. Jana had a few relatives, but she'd never been close to any of them.

Jana went back to the apartment to lock the door. She couldn't possibly do this by herself. She'd just wait for Olivia. Yet even as the thought came, she was crossing the room to get the cleaning supplies. This was hers, at least for the time being. It wouldn't hurt to clean up the place just a little.

Late Sunday night Tyler pulled into the four-car garage beside Olivia's SUV. Luckily, he'd overtaken her when she'd stopped for a red light just before Stemmons Freeway. He'd gotten out of his car and walked over to hers. Her hands had been clenched around the steering wheel.

She'd kept brushing the heel of her hand against her eyes. All he'd said was Griffin needed his mother as much as she needed him and then he'd asked her to pull into the service station across the street. Fortunately she hadn't argued. He understood her terror. Hearing that Griffin was all right and actually seeing for herself was a world of difference.

She didn't breathe easier until she saw Griffin. They raced to meet each other. Griffin had tried to be brave in front of his friends, but hadn't been quite able to make it when his mother had pulled him tightly into her arms, chastising him and telling him how much she loved him, then banning him from the water park for life if he pulled anything like it again.

It had been difficult for her to let him go back into the plunging pool of water, but she'd done it. She didn't want to baby him. Trying to balance between not being too strict and being too lenient was difficult for any parent, but especially for a single parent who had gone through as much as Olivia had.

"I'm hungry, Mother."

Olivia brushed her hand across Griffin's head. "You ate less than an hour ago."

"Feels like it was days," Griffin said as he got out of the car. "I bet Uncle Tyler is hungry too."

He wasn't, but he thought of Jana. He had thought of her a great deal since she'd come to him out of concern for Olivia. He'd gotten the impression that she was all about self. "Can't help you out this time."

Griffin's shoulders slumped. "How do you expect me to go to sleep hungry?"

Olivia smiled down at him. "You can have a glass of milk and a graham cracker, but that's all."

He looked up at her and grinned. "I was thinking more of cookies and ice cream."

"Nice try." She wiggled her finger on his chest. "Let's go inside and get you into bed."

Tyler went inside with them, then headed for the stairs. He told himself he just wanted to thank Jana and let her know Griffin was all right, but he couldn't deny that something about her puzzled him as much as it drew him. He hadn't missed the calculating way she had tried to come onto him last night, but she'd been genuinely worried about Olivia. It was almost as if she were two people. Shaking his head, he knocked on the door, then knocked again.

He glanced at his watch. 8:39. He frowned, turning away to check the family room downstairs as a thought struck. Wheeling around he reached for the doorknob. He started to open it, then lifted his hand. He'd been wrong about her once.

"Is Jana all right?"

Tyler turned to see his sister, her hand on Griffin's shoulder. "She didn't answer."

A frown flitted across her brow. "Perhaps she's still working in the apartment."

Tyler recalled the soft hands and broken nails. "I doubt it."

"She's not downstairs. Where else could she be?"

"Good question," Tyler said. The thought that leaped into his head of her with another man wasn't comforting.

"Would you please go check the apartment? I didn't notice a light when we came in."

Neither had he. From now on he was going to keep tabs on their houseguest until he had her completely checked out.

"I could go with you," Griffin offered hopefully.

"Your uncle can handle things. You're going to bed." Olivia turned him firmly toward the opposite wing.

5

Tyler started back down the stairs. He'd check the apartment, but he didn't think Jana would be there. She'd fallen too easily into trying to tempt first him, then Dr. Cortez. More likely she had changed her mind and decided to strike out on her own. That thought bothered him more than he wanted to admit.

He went up the stairs to the garage apartment and knocked. "Jana." He didn't expect an answer and he didn't get one. This time he didn't hesitate to open the door. The scent of pine-scented cleaning solution greeted him. He flicked on the light.

The room was immaculate. There were even rose cuttings in a water glass on the kitchen table. Closing the door, he moved further into the open room, then into the adjoining bedroom and clicked on the light . . . and forgot to breathe.

Wearing only his shirt Jana was stretched out on her stomach, asleep. The tail had worked itself up her long legs to just below her hips. Legs he could easily imagine locked around his waist. He drew in a shuddering breath.

"Jana." His voice was husky, rough.

She smiled, snuggling deeper into the bed. Walking over he gently shook her shoulder. His hand wanted to linger on the soft skin, to explore. Resolutely he kept his gaze on her face. She had to get some clothes on before he lost it. "Jana, wake up."

Sooty lashes lifted, her eyes beckoned, her lips smiled a siren's smile. Her body arched sensuously as she reached up and curved her hand around his neck and brought his head down. Seconds before their lips met and he gave into temptation, he jerked his head back. "Jana!"

She blinked. Her eyes widened. She shrank back in the bed.

No one had to tell him that she'd done this countless times. He pushed the anger and the image away. "Olivia was worried about you."

"I . . . I'm sorry."

He didn't know if her apology made him feel better or worse. "I'll wait in the other room while you dress."

Jana watched Tyler leave the room and closed her eyes. The image of his shocked face remained. She'd been so tired after cleaning the apartment she'd laid down and promptly fallen asleep. Tyler had awakened her from a dream, a dream in which they were lovers. Her response had been automatic and calculated to keep him enraptured of her. What she'd done was show him again how easily she could use her body.

Sliding her legs off the bed, she took off his shirt and draped it on the footboard. She slipped back on her dress, then stepped into her heels. She glanced into the mirror over the dresser and tried to bring some order to her hair, but gave up when finger-combing only made it worse. She laughed, then pressed both hands over her mouth, afraid the laughter would turn into tears. She looked a mess. She'd probably repulsed Tyler more than anything.

"Jana?" he called from the other room.

Impatience was in each syllable. She couldn't blame him. Well, she wasn't going to hide. Head high, she left the bedroom.

Tyler stood with the apartment door open. She continued toward him without a word. So he couldn't stand to be in the same room with her. It wasn't the first time a man had thought that. Her heel caught on something and she stumbled.

Tyler reached out to steady her, then just as quickly let her go as if he couldn't stand to touch her. That wasn't a first either.

Jana bit her lip and closed the door behind them. Tyler started down the stairs, leaving her to follow. She did, slowly, her thoughts on her ex-husband, Gray Livingston.

Gray was handsome, charming, and wealthy. She'd consciously sought him out because her father admired him. By marrying Gray, she had hoped to gain her father's love. It hadn't happened.

Her father had claimed he was ill on the day of her wedding. A family friend had walked her down the aisle and given her away. Gray had done everything in his power to make up for the hurt that day and every day of their short marriage.

Angry at her father's abandonment, and that she couldn't get back at him, she had made Gray her target. She'd taken a lover barely three months after they were married. She'd even planned to get caught. What was the purpose of cheating if it didn't get back to her father, hurt him as he had hurt and humiliated her?

She'd been so sure she could manipulate Gray just as she'd done every other man, but his love and devotion had turned into hatred. She hadn't been able to accept that he had moved on, that she couldn't get him back. Her return to Charleston a year ago to show him he still loved her had started her on her downward spiral. Her ex was the first man beside her father that she couldn't control. She had a feeling the third one was walking in front of her.

Tyler opened the front door to the house and stepped aside. He was far enough away so they wouldn't touch. "Come into my office."

Jana didn't even think of disobeying him. She stopped just inside the office door he'd left open. There were three computers on a long table, a massive desk with two phones and a fax machine, a stone fireplace with a picture of Tyler, Olivia and what must have been their parents, and Griffin as an infant over the mantel, a dark brown leather sofa, side chairs, and wall-to-wall bookshelves reaching to the high ceiling.

"Close the door," he ordered from behind his desk.

She tried to think of something, anything to explain her behavior and take that look of disgust from his face, but nothing came to mind. She closed the door and faced him, her hands clenched.

"Olivia is a respected businesswoman. She's worked hard to establish that reputation and make a success of Midnight Dreams. You try to crawl into the pants of every man that enters the store and her business will suffer," he said bluntly.

Jana flinched despite having a good idea of why he'd asked her into his office. "I must have been dreaming."

"Were you dreaming last night when we were outside the store or when you first met Dr. Cortez?" he asked, his voice tight with anger.

She thought briefly of trying to explain, then realized if she did she'd be out the door even faster. Tyler indulged Olivia, but if he knew about Jana's past she'd be out of the house in a heartbeat. "I was just flirting. It won't happen again."

If anything, his expression hardened. "It if does, you're history. No second chance, no financial help."

She nodded and turned to leave.

"Don't underestimate me, Jana," he warned.

Opening the door, she left. He had given her fair warning. She believed him.

Why should she care what Tyler thought of her? She had a job and a clean place to stay. The opinion of a man shouldn't matter. She paused on the bottom of the stairs and looked at the closed door of his study and realized that it did.

Another first.

Jana didn't have much of a choice of what to wear so by seven-thirty she was dressed in a black boat-neck top and a slim black skirt. She hadn't slept well lately so it had been easy to get up. Since the apartment was clean there was no reason not to go to work. Besides, the quicker she started working, the sooner she'd feel as if she had some control over her life.

Stepping into her shoes, she glanced at herself in the full-length cheval mirror in the room in the main house and grimaced. It was plain tacky to wear the little black skirt without stockings. It couldn't be helped. Grabbing the small Fendi bag, she slipped the thin strap over her shoulder and headed downstairs.

She smelled the coffee at the bottom of the stairs. She paused briefly, then continued walking. It wasn't likely Tyler was up cooking breakfast again. Yesterday had probably been a fluke. His calloused hands indicated he was used to manual labor. His new truck told her nothing. In Texas every other vehicle on the road was a truck.

Entering the kitchen she saw Olivia in a pretty blue suit talking with a slender black woman who was at the stove. The older woman wore a white uniform and spotless white thick-soled shoes. Jana couldn't imagine her mother laughing with the cook, but then Jana couldn't imagine her mother doing anything that didn't revolve around self-indulgence and men.

Like mother, like daughter.

Olivia reached for her cup on the counter and saw her standing there. "Jana, good morning."

"Good morning," Jana said, watching Olivia closely in an attempt to gauge her reaction to the way she was dressed.

Picking up the delicate cup, Olivia wore a welcoming smile on her face. "Jana Franklin, please meet Wanda Simmons, friend, cook, and housekeeper. She takes care of us. We couldn't get along without her."

Wanda beamed. "It's not hard doing for people you care about." She nodded in Jana's direction. "Nice meeting you, Miss Franklin."

"Pleased to meet you." Unsure what to do next, Jana stayed where she was.

Olivia solved the problem. "Please have a seat and I'll get you a cup of coffee. Breakfast will be ready in a minute." Opening the cabinet, she removed a cup and saucer that matched hers. "You must be tired after cleaning the apartment by yourself."

Wanda turned to look at Jana again. She barely resisted squirming. "You cleaned that place all by yourself?"

"Once I got started I didn't see any reason to stop," Jana said, which was the truth as far as it went. She hadn't expected to feel pride and satisfaction with each task she'd completed. Deep down she'd been afraid of not being able to take care of herself.

"Know what you mean." Wanda placed the eggs she'd been scrambling in a chafing dish, then brought the dish to the table. "Sit down, Olivia, and keep your friend company."

Jana was so startled by the cook's announcement, she simply blinked. She couldn't recall anyone she knew actually being a friend.

Olivia sat with a smile. "Wanda bosses all of us."

Wanda placed a large platter of bacon, link sausage, and hash browns on the table. "Got grits if you want them."

"No, thanks," Olivia said, spreading her napkin on her lap.

"More for me," Tyler said, entering the kitchen.

"Me too," Griffin said from beside him.

Jana froze in reaching for her cup. If she hadn't been so hungry she might have gotten up and left.

Greetings were exchanged. Griffin took a seat next to his mother, leaving the seat beside Jana for Tyler. She could have sworn he hesitated.

"Here you are." The cereal bowl Wanda sat in front of Griffin was lightly sprinkled with brown sugar. Tyler's was brimming with butter and a liberal coating of brown sugar.

"You do know how to tempt a man."

Jana tensed. Then Wanda giggled like a schoolgirl and swatted Tyler on the shoulder with the ease of a long and dear friend and Jana knew that he hadn't just taken a swipe at her.

"You want something else, Miss Franklin?"

Jana quickly shook her head. She didn't want to draw Tyler's attention. "No."

"I'll say the blessing." Olivia bowed her head to do so. Afterwards she picked up the serving dish to serve Griffin, then handed the dish to Jana. "You sure you want to come in today?"

"Yes." She made herself take a smaller portion than she wanted. She passed the dish without looking at Tyler. She did the same thing the next time Olivia handed her the platter of food. "I feel fine."

"You must have slept well. You look better this morning, doesn't she, Tyler?" Olivia asked.

Jana couldn't help it. Her head lifted. He was staring at her, his black eyes narrowed, his mouth tight. "Maybe it was her dreams."

Jana flushed and concentrated on finishing her breakfast. Tyler had her number all right. Smart man.

After dropping Griffin off at a day camp, Olivia parked at the end of the short block where Midnight Dreams was located. It was a quarter past eight and only a few cars were in the shopping center.

Grabbing a large insulated bag from the back, Olivia started toward the store at a brisk pace. "I like to get a jump on the day so I usually start out early. If you want to come in later once you've been here a while, you can."

"This is fine," Jana said, lengthening her strides to keep up with Olivia. She didn't mind. She was anxious to get the day started as well.

Opening the front door, Olivia headed toward the back of the store. "I'll put our lunch in the refrigerator and be right back."

"Thank you again."

"Think nothing of it," Olivia reassured her. "I've always eaten lunch at the store. When I first stared out five years ago it was to save money and because I didn't have any help."

"But that's changed now, hasn't it?" Jana asked, stopping at the entrance to the back when Olivia went into a room across from the restroom. If Olivia was cutting off the alarm Jana didn't want to see it. She didn't want to give Tyler any ammunition to throw her out.

"Business is fantastic. Now I don't have the time or the inclination," came the laughing answer. A few moments later Olivia appeared with the insulated container still in her hand. "Come on, I'll show you the lounge. It's rather small, but it is well equipped."

Olivia was right, the area was tiny, but the thriving greenery and window curtained with white sheers over a white porcelain sink made the room welcoming. On the dot of counter space next to the sink were an automatic coffee maker and a smoothie machine. Beside it were a refrigerator, a cart with a microwave, and a toaster oven.

Opening the refrigerator, Olivia wedged the bag between a jar of pickles and mayonnaise. To Jana it was a miracle, because it was stocked so well. All that food had been so close and she hadn't known.

"I know it's overkill, but I like to be prepared when Griffin or Tyler drop by or I'm running late and leave the house without bringing anything. Then too, since I like to handwrite receipts and it takes longer, I like to offer clients refreshments." She closed the door. "Now, let me show you around."

"Does Tyler drop by often?" Jana asked, trying to keep the anxiety out of her voice.

"Unfortunately, no." Olivia stopped in front of the cherry writing desk on the sales floor. "He's busy with his own company."

Jana felt instant relief. She didn't have to worry about him popping up and checking on her.

"I guess I'll start from the beginning." For the first time Olivia paused, and the perpetual happiness disappeared from her eyes. "You've been considerate enough not to ask, but I'm divorced."

"I was too busy trying to figure out why you wanted to help me," Jana answered truthfully.

"Because you needed help."

"Tyler doesn't think so," Jana blurted.

"Tyler is very protective of me. He'll do anything to keep me from being hurt again," Olivia said with unexpected bluntness of her own.

Jana now knew the reason for the brief flashes of hurt and pain in Olivia's face when she asked the other night if Griffin was her husband . . . a man. Jana envied her because she'd gotten her life back on track. Jana wanted to do the same. "You survived."

"Yes, because of Griffin. Because of my family."

Jana had nothing and no one. As if realizing that, Olivia briefly pressed her hand to Jana's shoulder. "You have us now."

Not Tyler, Jana thought, but left the words unsaid. "So how did you get started?"

The smile returned to Olivia's face. "When Griffin was six months old I was flipping through a magazine when he was down for a nap and saw an article on a boutique in Manhattan that sold Porthault linen. It was the only outlet in the United States for the French manufacturer and most of their clients were from Texas. A hand-embroidered custom set can cost as much as twenty thousand dollars."

Jana was familiar with the brand. "It's the bedding of choice for the royal Windsors."

"You know about linens?" Olivia asked, surprise and delight in her face and voice.

Jana didn't know whether to laugh or hang her head in shame. "A bit."

"I just knew this would work out! Come with me." Olivia went to a twelve-foot-high wall of shelving near the front of the spacious store. "These are Frette sheets, favored by Italy's royals and the Pope. The couple the other night purchased a set. We also carry Yves Delorome, another French manufacturer, and Pratesia sheets from Italy that are manufactured from the top two percent of the world's Egyptian cotton, which helps give them an extra long life span of fourteen to twenty years, and Rivolta, the bedding of choice for the Mansion on Turtle Creek, the only five-star hotel in Dallas."

Jana noted that the Pratesia king-sized set detailed with handmade lace went for five thousand dollars. "The sheets I slept on last night were identical to these."

"The sales rep let me have them for almost nothing when I told him they were going in my guest bedroom." She chuckled. "He was hoping he'd get another sale from whoever slept on them."

"He's out of luck."

"We won't tell him," Olivia said in a confidential tone. "For many people, fabulous linens are the splurge of choice which is understandable since so much time is spent in bed, relaxing or sleeping."

Or other activities Jana thought. "They're also another status symbol."

"Exactly—and self-indulgent." Olivia ran her hand across the luxurious sheet. "I love the feel of them against my skin, and admit to having a collection, but it wouldn't make sense to put them on Griffin's bed and Tyler would have a fit if he knew that Wanda and I sneak them onto his bed when he's out of town."

"Why does he mind?" Jana asked before she could stop herself.

"Wasteful, he said. He'd rather put the money to better use. Tyler can be very practical."

"I hadn't noticed." Jana's tone was droll.

Olivia's mouth twitched. "Let me show you the rest of the store. I've recently added bathroom accessories, candles, and soaps. Bliss is one my favorite manufacturers of bath and body products and a favorite among customers." Olivia picked up a red and black box and held it out to Jana. "This is one of their candles in pear-vanilla. It's so soft and wonderful. I have one in my bedroom as well as the bath."

Jana tensed at the mention of Bliss. It was the firm Gray's wife had started with two of her friends. Not only had she taken Gray from her, she was also successful in her own right and had the support of his family, especially his grandmother, Corrine Livingston. From the first time they'd met, Corrine had barely tolerated Jana. It was Corrine's threat of retribution that had started Jana's life on a downward spiral while Gray's new wife had a charmed life. She had the man, the prestige, the wealth, the love and respect while Jana had nothing.

"Jana, what's the matter?"

She couldn't answer. Too many conflicting emotions, none of them good, raced through her.

Putting the candle back on the shelf, Olivia took Jana by the arm and helped her to a seat in front of the desk. "Maybe you should go home and rest."

Rest wouldn't help. She didn't have a home. Her life was a shambles while Gray and his new wife were happy with a baby on the way.

"I'll get my keys."

"Wait." Jana grabbed Olivia's arm. "Give me a moment."

Olivia hunkered down beside her, for once as unmoving as her brother, but Jana saw the concern. Would Olivia feel the same way if she knew about her past?

"Let me get you some water."

Jana released Olivia's hand because she sensed the other woman felt the need to do something to help. She took the bottled water because Olivia needed Jana to. The water was trickling down her throat when another realization struck. She'd been thinking about Olivia, not herself, when she'd accepted the water. A small insignificant act to some, but to Jana it was a milestone. If it was possible to do one unselfish act, she could do another and another.

She realized something else. Her own huge ego and disdain of the woman

Gray was seeing had set her on a path of self-destruction. She'd let her own vanity overrule common sense. During the last five months her ego had been trampled underfoot, the anger toward Gray's wife and his grandmother hadn't. She still thought of them and they probably never gave her a thought. It was time to put the past behind her once and for all.

She came to her feet. "I'll put this back in the refrigerator and then you can show me the rest of the store."

"You're sure you're up to it?"

"Positive." Jana turned, her hand clamped around the bottle. She was taking her life back no matter how difficult.

A few minutes before the store was to open Olivia's sales associate came rushing though the door. The leggy young woman was dressed in black and white pinstripe pants and a white blouse with short sleeves. Several silver bracelets jingled on her left wrist.

"Sorry I'm late, Olivia. The car was running on fumes. I had to stop and get gas." She swept strands of thick curly blonde hair behind her ear. Large hoop earrings dangled from her lobes.

"That's all right, Stella. It gave me time to show the new sales associate around. Jana Franklin, meet Stella Banks."

The two women shook hands. "You're going to love working here. Olivia is the best boss I've ever had and I'm not just saying that since I'm late."

"I've already found that out," Jana said.

"Now, I won't feel bad about leaving so abruptly, but this is a once-in-a-lifetime opportunity to go backpacking through Europe with friends." Stella almost danced with glee. "I can't believe in less than two weeks I'll be in Paris."

"Paris is beautiful this time of year," Jana said.

"Olivia told me. She's been there on buying trips." Stella sighed and hugged her large bag to her chest. "I'll go put my things up or I'll never stop talking about my trip."

"Have you traveled extensively?" Olivia asked Jana when Stella disappeared into the back.

"Yes," Jana answered, hoping she didn't ask for any more information.

"One day I hope to do more, when Griffin can go with me." Olivia went to the door. "It's ten. I better turn the closed sign over."

Jana breathed a sigh of relief. Honesty was draining. It was so much easier to lie, but Olivia deserved the truth . . . up to a point.

Jana sold exactly one item her first day at work and that was because it was to a repeat customer who knew exactly what she wanted. Fearing someone she knew might come into the store, she'd been tense all day, tending to hang in the background. Thankfully, no one had recognized her.

"You survived your first day," Olivia teased as they took the curved stone walkway from the garage to the house. Griffin raced ahead of them.

"Thanks to you and Stella for being so patient with me," Jana told her.

"We all have to learn." Olivia opened the back door to the kitchen for Jana, then followed. "Griffin, come out of that refrigerator. I'll have dinner on the table in just a minute."

He closed the refrigerator. "But I'm hungry now."

"When aren't you hungry?" Olivia handed him her attaché. "Please put this in my room, wash your hands and come back down to help set the table. Wanda mentioned she was cooking lasagna."

He raced over to get the case, then ran out of the room.

Olivia laughed, washed her hands, then put on oven mitts. "He loves any kind of pasta."

"Can I help?" Jana asked, feeling awkward. In this new role, she didn't know what was expected of her.

"Please get the salad out of the refrigerator." Olivia slid the lasagna out of the oven, then set it on a metal trivet on the table. "Wanda and I coordinate time so dinner will be ready when I get home. Tyler becomes so wrapped up with his work that he wouldn't remember to check on the food even with a timer. Believe me, we've tried. It's not unusual for him to forget to eat at times."

Jana removed the tossed salad in a clear bowl. She didn't want to talk about Tyler. "Wanda is a great cook."

"She sure is," Olivia answered just as the doorbell rang. "Please get that. It's probably the painter for the apartment."

Jana spun around. "I can't afford a painter."

Olivia paused with a Pewter basket filled with breadsticks. "It's my responsibility as the landlord to ensure that the apartment is in good shape."

"No. You've done too much already."

"You need a nice place," Olivia said as she placed the bread on the table.

Griffin raced back in the room and to the drawer for the flatware. "I washed my hands."

Olivia smiled. "Thank you."

The doorbell sounded again.

"I'll tell him we don't need him," Jana said and turned, almost bumping into Tyler. Her heart raced. She backed away. "Sorry, I—I didn't see you."

"Tyler, please tell Jana that the apartment hasn't been painted in years," Olivia requested. "The cabinets might need to be refinished as well."

"No." Jana tried to ignore Tyler's silent presence. "The apartment looks fine the way it is." Marking a wide arch around Tyler, she went to the door and opened it.

A good-looking man in his mid-thirties, neatly dressed in dark slacks and a blue striped cotton shirt, stood on the step. On seeing Jana, his eyes widened with undisguised interest. Belatedly, he tipped his cap. "Good evening. Don Jeffries to see Mrs. Sanders, please."

"I'm Mrs. Sanders." Olivia stepped around Jana, extending her hand. "Please come in."

He stepped inside, his gaze flickering to Jana before going back to Olivia. "You have a beautiful home."

"Thank you. I'm afraid I might have wasted your time." Olivia glanced at Jana. "We may not want the apartment painted. Could I please call you tomorrow?"

"Of course," he said. "Would you like me to look at the place and give you an estimate?"

"No," Jana quickly answered. The only way she could afford a painter was if he was free.

His appreciative gaze settled on Jana again. He pulled out a card and handed it to her. "Call me if you want me to come back out. I'm available anytime."

Jana knew when she was being checked out. The tingling in the back of her neck warned her that Tyler was listening to every word. "Thank you, but your services won't be needed." She opened the door. "Good-bye."

He left, but not before he gave her a long measured look that said, "I'm available."

"I still think you should have the apartment painted," Olivia said on the way back to the kitchen.

Jana didn't say anything. She was too aware of Tyler watching her with unmistakable disapproval.

6

She had done it again. Confused him.

Tyler had always known women were a mystery to him, but none had ever been as complicated as Jana. She hadn't taken advantage of Olivia and she hadn't taken the painter up on his blatant invitation. Tyler thought she'd do both. He'd thought she'd take the easy way out. He'd been wrong about a woman before, with devastating consequences. He didn't plan on it happening again.

"Thank you for dinner. I'm going to get my suitcase and go to the apartment." Jana started to rise. "Excuse me."

"No," Tyler said.

She had avoided looking at him through dinner, but now her head snapped around, her eyes widening. She sank back in her seat. He wanted her to leave.

"Look. Olivia's right. The place does need to be painted," he told her. "There's no sense moving until it's done."

She closed her eyes in relief and swallowed.

The sight tore at Tyler. He didn't want to care that she looked vulnerable and alone, but he did.

Her lids fluttered upward. "I can't—" She glanced at Griffin.

Tyler sensed her embarrassment. Griffin was paying more attention to his lasagna than them. "Olivia was right. It's the landlord's responsibility."

Jana's back straightened. "If it needs painting, then I can do it."

He never would have pegged her as stubborn. Trouble was, he kept trying to pigeonhole her and she wouldn't fit. "Do you know how to paint? Strip and varnish cabinets or the floor?"

Fury leaped in her dark eyes. She'd like to take his head off. Good, Tyler thought. He much preferred anger to vulnerability. "No."

"A professional can do it quicker and correctly the first time." He picked up his fork. He had been thinking about Jana so much that he hadn't eaten very much. "Painters tend to get an early start. You're welcome to go over and learn. Do you have a color preference?"

"No."

He frowned. He didn't care for her one-word answers.

"How about a deep rose?" Olivia asked. "Mother has some beautiful rose pieces in the attic. I distinctly remember an ottoman and a lamp. There may even be a pretty patchwork bedding set with multiple rose tones and patterns. We can go up and look at them after we finish dinner. There's a home-improvement store nearby where we can check out paint samples."

Jana looked at Olivia, not at Tyler. "Thank you. I'd like that."

Seems the lady carried a grudge, Tyler mused.

Jana might have liked it better if Tyler hadn't driven them to the home-improvement store. At least she was in the back with Griffin. She was still too aware of Tyler and his warning not to take advantage of Olivia. He didn't have to worry. Olivia's innate goodness more than Jana's fear of Tyler assured that that wouldn't happen.

While they were checking paint colors, a man introduced himself as a painter. He had finished a job that day and was looking for his next client. That he was in his early sixties and had his wife with him probably helped get him the job. Jana hadn't missed Tyler's disapproval of the other painter, but she had to agree with him. The man had been too flirty.

The next morning when the painter, Arnold Blair, arrived at seven with his two-man crew, Jana was there with Tyler. Tyler stressed that he wanted the job done right, but he wanted it completed as quickly as possible. Jana linked her fingers together. She would not be upset that he clearly wanted her out of the house and soon.

"You still want to learn?" Tyler asked, catching her off guard. They'd said very little after dinner last night and had only spoken this morning. "You have some time before you leave for work."

"All right." She was going to learn everything she could. She didn't like feeling helpless.

Tyler turned to the painter. "Do you mind a helper at zero pay?"

Mr. Blair caught on. "Miss, you might want to put on something over your clothes. Paint has a way of going where you don't want it sometimes."

Jana bit her lip, then went to the bedroom where she'd left Tyler's shirt. Slipping it on, she couldn't help feeling an inexplicable sense of intimacy. Shaking off the feeling, she joined the men. "Ready."

Mr. Blair handed her a paintbrush and pointed to the paint in the pan. "Go for it."

Bending, she slowly dipped the tip of the brush into the paint, then spread it across the wall, then repeated the motion. The lush rose color was beautiful. The furniture pieces she and Olivia had looked at last night in the attic would be perfect.

Pleased, she glanced over her shoulder at Tyler. Her heart stopped, then beat wildly. Tyler was smiling at her. This new, supportive Tyler could be trouble.

Julian Cortez was a decisive man. He had to be. Hesitation, even for a second, in the operating room could cost a life. Julian had wrestled more than one patient back from the jaws of death with his legendary skills as a trauma surgeon. So when he made up his mind to seek out Olivia Sanders, he did so at his earliest convenience.

Shortly after twelve Wednesday afternoon Julian parked in front of the Ralph Lauren store and got out of his Maserati. The door closed with a satisfying thump. He'd stood over enough mangled bodies that had to be cut from pretty sports cars to want a solid frame around him. Pretty packaging only went so far.

The same could be said, he supposed, of a woman. Olivia Sanders was pretty, but it was her unbendable spirit, her loyalty, even misplaced, that captured his interest.

His dark eyes narrowed behind his sunshades as he stared at Midnight Dreams across the street. He must have been in the shopping center at least a dozen times and had never noticed the shop. Pity. He would have liked to have met Olivia under different circumstances.

Checking the traffic, he crossed the busy one-way brick street. He wasn't sure of the reception, but he was sure he could get what he came after. Julian wasn't conceited, but he recognized his appeal to women. They had flocked to him for as long as he could remember. His mother hadn't thought that was necessarily a good thing.

She had told him more than once that people who only looked at the surface were only surface themselves. To find a person's true self, one had to look deeper. His mother had known what she was talking about. She'd married a man that made women's heads turn wherever he went, but he had been autocratic and cruel, ruling his wife and two sons with an unbending hand instead of love.

Julian stuffed his hands into his pockets as an old anger surged through him. His mother had died senselessly because an incompetent doctor had misdiagnosed her appendicitis for gastroenteritis, and because of his father's unwillingness to seek another opinion even though Julian begged him to do so. Julian would never forgive him for the pain his mother suffered.

Drawing his thoughts from the past, Julian opened the door to the boutique and pushed his shades atop his head of thick black wavy hair. The spacious store smelled faintly of a citrus scent he couldn't name, probably because to his immediate left was a glass étagère filled with candles, sachets, and soaps.

"Good evening. Can I help you?" asked a young woman.

"I'd like to see Olivia Sanders, please."

"She's at lunch. Is she expecting you?" asked the young woman, her warm gaze flickering over his face with blatant appreciation and interest.

"No, but it's important," he said. Once he made up his mind he didn't like wasting time. "My name is Dr. Julian Cortez. Do you know where she's having lunch?"

"She's in the back," the woman said. "If you'll wait here, I'll get her."

"Thank you," he responded.

Stella walked normally when she wanted to run. The instant she brushed the half-louvered doors aside, she raced into the lounge where Olivia and Jana were just finishing their salads. "Olivia, the most gorgeous man in the entire world is outside wanting to talk to you."

Olivia paled. Her hand went to her racing heart. "He . . . he couldn't be."

Jana shot up from her chair and rounded the small table. "Olivia, what is it?"

The smile slipped from Stella's face. "Dr. Cortez seems like a nice man. . . ."

"What?" Olivia said, jerking upright in her chair. Jana straightened.

"I'll get rid of him," Jana said.

"Wait," Olivia called, trying to get her heart to stop racing. She had thought Stella had been talking about her ex-husband Aaron. The man with the face of an angel and the soul of a devil. "I'll take care of it."

"I'm going with you," Jana said.

"Me too," Stella said.

Olivia looked from one to the other. How could she explain that she'd thought it was her ex-husband without opening herself up to more questions, questions that could ruin Griffin's life if they were answered? "If you want, but I'm sure it's not necessary. I was just surprised."

Getting up, Olivia went into the store with Jana and Stella close behind. Dr. Cortez looked up the instant she entered. He placed the bottle of perfumed ironing water back on the shelf. Oddly, her heart raced even more on seeing him. "Dr. Cortez, what a wonderful surprise. I'm happy you decided to visit the store."

"Hello, Ms. Sanders," he greeted, then his dark eyes widened on seeing Jana.

"Please call me Olivia." She crossed to him, still puzzled why he was there.

"Making house calls, Doc?" Jana asked, her arms folded, her hip cocked.

Julian wasn't easily intimidated. His father had tried. "Olivia, if I could have a few minutes of your time I'd appreciate it."

"We can use my office."

Julian followed Olivia past the two watchful women and into her office. She waved him to a seat in front of her desk, then sat. "What can I do for you?"

"Have dinner with me Saturday night?"

She blinked. "I beg your pardon?"

He almost smiled at the surprise on her face. "Have dinner with me Saturday night. You choose and I will make reservations."

"You're kidding."

Ok, the situation was no longer comical. "Why is it so difficult to believe I want to take you out?"

She flushed and Julian knew he had said the wrong thing. He tried to backpedal. "It isn't often that someone surprises me. And you did Saturday when you stuck up for a complete stranger. I'd like to get to know you better."

"I'm sorry. I have plans for Saturday night."

She didn't look sorry. "What night do you think you might be free?"

She placed her delicate hands on the desk and lightly laced her fingers together. "The truth of the matter is that I don't date."

For a moment he was the one who was stunned. "Ever?"

"Not in years." She turned a picture in a crystal frame around for him to see. In the photo she was grinning into the camera, her arms locked securely around a young boy whose grin was just as broad. "Between my son and the store I don't have time for anything else."

There had to be a very strong reason a woman stopped dating. He recalled his statement in the emergency room. "I guess you did trust the wrong man."

Olivia flinched and came to her feet. "I don't mean to be rude, but I have work to do."

Julian had no choice except to stand. He placed his business card in the center of the neat desk. "Just conversation and dinner. No strings."

"The answer remains the same."

"Then I don't guess I have any choice but to change your mind. Goodbye for now, Olivia." Julian left Olivia's office. What gave him hope was the brief flare of interest he'd seen in her face just before the door closed.

He wasn't surprised to see Jana pacing just outside the door.

"Why did you want to see Olivia alone?" she asked.

"I don't think it's any of your business."

She clamped her hands on her slim hips. "You might not tell me, but her brother will make mincemeat out of you if you hurt his sister."

"You mean like you tried to do?" he said, then instantly regretted the words as she paled. "I'm sorry. I shouldn't have said that. Guess I'm not in a good mood."

"Are you ever?"

"Occasionally." He flicked his sunshades back over his eyes. "Until the next time."

"There might not be a next time."

"I'd bet on it." Brushing past her, he nodded to the other sales clerk as he left the store. Olivia might not know it, but she'd presented him a challenge he couldn't resist.

"He asked me to have dinner with him and I said no. End of story."

Despite the arrogance of the man and his quickness to come down on her, Jana had to admit he was one handsome package. "I bet he was surprised."

Olivia's hand paused over the keyboard of the computer. "I'm not sure. Anyway, it's over."

"Well, *I'm* not so sure."

Olivia lifted her head. "What do you mean?"

"I got the impression he wasn't giving up." Jana folded her arms.

"He was just talking." Olivia gave her attention back to the computer. "Drop-dead gorgeous men don't date women who look like me."

Jana was so surprised by the statement that for a moment she didn't know what to say. "Women like you? What's wrong with you?"

Olivia's hands paused briefly, then continued typing. "Jana, please see if Stella needs any help and remind her to let you write up the next sale. She'll be off tomorrow and it will be just the two of us."

It was a dismissal. Clearly Olivia didn't want to talk about Dr. Cortez's interest in her. The old Jana would have considered it was no skin off her nose and not given it another thought. She might even have tried to get the man for herself, but that was before Olivia had stood up for her when no one else would.

Olivia needed someone, a friend, something Jana had never been to anyone. Jana didn't know how to do what Olivia did so effortlessly.

"Is there anything I can do?"

"I'm fine."

Then why are your hands trembling? Why won't you look at me? Unsure if she should voice the questions aloud, Jana quietly left the office feeling as if she'd let Olivia down. Being a friend wasn't easy.

It took Jana most of the day to try and work up her courage to ask Olivia for an advance on her salary. She'd done so much for her already. The painters were due to finish today. Last night when she'd gotten home she'd gone to check on their progress. The transformation was amazing.

Jana had gotten a kick out of sanding a small area on the cabinet. This morning she had applied varnish to the spot. But she still had a long ways to go before she was in control of her life. The fact was evident by her need to ask for an advance.

She'd waited until the store was closed and Stella gone. Olivia was at the desk in the showroom going over the day's receipts.

Jana rubbed her sweaty palm on her short skirt, trying to rehearse a speech. She who had once spent with wild abandon only had a dress, two tops and a skirt to her name and she was wearing the skirt.

Olivia glanced up before Jana could get the words past her dry throat. "Another day in retail. How does it feel?"

"Fine." Jana tried to work up moisture in her mouth. "I . . . er . . . know I haven't earned very much and you had the apartment painted, but could you possibly give me an advance on my salary?" She flushed. "I don't have anything else to wear." She'd worn the faded sundress the day before.

"Of course, and I know the perfect place to shop." Closing the books, Olivia stood. "I'll ask Tyler to pick up Griffin while I'm in back grabbing our purses and setting the alarm. Unfortunately, my son is very male in that he hates shopping."

Jana stared after Olivia, unable to believe it had been so easy. Perhaps she shouldn't have been so surprised. Olivia was the most unselfish person Jana had ever met.

In minutes Olivia was back and they were on their way. It didn't take them long to pull into a shopping center filled with a mixture of upscale shops. "We can try a regular store, but I used to get some real bargains at Secrets," Olivia said as she parallel parked.

Jana's eyes widened in surprise. "You shop resale?"

"At one time I was going to two or three social events a week and needed a different dress each time. Secrets saved my sanity and my banking account." Olivia emerged from the SUV. "Now I send a check to charity functions and stay at home with Griffin or just relax."

"I used to go out every night," Jana admitted.

"I'd rather be at home." After a car passed, they crossed the street.

Jana easily recalled the loneliness of being alone every night. The loneliness was the worst part of her being ostracized. "Don't you get lonely?"

"Occasionally, but it beats the alternative."

"What's that?" Jana stopped in front of Secret's stained-glass door.

"Falling in love with the wrong man."

From Jana's viewpoint falling in love with *any* man was disastrous. She never stayed with any man for that very reason. She wasn't going to be miserable like her parents.

Olivia opened the glass door of the store. "Let's see what we can find."

They found two summer dresses, two pairs of pants, three tops, and a pair of heeled sandals. The next stop was a grocery store. Jana was lost, but Olivia guided her. It was after nine when Olivia pulled into the garage.

Tyler came out of the back door of the house to greet them. "Been shopping?"

Jana's arms around the sack of groceries tightened. Why did Tyler always catch her when she least expected to see him? Last night he hadn't been at dinner. Olivia said he often became involved in his work and lost track of time. Jana wished that was the case now.

"Yes." Olivia handed him the bag of groceries she carried. "Please help Jana. I'm going upstairs to see Griffin and see how long he can pretend to be asleep."

"You don't have to help," Jana said.

Tyler plucked the bag of groceries from her arms. "Lead the way."

Deciding the quickest way to get rid of him was to do as directed, she reached back in the car for the handled shopping bag from Secrets and started up the stairs, very aware that Tyler was behind her and of the snug fit of her short black skirt.

She pushed the door open. Faint fumes from the paint remained. Tyler brushed by her, tickling her senses with the citrus fragrance he wore.

"You can just put them on the sofa," she told him.

Tyler kept walking toward the kitchen. Jana gritted her teeth and closed the door. Determined to ignore him, she put the shopping bag of clothes on the counter. "Thank you. I can manage from here."

Folding his arms, Tyler leaned against the cabinet. "So, how did today go?"

"Fine." What he wanted to know was had she tried to seduce any men. He'd probably be surprised to know that men had plummeted to the bottom of her list. Turning her back to him, she began pulling perishables from the sack and putting them in the refrigerator.

"I see you went shopping."

The refrigerator closed with a loud thump. "So that's it. You just want to know how much I fleeced Olivia for." Opening the bag, she thrust the grocery receipts toward him. "$58.79 for the groceries and $78.96 for the clothes. Olivia is going to take it out of my check. Fifty a week for the clothes, seventy-five for rent and another twenty for the painter." When Tyler made no move to take the receipts Jana tossed them on the table and reached for the handled bag of clothes. "You want to check?"

His silence caused her anger to escalate. Without a second thought she upended the bag over the table and ticked off the items inside. "Any more questions?"

"Yes." Tyler nodded toward the pile of clothes. "What about those?"

Jana looked down and gasped. Laying on top of the pile were several sets of lacy bras and matching panties. She distinctly recalled looking at the new items at Secrets and silently bemoaning the fact that she didn't have money to buy them. She was so tired of washing the pitiful few she had every other day.

"No answer?"

Her frantic gaze went back to Tyler. "I didn't steal them. Maybe the sales woman didn't see them in the bag," she said. Even to her own ears it sounded implausible.

Tyler hooked one long lean finger through a pair of black thongs. "It would be a wild coincidence if these fit, wouldn't it?"

She snatched the panties from his hand, ignoring her racing heart. Picking up the bag she put the undergarments inside. "I'm telling the truth."

"Then this might explain it." He bent and picked up a white sheet of paper from the floor. "It fell out when you emptied the bag."

Jana didn't see how, but she took the paper anyway. Although there were only three words written on it Jana had to read them twice. *A gift. Olivia.* Slowly Jana lifted her head. "She must have purchased them when I was in the dressing room. She's already done so much to help me. Why?"

"Because that's the way she is," Tyler answered easily.

"But that's crazy," Jana said, a bit dazed.

"Not to Olivia's way of thinking," he said with a wry twist of his mouth. "The more she gives, the happier she seems to be."

"People will take advantage of her," Jana said, angered by the thought.

"Not anymore. Not if I can help it," he answered, his voice tight.

Jana didn't doubt him for a moment. He'd do whatever it took to keep his family safe. Perhaps if her parents had cared as much . . . her thoughts trailed off. It was time to stop blaming her parents for her problems and concentrate on being the kind of person who'd inspire the kind of loyalty Olivia inspired.

Reaching for another bag she began putting the groceries away. "I told Dr. Cortez as much when he came by the store this afternoon."

"Why was he there?"

"To ask Olivia out." She turned to get the next items from the sack and found Tyler holding two cans of tuna. He was much too close. Silently taking the items, she put them on the shelf. "She turned him down, but I don't think he's giving up."

"I suppose you think she should have taken him up on his offer?"

Olivia accepted the box of cereal and the can of coffee before answering. "He's gorgeous, young, and rich."

"Is that all you require in a man?"

The question was voiced as mildly as the first one. When she glanced over her shoulder at Tyler, his expression was unreadable, yet her heart thumped. Time seemed to stand still.

Why did she have to be attracted to a man after all these years, and worse, to one who didn't trust her? She opened her mouth to give him a flippant answer, but somehow the words wouldn't come. "At one time."

"What changed your mind?"

"Doesn't matter." She moved to the next bag. Once again Tyler helped until all the groceries were stored. "I can finish the rest by myself."

"You do that very well."

She frowned. "Do what?"

"Push people away."

He saw too much. "Apparently not you."

"It just makes me wonder why." He reached out and grazed a finger down her cheek.

Desire raced though Jana. She jumped and staggered back. "Why did you do that?"

"Curious I guess." Folding his arms Tyler leaned back against the counter. "It's in my nature to try to solve puzzles. It's also how I make my living."

"You're a private investigator?"

"Computer system analysis," he told her. He grinned at the look of astonishment on her face.

"A computer geek?"

The smile widened. "And proud of it."

"It's hard to imagine you into computers," she said.

"What can you imagine me doing?" he asked, aware the question was leading.

From her sudden intake of breath, he guessed that her imagination was right on target with his. Her beneath him wringing cries of ecstasy from her lips.

So the attraction wasn't one-sided. He wasn't sure if that boded good or bad. She was hiding something. "Are you sleeping in the house tonight?"

"Yes. Olivia suggested I wait to move in to let the paint fumes completely dissipate," she told him, her voice unsteady.

"Makes sense." He lifted the handled bag. "Ready?"

She hesitated, then nodded. She jumped when his hand closed on her upper forearm. Acting as if he hadn't noticed her reaction he continued to the door. Neither spoke as they went down the steps and into the house. He handed her the bag at the bottom of the stairs. "Good night."

"You're not coming up?"

"I want to put in a few more hours on a program I'm working on."

She nodded, turned, then whirled back, her hand gripping the bag. "I know you have no reason to believe me, but I wouldn't take advantage of Olivia. I needed these things."

"You aren't used to asking for help, or getting it, are you?" he ventured.

"No."

"If you stick around here you will be."

"I don't understand you."

He smiled lazily. "A lot of people feel the same way. Are you hungry?"

For once she could answer that question truthfully. "No. Olivia and I grabbed a bite earlier. Good night."

"Night." Tyler watched her climb the stairs and wished he was climbing them with her. He took a slow, deep breath and another until he could feel the desire lessening. He didn't understand his attraction toward Jana, but he planned to keep it in check.

7

Thursday morning Jana woke up thirty minutes earlier than usual, dressed, and went downstairs to the kitchen in the house. If she planned to be self-sufficient and take care of herself she needed to learn how to cook. As she expected, Wanda was already in the kitchen. "Good morning, Wanda."

The cook turned from the double sink with a potato in one hand and a potato peeler in the other. "Good morning, Ms. Franklin. Can I get you anything?"

"Please call me Jana," she said, trying to work up her courage. As Tyler had guessed, she wasn't used to asking for help. "I can't cook. I've never even used a can opener. If you have time and it wouldn't interfere with your schedule, could you please teach me how?"

Wanda's thin face softened. "Of course, child. I taught Olivia's mother and Olivia, too." She motioned Jana over with the potato peeler. "Ain't nothing at all to cooking. You just got to have patience and practice. I don't suppose you've ever done this?"

"No." She couldn't recall ever peeling anything with a knife.

"This is where the practice comes in. Just hold the potato in your hand and start at one end and go to the other. Just like combing your hair." She demonstrated what she meant, then placed the potato in a bowl on the granite counter and reached for another. "Tyler likes fried potatoes for breakfast with his biscuits and sausage."

The thought of surprising Tyler with foods she had helped prepare had an unexpected appeal. "Can I try?"

"Sure." Wanda handed the potato and peeler to Jana. "You can do that while I start making the biscuits."

Jana tucked her lower lip between her teeth as she concentrated on sliding the instrument just beneath the potato skin. The cut wasn't as clean or as straight as Wanda's, but the peels mounted on the counter. "Finished."

Wanda looked over and nodded her approval. "While I roll out these biscuits you can peel and slice those onions on the counter in front of you, sauté them in butter and add the sliced potatoes." She dumped the dough on a floured cutting board. "Peel the onion under running water and your eyes won't tear. Together we'll have breakfast ready in no time."

Jana wasn't so sure, but she was willing to give it a try. She reached for the onion.

"You sure you cooked these potatoes by yourself?" Tyler asked, polishing off his second helping.

Pleased and proud, Jana couldn't quite believe it herself. "Next time I won't scorch them."

"They taste fine to me." Tyler leaned back in his chair and picked up his glass of orange juice. "What do you plan to cook for breakfast tomorrow?"

"What?" Jana's eyes widened.

"Don't you go teasing her, Tyler," Wanda admonished from across the room where she was stuffing pork chops for dinner. "Jana is going to be a fine cook. She's got patience and she's a quick learner."

Jana had heard the same praise from Wanda earlier and it meant just as much the second time. There were few times in her life she had been praised for anything that didn't have to do with the bedroom. Her parents certainly hadn't. "Thank you, but it's because you're such a wonderful teacher."

"She certainly is," Olivia agreed. "No matter how many times I burned the green beans, she never became angry or impatient with me."

Chuckling, Wanda shook her head of graying hair and placed the meat in the refrigerator. "Seems like every time Olivia cooked green beans there was a program on TV she wanted to watch more than she wanted to watch her cooking."

"I'm glad she can bake chocolate-chip cookies without burning them." Griffin smiled at his mother. "I'd sure like some tonight."

"We're having fruit salad." Olivia placed her napkin on the table and stood. "You two ready to go?"

"Yes, ma'am." Griffin finished his juice and rounded the table.

Jana came to her feet as well. "Ready."

Tyler stared up at her. "I'm still waiting for my answer."

"What would you like?" she asked. The words were barely out of her mouth when she realized how flirtatious they were.

Tyler's expression was interested more than annoyed. "Surprise me."

Relieved that he hadn't misinterpreted her answer, the tension seeped out of her. "I just might do that." Feeling more in control of her life than she had in months, Jana left the kitchen very much aware that Tyler was watching her every step of the way and annoyingly pleased that he was.

That day at work was considerably better than the first for Jana. She'd finally stopped tensing for fear of being recognized every time a customer entered. Instead, she'd greeted customers as warmly as Olivia and Stella did. It wasn't a coincidence that the majority of the customers she approached were women. Even without Tyler's comment, she'd already decided to steer clear of men.

That wasn't too difficult as most of the men who came into the store were dragged there by their wives or girlfriends. They generally made a beeline for the seat in front of the desk as soon as possible. In between helping customers she watched the men check their watch or frown at the women with them, who in turn threw them annoyed looks. It was obvious that neither were enjoying the shopping experience, which could mean a lost sale for Olivia.

Successful businessmen hated to waste time. That afternoon, when it happened again, she decided to intervene.

"Excuse me, sir, but would you like anything to drink while you wait? We have wine, coffee, tea, or sparkling juice. Or perhaps the *Wall Street Journal*?"

The well-dressed man in a gray pinstriped tailored suit who had been drumming his fingers glanced up at her. In his mid-fifties, he was distinguished looking with manicured nails and polished wing tips. "The *Journal* would be great. There's an article I wanted to read."

"Coming right up. With or without a drink?"

He glanced at the leggy blonde in deep conversation with Olivia. "With a white wine, please."

"I'll be back shortly." Jana was good as her word, sitting the wine within easy reach on the desk and handing him the newspaper. "Please let me or the other associate know if there is anything else we can do."

"Thanks." He took a sip of wine. "You may have saved my sanity, and my wife from becoming even more annoyed with me."

"We want the shopping experience to be pleasurable for everyone." Jana moved away. Glancing around to see if there was a customer who might need her assistance, she caught Olivia giving her a thumbs-up. Jana inclined her head in acknowledgement. The next man who came through the door she wasn't so sure how to approach.

"Tyler, I didn't expect to see you here." Was he checking on her again or was she being paranoid?

He shrugged and glanced around the shop. "I'm stuck."

She frowned. "I beg your pardon?"

His gaze settled back on her. "The computer program I'm working on. When I'm stuck I go for a drive. How are things going here?"

When people went on drives they did just that. He *was* checking on her. This morning's lighthearted banter hadn't meant anything to him. She could be offended or give him the information he wanted. Seeing Olivia pass with two sets of sheets for the woman customer helped Jana reach a decision. She felt she had contributed in some small way to the sale.

"Wonderful," she finally answered. She nodded to the couple at the desk and told him everything.

Tyler rubbed his chin. "I know how he felt. I detest shopping."

"Most men do," Jana agreed, straightening the towels on a display.

"I have an extra laptop and Palm Pilot. It wouldn't take much to set up a little work sta—"

"No." Jana held up her hand to punctuate her statement. "A woman might not mind her husband looking at the newspaper which is easy to put down, but I think we'd create more problems if he's in the middle of checking e-mail or other data and she wanted his opinion on anything and he didn't want to be interrupted."

"You might have a point. I tend to get lost when I'm on a roll."

"So Olivia tells me." The door behind them opened and two women entered. "Please excuse me." Jana went to greet the mother and daughter who wanted to browse. Tyler appeared to be waiting for her and since Olivia was still working with the couple, Jana went back to Tyler.

"Good luck in getting unstuck," she said, hoping to get him to leave.

"I already have. I just have to do a reconfiguration of the mainframe."

"Sounds reasonable to me."

He flashed her a grin that caused her stomach to do a flip-flop. "You don't know what I'm talking about, do you?"

"I understood what you said, I just don't know how it's done." She smiled. "Checking e-mail is about the extent of my computer knowledge."

"Then I'll have to teach you," Tyler said. "Can't have you living with us and not know about computers. See you at home."

"Drive safely." Jana watched him leave, a warm glow inside. *Home.*

"Would you like to go to church with me tonight?" Olivia asked as they sat around the table at dinner that night.

Jana choked on the lemonade she'd just drank. Tyler's broad hand slapped her between the shoulder blades.

"Jana, are you all right?" Olivia asked.

Holding up her hand for Tyler to stop beating her with what she thought was entirely too much enthusiasm, Jana took a small sip of the lemonade, trying to gather her thoughts. She could count on both hands the number of times she'd been in a church, and that had been for weddings and a funeral. "Church? Tonight?"

"Yes. I'm working with a group of ladies, putting together gift baskets for victims of domestic violence," Olivia explained.

ANY RICH MAN WILL DO   89

"The children's Sunday-school class is collecting toys for their children." Griffin speared his last wedge of pineapple. "We have some great stuff."

"But those things won't make up for not having a home where they don't have to be afraid," Olivia said quietly.

"It's so they'll know that other people and God care about them," Griffin said. "I didn't forget, Mama."

"We could use an extra pair of hands," Olivia said. "But if you're tired I understand."

Jana considered lying, at least until she remembered being afraid and ashamed in the motel's office and having no place to go, remembered where she'd slept a week ago. Maybe a lightning bolt wouldn't strike her for what she was. Maybe the women would see her for what she was trying to be now. "Not any more tired than you are. Count me in."

"Can you be ready to leave in ten minutes?"

"Sure." Jana took her plate to the sink before coming back to slide her purse over her shoulder. "I'll be back as soon as I drop off my suitcase at the apartment."

"Need any help?" Tyler asked.

Jana lifted a brow. He knew very well that a five-year-old could carry her half-empty suitcase.

"Did you have time to change the linen on the bed or get fresh towels?" he asked her.

She hadn't. "That didn't even cross my mind."

"Wanda is way ahead of you." Olivia came to her feet, picking up Tyler's plate. Griffin followed with his. "She put your linen in a big plastic tote in the utility room. Tyler, could you carry it over for her, please?"

"No problem. I'll meet you back here." He rolled to his feet with that easy strength of his.

Aware it was a waste of time to argue, Jana hurried to get her suitcase.

"Haven't spent much time in church, have you?" Tyler sat on the thirty-two gallon tote just inside Jana's door.

"What a brilliant deduction." She placed the suitcase beside the tote and came back outside.

His brow knitted. He'd never heard that particular snide tone before. He studied her closely. She was trembling. "You're scared."

"Olivia is waiting." As soon as he came though the door, she closed it and started down the stairs. He caught her arm midway. "Let me go."

His response was to catch her other arm. "I'm no great biblical scholar, but I do know the one place where you don't have to be scared to go is church. People might judge you, but God doesn't. Thank goodness, I finally learned that."

That got her attention. "What could *you* have done?"

"Plenty. At least according to Courtney." His mouth in a narrow line, he released her arms. "God forgives our sins. All you have to do is ask. He doesn't keep throwing them up in our faces. Any person who has a true relationship with God will do the same. The rest don't matter."

"This Courtney woman judged you?"

"As you said, Olivia is waiting." Taking her arm, he started back to the house. He'd said too much already.

Jana had planned on staying in the background once they met with the group of women at the church, but that didn't happen. Olivia was too well respected and liked. Jana was welcomed with friendly hugs and warm hand-shakes. She couldn't remember all the names or who was related to whom, but one thing she was certain of, there wasn't a Courtney among them. Jana was curious about the woman who had seemingly thought Tyler didn't measure up to her standards.

Initially Jana worked with Olivia filling the baskets, then she volunteered to take them to the end of the large open area where they were to be wrapped. On her second trip she cringed on seeing the uneven paper, the tilting, mis-shapen bows.

"They're all pretty pitiful, aren't they?"

Jana's head snapped up to see a very pregnant young woman with her hands on her bulging stomach staring at the crooked bow she'd just tied. "God will have his way, but I sure hope this is a boy."

"If not?" Jana asked.

The woman grinned. "I'm going to buy every type and color of barrettes I can find." She extended her hand. "Maggie Palmer."

"Jana Franklin," she said, smiling without thought.

"Pleased to meet you, Jana. Are you a visitor to our church?

"Yes, Olivia invited me."

"There's a special place in God's kingdom for Olivia. She gets such a joy out of helping. This was one of her many community project ideas." Maggie moved her hands to the small of her back. "I hate to send these out to women who have already gone through so much."

Jana wasn't surprised that Olivia hadn't mentioned that this was her special project. Olivia generally cared about people. Jana sensed in the pregnant woman the same compassion Olivia seemed to have in such abundance. "Maybe we could fix them."

Maggie's eyes widened. She moved from around the table. "Please."

"We'll have to cut the ribbon," Jana said cautiously.

Maggie picked up the scissors on the table and clipped the bows away. "Now what?"

Jana studied the crammed wicker baskets. They had been stuffed with the idea of getting in as many items as possible. Presentation hadn't been a consideration. However, presentation, as her mother had taught her, *was* everything. Perhaps one lesson her mother had drilled into her head would finally help.

Removing all the items from the basket nearest her, Jana began rearranging the bath and body products and all the other items chosen to make a woman feel pampered and special. She paused only briefly when she saw the Bliss label. Finished, she gathered the clear wrap and held it for Maggie to tie a knot. Picking up a roll of red satin ribbon, Jana coiled it over her hand, secured it with a wire, then attached it to the basket.

"It's beautiful," Maggie said and hugged Jana. "You're a lifesaver. I defy anyone to say God doesn't send someone to those in need."

Jana started to dispute the claim, thinking of her life in the last five months, then she recalled standing in a motel office almost broke, with no hope. "Even if you don't believe He'll help," she said softly.

Maggie stared at her. "Yes. God's mercy and unconditional love is for everyone."

"Amen." A tall, dark-skinned man in his mid-thirties came up to them. He curved his long arm lovingly around Maggie and extending his hand toward Jana. "Pastor Palmer. Welcome to Concord."

Realization hit Jana. Maggie was the pastor's wife. She glanced upward quickly, wondering about that lightning bolt. "Jana Franklin."

"Didn't she do a beautiful job on the basket?" Maggie reached for the basket, but her husband moved her hands aside. She made a face. "He thinks I'll break."

"I think you're eight months pregnant with our child." He held up the basket, then looked at Jana. "You did a wonderful job. We want to do two hundred of these. We plan fifty a night. If you don't mind I can have the other women in charge come over and you can teach them."

Jana wondered if he would want her help if he knew her past? Probably not.

He must have sensed her hesitation. "You'd be helping women, many of whom have lost hope," he said softly.

A woman like she had been just a short week ago. And since lightning hadn't struck, maybe there was hope for her yet. "Make the call."

Jana once had prided herself on her ability to enter a room and draw the gaze of every man there. It didn't matter if he desired her or not, it mattered that he had looked and for that space of time, she had more power than he. Yet somehow, as she listened to Olivia tell Tyler what had happened that night at the church, Jana wanted to squirm.

"You should have seen the beautiful baskets she created. Everyone was raving over them."

"So you're a hit?" Tyler leaned back lazily in his chair and smiled at Jana.

Jana moistened her lips. That man had a killer smile. "I just helped."

"She's being modest," Olivia said. "But the baskets started me thinking. Jana could do a few up to offer as gifts and see how they go. If they prove successful, we can offer them seasonally beginning with the Christmas holidays. What do you think, Jana?"

Jana was too stunned to think anything except Olivia's offer of help wasn't temporary. "I don't know, Olivia."

"I'm counting off the days until Christmas," Griffin said. "I've already started on my list."

"Why am I not surprised?" Olivia rubbed her hand across his head. "Think about it, Jana, and we can talk later. For now, it's bedtime for Griffin."

"I want to tell Uncle Tyler about what we did." Griffin started for his uncle.

Olivia caught him by the shirt collar. "You can tell him tomorrow. Good night." She herded her son out of Tyler's office.

Jana stared after them.

"Surprised?" Tyler pushed up from the chair.

"Yes," she answered without trying to guard her answer. "I haven't made any long-range plans in a long time."

"Well, now you can. But what about my surprise for breakfast?"

The realization slowly sank in that she had a job, a place to stay, but most importantly she was wanted. "You'll just have to wait until the morning. Night."

"I'll walk you to your place."

"You can't walk me out every night," she told him. "If you don't mind, I'd rather go by myself."

"I'll walk you to the back door and wait until you're inside."

Knowing that was as good as she was going to get, she accepted his offer. At the back door of the kitchen, she sprinted across the lawn. She'd never hurried anyplace except to spend money. Laughing, she went up the stairs, opened the door and stepped inside.

Her place. She allowed herself to bask in that knowledge for all of thirty seconds before she recalled she had promised Tyler a surprise for breakfast. Whatever it was, it wouldn't be the erotic scene she'd dreamed the day after they met.

Sternly chastising herself, she took her suitcase and the tote into the bedroom. She'd sworn off men, and Tyler was at the top of that list.

———

Tyler came downstairs the next morning unsure what Jana's surprise for breakfast would be. When Jana had asked him what he wanted, it was a good thing he'd been sitting down or she would have known exactly what he wanted. The two of them naked in bed. If he wasn't careful he'd be in just as much trouble this morning.

Nearing the kitchen he caught the scent of coffee. He sniffed the air, trying to see if he could detect what she'd cooked. Somehow he couldn't imagine Jana as the homemaker type, but he could easily imagine them wrapped in moonlight and in each other's arms.

Annoyed that he couldn't stop thinking about the two of them in bed, he entered the kitchen and saw Jana, Wanda, Olivia, and Griffin huddled together. They all looked like the cat that swallowed the canary. "Good morning and where is my surprise?"

Griffin giggled. "Good morning, Uncle Tyler. You're really going to be surprised."

Tyler pulled out a chair and sat. "Well?"

Olivia pressed her fingertips over her mouth. Wanda folded her arms. Jana turned away from him then turned back. In her hands were a cup and a small porcelain pot.

"Tea?"

"Perhaps." Jana sat the cup in front of him and poured.

He looked from the rich chocolate streaming from the sprout to Jana. "You're kidding, right?"

"You're surprised, aren't you? After all you didn't *specify*."

Griffin laughed. "You always have to be specific when you want something. I learned that from watching the genie cartoons."

"I stand corrected and chastised." Tyler picked up his cup. Steam curled upward. "You made this by yourself?"

"Yes, and since you're being such a good sport, you can have your second surprise."

"Marshmallows?" He'd never seen that sparkle in her eyes before. It intrigued him and beckoned, and he was pleased he was the cause.

Smiling impishly, she opened the lid of the creamer in front of him with a flourish. It was brimming with miniature marshmallows. He promptly put several in his cup, fascinated by the becoming change in Jana. She could definitely be trouble if he wasn't careful.

Later that morning Olivia paused in making the bed on the showroom floor with hand-embroidered linen and thought she shouldn't have a care in the world. Griffin was healthy and happy. She had a wonderful family who loved her. Business was booming. Jana was settling in nicely.

Yet Olivia continued to be restless, especially at night. She couldn't ignore any longer the very annoying reason. Dr. Julian Cortez.

She snapped the sheet tight and tucked it in. She was attracted to him, and no matter how busy she kept herself, thoughts of him would slip into her mind when she least expected them to. Worse yet were the wildly erotic dreams that each morning left her body yearning and tangled up in the sheets.

The cold, brisk showers weren't helping. It was becoming more difficult to keep a smile on her face and concentrate on the conversation at home and at work. Last night at the dinner table, Tyler and Griffin kept having to repeat themselves. That was unacceptable. Nothing could come between her and Griffin, least of all a man.

She was aware that Tyler was becoming concerned about her, but how could she admit that she was almost afraid to go to sleep for fear she'd dream about a man she'd met twice. It was Dr. Cortez's fault for disrupting her orderly life. She'd been content without a man. One heart-stopping smile from Julian and that had changed. She picked up a neck roll, but instead of placing it on the bed, simply held it to her chest.

"Are you all right?"

Olivia glanced around to see Jana staring at her with a puzzled frown on her face. "Did you say something?"

"I asked if you were all right. You've been staring into space, clutching that pillow for over a minute. That isn't like you."

Olivia placed the pillow on the bed. "Just thinking," she said, trying to stick as close to the truth as possible, but Jana didn't look as if she believed her any more than she had the other times she'd asked during the day. "How does the bed look?"

"Comfortable and inviting," Jana told her. "I'd certainly drop the three thousand dollars to take the complete set home with me."

Olivia looked at the wide bed with the covers turned back. On the night-stand was a pear-vanilla candle in a crystal holder, a book of poems, and a crystal lamp. The scene was set for lovers. Her thoughts veered to Dr. Cortez and her body heated. She clenched her hands again.

"You're thinking about him, aren't you?"

Olivia whirled around. "Yes." It was almost a relief to say it.

"I'd think something was wrong with you if you weren't," Jana said. "You probably threw him when you refused to go out with him. He's probably not used to women saying no."

Olivia smoothed her hands over the already neat bed. "Then he shouldn't come back."

"Is that what you really want?"

Olivia straightened, opened her mouth, then closed it. "Yes, especially af-ter the dreams I keep having."

"That bad or that good?"

Olivia blew out a breath. "Depends on how you look at it. They're very erotic."

"Those are the only kind to have."

"Not for me. I'm a mother."

"You're also a woman. You're young, pretty. It's reasonable to be attracted to a man."

Olivia was already shaking her head. "I won't go through that again."

"Through what?"

Olivia started as if just realizing what she had said. "Nothing. I need to make a few phone calls."

"Olivia, I'm probably the last person in the world to try and give advice about men, but don't let one bad experience turn you off from all men," Jana told her.

"I need to do some work in the back." This time Olivia made good her es-cape.

The door opened and a middle-aged woman came in. Her bag was Her-mès, her suit Dior, the pearls at her throat large and lustrous. Her hair was perfectly coiffured, her posture finishing-school correct. It had taken only seconds for Jana to size the woman up as being able to afford anything in the store many times over.

Most of her sales thus far had been low-ticket items. This customer could change things dramatically and pay Olivia back a little for all she'd done for Jana.

Smiling her brightest, Jana went to the woman. "Good evening, and welcome to Midnight Dreams. Can I help you with anything in particular or would you like to browse?"

"I was just . . ." Her voice trailed off, her eyes narrowed, "Excuse me, but have we met?"

Jana felt as if her heart had dropped onto the floor. She didn't remember the woman, but she'd never paid that much attention to the women, only the men. She kept the smile on her face with an effort. "I don't think so. I seem to have one of those faces."

"You look so familiar."

"Mrs.—"

"Fulton. Mrs. Robert Fulton."

Jana recognized the name, but thank goodness had never been involved with the real estate developer.

"Mrs. Fulton, what an honor. I'm sure I would have remembered meeting you. I haven't been in Dallas long, but Mr. Fulton is very well known throughout the country," Jana gushed. She might not have played the game, but she knew how it was done.

Mrs. Fulton preened. "I'm involved in a great many charities. We believe in giving back."

And what's the sense of giving money if no one knows about it? "The community is fortunate to have two philanthropic patrons such as you and your husband. If there is anything I can do to make your shopping experience at Midnight Dreams more enjoyable, please don't hesitate to let me know."

"Robert recently purchased a yacht and I understand Frette sheets can be custom made with monograms," Mrs. Fulton said.

Only because Jana was used to the extravagance of people and had been indulgent herself was she able to keep from showing her excitement. "Frette sheets are sublime and can be made in a wide range of fabrics and colors to complement the yacht interior. If you'd come this way and have a seat, I'll get the owner, Olivia Sanders, and she can show you the sample book."

"That would be wonderful." Mrs. Fulton took her seat, setting the ten-thousand-dollar bag in her lap.

Jana plucked a little table from a display and set it beside her. "Would you like Perrier, wine or sparkling juice?"

"White wine, if you have it?" She placed the bag on the table.

"We do. I won't be but a moment." Jana headed for Olivia's office, closing the open door behind her. "Mrs. Robert Fulton is outside. She wants Frette monogram sheets for the yacht her husband recently purchased."

Olivia's eyes gleamed. She immediately came to her feet. "Then she's come to the right place."

"Same thing I thought. I'll get her wine." Jana said, heading to the lounge. By the time she placed the glass of wine on the small table next to the handbag, Mrs. Fulton had several swatches in her lap.

"Thank you," she said. "You've been very kind. I didn't get your name."

She hesitated a beat too long.

"Jana Franklin," Olivia supplied.

"Thank you, Jana," Mrs. Fulton said, then returned at looking through the sample book.

Jana left the two women alone. She'd dodged that bullet, but what about the next time?

She bit her lower lip. The people who traveled in the wealthy circles where she had once been welcome were relatively small. Many of them were self-indulgent, bent on one-upmanship and reigning supreme as the wealthiest of the wealthiest. Midnight Dreams catered to that need to say "Hey, look at me. I dropped sixty thousand dollars on sheets for my yacht." Sooner or later a customer would walk though the door and recognize her.

And when that happened, she'd have to leave.

8

Jana did her best to join Olivia in the impromptu celebration of the sale. Mrs. Fulton had come prepared with the measurements and used her black American Express credit card that cost ten-thousand dollars a year for the privilege to carry it to pay for the order. But Jana couldn't shake the worry that time was running out for her.

"You're the reason for the sale," Olivia said, touching her glass of sparking juice against Jana's. "She told me just before she left that she was impressed with your friendliness and knowledge."

"It was nothing," Jana mumbled, taking a small sip, thinking of all the times sales associates had stroked her ego and she'd fallen for it.

"You're too modest. I've already called in the order and put a rush on it since she wants them for the launch party in a month." Olivia finished the juice and began rinsing the glass. "I better get back out there."

"I'll go." Jana finished her drink and took over rinsing both glasses.

"All right, but you don't seem very excited about the commission."

"Commission?" Jana turned around, her eyes wide.

Olivia laughed. "I thought that would get your attention. I didn't mention it because some people I've hired have tried to pressure customers. This way, it's a nice surprise and we both see if the fit is right."

Jana's heart raced. "How much?"

"Five percent of this." Olivia held a piece of letterhead paper.

For a moment Jana couldn't catch her breath. The sale was more than she had estimated.

"Sit down." Olivia helped her to a chair. "I'm sorry. I thought you'd be happy."

"I am . . . it's just . . ." Jana shook her head.

"I heard the front door. Will you be all right?"

"Go." Eyes closed, Jana took one slow breath after the other. She had money. She wasn't destitute any longer.

"Does good news always affect you this way?"

Her eyes snapped open to see Tyler, tall, lean, and male. The pulse that had been trying to settle sped up again. Would there ever be a time he didn't affect her? He crouched down in front of her. "A customer came in with me or Olivia would be back here with you. You all right?"

"I have money," she said, her voice shaky and filled with wonder.

"Yes, you do." His hand swept her hair back from her face. "What's the first thing you plan to do with it?"

She shook her head, swallowed. For so long she hadn't had the freedom to have choices. "I don't know."

He smiled gently at her. "That's a first coming from a woman."

Before she knew it she was smiling back at him. "I can't believe it myself."

From one moment to the next Tyler became aware that they were holding hands, their breaths mingling, her lips close to his. His breath snagged. The desire that was never far from the surface when Jana was near emerged. Her smile dissolved and he knew she was as aware of him as he was aware of her. He forced himself to release her hands and come to his feet. "I better let you get back to work."

"Y-yes." Jana stood, some of the happiness she'd felt earlier gone. Tyler might be attracted to her, but he wasn't going to follow through on it. And she knew it was because he still didn't trust her.

Olivia had just finished writing up the sales of several bath and body products to a repeat customer when she heard the front door open. "Thank you, Elaine. As always it was a pleasure helping you."

"Thanks, Olivia. Goodbye." The woman turned and stopped dead in her tracks.

Olivia looked beyond the woman and saw the reason. Julian Cortez was back. He looked mouthwatering and sexy in a white shirt, navy blue blazer and slacks. He would attract admirers wherever he went just as her ex-husband had. She wanted to believe he was just as superficial, but somehow she couldn't.

"Hello, Olivia," he greeted, then nodded at the customer.

"Well, hello." The woman extended her hand. "I don't think I've had the pleasure. I'm Elaine Parsons."

"Julian Cortez." The handshake was brief, although it was obvious Elaine wanted to prolong it. "Let me get the door for you."

Olivia saw Elaine's quick frown. She hadn't expected that. Elaine was single and beautiful, and one of the new breed of women who didn't wait for the man to make the first move.

"Thank you." As she passed him, she shoved her card in the pocket of his coat. "Call me sometime and we'll have drinks."

"That would be nice. Goodbye." Julian closed the door and turned to see Olivia frowning at him. "I told you I'd be back," he said with a slow smile.

"Since you just made a date with Elaine, I can't imagine why."

Now he was the one frowning. "No, I didn't."

"I heard you say 'that would be nice.' You can't deny it."

"I don't intend to," he told her. "It's a nice way of saying thanks, but no thanks. I only want to go out with you."

Olivia flushed with embarrassment.

"Dr. Cortez, who is taking care of your patients while you're here?" Jana asked, entering the room from the back, with Tyler behind her.

"I'm between appointments," he told her. "Ms. Street. Mr. Maxwell." He didn't know why they all traded a look. He just hoped they weren't going to gang up on him to keep him from dating Olivia. He was having a hard enough time without their interference.

"Call me Tyler." Olivia's brother took Jana's arm. "I'll be going. Walk with me to the door."

She resisted for a moment then allowed him to lead her away. At least the brother was on his side, Julian thought. "I thought I might buy some new sheets for my bedroom."

Olivia flushed. He hoped that meant she had imagined him sharing the bed with her. "What size?"

"King." Wouldn't she be surprised to know he'd never made love to a woman in his bed? And only a handful had ever been in his penthouse apartment. He didn't like tearful good-byes.

"This way please."

Julian followed, noting the sway of her hips, the shapely body. He'd never thought of a woman as being cuddly, but Olivia was and it wasn't because she barely came to his shoulder. It was something innate about her that made him want to hold her, keep her safe, and keep that beautiful smile on her face.

"Are you trying to coordinate with any particular color or theme?" She stopped in front of a shelf filled with sheets ranging in different hues and patterns.

He hadn't thought that far. "I like yellow."

She frowned up at him. He smiled, wondering if she recalled that she had on yellow when they'd first met. "But I'm open to suggestions."

"I'd say stick with a neutral tone to make them more visual and less tiring." She opened a package of sheets. "These are Yves Delorme. They are one hundred percent Egyptian combed cotton. Feel."

He'd rather feel her and she him. Her hands were small and dainty. It didn't take much effort on his part to imagine them on his body or his on her. His hands joined hers on the sheet, noting the difference, his hard to her soft, just like their bodies would be when they came together and blended into one.

Olivia knew he had intentionally touched her. She snatched hers away. His remained on the sheet, deliberately gliding over where hers had been.

"I don't think I've ever felt anything as soft."

She swallowed, linking her fingers together in front of herself. "This set is fifteen hundred dollars."

He blinked. "I beg your pardon?"

She smiled, a slow heart-stopping smile, for the first time. "Shall I get you a glass of water?"

He looked back at the king-sized set and shook his head. "Guess I forgot where I was."

"Don't feel bad. I've been in business for almost six years and Tyler still has the same reaction," she said.

"Thanks. That does make me feel somewhat better."

She moved to another shelf. "These are from the same manufacturer, but plain. They retail for three hundred dollars." She opened the package. "If you close your eyes you won't be able to tell the difference. The weave is what makes the other set costlier."

"I'll take these."

"Please come with me and I'll write you up." She pulled the sheets from the shelf.

Julian caught the other end. "I'll take them."

"I'll need them for the stock number."

"You won't be writing the number now," he said reasonably.

It seemed silly to argue over who would carry the sheets. Besides men had offered to carry things for her before and she hadn't thought a thing about it. That was the problem with Julian, she thought too much about him. "Thank you."

Stepping around her desk, she waved him to a seat. Dutifully he placed the set on the far corner of the desk. "Please have a seat. Can I get you anything to drink? Wine, tea or water?"

"Yes," he said still standing.

"What would you like?"

"I'd like wine tomorrow night with our dinner."

She took her seat and reached for the receipt book and pen. "I've already given you my answer."

"One I refuse to accept."

Her head came up. "Arrogance is not an endearing quality."

"It's not arrogance to go after what you want," he told her. "If I gave up every time there was an obstacle, I wouldn't be a doctor."

"How so?"

Julian didn't like talking about his past. Even his friends and associates knew very little about him. It had been a slip of the tongue. "It's unimportant."

"Sorry, I didn't mean to pry." She went back to writing the receipt.

"Why don't you have a computer?" he asked, oddly irritated with her.

"Because it's too impersonal," she said, still looking down. "I apologize if it's taking too long."

"It's not taking too long," he snapped.

Her head came up again. "Which one of us are you angry with?"

The question was so blunt and dead on, he was speechless for a moment. "Well?"

"I don't like to talk about my past or remember it," he admitted to her.

"Then we have something in common." She tore off the receipt, picked up the sheets and slid them into a white shopping bag strewn with poppies. Rounding the desk, she gave him the bag and receipt.

"Thank you. Improper laundering can shorten the life of sheets, so I've included laundering instructions or you can return them to us and we'll have them done for you."

"I need proper care too."

She folded her arms across her chest. "Women probably fall at your feet like ripe fruit."

"They see this face and not the man. I thought you'd look deeper than that," he said, unable to hide his annoyance with her. "How would you like to be judged on what others thought?"

She didn't have to think long for the answer and recall that she had been. "I wouldn't like it."

"Then why are you judging me that way?" he asked.

If he hadn't looked so frustrated, she might have evaded the truth. "Because it's safer."

"But is it fair? You struck me as a fair woman."

"Why are you pushing this?"

He started to shrug, then stopped. "You intrigue me."

"Because I said no?" She needed the answer and hoped he was honest enough to give it to her.

"That just made me more determined. Almost from the moment I saw you in the emergency room, I wanted to ask you out." He smiled. "I was tired and on my way home, but seeing you made me feel . . . I don't know. Refreshed."

He frowned and Olivia knew he hadn't meant to say the word. More importantly it meant he was telling the truth. "Why haven't you tried to persuade me to go out with you by reminding me that you helped me at the hospital?"

"Because one had nothing to do with the other."

The front door opened and a couple entered. Jana, who had been trying to look busy, moved to greet them. Olivia turned back to Julian. He appeared sincere, but so had her ex-husband. Her hands dropped to her side. "The answer remains no. Now, if you'll excuse me."

Julian stared at her a long time, then he nodded abruptly and spun on his heels. He reached the door the same time the customer who had just come in was leaving. The door had barely closed before Jana rushed over to Olivia. "Please say you accepted this time?"

Olivia wrapped her arms around herself and watched Julian jaywalk across the street. "It wouldn't have worked."

"How do you know if you don't give it a chance?" Jana asked. "Men like that don't have to go to this much trouble to get a date. And purchasing bed linen is not high on the list for single men."

"He almost had a coronary when I quoted fifteen hundred dollars for a set." Olivia glanced at Jana before looking back at Julian. He opened the back door to his car, tossed the package into the seat, then slid inside. She didn't expect the pang of regret to hit her so fast or so deep.

Jana watched him as well. "As I said, I'm probably the last person to give advice about a man, but if Tyler trusted him enough to give you two time alone, I'd say go for it."

Olivia bit her lower lip. "I won't be used again."

"Despite his ticking me off, I'd have to side with Tyler. Dr. Cortez is not playing with you. Believed me, I can tell," Jana said.

"I guess you've had a lot of experience with men."

"Enough," Jana answered, finding it easier to be more open each time she talked with Olivia. "If you want Julian, go after him."

Olivia started for the door. Julian backed out and sped off. "It's too late." She couldn't keep the misery from her voice.

Jana came to stand beside her. "Call his office."

Olivia was already shaking her head. "It's probably for the best." She firmly turned away from the window. "Enough talk about Julian. After we close I'll drive to my bank on the way home for your money. Have you decided what you plan to do first?"

"Pay my hospital bill and the painter. And I don't want an argument out of you about the painter."

A pleased smile washed across Olivia's face. "You sure? It will take a big chunk out of your money."

Jana sighed. "Yes, and I better take care of them before I weaken. I've been sneaking peeks at the black leather dress in the Gucci window every time we pass."

"I've learned not to look, but I've had more practice," Olivia said.

"You have a way of making me feel normal when I'm not sure I've ever been," Jana confessed. "If you hadn't helped, I don't know where I'd be today. You saved me."

"I'm just glad I was there."

The door opened and Julian rushed into the store. "I'm double-parked. How about drinks?"

Olivia saw the Maserati parked directly in front of the store. "The police are very diligent and unforgiving in this area," she warned him.

Julian took a step closer. "How about a walk in the park?"

"I'll be in the back," Jana said, and hurried away.

Neither Julian nor Olivia took their eyes from each other. "You'll be towed."

"Coffee before work at Starbucks in the morning?"

His handsome face was etched with determination. Jana was right. Perhaps it was time she stopped remembering the past and started living in the present. She did want to go out with him. All men weren't like her ex-husband and it was unfair of her to keep thinking so.

She took a deep breath. "I distinctly remember you asking me out to dinner and I'm holding you to it."

A slow grin spread over Julian's face. Olivia barely kept from sighing dreamily. "How about eight tomorrow night at Chamberlain's?"

"Sorry, I promised Griffin we'd go to a carnival. Is next Saturday all right?"

"It will have to be, but feel free to call me if you and Griffin want company or you want to go out earlier," he told her.

"I'll keep that in mind." Quickly going to the desk, Olivia scribbled her address and phone number on the back of a business card. "Now get going before you get a ticket. Here are my address and phone number, in case something comes up."

He would have liked to say it wouldn't, but he knew better. Emergencies didn't care what doctors had planned. He clutched the card in his hand. "You won't regret it."

"If I thought that, I wouldn't have said yes."

He laughed. "You're something. Until next Saturday night."

Olivia watched him through the window as he hurried to his car and drove off. She'd done it now and she couldn't wait to see how it turned out.

Tyler couldn't concentrate. He kept making stupid errors on the program he was working on. His team was scheduled to meet in a week to compile data for the systems program for one of the largest manufacturing firms in the country. Errors were unacceptable. He knew that, yet he couldn't clear his mind and work.

Finally accepting he wasn't going to do any more for today, he hit save, then exited the program. He was a man who saw solutions when others saw chaos. So why was he having so much difficulty trying to figure Jana out? And why was he worried that with the commission she might leave?

Tyler rubbed the back of his neck and admitted what he'd been trying to ignore. He was seriously attracted to the woman. Perhaps because she was such an enigma. Bad girl one moment, vulnerable the next. With a commission of almost three thousand dollars, she wouldn't have to stay in a garage apartment or buy secondhand clothes. And that's what bothered him. The possibility of her leaving.

He heard the front door open and got up and walked out of his office. Olivia and Jana were laughing and talking like old friends. "I thought you two would be home an hour ago."

Both women wiggled their hands, then held out one foot, then the other.

On their feet were jelly flip-flops. "We stopped by this little salon on Preston," Olivia replied. "Jana insisted on treating us to a pedicure and manicure."

"She has to be ready for her date," Jana explained.

"Dr. Cortez?" Tyler guessed.

Olivia's smile slipped a fraction. She stared at Tyler. "We're going to Chamberlain's for dinner next Saturday night."

"He double-parked to come back and ask Olivia again." Jana grinned at Tyler. "He was so desperate he suggested a walk in the park."

"A man who looks like Julian isn't nor ever will be desperate," Olivia said.

"We'll let Tyler decide," Jana said. "When is the last time you asked a woman to go for a walk in the park?"

"I can't recall ever doing so."

"We'll take that as a no." Jana went to the front door. "Good night."

"You aren't staying for dinner?" Tyler asked.

Jana held up a handled bag with the logo of a popular restaurant. "I stopped on the way. Good night."

Tyler was reluctant to let her go. "Will it keep? I told Wanda about your sale and she made a special dinner."

Jana stopped and stared.

"Shrimp étouffée," he said. "Of course Griffin wanted his shrimp deep fried."

"You're kidding, right?"

"Why don't you come see for yourself?" Feeling inordinately pleased, he took her arm. "Olivia, Griffin is in the media room playing computer games."

"I'll get him and be right back." She took the bag from Jana. "Let me put this in the refrigerator."

"Thank you," Jana said as Tyler swept her along. "This isn't the way to the kitchen."

"I thought we'd eat on the portico."

She stopped again the moment she stepped on the terrazzo floor and saw the table draped with an ecru linen tablecloth and lotus candles. The backyard was lush with blooming flowers and dense greenery. The tranquil blue water of the pool was twenty feet away.

He felt her tremble. She looked up at him. His heart clenched at the glimmer of tears in her eyes. He had never felt so helpless. He'd never before felt anything so right. "It's just a celebration dinner."

She swallowed and swallowed again. "I guess I'm still excited about everything. Don't mind me."

It was more than that, but he let it slide. "Have a seat and I'll get you a glass of wine."

He popped the cork and filled her glass, then his. Griffin and Olivia came out and he filled their glasses as well. Griffin would have cranberry juice as usual. Hoping he wasn't too obvious, Tyler took a seat beside Jana, blessed their food, then lifted his glass. "To more great sales and commissions."

Glasses clinked, and they drank. Picking up the serving dish, he served Jana.

"That's enough," she told him.

"Wanda's feelings will be hurt if this is in the refrigerator in the morning." He intended to make sure she ate and took care of herself.

Jana frowned at the large chunk of French bread he put on her bread plate. "I won't be able to fit into my clothes if I keep eating like this."

"Adding a few pounds never hurt anyone." He passed the dish to Olivia.

"Spoken like a diplomatic man," Jana said with a smile.

"Mama, did you know children in France drink wine?" Griffin speared a giant, batter-fried shrimp. "Rene in my class is from Paris and he says his mother lets him have wine with the grown-ups."

Olivia picked up her fork. "When we move to France I'll give it all the consideration it deserves."

"That means no," Griffin said to Jana.

Jana paused in eating, the happiness of moments ago muted as she recalled drinking with her mother. No matter how she tried, she couldn't remember them eating together. They had never shared the deep bond Griffin and Olivia shared. What might have life have been like if an adult had stepped in and tried to help her?

"The food taste all right?" Tyler asked, his brow puckered in a frown.

"It's fine." Jana caught Griffin's attention. "You're very fortunate to have a mother who loves you. When you're grown you'll learn that drinking before you're old enough isn't that much fun."

"Did you?" he asked with wide-eyed curiosity.

"Griffin, don't ask personal questions of adults," Olivia admonished.

Jana refused to look at Tyler. She made her tense body relax. "It's all right, Olivia. Yes, I did, but I wish every day that I hadn't. You'll be happier and have more friends if you wait."

Griffin screwed up his face. "I like having friends. I guess I'll wait." He turned to his mother. "Wanda fixed a chocolate cake for dessert."

"And since I know you're going to stop playing with your broccoli and carrots and eat them, you can have a slice." Olivia smiled sweetly.

Griffin pierced a floret. "My team won the soccer game today. I scored right between Anthony's legs." He giggled. "It was great."

The conversation soon revolved around Griffin's day at camp. No one looked at Jana differently. Slowly, she started to eat again. Tyler and Olivia weren't condemning her, but they might if they knew what else she had done.

How do you explain to a seven-year-old boy that his mother is going on a date? Olivia had thought about the answer to that question all afternoon and now that they were finished with Griffin's bath, his prayers and story time, she still hadn't come up with an answer. She saw no reason to put off telling him.

She tucked the covers under his arms and smoothed her hand over his head. Her heart swelled with love. She'd do anything, go though anything to keep him safe and happy.

"Griffin, I want to talk to you."

"I'm not going to drink wine until I'm older, I promise," he told her.

"It's about something else." She took a deep breath and decided to go for it. As long as he didn't have to go to sleep Griffin would happily let her sit there half the night. "Do you remember when Uncle Tyler was dating Courtney last year?"

His face scrunched up. "She wanted you to take away my video games."

Olivia had forgotten that. Courtney hadn't approved of video games or much else as Olivia remembered. Tyler might have been serious about her, but she was too rigid in her Christian beliefs. "Remember they went to the movies, to dinner, church? When a man takes a woman out by themselves it's called a date. A man has asked me on a dinner date with him next Saturday night."

Griffin sprang up in bed. "He's not going to want you to take away my video games, is he?"

Olivia briefly wondered if her son was too deeply involved in his games, then recalled him giving up the money he had been saving for a new game to the children with their mothers in the shelter. "No."

He stared at her a long time. "Cindi in my class said a boy stood up her big sister and she cried herself to sleep."

When Olivia had been seven, she and her friends had talked about dolls and tea parties. "Julian, Dr. Cortez, is a doctor. There's always the possibility that he'll be needed to help someone who is sick, but otherwise he won't stand me up."

"Cindi said the boy who stood her sister up said he was sick, but their cousin saw him at the movies with another girl."

Olivia felt on firmer ground. "Then Cindi's sister is better off. Anyone who would lie is not worth her time."

"Will I meet him?"

Smiling, she hugged him. "Yes."

"Does Uncle Tyler know him?" he asked, apparently still a bit apprehensive.

"Yes, and he likes Dr. Cortez," she said, hoping to ease the concern she saw on her son's face.

"If Uncle Tyler likes him, I guess you can go out with him," he said, lying back down.

Olivia almost expected him to give her a curfew. "Thank you, Griffin, but if you don't like him I won't go out with him."

"You must like him since you've never gone on a date before."

Brilliant child and I wouldn't have it any other way. "We're just getting to know each other."

"He better not make you cry."

"He won't. Now, close your eyes and go to sleep." Olivia didn't have any doubt she could keep the promise. She'd never cry over a man again. Kissing Griffin on the forehead, she turned off the lamp on the nightstand and tip-toed out of the room.

Saturday morning Jana was showered and dressed by seven thirty. Last night Tyler had received a phone call while they were clearing the table and she had helped Olivia with the dishes. She had been glad. She hadn't wanted him asking questions about her past. Olivia was too well mannered. Tyler was too inquisitive not to want to know more.

In the kitchen she prepared toast and scrambled eggs, congratulating herself even though a good portion of the eggs stuck to the skillet. She'd do better the next time. Wouldn't her mother be surprised, she thought as she munched on the toast.

Jana had left a message about the commission on her answering machine and told her not to worry. Her mother hadn't called back. Jana hadn't been surprised. Her mother seldom called. She always said she was so busy.

The knock on the door caused her to frown. She glanced at the clock on the stove. 8:04. Olivia didn't usually leave until 8:10. They'd gotten into the habit of leaving early and had stuck with it.

Opening the door, she saw Tyler in his usual dress of shirt and jeans. "Can I come in?" he asked.

She hesitated, then stepped back. They may as well get the drill over. "Of course."

"You sleep all right out here?" he asked, stepping inside. "The fumes all gone?"

"Yes." Tyler made her nervous. "Would you like a cup of coffee?"

His mouth twitched. "No chocolate?"

"No." She started for the kitchen and sensed him following.

"You make it?"

"Unless there's a genie somewhere that I'm not aware of." She opened the cabinet and took down a mug. "Have a seat. I'd offer you breakfast, but I haven't got the hang of making eggs yet."

"Coffee's all right."

Pouring him a cup, she took it to the table where he was seated. "Black?"

"Fine." His large hands wrapped around the mug.

Jana stared at his long fingers. A week ago, the first thing she would have thought about was how they might pleasure her.

"Something wrong?"

She almost jumped, annoyed that that was *exactly* what she had been thinking. "Not at all." She picked up her cup. "Now that we're finished with the small talk, what is it you want to tell me?"

"For starters, I want to thank you. You didn't have to tell us about your past to help Griffin."

Jana was taken aback. She shrugged to cover it. "He's a good kid. Someone should learn from my mistakes."

"Olivia can't stop singing your praises. Seems you have a knack for satisfying customers," he said, watching her over the rim of his cup.

She flinched in spite of herself. She didn't doubt Tyler had seen the reaction. Very little got past him. "I hate to rush you, but I don't want my boss thinking I'm getting lazy."

"Can't have that." Getting up, Tyler rinsed the cup in the sink. "I'll walk you down."

"That isn't necessary."

He cocked his head to one side. "I didn't say it was. Get that little purse of yours, and let's go."

He was bossy and pushy, but she did as he requested. As soon as she returned, he took her arm and started out the door. His touch was light, but she felt the imprint of his strong-fingered hand almost as if it were a brand, and smelled the citrus cologne that made her want to investigate. She couldn't deny that he excited her. Men had only been useful in the past if she could use them to her benefit. It was strange, but Tyler appealed to her because she couldn't.

Just as they reached the bottom of the steps, Olivia and Griffin came out of the house. "Good morning. I see you're ready to go."

"Morning, Ms. Franklin," Griffin said.

"Good morning, Griffin, Olivia." Jana shoved the strap of her purse higher on her arm. She turned to face Tyler and found him much too close and too tempting. "Goodbye."

"See you tonight."

There was a promise, almost a caress, in his deep voice, in the way his hands slowly trailed from her arm. Jana couldn't stop the shiver of awareness that raced through her. She'd never been attracted to the brainy, studious type. She'd considered them boring and suspected they'd be the same way in bed.

Somehow she knew that wouldn't be the case with Tyler . . . if she let things get that far. He didn't know who she was and, if he did, he wouldn't be staring at her with need just beneath the surface. He was possibly the only man who'd ever wanted her for her, and not just because of her bad reputation.

And he was the one man she dared not become involved with.

9

Throughout the day, Jana tried to remember that Tyler was off limits, but it was difficult. They were too aware of each other. As soon as they arrived home from work, Jana escaped to her apartment. She didn't want to see Tyler. Caring about any man was asking for trouble.

She'd barely entered the bedroom before there was a faint knock on the door. She tensed, fear and anticipation pulsing though her. She caught herself checking her lipstick and hair in the mirror over the dresser. Annoyed with herself, she went to the door. Instead of Tyler, Griffin stared up at her. She tried to convince herself she wasn't disappointed.

"Mama said dinner is ready. Uncle Tyler had to go out of town, so it's just us." Griffin grinned up at her. "I can have his slice of chocolate cake."

She smiled down at the child. It was so easy to like him. "I think your mother will have something to say about that."

His smile disappeared, his head lowered. "You're probably right," he said, then he looked up again with a grin on his face. "But it won't hurt to ask her." Then he turned and ran back down the stairs.

Jana followed. What wouldn't she give for his enthusiasm and optimism.

Jana decided later on that night that Olivia should have been a politician as she watched Olivia and Griffin riding in the box cars of the slow moving train around the track at the small carnival in a field near their church in Oak Cliff. The happy sounds of children's laughter, the beckoning spiels of barkers, and the screams of those on more adventurous rides filled the air.

Jana hadn't stood a chance of staying home alone and working on getting her apartment in order with the pieces from the attic. That could wait, Olivia had said. She and Tyler could help her with that later. She hadn't wanted Jana to be home by herself. Jana hadn't put up too much of an argument.

Jana didn't like being alone or that Tyler kept intruding into her thoughts. No man had ever done that before. But then, she'd never known a man as complicated and as unpredictable as Tyler.

"Hi, Jana," Griffin called as he and Olivia passed her.

Smiling, Jana waved. She'd finally convinced Olivia to let him call her by her first name.

"Excuse me. Don't I know you?"

Jana tensed. Slowly she looked at the man who had spoken. Thankfully she didn't recognize him. "No." She turned back to the ride, which was coming to a halt.

"Then I'd definitely like to. You here with anyone?"

She threw him a disinterested look. "Yes. Have a great night." Then she walked over to meet Olivia and Griffin. She hadn't even sized the man up to figure out if he could afford her. Jana smiled. What had once been automatic was no longer that way.

"What's next?" she asked Olivia.

"Home," Olivia answered.

"Mama, can I ride the mini roller coaster?" Griffin asked. "I promise I'll get up the first time you wake me up for Sunday school."

Olivia's mouth twitched. "The *first* time? You mean I won't have to come back and drag you out of bed by your feet?"

He giggled. "You never do that."

"I might if you don't get up in the morning." She handed him the tickets to the ride a few feet away. "No running."

Griffin didn't run, but he did a fast walk. Olivia and Jana followed. "Hold tight," Olivia called out to Griffin, stopping at the rail.

"He's a great kid," Jana said, meaning it. Olivia had a right to be proud. Briefly she thought of her own childhood. "He's lucky he has you."

"Thanks, but I'm the one blessed." Olivia kept her eyes on Griffin as the roller coaster climbed twenty feet in the air before swooping down again. The joyful screams of the children followed.

Jana knew Olivia wasn't just mouthing words. Despite the pain of her divorce, she'd turned her life around. Jana was determined to do the same.

"You want to go with us to Sunday school in the morning?" Olivia asked. "Afterwards we're going to the shelter to distribute the baskets."

"I really need to get the apartment in order," Jana said. The more she went out, the more chance there was of being recognized. Then, too, no matter what Tyler said, if Olivia's congregation learned about Jana's past they might not like it that she'd brought a woman like Jana into their midst.

"Maybe next time." Olivia went to meet Griffin as the ride came to a slow halt.

Jana blew out a breath and stuck her hands in her pockets. She'd disappointed Olivia, but that was better than her friends turning against her. Jana was an expert on how people smiled in your face then cut your throat.

She'd been one of them.

Jana didn't get out of bed until after ten Sunday morning. She'd suspected Olivia would invite her over for breakfast and she had. Jana had been able to truthfully say she hadn't gotten up yet. If Courtney had been critical of Tyler, what would she and those like her at the church say about Jana? It didn't bear thinking about.

Jana dressed and went to the house. She might as well make good use of the time and bring the things out of the attic. Unlocking the door with the spare key Olivia had left in a flowerpot near the back door, she went inside.

On the second floor, she couldn't help but look longingly down the hall toward Tyler's room. It was too easy to imagine them together. Shaking away the thought, she continued to the attic. The crammed space resembled an antique store. Oriental rugs, chests, tables, and lamps abounded. Olivia said the various pieces represented her mother's change in taste though the years.

Deciding the best way to go about transferring the things she had picked out was to put everything near the door, she began doing just that. The rose velvet ottoman trimmed with fluffs of ribbon fringe was first. Next came the sleek console table she planned to put behind the sofa. She admired the six-arm handcrafted wooden candelabrum lamp with scalloped shades, then picked it up, turned to add it to her pile, and bumped into someone.

She gasped, losing her grip on the lamp. Tyler moved quickly to take it from her. Her hand pressed to her rapidly beating heart. She wasn't sure it was entirely due to fright. "You scared me."

"Sorry." He placed the lamp on the floor. "I heard noises and came to investigate."

"I decided to finish with the apartment," she explained, wishing he had on a shirt. Apparently he'd been asleep. At least he'd taken time to pull on his jeans. Now if he'd just fasten them.

"I thought you might have gone to church with Olivia. They're distributing the baskets afterwards, aren't they?"

The guilt came hurtling back. "They don't need me."

"Everybody needs someone," he said softly.

She certainly couldn't argue that point.

"Want help?"

He wasn't going to make her feel guilty, but he was making her hot. "Don't you think you should finish dressing?" He was too distracting with his roped muscles and tempting mouth.

His smile was slow, lazy and sexy as hell. He had the audacity to absently run his hand across his muscled chest. "Sorry. Be back in a minute."

Jana discovered he was just as tempting from behind. He had a tight butt. She easily imagined her nails pressed into his flesh as they came together. Her pulse quickened.

She swiped her hand over her face. Tyler certainly was making it difficult to stick to her promise of no men.

"What do you want to move first?" he asked when he returned.

You to the North Pole. "Can you take the tufted area rug? I'll finish putting things together while you're gone."

He hefted the 8 x 11 foot flowered rug on his broad shoulder as if it weighed nothing. "Be back in a sec."

Don't hurry on my account, Jana thought. *Perhaps I'll cool down by the time you return.* Blowing out a breath, she went to get the patchwork bedding set.

Working together, they were able to get everything in place in less than an hour. The rose tones worked beautifully in the open room and were repeated in the bedroom. With the pieces she'd been able to add, the place took on a stylishness it had lacked before. She'd even been able to fashion blush pink draperies over the sofa and chair as slip cover.

"You certainly know how to spruce up a place," Tyler said. "But it's missing something. Be right back."

Jana frowned, then went to fluff the patchwork pillows on the sofa. They'd been a part of the bedding group and helped tie the bedroom to the living area.

"Here you are."

Jana looked up and her breath caught. He had a large bouquet of red and yellow roses.

"I remembered you had flowers on the table the day you cleaned the apartment."

Jana wondered if he also remembered her trying to seduce him. Her question was answered in the next second when his eyes narrowed, his gaze going to her mouth. Heat and desire shot through her. She swallowed.

"Where is the vase?"

Jana snapped out of her daze. "I'll get it." In the kitchen she took the vase from beneath the sink, with hands that refused to steady. When she straightened, Tyler was there to put the roses inside. Jana filled the tall glass cylinder with water.

"We work well together," he said.

Jana didn't want to think of what else they might do well together. She was not going to repeat the pattern of going to bed with any man she found attractive. "Thank you."

"Anytime. Now that the place is finished, you want to go grab a bite to eat?"

It hit her at once. "You haven't eaten, have you?"

"No."

She couldn't recall anyone putting her needs before their own, unless they wanted something in return. Could she do any less? No matter how busy she was, she couldn't stop thinking about Olivia. She'd done so much for Jana and asked for so little in return.

Jana took a deep breath. "What time do you think they'll deliver the baskets?"

"Around twelve."

She glanced at the clock on the stove. It was seven minutes after eleven. "If we grab something quick, maybe you could take me to church."

His smile made her breath catch. "It will be my pleasure."

"Thanks." She turned, then spun back. "What should I wear?"

"Doesn't matter," Tyler told her. "God looks at the heart."

"He might, but others might not share His or your view." She almost added that she'd bet Courtney wouldn't.

"The blue pinstripe blouse and black pants you had on Tuesday will work," he said.

That he remembered what she had worn caused warmth to curl through her. "I'll hurry." Jana went to get dressed, taking her roses to the bedroom with her.

Jana quickly discovered that thinking about something and doing it were entirely two different things. They'd arrived just as the two-story white brick church was dismissing. As Tyler had indicated, the parishioners' clothes ranged from simple to elegant. Jana hadn't seen so many hats since she attended Derby Day in London last year. When the match was over, she'd left with the winning team's captain, an Italian count.

"You all right?"

She could lie, but the death grip on her purse said differently. "I'll get there."

He nodded and they went inside. It became apparent immediately that Tyler was as well liked as Olivia. He was greeted repeatedly with handshakes, pats on the back and one-armed masculine hugs.

Jana noticed he also received his share of longing looks from women. She was the recipient of a few glares. It seemed she wasn't the only one dealing with issues. "I can't do this." She wasn't aware she'd said the words aloud until she felt Tyler's hand close gently around her arm. She couldn't bring herself to look at him. "I have to leave."

"Jana, I'm so glad you changed your mind!"

Jana lifted her head. Olivia and Maggie were making their way through the crowd toward them. She was trapped.

"You'll have another friend if you'll give Maggie a chance," Tyler whispered.

Jana bit her lip and said nothing. People like her didn't have friends. Did they?

Both women wore pleased smiles when they stopped directly in front of her. Greetings were exchanged.

"Jana, we had some last-minute donations. Do you mind making a few more baskets?" Olivia asked.

"I was afraid I might mangle them," Maggie said with a smile, her hand on her stomach. "I should have known you'd show up."

Jana recalled what she had said about God sending someone to those in need. If He did, it wouldn't be a woman like Jana.

Olivia frowned. "Jana, are you all right? You didn't hurt yourself moving stuff, did you?"

"Do you want to sit down?" Maggie asked, her voice just as concerned as Olivia's had been. "The lounge is down the hallway."

"Do you want to leave?" Tyler asked.

It was her choice. She could stay and help as she wanted to or let her past continue to trample deeper underfoot what little self-respect she had left. She opened her mouth to say she was leaving, then remembered something else: Tyler saying the one place she was always welcome was the church. The other was his and Olivia's home.

Jana made herself meet his gaze. His was filled with understanding and patience. If she had somehow gotten Tyler on her side, perhaps there was a chance for her not to mess this up as she had messed up her life.

Her gaze went back to Olivia and Maggie. "I'm staying. Let's get started on those baskets."

Each woman joyfully took her arm. "Let's go," Olivia said. "Men can't come because of the security of the shelter. Thanks, Tyler, for bringing her. We'll see you later. Bye."

"I'll be waiting," he said softly.

Jana couldn't help but think the words held a special meaning just for her. If she was right, what did she plan to do about it?

There were few dry eyes at the women's shelter by the time the last basket and toy had been given out. Olivia's effort made a lot of women and their children happy. During the presentations and the reception that followed, Jana noticed Olivia stayed in the background. If Maggie was right about God sending someone to those in need, He couldn't have sent a better person than Olivia to Jana.

"Olivia, you did it," Jana said on the drive home.

"God did it," Olivia said. "I was just a conduit. At least for a moment or two the women and children were able to forget they were in a shelter and why." She glanced in the rear-view mirror at Griffin dozing in the back seat. "Children understand the least and suffer the most."

Jana knew that firsthand. "But not today, thanks to you."

Olivia nodded and turned onto their street. "We were so busy I didn't get a chance to ask about the apartment. How much did you get done?"

"Everything." Excitement rang in Jana's voice. "Do you have time to come and see?"

"I'd love to." Olivia turned into the driveway and parked in the garage. "Griffin will probably be fully awake by the time we hit the back door. But if not, I'll get him settled and come right back out."

"Do you need any help?" Jana asked, unbuckling her seat belt.

"Thanks, but I can manage." Olivia reached for the door handle.

"See you in a bit." Jana got out of the SUV, waited until she saw that Griffin was walking on his own, then went to the apartment.

She was just as pleased with the results as she had been earlier. A moment of doubt hit when she saw the improvised chair covering. She heard someone on the stairs and went to the door. Griffin led the way. Behind him were his mother and Tyler.

"I came to make sure you don't start talking about decorating and lose track of time," Tyler said. "Griffin and I are hungry."

"Not after two pieces of cake and no telling how much punch," Olivia countered.

Griffin seemed resigned rather than surprised by his mother's announcement. "Grandmother Maxwell says mothers have eyes in the back of their head," he said to Jana. "Did yours?"

"No." Jana's mother had been too busy with her lovers to pay any attention to her only child. Jana stepped aside for them to enter.

"Oh, Jana, it's beautiful." Olivia's warm gaze took in everything. "It doesn't seem like the same place. I want to see the bedroom." She took off in that direction.

"Where's the television?" Griffin asked, his brows puckered.

Jana smiled with Tyler. "I've never watched much television."

"Then what did you do?" he asked innocently.

Her smile vanished.

"Anything she wanted to," Tyler answered for her. "I've told you you're only limited by your imagination. Come on, let's go light the fire."

Griffin took off in a flash, only to stop at the door and face Jana. "Jana, if Mama says it's all right you can borrow my portable DVD or my books."

Jana was stunned, touched and almost speechless. "Thank you, Griffin. I may take you up on the offer."

Smiling, he took off again. After a long look, Tyler went with him.

"He's never offered before to loan out his things." Olivia crossed from the bedroom door to Jana. "He likes you. We all do."

But would they if her past were revealed? "I like you too."

Olivia looped her arm with Jana's. "Come on, let's go laze by the pool and watch Tyler grill."

Tyler kept one eye on the steaks and burgers and the other on Jana. He hadn't missed the startled expression on her face when Griffin asked what she did, nor the uncomfortable silence that followed.

"Uncle Tyler, is it ready yet?" Griffin asked for the third time in less than a minute.

"Let's see." Tyler turned over the ground chuck patties. Smoke wafted up. Olivia and Jana laughed and he glanced in their direction. He went still as he looked at Jana though the smoke. He suddenly remembered where he'd seen her. Blood pounded in his veins.

"Uncle Tyler?"

"Sorry." Scooping up the meat with the long-handled spatula, Tyler slid the patty onto Griffin's bun. "Come and get it, ladies."

Olivia and Jana got up from the cushioned lounge chairs by the pool and started toward them. The pinched expression Jana wore earlier was gone. She appeared relaxed . . . until she caught him staring at her.

She went as motionless as a deer caught in the beam of headlights. "W-what is it?

"Just thinking. Grab a plate," he instructed. He was glad to see she did just that, but she kept throwing cautious looks at him.

To put her at ease, Tyler busied himself preparing his own plate. He could use his skill on the computer to find out about her past or he could let things play out.

At the table, Jana was the first one to bow her head for the blessing. Afterwards she lifted her head and stared across the table at him as soon as Olivia finished saying the blessing. Her eyes were filled with wariness. The sight tore at him and he thought, whatever her story, it was obvious she was trying to get her life together now. After all everyone deserved a second chance.

"Ladies, since the men did the cooking, you're doing the dishes, right?" he said.

"That's right," Griffin said around a mouthful of food.

Olivia cut into her ribeye. "Women cook *and* wash dishes all the time. Why can't you two?"

"What do you think, Jana?" Tyler asked, loading his baked potato with sour cream, chives, cheese, and bacon bits.

For a moment he thought she was going to keep playing with her garden salad. "I think Wanda would appreciate Tyler and Griffin's help with dishes in the morning."

Griffin straightened in his chair. Tyler scowled. Olivia and Jana laughed.

"I don't think there's any need to go that far." If he could keep that smile on her face he wouldn't mind kitchen duty. "I'll handle the dishes."

"I'll help," Griffin offered, but clearly his heart wasn't in it.

"I'm doing the dishes," Jana surprised them all by saying. "It's the least I can do. If someone will show me how to work the dishwasher."

"I'll show you," Griffin volunteered. "Afterwards we can watch a movie. Have you ever seen *Aladdin*?"

Tyler and Olivia groaned.

"No, but I'd love to," Jana said.

"Great," Griffin said, finishing off his burger. "I'll show you how to use the DVD player, too."

"Thank you, Griffin."

Jana was smiling again. For that pleasure, Tyler could sit through the thousandth showing of Griffin's favorite movie.

Jana couldn't believe she was actually watching an animated movie and enjoying it. Or did her enjoyment stem from the people around her?

This is the way a family is supposed to be ... warm, supportive, loving, tolerant ... and for a while I'm part of it.

Jana snuck a peek at Tyler, slouched in the side chair next to her, his long legs stretched out in front of him, his hands linked over his flat stomach. Her lips twitched at the glazed look in his eyes. Obviously he'd rather be watching something else. He was there because Griffin had insisted the entire family watch Aladdin. Jana would never forget Griffin catching her hand and saying, "You, too, Jana."

She'd taken a seat on the sofa in the media room with Griffin next to her and Olivia on the other side of him. Griffin had accepted her. That complete trust coupled with that of Olivia was humbling. Jana would do anything to keep their faith in her.

Tyler was another story. He kept confusing her. This afternoon at the cookout when he'd looked at her, his eyes piercing, she had felt threatened. She couldn't explain why she sensed that emotion. She just knew she had.

Suddenly Tyler looked at her and winked. The apprehension that had begun to build again disappeared. She winked back, then sobered. Tyler wasn't for her. She returned to watching the movie, unable to deny that she was beginning to wish he was.

Tyler sensed Jana was watching him more than the movie, and that was all right with him. He was doing the same thing.

Too bad real life couldn't be wrapped up in a pretty package like a lot of movies. The good guys didn't always win. Often they were kicked in the teeth again and again, or went down for the count and never got up.

Without friends or family to help you through the rough times and be there with you to celebrate the good times, life could be vicious and cruel. It certainly had been to Olivia, but Griffin had been the result. No one had to tell him she'd go through it again because it had given her the most precious thing in her life, her son. It had also made her more self-assured.

He'd often heard the saying that "What doesn't kill you will make you stronger." He had to agree. Courtney walking out of his life had torn him apart at the time, but now he was a better man, a more tolerant man because of it.

On the fifty-one-inch screen he watched the wedding scene of a thief and a princess. Aladdin had been redeemed. Most people weren't all good or all bad. There were degrees.

"We can watch *Finding Nemo* next." Griffin took Jana's hand and went to find the DVD. "It's the story of a father fish that goes searching for his son who was kidnapped. My dad would do that if I got kidnapped, wouldn't he, Mama?"

Olivia's smile was strained. "Yes, he would and so would your uncle, your grandparents and all the people who love you, and most of all, so would I."

Tyler knew some people changed. Others, like Griffin's father, would be bastards until the day they died. Tyler threw a glace at Jana who patiently sat on the floor with Griffin as he told her about the various movies in his collection. She wasn't the same woman she'd been a week, or even a day ago.

She'd have her chance.

Jana had never been nervous when a man walked her to the door. It was a foregone conclusion where they'd end up. With Tyler that wasn't going to happen no matter how her body yearned and heated when he was near her.

Opening the door, she moistened her lips. "Thank you for helping me with the apartment."

"You're welcome."

She swallowed. "Good night. I'll see you in the morning."

He shook his head. "I'll be busy working."

"Because you helped me and spent time with Griffin," she correctly guessed.

"And I'd do it again," he told her easily.

She didn't doubt him. Tyler was a man of principle.

"I better let you get to bed, but there is one other thing I need to do," he said, staring at her lips.

His head slowly descended toward hers. Jana quivered in anticipation. His warm lips touched hers. She simply melted in his arms. She didn't try to think of the best way to manipulate him, how to tease him until he was crazy with desire or how much she could get out of him. The truth was she couldn't think at all, but she could feel.

Wild emotions surged through her, heating her blood, deepening the craving in the junction of her thighs. The kiss was like nothing she had ever experienced before. Her hands curled in the fabric of his shirt, then moved around his neck to bring him closer, closer still. Her body pressed against his, needing, wanting.

His head lifted, his breathing harsh and labored. "I knew you'd take the top of my head off," he rasped, his voice rough and incredible sexy.

"I'm not sure mine is too steady," she said, trying to get her breathing under control.

He laughed, a wonderful sound that made joy dance in her heart. "Your beautiful head is still attached to your incredible body." He kissed her quickly on the lips. "Sleep tight. I'll be underground for a few days."

She didn't want to let him go. She had the incredible urge to ask him just to hold her again.

His eyes narrowed. "You all right?"

She drew her arms to her sides. "How can you ask after a kiss like that?" She'd meant it as teasing. He didn't smile as she'd wanted him to.

His thumb tenderly grazed her bottom lip. "My mother has a saying. Take joy where you can find it. Don't waste it looking for trouble."

Men didn't mention their mothers to her. Nor did they hold and look at her as if she were precious. "Don't forget to eat and take care of yourself."

That time he smiled. "Yes, ma'am."

"Good night," Jana said and went inside. She was turning back the floral duvet on her bed when she thought of another difference between the past men in her life and Tyler. He respected her.

Jana hadn't known she could miss a man as much as she missed Tyler. They'd only kissed, but a kiss like none other she'd ever experienced. She hadn't thought she was the type to go weak-kneed over a man. The second their lips fused Tyler had shown her how wrong she was. The revelation was frightening and exhilarating. She wasn't as jaded as she'd thought.

It was Wednesday and she hadn't seen him since Sunday night, but each day she'd found a note slipped under her door.

The words were simple, but telling. *Hope you had a great day,* on Monday. On Tuesday he'd written, *How about a non-animated movie when I come up for air?* Jana saved the notes like a schoolgirl and didn't feel silly for doing do.

At least she didn't have time to brood. The shop had been busy most of the day. Both she and Olivia were needed on the floor. She'd just finished writing the receipt for a customer who'd purchased two sets of towels when Priscilla Haynes walked in. Jana stiffened in shock and fear.

With Priscilla was Mrs. Robert Fulton. Both women's mouths were pinched. Priscilla's eyes were filled with hatred, Mrs. Fulton's with annoyance. Their gazes raked over her, then they moved toward Olivia who was helping a couple select bedding.

"Hello, Olivia. We need to speak with you at once," Priscilla told her, not bothering to keep her voice down.

Jana began to tremble. Of all the scenarios she'd envisioned, she had never thought Priscilla and Olivia would be on a first-name basis.

Olivia's smile was strained. "Hello, Priscilla. Mrs. Fulton. As you can see I'm with a customer. I'll be with you when I finish."

"If you don't stop and hear what we have to say, you may not have any customers," Priscilla snapped, her gaze cutting back to Jana. Her threat brought activity in the shop to a halt. The young couple with Olivia edged away as if expecting an altercation.

"Please excuse me," Olivia said to the wary couple, then spoke to Priscilla. "I can tell you're upset, but whatever it is will have to wait. Please come back later."

Priscilla's chin lifted. "Perhaps I was wrong to come here and warn you about the slut you have working for you."

Jana wasn't sure if the gasp came from her or Olivia. Slowly, one by one, everyone in the shop followed the direction of Priscilla's hate-filled stare.

"Priscilla, please leave," Olivia said, her voice tight with anger.

Priscilla whipped back around. "You'd defend *that slut* after she's whored her way from one end of the country to another? Her first husband threw her out of their bedroom naked when he caught her with his business associate."

Jana wanted to sink through the floor in shame. She wanted to run, to escape, but her feet were glued to the floor.

"She'll go after any man with money. She doesn't care how old or how lewd the act. She shouldn't be allowed to be in the room with decent women," Priscilla ranted. "Last year she dared attend the funeral of a man she'd been mistress to, flaunting herself in front of the grieving woman and her children."

Olivia stared at Jana mutely, begging her to deny the claims. Jana couldn't, and she knew it was about to get worse.

"Her own father has disowned her. She and her mother are cut from the same dirty, amoral cloth." Priscilla took two steps toward Jana. "But she underestimated her appeal when she tried to get her ex-husband back. His grandmother let it be known that whoever was a friend of Jana was not a friend of hers. Since then Jana has been on a slow descent into the cesspool where she belongs."

"Jana?" Olivia finally managed to say. "Is this true?"

Jana's throat was so tight she couldn't speak.

"She'd as soon as lie as look at you. You don't socialize much since you had Griffin, but don't take my word for it, ask any of our crowd. She's no good. She had the nerve to crash a party at my house. I had her thrown out." Priscilla spoke to Olivia. "No one is going to shop here as long as she stays. Isn't that right, Cynthia?"

Mrs. Fulton, who had ignored Jana since Priscilla spoke, didn't hesitate. "Unless she goes, you can cancel my order."

"No," Jana said, her voice choked. She stepped forward, finally able to move. "No. I'll leave. It's not her fault. She . . ." Jana felt the tears clog her throat and fill her eyes. To cry in front of these women would be the ultimate humiliation. "I'll go." She quickly walked into the back for her purse, then ran out the front door, knowing as she did that she couldn't run fast enough to leave her past behind.

10

Tyler beat his deadline by a hair's-breath. Kicking back in his chair, he
called his team members, checking to ensure that they were all on
schedule and ready for the job Friday in Las Vegas. They were.

He decided to drive to Midnight Dreams. He didn't try to deny that the
reason was to see Jana. He'd missed her. When he came downstairs this
morning, she had already left.

He was on the walkway leading to the garage when he saw Jana heading
for the stairs leading to her apartment. She was sobbing. His heart jumped
into his throat. He glanced wildly around for Olivia before running to Jana.

"What's the matter? Where's Olivia?"

Jana fought against his hold, shaking her head. Realizing she was hysterical, he shook her. "Jana, where's Olivia?"

She shuddered, her head remained downcast. "At the shop."

"What happened? What is it?"

She pushed against his hold. "Let me go."

"No! Not until you tell me what's going on."

"It's over. My past finally caught up with me," she said.

"You're not making sense."

She pushed ineffectively against him again. "Ask Priscilla Haynes. She
would be happy to explain everything to you. She had everyone at the store
hanging on every word."

His stomach knotted, but he didn't let her go. "I'm asking you."

She looked up at him, her dark eyes flared. "All right, I'll tell you. Any
man with the right price can have me and I'm never cheap. You could never

afford me, Tyler. I thought it was ironic, my line of work now, considering all the time I've spent in bed."

Tyler let his hands fall away from her.

Her laugh was ragged. "Didn't want to hear it after all?" She turned around "It won't take me long to pack and you can fumigate the place." She ran up the stairs to her apartment.

For a long moment Tyler couldn't move. He'd always known she was hiding something dark in her past, but hadn't dreamed it was that. Sure, she'd initially come on to Julian and him, but not once since then had Tyler seen her act inappropriately with any man. If anything, she tended to avoid men when she first began working at Midnight Dreams.

His thoughts veered to Olivia. Priscilla was status-conscious and could be vindictive. He threw a glance toward Jana's closed door and started toward his truck.

He was halfway to the garage, when Olivia pulled up. By the time he reached her she had gotten out of the SUV.

"You know," she said.

His gut clenched. "Jana told me."

Olivia placed a hand on her arm. "The person Priscilla described is not the woman we both know."

The knot in his gut eased. "You don't have to convince me. Come on. She's packing."

"She can't leave," Olivia said, her brow creased with worry.

"She's not," Tyler said, heading for the stairs. Without knocking, he opened the door.

Jana, her suitcase in her hand, stopped abruptly on her headlong flight out of the apartment when she saw them. "Come to fumigate already?"

Tyler ignored her baiting words. "Running away won't solve anything."

Jana tossed her head. "I'm just moving on. You couldn't have expected me to stay here. I'm used to better," she said, but her voice trembled.

"You didn't seem in a hurry to leave before now," he pointed out.

She shrugged carelessly. "Priscilla just made me move up my time schedule. Besides, you should be throwing a party."

"How about throwing one if you stay?" Tyler asked softly.

Longing darkened her eyes. She swallowed.

Olivia came to stand beside Tyler. "You don't have to go."

"Priscilla doesn't make idle threats. You'll lose business. If I go, perhaps Mrs. Fulton won't cancel." Her grip on the suitcase tightened. "Both women wield a lot of power. I've learned the hard way that you can't go against them."

"I've already given Mrs. Fulton a full refund despite her signing a sales receipt that said there was no refund on special orders," Olivia told her. "I don't want her business. No one threatens me."

"They woke the sleeping tigress," Tyler said, proudly grinning down at his sister.

Jana stared at them as if they had lost their minds. "You'll lose customers. Don't you understand that?"

"No one dictates to me who I can hire or who my friends are."

Tears streamed down Jana's cheeks. "Don't you understand? She was telling the truth. I don't inspire loyalty in anyone, not even my parents. And I've never had a friend."

"You do now," Tyler said, brushing the tear from Jana's cheek with his thumb.

Longing went through her. She wanted to accept the comfort he offered, but she couldn't. "I'm not worth Olivia putting her business in jeopardy. One of the owners of Bliss is my ex-husband's wife, Claire. If I stay, you won't get another product. I can't blame her."

Jana made herself look at Tyler. "He caught me cheating on him. When I didn't get the divorce settlement I wanted, I tried to hurt him by embellishing details of affairs with as many men as I could think of. I was vicious and mean and very convincing."

Tyler tried to absorb what she was telling him and he did to a certain point, but he was more concerned with the tears shimmering in Jana's eyes, the way her voice kept breaking. She was hurting. How could he condemn her? He hadn't lived the life of a saint.

"I've always done business with Brooke," Olivia said, referring to Bliss.

Jana hated what she had to do next, but she had to make them listen. "Brooke hates me just as much as Claire. I used the man she thought she was in love with to pass the time while waiting for my next victim." She swallowed the tears clogging her throat. "I'm no good. Men were playthings to me."

"Were," Tyler repeated. "What changed your way of thinking?"

He deserved that much truth. "I finally realized that all the time I thought I was using men and being in control of my life, they were the ones in control. Worse, they were using me."

Tyler wanted to reach out to her, but sensed she'd fight like a cornered animal. "You learned. You told me you wanted a chance to start over. You have that here. You can be strong enough to face up to your past and accept the blame or you can run."

Tears she couldn't control no matter how hard she tried streamed down her cheeks. Angrily Jana brushed them away. "You don't know what you're asking. People look at me as if I'm filth on the bottom of their shoes, and they're right."

"I don't, and neither does Olivia," Tyler said, gently.

"Tyler's right. I'm going back to the store. The last time it closed in the middle of the day was when Griffin had the chicken pox and wanted me to come home and Stella had gone to lunch. I need you at the shop since Stella resigned." Olivia opened the door. "I'll be waiting."

"People won't shop if I'm there," Jana tried again.

Olivia's gaze didn't waver. "People make mistakes. I wouldn't be much of a Christian if I didn't understand that. I'll be waiting for you." Turning, she went out the door.

Tyler remained unmoved. "Are you going to let her do this alone?"

Jana took a deep shuddering breath. "She'll be fine once I'm gone."

"Do you honestly believe she'll let them think they've won?"

Olivia was sweet, but she wasn't a pushover. "No."

"At least you have that right."

Jana dropped the suitcase and paced in frustration. "You were right about me. How can you want me anywhere near you or your family after what I've told you?"

"Because not one of us is sinless, because you're not the same woman," he said quietly.

Her gaze cut to him. "I came on to you *and* Dr. Cortez."

"That you did." His head tilted to one side. "You were trying to get under my skin enough to let you go. I imagine most women try to come on to him because of the way he looks."

"You're just as handsome," she blurted. Her eyes widened at her blunder. "You're trying to make me out as this good person. You're wrong. I only look out for myself."

"If so, Olivia and I were wrong about you. Our mistake." Tyler stepped back and opened the door. "If you want to go back to your old life, I can't stop you."

Frustration welled up within Jana. "You're better off without me."

He left the door open and walked over to her. "Would the Jana you described have been concerned with other people's welfare? Would she have given back money?" Stepping around her, he picked up several large bills on the coffee table. "Your commission?"

She wrapped her arms around herself when she really wanted to wrap them around him, understanding at last the full extent of what her lifestyle had cost her. "The money wasn't mine any longer. The order has been canceled."

"But you weren't aware of that before Olivia told you. At least give yourself credit for not wanting to take money that you hadn't earned. It never would have crossed the mind of the woman Priscilla was talking about." He went to her. "I know it's not going to be easy. You hurt a lot of people and they aren't going to easily forget, if at all. All you can do is show them that that person is gone."

"They hate me." She couldn't stand it if he hated her.

"Can you blame them?"

"No. No, I can't."

"Then don't waste time or tears on something you can't change, use it on something you can fix and that's showing them the woman Olivia and I have come to know and respect. I'm going to the shop to help Olivia. You want to come with me?"

"I can't." Stepping around him, she picked up her suitcase. "Please thank Olivia for me. Goodbye, Tyler."

"I don't want you to go," he said softly.

She stopped, hesitated, then continued. He followed and watched her determined steps across the yard. "If you want to change, why are you running away?" *Why are you running away from me?* he wanted to ask.

She turned and stared at him with tortured eyes. "Can't you understand this is the first unselfish act in my life?"

Tyler thundered down the stairs to her. "Are you sure that's the reason, Jana? Or is it because you don't have the courage to face the people you wronged? Once again, you're taking the easy way out, leaving Olivia to be the brunt of snide remarks."

"I can't stay!" she screamed.

"Then go," he said. He pulled out his wallet. Angry at her refusal to stay and fight, he snatched up her hand and slapped the money into her palm, closing her fingers over the bills. "Take it. I don't want you sleeping in a rat trap."

Not waiting for her to say anything, he went to his truck and drove off. He refused to look back.

Midnight Dreams was eerily quiet. Olivia walked around the shop, rearranging, straightening where there was no need. This was her dream, her chance for financial independence. She'd started with a loan of five thousand dollars from Tyler. Last year she had grossed close to $2 million dollars. The downturn of the economy hadn't affected her business.

Priscilla's revelation could.

Olivia turned from smoothing her hand over the linen on the bed and glanced out the window. There were quiet periods in any business. Was this one of those times or had the grapevine already started? If so, so be it. Never again would she shy away from the truth to save face. She'd done that when she refused to tell anyone the real reason she filed for divorce from Aaron.

She sighed. She could just imagine the field day gossipers like Priscilla would have if they learned her horrible secret. She'd do anything to keep that from happening. Griffin would be safe at all cost.

The door opened and she looked around as Tyler came through the door. "Jana?"

"She's gone," he said, unable to keep the despair and anger from his voice.

Olivia went to him. "I wanted her to stay, but it had to be her choice. I think you were beginning to like her."

He shrugged, picked up a candle from a shelf in an uncharacteristic nervous motion. "Doesn't matter."

She curved her arm around his waist and leaned into him. "Relationships have never been easy for either of us."

"Seems that way." He held her away from him. "If this gets ugly, can you stay afloat?"

The corner of her mouth tilted. "With a penny-pincher for a brother, what do you think?"

He almost relaxed. "But money is only part of it. You've put so much into this place to make it successful. It's a part of you."

"You'd understand that better than most people." She looked around the shop. "If I can survive Aaron, I can survive this."

The door opened; both turned. An elderly couple entered.

"I thought it was Jana," Tyler said.

"I'm sorry," Olivia said before going to the couple.

Tyler looked though the plate glass window. "Jana, where are you?"

Jana sat on the concrete bench at the bus stop with her suitcase in her lap. On one side of her was a young woman with a baby asleep in a stroller. On the other was a robust woman in a white maid's uniform. Neither had said a word since Jana sat down between them twenty minutes ago. Why should they? They were strangers. Nothing connected them except they were all waiting for the same bus.

Jana swallowed the painful lump in her throat. She hadn't been foolish enough to not take any of the money. She'd left the money Tyler tried to give her and all of the commission except $100. Although it was considerably more money than she had the night she met Olivia and Tyler, it wouldn't last long.

I don't want you sleeping in a rat trap.

Tyler's words came back to haunt her. She'd taken enough from them. She just wished she knew what to do next.

A late-model convertible sports car cruised to a stop in front of the bus bench, ignoring the angry blasts of horns behind it. "A woman as gorgeous as you shouldn't be waiting for a bus. Hop in," urged the driver.

The full-figured woman sitting on Jana's right nudged her with her elbow. "He's talking to you."

"Why can't he be talking to me?" the young girl in a halter and shorts asked, her voice peeved.

"Because, although that baby might prove you don't mind what he has in mind, the car's a two-seater," the older woman said.

"I don't want him anyway," the young woman said, crossing her legs.

"Come on, honey. Let's go have drinks and talk," the driver cajoled.

The woman harrumphed and mumbled, "Who does he think he's fooling?"

"Well, go on," the young woman said. "But don't get caught like I did. Babies sure cut into your fun."

Jana looked down into the carriage. The baby was sleeping peacefully. She couldn't imagine Olivia thinking Griffin spoiled her fun.

"Screw it. You aren't the only woman in town." The car sped off.

Jana didn't even bother to lift her head. "How old is your baby?"

"Two months," the young mother sighed. "Mama has to spend the night where she works. She broke her glasses and I brought her extra pair." She pouted her deep red lips. "I had planned on going out with my friends tonight, but now I have to keep Yamika. It isn't fair."

"She probably feels the same way," the older woman said.

The young woman's head whipped around. "What's that supposed to mean?"

"Just what it sounded like." The older woman stood as the city bus pulled up.

"At least a man wanted me." The young mother efficiently broke down the carriage, ignoring the unhappy cries of the abruptly awakened baby that was tucked under her arm like a football. "You'd have to *pay* a man."

"That's what you think." The older woman tossed over her shoulder as she got on the bus.

Mumbling, the young mother and crying baby followed. For a crazy moment Jana wanted to snatch the baby from its mother. No child should have to grow up as she did, knowing they were unwanted, winding up so desperate for that love they'd do anything.

"You coming, miss?" asked the driver.

Jana came upright, but couldn't make herself get on the bus. She was afraid if she did she'd end up miserable, alone, and bitter.

"Guess not," the bus driver said. The door closed. The bus pulled off, leaving Jana staring after it.

11

Julian had called Dallas home since he'd been in medical school. He loved the city, but detested the heavy traffic, which seemed to grow worse with each passing month. On his way home from his office, he eased to a stop behind another car in the stop-and-go, bumper-to-bumper traffic on Preston. If he took a right at the next light he'd run into Highland Park Village. Perhaps he could talk Olivia into a latte. It was time for her store to close.

The traffic light changed and he pulled off. That might not be a good idea. He didn't want Olivia to think he was crowding her. One wrong move and he was history. He planned on being on his best behavior. He couldn't recall ever being so anxious for a date or so concerned about making a good impression.

Women had been coming on to him since he was old enough for the first adolescent urges. He'd never been bothered by the prospect of one leaving because there was always another to take her place. Inching up in traffic he winced at how callous that sounded. He'd be very disturbed if Olivia walked away and he had yet to even kiss her.

He wanted to. Badly. Perhaps he'd catch her in a weak moment. Flicking on the signal, he took the next turn onto Mockingbird. No guts, no glory.

To help put her at ease about his unexpected visit, perhaps he'd tell her how much he enjoyed the sheets. On second thought that might not be wise since he didn't seem to be able to stop thinking about her on those sheets with him. His body reacted predictably. He shifted to ease the sudden uncomfortable fit of his pants and tried to think of anything to get his mind off Olivia, her arms open, her eyes hot and filled with desire as she reached for him.

He glanced around, trying to find anything else of interest. The condos, the flowers, the trees lining the two-lane street, the man and woman at the bus—He whipped his head back around to do a double take. That couldn't have been Janet with a suitcase. He looked into his rearview mirror, but the thick crepe myrtle bushes next to the street obscured his view. But what if it had been?

He was more anxious than ever to see Olivia. No one had to tell him that, if Janet had betrayed Olivia's faith and trust in her, Olivia would be deeply hurt. Like his mother, Olivia was a sensitive and compassionate woman. No one should take advantage of her. Even as the thought swept through his mind, he fought with the knowledge that whatever it was that drew him to her probably wouldn't last and he'd move on. Or would he?

"It was business as usual as far as I could tell." Olivia looked at the receipts for the day. "So you can stop worrying."

Tyler gave Olivia a thumb's-up although they both knew that that might change tomorrow or the next day, but there was so sense worrying about it now. "We better get home."

Putting the receipt book in the desk drawer, she came to her feet. "Are you going to look for her?"

"I wouldn't know where," Tyler said, frustration in his voice.

Rounding the desk, Olivia lightly touched his arm. "At least she knows where to find us."

He nodded, but the knowledge didn't help. Each time he thought of Jana having to go back to that hotel, his stomach clenched. He'd called twice. If she was there, she wasn't registered under either name.

"Let me lock the door and I'll get my—" All of a sudden Olivia went still and stared.

Tyler turned around. Disappointment hit him hard when he saw it was Dr. Cortez and not Jana.

"Hello," Julian said, thinking he should have followed his first instincts and kept on toward home. Neither looked pleased to see him. "I hope you don't mind me dropping by."

"I'm sorry, Julian." Olivia went to him. "I didn't expect you."

His gaze went from Olivia's unhappy face to Tyler's tight-lipped expression. "Guess I was right."

"Right about what?" Twin furrows raced across Olivia's forehead.

"The reason Janet was sitting at the bus stop with her suitcase," he answered.

"What? Where?" Tyler asked, striding toward Julian.

"Julian, please, where did you see her?" Olivia asked, her voice just as anxious.

"About five blocks up Mockingbird," he told them. "At least I think it was her. I only caught a glimpse of her when I passed. She had a suitcase . . ." His voice trailed off as Tyler raced for the door. Frowning as deeply as Olivia had earlier, Julian turned back to her. "Do you mind telling me what's going on?"

Olivia shook her head. "I'm not sure I can do that, although I appreciate you telling us about Jana. We were worried about her."

"Jana? I saw Janet," he corrected.

Olivia threaded her hand through her hair. "Jana is Janet."

"If you're trying to confuse me, you're doing a good job."

She signed, realizing there was little sense in not telling him everything. "All right, I'll explain, but on one condition."

"Name it?"

"That you listen objectively and keep an open mind."

He didn't hesitate. "All right."

Olivia glanced at her watch. "If I'm not home in ten minutes for dinner, Griffin will call. After dinner we're playing his new video basketball game."

Julian was as surprised as he was intrigued. He was also a man who took opportunity when he saw it. "Perhaps if I followed you home there'd be a few minutes for us to talk. Then, too, I could meet Griffin and let him know his mother will be in good hands since you said you haven't dated much."

Olivia tilted her pretty head to one side. "It sounds reasonable, but why do I get the feeling you have an ulterior motive?"

Julian grinned. "Because you're a perceptive woman. I already plan to wrangle an invitation to stay for dinner."

His honesty coupled with that engaging smile made her laugh. Perhaps Julian would be good for her. "Consider yourself invited."

Tyler didn't draw an easy breath until he saw Jana sitting on the bench at the bus stop. He whipped into a driveway of a neat pink brick home and slammed out of the truck. Her head down, her shoulders slumped, she looked to be a woman mired in hopelessness and despair. If she'd let him, he'd show her that her life didn't have to be that way.

"Jana," he called to her when he was several feet away.

Instantly she looked up. Her lips trembled. By the time he reached her, tears were streaming down her cheek. His arms went around her, holding her tight against him. "It's all right."

She held him just as tightly. "I didn't have anyplace to go."

"You do now." Ordering himself to let her go when he had been so afraid that he'd never get the chance to hold her again, he picked up her suitcase and started for his truck.

She was still sniffling when he gently urged her into the truck and gave her his handkerchief. Rounding the truck he climbed inside and fastened his seat belt. When she made no attempt to fasten hers, he did it for her, then started the motor. "We're going home."

She glanced up with the remnants of tears glittering in her eyes. "The police passed twice and looked me over. I was afraid they'd stop the next time."

Tyler shifted the truck into reverse, backed out into the street and took off the way he had come. "How long have you been there?"

"Since I left the house." She crumpled the handkerchief in her hand. "I couldn't seem to make myself get on the bus."

"I'm glad." In a matter of minutes he turned the corner onto his street. "Julian saw you at the bus stop."

She swallowed. "After a while I stopped paying much attention to the cars passing by."

Tyler knew men often trolled the area looking to pick up coeds from nearby Southern Methodist University. Traffic was always extremely congested. "Turned them all down, huh?"

She looked up. "It never crossed my mind to do otherwise."

"Of course not," he said and pulled into the driveway that curved around the side of the house to the garage in the back. "Want to bet that car in front of the house belongs to Julian?"

Jana twisted uneasily in her seat. "I don't want to see anyone. Could you please let Olivia know I'm all right?"

Parking the truck in the garage, Tyler opened her door. "She'd feel better and believe it more if it came from you."

"I have to face people," she said.

"Exactly." His hands spanned her small waist and lifted her out of the truck. "Come on. You need some fluids after sitting outside for three hours."

"The bench was shaded."

Holding her hand, he continued into the house. "It was still in the nineties today, and the bench was stone."

She rubbed her posterior. "Don't remind me."

He stopped and looked down at her. "I'd be glad to do that for you."

Her mouth opened, but nothing came out. She blinked rapidly as tears formed.

"I'm sorry," he quickly said, using his thumb to wipe away the moisture. "I was trying to make you laugh. Courtney always said I had a weird sense of humor."

The tears stopped immediately. "You mentioned her before."

"So I did." He entered the kitchen and saw Olivia, Julian and Griffin at the table eating. "I see you started without us."

Olivia squealed and was up in a flash. She and Jana hugged and wiped way tears with the tissues Tyler handed each of them.

"Those are happy tears, right, Mama?" Griffin asked, rising as well.

With one last sniff, Olivia held out her arm and her son came. "Yes, they are."

"I'm glad," he said. "Jana can play the video game with us if she wants."

"Trying to get another victim?" Tyler pulled out a chair for Jana.

Griffin grinned. "I'm playing Dr. Cortez after Mama. He promised he can take losing."

Julian smiled and casually sipped his iced tea. "A bit confident, aren't you?"

"That's the only way to be, Mama says." Griffin rounded the table and took his seat. "But considering you're a guest and you're taking Mama to dinner, I'll go easy on you."

"Griffin!" Olivia admonished, but she was laughing.

Jana took the seat Tyler held out. This felt right. Her gaze went to Olivia, then Tyler sitting beside her, piling food on her plate. They cared. Hearing about her past hadn't made them care any less. "Griffin, thanks but I think I'll just watch."

"How about you, Uncle Tyler?"

Tyler filled Jana's glass with iced tea. He was sticking as close to Jana as possible. "I'll sit with Jana and watch."

Julian looked at the score on the wide-screen television, which made it all the more glaring. Griffin had decimated him. The media room was ominously quiet. Griffin, who wore a big grin on his face, apparently wasn't concerned with or cared that grown-ups were supposed to win, which meant double for guests.

"I tried to warn you."

Julian looked at little boy sitting cross-legged in a pair of shorts and Polo shirt, the instrument of Julian's destruction still in his small hands. Apparently Griffin wasn't concerned about rubbing it in either.

"Griffin." Olivia said her son's name softly, but he lowered his head as if in contrition.

Julian was close enough to see that the smile remained on the young boy's face. Griffin was fiercely competitive with a keen intelligence, nerves of steel and uncanny instincts. Julian had liked him immediately.

"I want a rematch," Julian finally said.

"Not tonight," Olivia said, talking over Griffin's protest. "It's thirty minutes past your bedtime. Protest and the next time you'll go to bed whether or not the game is over."

Griffin began putting up the video equipment. Apparently Olivia didn't bluff.

"Good night, Julian." Tyler stuck out his hand. "Griffin is a whiz with video games and seldom loses."

"Now you tell me," Julian laughed. "Good night."

"Good night, Julian, Olivia," Jana said, then to Griffin. "Perhaps you can teach me sometime."

His grin broadened. "I sure will."

"Good night, Jana. We'll expect you for breakfast in the morning." Olivia told her, her hands on Griffin's shoulders.

"I'll see you then." Jana left the room with Tyler by her side.

"Julian, we haven't had a chance to talk and getting Griffin down for the night during the summer can be an experience." Olivia lovingly wrapped her arms around Griffin and pulled him back against her. "Perhaps if you have time you can come by the shop tomorrow."

"I have surgery in the morning," he said as they slowly walked to the front door. "It would have to be late afternoon."

"You cut on people?" Griffin's eyes widened with awe and pleasure. "Wow!"

"Griffin!" Olivia shook her head. "I'm sorry, Julian."

"It's all right. I've a feeling Griffin is an unusual young man." Julian stopped at the front door. "Are you going to be a surgeon when you grow up?"

"No, sir. I'm going to be like my father," Griffin supplied. "He's a financial planner and owns his own company with my grandfather."

Olivia tensed, her hold on Griffin tightening possessively. Julian knew he had stumbled into forbidden territory, but he didn't know how to back out without causing Olivia any more discomfort or hurting Griffin's feelings by ignoring the comment.

"My dad couldn't make it for Christmas, but he sent me a ton of cool games I wanted." Griffin stared back up at his mother. "Didn't he?"

"Yes," Olivia answered, her face and voice strained. "Your father loves you very much."

"He sure does." Griffin's attention switched back to Julian. "He couldn't make my birthday last year, but he will this time because I'll be eight in September and I'm not a baby anymore."

It wasn't difficult for Julian to figure out that Griffin's father didn't have much, if any, involvement with his son. Julian's father had been the same way. The army had been his first priority, not his family. "You certainly aren't a baby," Julian agreed. "A baby couldn't have beat me so badly, but I'll do better next time."

"How about Saturday night when you pick up Mama?"

Julian glanced at Olivia, glad to see the tension gone from her face. "If your mother doesn't mind, I could come fifteen minutes early."

Griffin whirled around. "Could he, Mama? Please?"

She brushed her hand tenderly over his head. "I suppose."

"Yippee!"

Julian smiled, enjoying the enthusiasm and spontaneity of the young boy. "I'll call tomorrow and let you know what time to expect me. Good night." With his hands in his pockets, Julian strolled to his car. Olivia might want to tell him what was going on with Jana, but he was more interested in the story behind her divorce.

Tyler gripped the money Jana handed him seconds after they entered her apartment. "You should have taken this."

Jana linked her fingers together. "I couldn't. Besides, I didn't need it."

He tried to look at it the way she did, but couldn't. Things might have turned out differently if Julian hadn't seen her. Just the thought of her being alone and in need knotted his stomach. She was safely back, and he had to fight the urge to crush her to him and make love to her. He couldn't. Not until Jana saw the woman he saw. "I have to go out of town tomorrow. I don't expect to be back until Sunday. I'd postpone it if I could."

"Somehow I know that. Have a safe trip."

"I'll see you in the morning." He pulled her into his arms, giving in to the desire to taste her lips, to hold her again. "Good night."

"Wait." She touched his arm.

Tyler stopped immediately, becoming worried when Jana didn't say anything. "What is it?"

She shook her head. "Nothing. Good night."

His finger lifted her chin. "You can ask or tell me anything."

"I just . . . just wondered why Courtney thought you had a weird sense of humor."

That was the last thing he expected her to ask. "I suppose because we never laughed at the same jokes. Come to think of it, we never agreed on much of anything."

"Was she important to you?" Jana asked, knowing she had no right to, but unable to stop herself.

"I was very close to asking her to marry me when she broke off the relationship."

A myriad of emotions pummeled Jana. She tried to feel sorry that the relationship hadn't worked, but couldn't. "Do you still care about her?"

He swept a finger down the side of Jana's face. "No. It just took me a while to realize that it wouldn't have worked."

"Why?"

"We were totally different people. Courtney wanted a perfect man, a man who had no vices. I like to play nickel poker occasionally, drink a beer, laze on the couch, and watch the Sunday game on television."

Jana's eyes widened. She couldn't believe a woman had actually walked away for such minor infractions. "Then she'd crucify me."

"Probably." His mouth twisted wryly. "No matter how I tried I couldn't quite come up to the level Courtney expected of me. It made me more tolerant of other people."

"Like me?"

"Like anyone. No one is perfect in this imperfect world. The best you can do is try. Anything else?"

"No, thank you. And thanks for being there for me. I won't let you or Olivia down."

"Don't let yourself down." His lips brushed gently across her. "Get some rest. Welcome home."

Trembling fingers pressed against her lips, then she smiled and whispered when the door closed behind Tyler. "Thank you, Courtney."

12

Jana went to sleep feeling as if she could conquer the world. However, by the time she followed Olivia into Midnight Dreams the next morning, her knees were shaking, her hands sweaty. Not even remembering Tyler's unshakable support that morning during breakfast helped. "I'm not sure I can do this anymore."

"You can." Olivia took her arm and kept going to the back. "Take a deep breath, push it out slowly, and relax."

"I don't think that will help," Jana said, but she did as Olivia instructed. "Maybe I should have waited a couple of days before coming back."

"Nonsense." Releasing her arm, Olivia took a seat behind her desk and put their purses in the bottom drawer. "You're a friend and a valuable asset to the store."

Friend. Her very first one. "I didn't know what having a friend meant until I met you," she confessed. "As for being an asset . . ."

Olivia booted up the computer before she spoke. "You're staying. I have an eleven-fifteen appointment and I'm leaving you in charge."

Jana's eyes widened. "Me?"

"You'll do fine." Olivia's slim hands danced over the keyboard. "And you can always reach me on my cell."

Jana opened her mouth to argue, then closed it. It was about time she acted as if she had as much confidence in herself as Olivia and Tyler had. "All right. I'll start on dusting."

"Thanks. That's definitely my least favorite thing to do."

Smiling, the tension slowly ebbing, Jana left the office.

Moments after Olivia left, three fashionable women entered the store. Hoping fervently they didn't know her, Jana went to greet them. "Welcome to Midnight Dreams. Is there anything I can help you with or would you like to browse?"

All three gave Jana the once-over. "We'd just like to look," the one in the middle said.

"Please feel free." Jana kept her smile in place although she was sure they'd come to look her over and not the merchandise.

The women went through the motions of picking up a candle here, bath soap there, then inspecting the linen on the bed, all the time their gazes sliding back to Jana.

They knew.

Jana's first instinct was to duck her head in shame and embarrassment; her second was to ask them to leave. She dismissed both inclinations. Yesterday Tyler had asked her if she had enough courage to face up to what she had done. She realized until she did, she'd never put her old life behind her or have the new life she craved.

Putting on her brightest smile, she walked over to them. They crowded together like a covey of quails, apprehension replacing speculation on their faces.

"Are you sure there isn't anything I can show you? I can tell by the way you carry yourselves and those stunning couture outfits you have on that you are discriminating buyers with impeccable taste. Armani, Ralph Lauren, Prada?" Jana said, ticking off the designers. The Kate Spade handbags were almost identical and matched their outfits in hot pink, sun yellow and apple green. "I love Kate Spade bags. I've met her."

"So did we, at a private showing at Neiman's," the one in green, apparently the leader, said. The other two made sure Jana could see the logo on their bags.

"I just love Neiman's, but when it comes to pure indulgence in linen you can't go wrong shopping at Midnight Dreams." Jana ran her hand over the eight-hundred-thread count sheet. "Feel. Can't you just imagine slipping between these after a long day? This is one purchase your husband will thank you for." She'd also noticed the wedding rings. All were more than three carats, but they weren't A-1 colorless. Obviously they were still trying to belong.

One by one, the women brushed their hands across the sheets. Jana could almost hear their sighs. "At five thousand dollars this is the best investment you can make."

"We're just looking," the outspoken one said, but she kept looking at the bed.

"We also have D. Porthault sheets. I'm sure you've heard of the Paris manufacturer." From their blank looks Jana knew they hadn't. "Who in society doesn't know they're the choice of English royalty? Being able to say you have on your bed the same sheets as those Queen Elizabeth sleeps on is priceless. Oprah prefers Anichini. Those are so fabulous the company doesn't even put the thread count on the package. Once you've felt them, you'll know why. They're sublime."

"Where are they?" asked the one in yellow.

Jana almost rubbed her hands together. "This way."

Thirty-seven minutes later the three women left the store, each carrying a shopping bag with a set of sheets. Jana couldn't wait to get to the phone. She didn't want to disturb Olivia, but there was one person she could call. "Tyler, I did it!"

"I could join in the celebration better if I knew what's made you so happy."

Jana laughed out loud. "Three women came in to scope me out and they all left with bed linen."

"Good for you."

"After seeing the set on display for five thousand dollars they considered it a steal to buy a set for nine hundred, especially when they can name drop that Oprah buys the same brand."

"I'm proud of you."

Her chest felt tight. No one had ever said those words to her, but then she couldn't think of too many things she'd done in her life to be proud of . . . until she met Tyler and Olivia.

"Jana?"

"I'm here." She took a steadying breath. "Just thinking how different my life might be if I hadn't met you and Olivia."

"You did. That's all that matters."

"Yes, I did." The door opened and a middle-aged man entered. "Customer. See you when you get back."

"Count on it."

Jan's heart fluttered. "Bye." She hung up the phone, and walked out to meet the customer. "Welcome to Midnight Dreams."

Jana met Olivia at the front door of Midnight Dreams waving sales receipts. "$3,430.98." She was bubbling. "I can't believe it!"

"You have the proof in your hand." Olivia placed her attaché case and sample books on the desk on the sales floor. "With the sale I just completed, we're having a banner day."

"I actually enjoyed selling, even to the three women who came in to size me up." Jana quickly told Olivia everything. "I may make a copy of the sales receipts and frame them."

"You should. It will remind you that you're stronger than you think," Olivia said. "God has a way of reminding us of that from time to time."

Jana didn't know about that. She wasn't high on religion. The people at the church she'd met were nice, but it could have been surface just like she'd been. Gray's grandmother was reportedly a staunch Christian, yet she had tried to ruin Jana's life. "Some of the biggest churchgoers are probably the biggest sinners."

"God understands that all of us can backslide now and then. Regardless of the women's initial motives, you both won."

Jana frowned. "How do you figure that?"

Olivia's smile was patient. "They learned not to be so harsh or quick to judge others, and you learned that with God in the mix, good can come out of bad."

If Jana had ever met a person as optimistic as Olivia, she didn't remember. "You're incredible."

"Not by a long shot. It took me a long time to get where I am and every step was difficult." She leaned against the desk. "When my marriage disintegrated I felt as if my heart was ripped from my body. I couldn't understand why God had given me so much pain. I didn't even begin to understand until I felt Griffin move." Her hand briefly cupped her stomach. "Without the marriage, he wouldn't have been born. He more than makes up for anything I had to endure."

Jana's eyes hardened. "My life is in shambles. I can't see the good in that."

"I don't mean to belittle what you've gone though, but you're more blessed than many people." At Jana's look of disbelief, Olivia continued. "You're safe and healthy. You have a place to stay, a job, food, friends, and you're making more. The women we prepared the baskets for can't say as much," she said.

"Perhaps your defining moment hasn't come or, if it has, you don't realize it yet," Olivia continued. "Just ask yourself one thing, and you don't have to tell me: Would you rather return to your old life or continue to build this new one?"

Jana thought of her privileged and luxurious jet-set life and the people she'd met, most of whom were as superficial and shallow as she, a life where no one cared if she lived or died. "I want to build a new life," she declared firmly.

Olivia didn't act surprised by the answer. "Then, whatever the reason or person that started you on this path did you a favor."

Jana's first instinct was to argue. Corrine Livingston had meant to crush Jana. Wait. Maybe she had simply been trying to protect her family. Wouldn't it be ironic if Jana owed her new life to Gray's protective grandmother. "She probably didn't mean it that way."

"What did I tell you about how God being in the mix changes things?"

The pastor's wife thought the same thing. "Maybe for some people, but not for me."

"For everyone." The phone on the desk rang and Olivia picked up the receiver. "Hello, Midnight Dreams." Her gaze flickered to Jana. "Hello, Julian."

Smiling, Jana moved away.

"If you like we can have lunch here. I'll see you in thirty minutes." Hanging up the phone she told Jana, "Julian will be here in thirty minutes for lunch."

"That will give you enough time to run to the store and get a fresh bouquet of flowers for the table. The tablecloth and candles are already covered."

Olivia frowned. "That's going a bit far. I'm not sure if I want this to go past a couple of friendly dates."

"Yes, you are. You're just scared." Jana handed Olivia her purse from the desk. "Go. I'll set the table."

Olivia didn't move. "There's linen on the top shelf in the back room."

Jana escorted Olivia to the front door. "I know where everything is. Get going. You want to be back in time to freshen up your makeup."

"I wish I knew where this will end. How's that for optimism?" She bit her lip. "I prayed about it, but I just don't know."

"I've been a player long enough to spot another one. Julian is for real, but that doesn't mean things will last," Jana told her frankly.

"There's more to think about than just me. I hadn't considered how much Griffin would like Julian," she said, her voice troubled.

"From what I saw last night, Julian is just as taken with Griffin as Griffin was with him." Jana opened the door. "Scoot."

"All right, I'm going. I'll just have to play this through." Closing the door behind her Olivia was gone.

"You didn't have to go to this trouble, but I appreciate it." Julian sipped his iced tea. On the ecru-draped table was a bouquet of fresh-cut flowers with roses, daisies and lilies and silver flatware. The air was gently scented with a vanilla candle.

"This is Jana's idea," Olivia admitted.

Julian lifted a brow. "You sure know how to burst a guy's bubble."

Dark chocolate eyes stared back at him. "But if I hadn't wanted the table to look nice, I wouldn't have let her talk me into it."

"You're such a mixture of courage and vulnerability." Julian commented, his fork poised over his salmon salad.

"I'm not vulnerable," she said, pushing her salad around on her plate. "Or very courageous."

Yes, you are, he wanted to say, but he let it slide. He had a pretty good idea both were because of her ex-husband. "I made reservations for eight at Chamberlain's. I thought I'd come by around half past seven."

Her head came up. For a moment there was fear in her eyes. "Griffin likes you. The game with you Saturday is all he talked about."

She'd fight a bear bare-handed to protect her son. "There haven't been many men in his life, right?" Julian said.

Lines radiated across Olivia's forehead. "Griffin has family who love him. My brother and his grandfather are all the men he needs," she said a bit defensively.

"And a mother who would give him the world if she could."

"Of course," she answered immediately.

"So simple and so complex, but then a mother's love always is." He smiled in remembrance. "You remind me of my mother." He chuckled at the shock on Olivia's face. "She loved us unconditionally, and wanted the world for us."

"You have sisters and brothers?"

"A brother." He picked at his salad. "He's a corporal in the army, stationed in Germany. My father is a drill sergeant and he's there as well."

"And your mother?"

His hand flexed. "She died when I was sixteen."

Her small hand covered his. "I'm sorry. That had to be devastating."

"She didn't have to die." He'd never discussed her death with anyone, but the quiet patience and understanding in Olivia's face drew the words from him. "We were on vacation and the doctor misdiagnosed her appendicitis. He sent her home with Maalox." His mouth tightened.

"I begged my daddy to take her to another doctor, but he didn't believe in coddling his soldiers or his family. She lay in bed for almost six hours in excruciating pain, then she seemed fine, the pain gone.

"We found out what was going on a month later when she became ill. The reason the pain subsided was that her appendix had ruptured. The last days of her life were spent in misery that didn't have to happen."

"So you decided to prevent other mothers and children from going through what your family had," she correctly guessed.

"Yes."

"You make her proud."

That had always been his goal. Feeling a little exposed, he pulled his hand back. "What about Jana?"

Olivia slowly put her hand in her lap. If he didn't want her comfort, it shouldn't matter. "I asked Jana if she minded me telling you. Remember your promise not to prejudge." At his nod, she told him of Priscilla's visit. "Jana is no longer that woman. She's proven that each and every day."

"So you keep Jana on despite a threat of losing business?" he asked.

She straightened. "I didn't say anything about losing business."

"You didn't have to," he said tightly. "It's no big jump to know the woman and her cronies wouldn't want around a woman known to go after any man she wants."

"I told you, Jana isn't like that anymore," Olivia defended.

"You've had a chance to see that. They haven't."

She leaned back in her chair. "You're right, but neither did they try to find out. They just assumed and crucified. She had the label, and they didn't look any further."

Julian stared at her a long time and she was afraid she'd revealed too much. "Is this all about Jana or something else?"

"I was just making an observation." Olivia rose and began picking up the plates. "I'm sorry to rush you, but I need to get back on the sales floor."

Julian gathered the flatware. "Despite my reputation as having no bedside manners, I'm a good listener."

She took the things from him and placed them in the sink. "I'll remember that if ever there is a need."

He wasn't going to push it. He had a feeling he might wind up dateless for Saturday night if he did. "You're very loyal. Griffin is a lucky boy."

"I'm the one who's lucky. I can't imagine how my life would be without him in it," she said.

She looked so sad. Julian wanted to hold her, take whatever worried her away. "See you Saturday night. Tell Griffin to get ready."

"I will. But he's already plotting your demise."

He'd gotten her to smile. "I better rent a game or two and practice." His beeper went off. He recognized the number. "Excuse me." He dialed the number on his cell phone. "Dr. Cortez." He listened, then said, "I'm on my way."

His face grave, he turned to Olivia. "I'm needed at the hospital. Care flight is bringing in a patient."

"Go." She briefly touched his arm. "I'll pray for both of you."

"Thank you." He headed for the door at a fast clip. From what the surgical resident had told him, they'd need all the prayers they could get.

Several hours later Julian sat in the doctor's lounge, his head bowed, his fingers laced together between his legs. Tonight their prayers hadn't been answered. Death had won.

For the better part of an hour for the second time that day he'd desperately fought to repair the broken body of a young woman cut from the wreckage of her car. She'd lost control when she tried to go around another car and skidded off an embankment.

He'd known before she was rushed into surgery the first time that the damage to her internal organs might be too severe, the blood loss too great. She'd made it through the first surgery, but had begun to hemorrhage in ICCU and was rushed back into the operating room. Her body had been too weak to survive. She'd never regained consciousness. She'd died while he was still trying to tie off bleeders.

"You did everything you could, Julian."

He lifted his head. Anger snapped in his dark eyes. "It wasn't enough."

Frank Jamison, the surgical resident who had assisted him, merely patted Julian on the shoulder and walked out of the doctor's lounge. They were taught in medical school that you couldn't save them all.

Julian wanted to rage, felt the words clawing at his throat at the senseless waste of life. The girl had been speeding home for her mother's birthday party. He'd had to tell her parents that their eighteen-year-old daughter wouldn't be coming home.

Too keyed up to remain sitting, he got up, paced. The mother had become hysterical. The father had looked dazed, utterly broken.

Julian walked to the window and looked out at the night skyline of downtown Dallas in the distance. Life went on, but not for Patti Ann Young. And for those she left behind, their lives would never be the same.

Changing out of his surgical scrubs into his street clothes, he left, got into his sports sedan and punched in a Sade CD. The singer's mournful voice and sad songs suited his mood. He thought he was driving aimlessly until he turned onto Olivia's street.

He stopped in front of her house. Lights shown from windows on the first floor and upstairs. Leaning his head back, he stared up through the moon roof. The night was beautiful. Death hadn't changed that. The day Julian's mother died the tulips she'd planted bloomed. He'd carried her outside to see them. An hour later she was dead.

Sitting up, he picked up the car phone and punched in Olivia's phone number.

"Hello." Just the sound of Olivia's voice somehow soothed the rough places.

"Hello," she repeated.

"Olivia, it's Julian."

"Julian?" There was a question in her voice, a slight hesitation as if she already knew.

"I wasn't able to save her."

"Oh, Julian, I'm so sorry. Are you still at the hospital?"

He rubbed his hand over his face. "No. I'm parked in front of your house."

"Would you like to come in?"

His getting through the night might depend on it. "Yes."

"I'll be right down."

Julian disconnected the phone and got out of the car. By the time he reached the front porch Olivia was there. He felt an almost overpowering need to hold her. Instead he stepped inside and closed the door behind him.

"Thank you." He rubbed the back of his neck. "As a trauma surgeon you expect the odds to be against you going in. We're trained to put our emotions on automatic."

"You value life, Julian. The person should be mourned."

He slipped his hands into the pockets of his slacks. "You never know the ones who will affect you. Young, old. They all want to live."

Gently she touched his arm. "Come into the kitchen. I'll get you a cup of coffee."

He nodded and followed. Taking a seat at the table, he watched her gather the things needed, her motions quick and efficient. She wore a long pink silk robe with three-quarter length sleeves. She looked adorable.

"I take it Griffin is asleep."

Olivia tossed a smile over her shoulders. "About ten minutes ago." Picking up the tray, she came to the table. Julian stood and helped her, then held out the chair next to him for her. She didn't hesitate to take it. "Thank you. Cream and sugar?"

"Black." He accepted the rose-patterned cup. "Sorry, I probably got you out of bed."

Olivia flushed prettily. "You didn't. I was working on plans for the store."

He nodded toward the pot. "You're not having any?"

The corners of her mouth tilted upward invitingly. "I'd be up half the night if I did."

He sat his cup down. "Yet you went to the trouble to fix coffee for me."

"It was no trouble." She sent him a teasing look. "Don't tell me you're one of those bachelors who can't cook?"

"My mother would have disowned me," he said. "She was from New Orleans and could cook like nobody's business. Her peach cobbler would make your drool. She taught me and my brother to cook and clean."

"Smart woman."

He couldn't agree more, except when she'd chosen her husband. "I take it you are doing the same with the Whiz Kid."

"Absolutely." She smiled at him. "One day a lucky woman is going to get a wonderful man."

"All trained." He relaxed in his chair.

She placed her folded arms on the table. "We're still working on putting the toilet seat down."

He grinned at her. "My money is on you."

She grinned back.

Somehow his gaze dropped to her lips, soft and inviting. He didn't think. He just leaned forward and brushed his against hers. She stiffened.

Before she could draw back, his hand cupped her head, keeping her in place with gentle persuasion instead of force. He felt the tremor that went through her body, felt his own heart rate increase.

Everything within him wanted to deepen the kiss, explore her sweet mouth. Instead he pulled back. Her eyes slowly opened. They were dazed. His weren't much better. The lady packed a wallop. When he really kissed her, it was going to be mind-blowing.

Slowly releasing her, Julian stood and stared down at Olivia. "That wasn't my intention when I arrived, but I'm glad it happened." He held out his hand. "Come on and lock up."

Olivia circled her lips with the tip of her tongue as if searching for the taste of him. Julian's hand clenched, then opened. "If you do that again, I may not be responsible."

Her eyes widened. She seriously thought of repeating the motion. Instead she took his hand and stood.

He squeezed it gently. Without a word he went to the front door. "I'll see you Saturday night. I'll be on my best behavior."

She wasn't sure she wanted him on his best behavior. She'd never known a kiss could empty your mind and fire your body like that.

"Good night and thanks." Opening the door he closed it after him.

Olivia pressed her trembling fingers to her lips. Julian could turn her inside out, transform her brain into confetti, make her knees week. She grinned and raced up the stairs to her room.

What a man, what a man.

"What's the matter?"

Saturday evening, Olivia spun around in the kitchen with the telephone in her hand. "Wanda's daughter came up unexpectedly from Lubbock. She can't make it to babysit Griffin." Sighing, she hung up the phone.

"I bet she wanted to, and you insisted she not come," Jana guessed.

"Family is important." Olivia removed Griffin's favorite cookies, chocolate chip loaded with walnuts, from the oven and placed the pan on the cooling rack. "I'll just have to cancel. Tyler isn't due home until tomorrow."

"Whoa." Jana turned Olivia around to face her. "You are not canceling your date with Julian. I have the perfect answer."

"I'm open to suggestions." Olivia removed her oven mitts. "I was kind of looking forward to going out with him tonight."

"If you weren't, I'd check your pulse. He's a dish. I'll keep Griffin. Unless you don't trust me with him," Jana added.

"I'll pretend you didn't say that. You don't know how energetic he can be." Olivia thrust her hand through her hair. "He's never still for more than a minute."

"Like his mother."

She smiled. "I'm afraid so."

"Why don't we let Griffin decide?" Jana suggested. "He can teach me how to play the video game."

"With that as a lure, he'll be your new best friend."

"Never can have too many. Let's go find out."

The two women left the kitchen together and found Griffin sitting crossed-legged in the media room playing a video football game. Jana saw no reason not to be up-front. "Griffin, Wanda can't make it. Looks like I'm your sitter, if you don't mind. You can start teaching me how to play."

"Great!" He scooted over on the carpeted floor. "Those are your controls."

Jana threw a quick look at Olivia, then sat beside Griffin and picked up the controls. "I don't suppose you'll take it easy on me because I'm a beginner?"

He looked at her sideways. "I might if we can have cookies and ice cream once Mama leaves on her date with Julian."

Jana laughed. "Nice try. I already heard her tell you at dinner that you can have two cookies, but no ice cream."

He shrugged carelessly. "Uncle Tyler and Grandpa always say you don't get anywhere if you don't try."

Even a seven-year-old had learned that valuable lesson. She was playing catch-up. "What do I do first?"

Griffin proceeded to show her how to work the controls. She quickly caught on, but no matter what she did, Griffin kept her scoreless.

Several minutes later the doorbell interrupted Griffin's total defeat of Jana. Laying the controls aside, he was up in a flash and racing for the door. Jana caught up with him at the door, admiring his restraint when he asked who was at the door since he wasn't tall enough to look through the peephole.

"Is that you, Dr. Cortez?"

"Yes."

Griffin unlocked the door and grabbed Julian's hand, dragging him over the threshold. "Come on, I've been waiting."

He nodded in passing. "Hello, Jana."

Jana tipped her head. They were still unsure of each other and both were aware that Olivia was the only link they shared. "Doc."

"I've been warming up with Jana." Griffin didn't release the doctor's hand until they were in the media room.

Julian glanced at Jana lagging behind. "How did you do?"

"I didn't score one point," she said, taking a seat in the deep burgundy leather sofa facing the television. "Griffin might be unbeatable."

"We'll just see about that." Julian rubbed his hands together, hitched up his pants and sat.

"You want a chair?" Jana asked.

"No, I'm fine. You can get into the swing better sitting on the floor."

"Prepare to be crushed," Griffin said.

The challenge was on. Amid giggles and verbal sparring, the two played. Olivia found them that way, sitting side by side. Her heart twisted. Griffin so much wanted a father. Tyler and their father tried to make up for her ex-husband's absence, but couldn't really. And there was no way Aaron would ever be a real father.

"I won!" Griffin shouted.

Julian groaned. "I'll never be able to hold my head up." Griffin giggled louder. "I bet I know a game I can win," Julian said.

With that warning, Julian pounced on Griffin, tickling him. In a matter of moments they were rolling on the floor. Julian looked up and saw Olivia with a wistful smile on her face. He went completely still. Griffin took advantage of Julian's inertness to climb on his back, his arms going around his neck. "I won again."

Julian barely noticed the boy's weight. He was too busy absorbing the stunning impact of his mother. She wore a tangerine sleeveless sheath that made her flawless cinnamon complexion glow. "You look beautiful."

"Thank you," she said shyly.

"Oh, Mama, you can't take him now." Griffin unclamped his arms from around Julian's neck and stood.

"A man can't stand up a woman." Julian came to his feet as well.

"I know or they'll cry," Griffin said, his expression grave.

Julian frowned down at him, then looked at Olivia for an explanation. "He and his classmates have been discussing dating," she explained.

"I'm glad you're not like the boy who stood Cindi's big sister up. She cried," Griffin told him. "But Mama said Cindi's sister was better off without him."

"Your mother is right." He stuck his hand out to Griffin. "I'll take good care of her."

Griffin looked enormously pleased by the gesture. "It's all right if she gets two desserts."

They all laughed. "I'll remember that. You ready to go?"

"Yes." She went to Griffin and kissed him on the cheek. "My cell is on. Two cookie limit and once Jana puts you in bed stay there, and no cutting off the monitor or you'll have me to deal with."

"Yes, Mama," he said dutifully.

Smiling Jana put her hand on Griffin's shoulder. "He'll be fine. Have fun."

"Good night." Julian's hand on the small of Olivia's back, he led her to the door. The heat of her body caused his hand to tingle, his body to want. Ruthlessly he brought his desire under control. If he wasn't careful, his first date with Olivia would be his last.

13

Chamberlain's, a four-star restaurant in a sprawling upscale shopping complex, has the best steaks in Texas, so Julian wasn't surprised when there was a wait for valet parking in front of the red brick structure. Three cars were ahead of them. "Sorry about this, but we won't have to wait for our table."

"If there wasn't a wait on a Saturday night, I'd suggest we find another place to eat," Olivia said.

Julian threw her a look. "Why do you always surprise me?"

"I'm not sure. Could it be because you expect so little from women?"

He frowned. She'd done it again. The women he dated were beautiful and charming, good in bed, and able to walk away from him as easily as he walked away from them. He hadn't thought of any of them last night when he was dealing with the loss of his patient. He'd called Olivia.

"The valet is motioning for you to pull up."

Julian eased up behind a Corvette. "You think I'm shallow, don't you?"

"I haven't formed an opinion past dedicated and determined. However, it wouldn't speak well of me if I dated a shallow man."

Julian stared hard at her. He couldn't tell if she was laughing at him or not. He'd never had this much difficulty gaining a woman's trust. Or was it that they hadn't interested him enough to think about them past the time they'd spend together.

He moved up. Perhaps he was shallow. "Have you ever been here before?"

"No." She smiled. "Griffin is more into places like Chuck E. Cheese's."

"You've done a great job with him," Julian said. "He's not shy about speaking his mind."

"No. No one will ever take advantage of him," she said, her expression set and determined.

"His father didn't send those games, did he?" he guessed.

Her brown eyes widened, then she glanced out the window. "No."

He placed his hand on hers clamped together in her lap, waited until she looked at him. "My father and I didn't get along. Without my mother's love, I wouldn't have made it."

"Thank you." Her hands beneath his relaxed.

Releasing her hand, Julian pulled up to the valet stand. Almost immediately two smiling attendants opened their doors. "Good evening, folks. Welcome to Chamberlain's."

Julian rounded the sports sedan and took Olivia's arm. Wearing the same friendly smile as the valet attendant's, the doorman held open one of the double wooden doors. "Good evening. Enjoy your meal."

"Thank you," Julian and Olivia said simultaneously.

As Julian has predicted, they were immediately shown to their intimate table near a stone fireplace. On the pristine white tablecloth was a deep red hibiscus in a bud vase. The waiter appeared and took their orders. In minutes he was back with a small French loaf and the wine Julian had ordered.

"You aren't on duty tonight?" Olivia questioned.

"Nope. Tomorrow either." Julian sipped the red wine and nodded his acceptance. The waiter filled their glasses and withdrew.

Julian lifted his glass. "To becoming better acquainted."

Olivia touched her glass to his and sipped. "This is delicious."

"So is the food and the cheesecake is marvelous." He placed his glass on the white tablecloth. "You can have two desserts, remember?"

"Since I only had a few crackers for lunch, I may take you up on your offer."

Julian immediately signaled their waiter and ordered the appetizer sampler. "So business is good."

"Yes. Jana is the reason." She reached for the bread. "Do you want any?"

"No, thanks."

Olivia placed the sliced bread and then a pat of butter on her bread plate. "She's a natural at sales. She friendly and knowledgeable."

The waiter placed their salads and appetizer of jumbo shrimp, scallops, and portabello mushrooms on the table, then left.

She frowned. "I think you might have overdone it. I hate wasting food."

"We'll ask for a take-away box." He picked up a skewered sesame shrimp and held it out to her.

Olivia eyed the shrimp, then Julian. He smiled. "It won't bite."

Cautiously she leaned forward and bit. "Delicious." She moaned in pleasure and Julian's body reacted to the sound, a sound he could easily imagine coming from her when they were in bed making love.

She offered him a shrimp. He didn't hesitate to take the food. Perhaps it would get his mind off making love to Olivia until neither one of them could lift their head from the pillow. Somehow his lips brushed against her fingertips.

Olivia's sharp intake of breath went through him. She stared at him. Julian smiled despite the need that rushed though him. "I agree. Delicious."

Olivia blinked and busied herself with her salad. "How long have you lived in Dallas?"

"Since medical school at UT Southwestern," he answered, willing to take it slow. Olivia was worth the cold showers. "You?"

"All my life. I went to college at UT in Austin." She glanced up at him. "So I guess that makes us college mates or something."

He knew what he'd like them to be. His expression must have shown as much because she dove back into her ceasar salad. He almost sighed. If he kept this up, he'd be lucky to get her to go out with him again. He searched his mind for a safe topic. "Why luxe linen?"

Her head came up and Julian was determined that it remain that way. She explained how she'd read an article in a magazine. "Three years ago I relocated to where I am now. It's a prime location, near my home, and Griffin's school."

The waiter served their food, replenished the bread, topped off their wine, and disappeared.

Her eyes sparkled when she mention her son. Julian cut into his rare kobe filet mignon. "He's something."

"He is, isn't he?" she laughed. "He doesn't know fear."

There it was again. Her deep need for Griffin to care for himself. Just the thought of her possibly being abused sent rage through him. "Your marriage—"

"Is not open to discussion," Her words were sharp, unconditional.

Instinctively he knew she'd leave if he pushed it. "Has anyone ever beat Griffin at video games?"

She relaxed. "Tyler. But no one has ever beaten him two games in a row."

"Figures," Julian said with just enough grumpiness to ensure Olivia would laugh.

"I must admit he likes playing with you." She bit into her asparagus.

"Because he beats me," Julian guessed.

"No," she said, her face troubled. "He likes you."

"And that worries you?" Julian paused in reaching for his wine.

"Yes." She looked across the table at him. "I didn't realize how much he'd be taken with you or think about how he'll feel when this is over."

Julian didn't expect his gut to clench. "This is our first date and you're dooming us already?"

She placed her fork on her plate. "You'll move on, Julian. It's inevitable."

He didn't like the calm way she'd said that. "You don't seem disturbed by the thought."

For a moment she looked incredibly sad. "I learned long ago to be realistic."

He suspected her marriage had taught her many hard lessons. He easily recalled the hell his father had put his mother though. Rage at Olivia's ex-husband swept though him. "Perhaps you learned the wrong lesson from the wrong man." He shoved his plate away.

Her eyebrow lifted at the harshness in his tone. "Perhaps."

Immediately contrite, his hand closed tenderly over hers. Olivia had been through enough. "I wouldn't hurt you or Griffin."

"Not intentionally." Withdrawing her hand, she smiled. "Now, about dessert."

She was pushing him away again. Julian straightened and signaled the waiter. He'd let it go for now. He'd just have to show her he wasn't going anyplace anytime soon.

Griffin was as difficult as Jana had anticipated in getting to bed and closing his eyes. There was always one more thing he needed to do: check his goldfish, get a glass of water, find his favorite book. Still, they were only thirty minutes behind schedule. Best of all, he'd fallen asleep almost immediately.

Making sure the monitor was on, she picked up the portable receiver and went downstairs to the pool. Placing the monitor out of harm's way and where she could see it on the glass table several feet from the pool, she turned up the volume and slipped out of her pants and blouse. Underneath was a black one-piece swimsuit she'd purchased the day before.

She dove into the tranquil blue water of the rectangular pool, barely creating a ripple, swam several feet away, and then back to the edge. She didn't want to get so far away she couldn't hear the monitor. Olivia couldn't possibly know how much it meant to Jana that she let her watch Griffin. She was trusted.

Reaching the end of the pool, Jana listened, then floated on her back, staring up at the huge half-moon above. It almost looked as if she could touch it. The sight made her feel small and miss Tyler like crazy. She hadn't realized how much his presence had come to mean to her until he was gone.

"Hello."

Tyler. Jana's pulse accelerated. She came upright, floating in place, and simply stared at Tyler, who stood at the edge of the pool. He had on snug-fitting jeans and a white shirt. He looked wonderful and sexy as hell. "Hello. We didn't expect you until tomorrow afternoon," she managed, her voice breathless.

"Finished quicker that I thought. I didn't see any reason for staying."

She didn't know what to say. He was hunkered down by the edge of the pool, the light from the house silhouetting his well-built body. He was a tempting man.

He stood, still staring down at her. "I think I'll join you." His hands went to the button on his jeans. Jana's eyes widened, but she couldn't look away. She told herself she was glad when he shoved his pants down his long, muscular legs that he had on a pair of brief black swim trunks.

So she hadn't quite stopped lying.

He grinned devilishly. "I saw you when I came home. I make it a practice to check the house when I get back."

"You checked on Griffin?" she asked, a safe subject.

"Sleeping." He slipped into the water. "He can usually talk Wanda into extending his bedtime."

Her pulse hammered like crazy. "Wanda couldn't make it."

He brow puckered then cleared. "You?"

"Me," she said.

"It seems you're a woman of many talents."

Once she might have taken that as an insult. "It does." She swam easily beside him. "I made good grades in school until I learned I got more attention if I screwed up. I was very good at screwing up."

"A lot of children do that."

"I suppose, but at the time I was so angry with my parents for ignoring me, I just wanted to disrupt their lives and make them look at me. My mother finally did when I was fifteen, but it was to make me a clone of her." She reached the edge of the pool, hoisted herself out and reached for a towel to dry her face while she left her lower legs in the water. "I remember being so happy that she was paying attention to me, teaching me about boys, and how to always be in control."

Shock, then anger swept across Tyler's face. He'd never understand her parents. She wasn't sure she ever would either.

"My mother is one of the most beautiful women I've ever seen. Having her pay attention to me was the most important thing in the world. We became friends, or so I thought."

"What happened?" He climbed out and accepted the towel she handed him.

"She liked listening to my escapades, but we never shared anything if it didn't involve conquest. To her, control was everything and I was her willing pupil."

He sat beside her. "It's natural to look up to your mother. It's the parent's responsibility to teach the child right from wrong. You weren't taught."

"I was so busy racking up scores, I didn't care. The more my father ignored me, the worse I became." Somehow she found the courage to look him in the eye. "The night we met I'd been to Priscilla's house, looking for a man to take care of me."

"Did you find one?"

"In a matter of speaking." She told him about being tossed out of Priscilla's house and being picked up by Douglas Gregory. "In that car in the darkened parking lot, it finally hit home that I had sunk to rock bottom. I ran."

Reaching over, he squeezed her hand. She squeezed his back. "There hadn't been a man in my life for the past five months. To survive I sold almost everything."

"You're not the woman Priscilla or the others knew."

"I finally believe that. Perhaps my father will believe it too and stop hating me. Heaven knows, I've given him and his new wife reasons." She sighed. "I've done so many unspeakable things in my life."

"In the eyes of God, sin is sin. He's not going to keep throwing them up in your face, so neither should you. You won't get very far in life if you don't let go of the past and stop dragging it with you every step of the way."

"I don't want that life anymore, but I realize it will be difficult for some people to accept that I've changed."

"If you try to live for other people instead of yourself, you're doomed to be miserable," he told her.

"I think that's what I did with my mother. I imitated her in hopes she'd love me." Jana stared up at the moon again. "I wonder if she ever did. I called her the night I fainted and ended up at the hospital. She wasn't interested."

"So, what do you plan to do now?"

She looked at him. "Be the best that I can be. I was great today in the store. I don't need a man to take care of me or make me feel special."

"Well, that all depends on the man don't you think?" Tyler replied, his voice dropping to a husky pitch.

"Beside my ex, I've only known one kind," Jana said, regret making her voice strained.

"Then you're long overdue. It will be my pleasure to reacquaint you." His fingertip softly traced her lower lip. "If you'll let me."

Her body quickened, yearned. She was caught between desire and wanting more than sex with him. "Tyler, too many things in my life are unsettled now."

"I understand." He stood and tugged her to her feet. "I have a present for you." With his free hand, he lifted a rose print gift bag from the glass table.

Her eyes rounded. She'd been so intent on him, she hadn't noticed anything else.

"It won't bite," he teased.

Finally accepting the bag, she lifted the tissue wrapped box out and gasped. Her gaze bounced from the bottle of Joy to him. She blinked, and then blinked again.

"If you cry, I'm taking it back."

She managed a shaky smile. For a practical man like Tyler to buy the expensive perfume was more precious than any gift she had ever received. "Thank you."

"You're welcome. How about that movie Monday night in the media room around eight-thirty? I'll bring the buttered popcorn."

For a moment Jana visualized them on the sofa, not making love, simply holding each other. "I'd like that. Good night."

"Good night, Jana. Sweet dreams."

Handing him the monitor, she walked away. With Tyler home, sweet dreams were the only kind she'd have.

Olivia hadn't meant to be quite so frank about the outcome of her dating Julian. Maybe because Aaron's dishonesty had been so devastating she'd overcompensated. Now, walking beside Julian to the front door, she wished she'd kept her mouth shut. Before and after her blunder, she'd enjoyed being with him.

She unlocked the door and turned, lifting her hand. "Thank you for a wonderful evening."

Julian looked from her outstretched hand to her face. "Thank you." His hand closed over hers and he pulled her into his arms.

His warm, persuasive mouth covering hers cut off her startled cry. This time there was no gentle brush of lips. This was a wildly erotic and bold taking of her mouth by a man who knew what he was doing.

His tongue ravished her mouth, the heat of his hand burned though her dress, his hard body excited her. She couldn't think and gave up trying and just enjoyed Julian driving every thought from her head except the incredible pleasure he was bringing her. Much too soon he lifted his head.

"Have you or Griffin ever driven bumper cars?"

It took a long moment for her brain to work, for his words to sink in. "No."

"Great. If you don't have plans for tomorrow afternoon, how about I pick you and Griffin up around five. We can eat before or afterwards, whatever works best for you," he said.

"You want Griffin to go on a date with us?" she asked.

"Yes." Julian smiled. "At least he won't beat me this time."

A knot formed in her throat. When he moved on it would be difficult for both mother and son, but not for anything would she deny either of them the prospect of being with Julian. "He'll be so excited. We'll be ready."

"See you then." He kissed her quickly on the lips, urged her inside, then closed the door.

Olivia heard him whistling. She smiled.

Sunday morning Jana stared in the mirror and assessed herself. Nothing about her hinted at the kind of life she'd once lived. After two weeks the dark circles were gone, her cheeks had filled out, her hair was styled, her nails manicured, her feet enclosed in heeled sandals. She wore a white silk blouse and black gabardine slacks. The look could have been improved with a jacket, hoop silver earrings and a silver chain necklace, but she hadn't made her decision until that morning.

She was going to church with Tyler and Olivia. She'd told them at breakfast. Olivia had hugged her. Tyler had given her a smile that she'd always treasure. That they could forgive her and want her around after what they'd learned about her past was nothing short of miraculous. Church was important to them and although Jana wasn't sold on it for herself, it wouldn't hurt to give it a try. She'd certainly screwed up on her own.

Picking up her purse, she went downstairs. They were waiting for her by Tyler's truck. "Sorry to keep you waiting."

"For this we'd wait all day," Olivia said, getting in the back seat of the vehicle. Griffin climbed in behind her.

"You look beautiful and smell wonderful." Tyler opened the passenger door for her.

"Thanks to you." She climbed inside. "But I have to admit I'm shaking in my shoes." She never wanted to lie to him.

"You'll be fine." He closed her door and went to the driver's side and got in.

Jana wasn't so sure, but she was willing to give it a try.

If you expect God to forgive you of your sins, you have to forgive others.

Pastor Palmer's words replayed themselves over and over in Jana's head long after they'd returned home from church. After lunch, she'd excused herself and gone outside to sit by the pool and think. Her motto had always been, "Don't get mad, get even." No one crossed her and got away with it. No matter how long she had to wait she'd eventually pay then back.

And because of the way she'd treated people, no one had helped her when she was down. Every person she'd wronged and those close to them had been standing in line to pay her back.

Their motto had been the same as hers.

"What are you thinking?" Tyler asked, sitting on the lounge chair next to her.

She sighed. "You reap what you sow." That had been in Pastor Palmer's message too.

"True, but you're fast racking up points in your favor." He took her hands in his. "Pastor Palmer thanked you from the pulpit."

She'd been surprised and a bit embarrassed to stand up. "I'm sure Maggie had a hand in it."

"Probably, but you deserved to be recognized for helping," he told her. "Some people only want to help themselves."

"I was at the head of that line," she reminded him.

"*Was.*" Standing he pulled her to her feet, his arms going around her waist as he nuzzled her neck. "You always smell and taste sensational."

Boneless she sank against him, arching her neck to allow him better access. "It's the perfume."

"It's the woman," he said, brushing his lips across hers again and again, teasing both of them before taking her mouth in a deep, hot kiss.

Their breathing was off-kilter when he lifted his head. "Want to go see a Rangers' game?"

Her hands on his wide chest, she stood easily in his arms. "Baseball, right?"

His sinful mouth twitched. "Right. We'll stuff ourselves with junk food since we don't have to set an example for Griffin. It will just be a lazy afternoon of fun."

She couldn't think of anything she'd like to do more. "It sounds wonderful."

Olivia and Griffin were waiting in the living room when Julian drove up. She couldn't deny she was anxious. Julian could make a woman throw caution to the wind. She didn't like to recall that she'd done that once with disastrous results.

Aaron had been a chameleon, sly and devious. He and Julian were worlds apart, but Julian could hurt her just as badly if she allowed herself to care for him too much.

"Julian is here." Griffin was out the door in nothing flat.

Olivia followed. Julian in worn jeans that molded to his muscular thighs and a blue pinstriped shirt emerged from the sports sedan and waved. "Hi, Olivia. Griffin."

Fifteen feet from the car, Griffin stopped dead in his tracks. "Wow!"

Julian smiled. "That was exactly my reaction when I first saw the car on the showroom floor." He put his hand on Griffin's shoulder and walked closer to the car, pointing out details. "The front has a chromed mesh-front grill and side vents."

Olivia hung back. How could she not care for a man who treated her son with such care and affection?

"Would you like to sit in the driver's seat for a moment?" Julian asked.

Olivia saw that Griffin was torn. Like most little boys he loved cars, but he was also excited about the bumper cars.

He looked at her. "Can I, Mama?"

She didn't hesitate. "Yes."

Griffin cautiously sat on the custom handcrafted ivory leather with bordeaux piping, the same color as the car, and wrapped his hands around the leather-covered steering wheel. His legs weren't long enough to reach the pedals and he could barely see over the gauge-filled dash, but he was grinning for all he was worth.

"How fast will it go?"

"With a V-8 engine it can take you from zero to sixty miles per hour in five point one seconds and reach speeds of one hundred seventy miles per hour." Julian hunkered down beside the open door. "But that's not why I bought it." He waited until Griffin looked at him. "It's one of the safest cars made. Driving fast is dangerous. Remember that when you start driving."

"I will."

Julian pushed to his feet and turned to Olivia. "Ready?"

"Yes, if we can get Griffin out of the driver's seat."

"I got it covered." He seated her and went to Griffin. "There's a Chuck E. Cheese's near where we're going. You think we can talk your mother into eating dinner there?"

"I bet we could."

"Great. Hop in the back seat and fasten your seat belt. Women don't like to be kept waiting and we want to make sure she stays in a good mood."

Griffin quickly got into the back seat and fastened his seat belt. "Mama, are you in a good mood?"

She looked at Julian next to her. "Yes, Griffin, I'm in a very good mood."

"And I plan to keep you that way," Julian whispered softly as he pulled away from the curb.

If only he could, she thought. *If only he could.*

14

By Monday Olivia was ready to move forward with her idea of having gift baskets available to customers. Theirs would be different and distinct. They'd put bath products with towels or bathrobes; pair perfumed ironing water with sheets.

Julian was even coming over later to help. Yesterday had been filled with fun. Griffin had enjoyed himself. He was so tired he had fallen asleep when his head hit the pillow. That had given her the opportunity to go back downstairs and kiss Julian goodnight. Several times as she recalled with remembered pleasure.

Olivia paused at the desk on the sales floor, her eyes going dreamy. The way Julian kissed and made a woman feel should be illegal. But she was grateful it wasn't. During their outing she had made up her mind to enjoy the time with Julian and let tomorrow take care of itself.

She went back to the list Jana had given her. As soon as they closed, she and Jana were going to the floral wholesale warehouse. They'd already loaded the merchandise in her SUV. She had a feeling this was going to be great for business.

The door opened and she looked up and saw Mrs. Fulton. Olivia stiffened. The woman hesitated, then came directly to the desk, her hand clenched around the gold chain strap of her Chanel bag.

"Mrs. Fulton."

"I, er . . ." Mrs. Fulton's voice trailed off, she moistened her lips. "I've come to give you another chance."

Her gaze direct, Olivia came to her feet. "I run my business as I see fit. Good day."

"I—" Mrs. Fulton stopped and took a step back.

Olivia heard the swinging door behind her and knew Jana had entered the room. "There is nothing more to discuss."

The older woman didn't move. "I'm sure we can work something out to both of our satisfaction."

Olivia stepped around the desk "There is nothing to work out." She glanced at her watch. "I'm sorry. We closed as of three minutes ago and we have an appointment."

"You'd take her over the kind of business I can bring you?" Mrs. Fulton asked, her chest puffed out in her pink and black mini-check Chanel suit.

"I'd close before I turn my back on a friend," Olivia told her without hesitation.

Mrs. Fulton stared at Olivia, then seemed to crumple in the Queen Anne chair in front of the desk. "You have to help me. My husband wasn't . . . wasn't pleased when I told him we wouldn't have the linen for the launch. He has some very important guests coming." Her grip on her bag tightened.

"You could try another store or another manufacturer," Olivia suggested.

"Don't you think I've tried? My husband wants Frette sheets, but since I canceled my order the company won't even attempt to finish the order unless I'm willing to pay triple because they have to push my order ahead of others."

Jana whistled softly.

"Robert won't pay such an exorbitant amount. Please, you have to help me," Mrs. Fulton pleaded.

"I'm sorry, Mrs. Fulton," Olivia said. "You put me in a terrible position when you canceled and I had to notify the company. The manufacturer prides itself on top-quality workmanship and customer satisfaction. I pride myself on customer satisfaction as well. Money and many man-hours were lost in cutting those custom sheets."

"What am I to do?" Mrs. Fulton asked, her face drawn as she battled tears.

"There are two possible solutions." Olivia folded her arms. "You can postpone the launch or have someone monogram regular sheets."

Tears crested in Mrs. Fulton's eyes. "I told everyone about the sheets. I'll be ruined."

And you brought it on yourself by bragging, Jana thought. Mrs. Fulton knew as well as Jana that women would be checking to see the Frette label. When they didn't see it, the news would spread that she had lied. Jana took satisfaction in the other woman's misery until she remembered the pastor's message the day before. Most of all, she remembered that Tyler and Olivia had forgiven her and what might have happened to her if they hadn't.

If you want God to forgive you, you have to forgive others. Jana didn't know if God had forgiven her or if it was He who had directed her to Midnight Dreams, but she was willing to give Him the benefit of the doubt.

"Olivia, if the sheets are ready except for the monogram could the company overnight them and you hire a seamstress to do the monogram?" Jana asked.

Mrs. Fulton perked up. "Could we do that?"

Olivia tried to hide her surprise at Jana's attempt to help a woman who had wanted to ruin her. She stared at Jana a long moment, then unfolded her arms, picked up the phone and dialed. If Jana could forgive Mrs. Fulton, then so could she. "Their rep is in New York this week," she said, then moments later. "Yes, Henri, Olivia Sanders. Fine, thank you. I need to speak with you about Mrs. Fulton's order."

Olivia hung up ten minutes later. "The sheets should arrive by Friday. It will be an additional ten thousand dollars. I assumed you wouldn't mind paying."

"Thank you." Mrs. Fulton fumbled in her purse, pulled out her American Express credit card, and handed it to Olivia. She didn't take it.

"The seamstress we use charges by the letter, the intricacy of the lettering, and the type of thread. A ballpark estimate would be an additional two to three thousand dollars," Olivia said.

"Whatever you say," Mrs. Fulton agreed, the credit card still in her hand.

"There is one other thing before the sale is written up. You owe Jana an apology."

Mrs. Fulton's eyes widened. She shrank back in her chair.

Olivia's eyes narrowed. "If you can't do that, then this conversation is over."

"I'm sorry," the woman whispered.

"Apology accepted," Jana said, seeing Olivia in a new light. Tyler had indicated she was a tigress and he was right.

Olivia took the card and gave it to Jana. "Jana will assist you."

Mrs. Fulton's lips pressed tightly together.

"Is there a problem, Mrs. Fulton?" Olivia asked.

"No." She quickly shook her head.

"Good, because this is to help you and not because I need the business," Olivia said. "I'll pull the old order from the back."

Jana sat and stared across the desk at the haughty, miserable woman who had been taken down a notch or two. "You didn't ask for it, but I'm going to give you some advice. Cultivate the friendships of those who could care less about the manufacturer of your linen or how much money you have."

Mrs. Fulton nodded slightly, then glanced away, dismissing Jana.

Instead of thinking what satisfaction snatching every frosted hair out of Mrs. Fulton's head would bring or dwelling on how ungrateful she was, Jana thought of Tyler. He always saw the best in her. "You better be glad I'm not the person I used to be."

Mrs. Fulton glanced around sharply. Fear leaped in her eyes.

"Don't worry. What I'm trying to build is more important than revenge." She picked up a pen. "But if I were you, I'd watch my back with Priscilla."

Working together that evening it didn't take long to wrap the baskets and load them in Olivia's SUV. Griffin wanted Tyler to see Julian's car and somehow talked them into going for a drive with the moon roof down and a stop at the Marble Creamy for ice cream. The took their ice cream outside where they could sit in the black wrought-iron enclosed patio in front of the store.

Olivia looked across the table at Tyler with his arm around Jana, her feeding him a mixture of fresh strawberries and vanilla ice cream with a spoon. She smiled.

"Next time we'll have to try that," Julian said softly.

Olivia glanced at Griffin beside them, licking his chocolate ice-cream cone. "I'll hold you to it."

"How about Wednesday night?" he asked, his gaze warm and full of promise.

Olivia didn't hesitate. "I'll be ready at eight."

"Hello, Tyler, Olivia," greeted a tall, slender man with graying hair. "You too, Griffin."

"Hello. Mr. Callier," Olivia and Griffin said.

Tyler stood and extended his hand over the three-foot railing. "Good evening, Mr. Callier. This is Jana Franklin and Dr. Julian Cortez. Lionel Callier."

The older man nodded to Jana and shook Julian's hand, but clearly his attention was on Tyler. "How are things going?"

"Great. Would you like to join us?" Tyler asked.

He held up the quart-sized white sack. "No thanks. I better get home with Courtney's ice cream before it melts."

"She and her husband are back from Africa?" Olivia asked.

There was a long pause. Mr. Callier glanced away then looked at Tyler. "She's by herself," Mr. Callier said quietly.

Tyler was not going to speculate on the reason. He took his seat, repositioning his arm around Jana's shoulder. "You must be glad to have her home."

"Yes, I am," he confirmed, a frown on his angular face as he studied Jana. "Well, I better get going." He continued toward the parking lot.

"Uncle Tyler," Griffin whispered when Mr. Callier was several feet away.

"Yes, Griffin."

Griffin watched Mr. Callier get into a late model black Cadillac, then asked, "You aren't going to start dating her again, are you, Uncle Tyler?"

"No, Griffin. She's married." He turned to Jana sitting quietly beside him and tightened his hold. "I'm interested in another woman."

Jana had rolled over her competition in the past. She'd used every sexual trick she could think of to get the man she wanted. Even if she thought that would work with Tyler, she had left that life behind.

"You aren't paying any attention to the movie." Tyler sat beside her in the media room later that evening. Olivia had put Griffin to bed as soon as they returned, then retired herself.

They'd chosen a comedy from the wide election of DVDs. As she'd expected, it was nice just sitting beside Tyler on the sofa, his arm around her. But she couldn't relax. "Just thinking."

Tyler turned off the movie and dimmed the lights in the room. Her breath quickened even before he turned, his mouth unerringly finding hers.

He took his time driving her slowly out of her mind with need and pleasure. She couldn't get enough of his hot mouth, his inventive tongue that teased and beckoned. His large hand stroked her stomach, going higher and higher until he cupped her breast. She shuddered, then arched.

He groaned. She moaned.

Her hand swept beneath his shirt. His skin was smooth with muscled hardness beneath.

"You taste sweeter each time I kiss you," he said.

She wanted to. She wanted to be everything he had ever wanted in a woman. His mouth took hers again. It was a long time before he lifted his head. "If I don't stop now, I may not be able to."

She didn't want him to stop and almost voiced her objection aloud. "You're doing this for me, aren't you?"

He tipped her chin up with his finger. "You deserve to be cherished, and I'm the man to show you just how much."

She recalled his promise. "You already have."

"Honey." He pulled her back in his arms and just held her.

She snuggled closer, content to lie in his arms. This was the life she wanted. She just hoped and prayed, yes prayed, it wouldn't be taken from her.

"What about Courtney?" she asked, barely breathing as she waited for his answer.

He stared down at her. "It's over between us. I wouldn't lie to you."

The fear receded. Tyler was too honorable to lie to her. Her hand circled his neck and she pulled his head down to meet her lips.

———

Jana didn't notice Mitsy and Sherilyn were in the store until she handed the customer in front of the desk a large-handled shopping bag containing the gift basket she'd just purchased. Jana's smile froze. Frantic, she glanced around the store, searching for Olivia.

Jana located Olivia near the front of the store showing a matronly women the last of the five baskets Jana had made. They'd proven as popular as Olivia had predicted. The only other customers were a young couple in their mid-twenties browsing in bath accessories. There was only one reason for the two troublemakers to come into the store. It was exactly a week since the altercation with Priscilla.

"Can I please have my bathrobe gift basket?"

The woman's rather amused request snapped Jana's attention back to her. "Of course. I'm sorry."

"That's all right, dear," the older woman said, a twinkle in her dark eyes. "The older I get, the more I catch myself drifting, but you're rather young."

"I'm older than I look," Jana bantered. "Enjoy."

"Thank you. I will." The woman started for the front door.

Jana noted that Olivia had greeted Sherilyn and Mitsy but, aware that Jana was finishing up a sale, she had remained with the customer. Apparently Olivia didn't know the two women or sense the trouble they might cause. Jana thought of taking Olivia's customer, then dismissed the idea. She might as well let them get their jab in and get it over with.

Besides, Tyler said he'd drop by on the way to a project he and his team were working on. She didn't want him there if things got nasty. After being around Olivia and Tyler, Jana now understood what real friendship meant. They deserved their pound of flesh.

Taking a deep breath, Jana moved toward the two solemn faced women. "Welcome to Midnight Dreams. Can I show you anything?"

Mitsy looked down her long nose at Jana and shoved the leather strap of her black Chloé bag over her shoulder. The chic black and white suit was also Chloé. The double string of pearls, a prerequisite for women in the Junior League, were perfectly matched and lustrous. "I want to see those towels on the top shelf."

"Which color?"

"Every color," she ordered.

"And style," Sherilyn added. She wore Prada, but the light blue designer suit couldn't make up for slimness that bordered on gauntness. It was rumored at one time that she had an eating disorder.

"Those are for display. I can get you a set from the back," Jana told them.

"I want to see *those*." Up went Mitsy's nose again.

Jana hadn't thought it would be simple or easy, but they might as well learn that she wasn't running or hiding. She'd done enough of that. "Of course."

Glad she'd worn pants, she pulled the sliding ladder over and climbed up. She was reaching for the towels when there was a hard bump against the ladder. Almost toppling, Jana frantically grabbed the ladder to steady herself. Her heart racing, she looked down. Both women gazed innocently up at her. They wanted more than retribution, they wanted Jana broken and bloody.

"Hurry. We haven't got all day," Mitsy snapped.

Gathering a set of plush towel in berry to her chest, Jana carefully came back down the ladder. "Here you are."

"Are you dense?" Mitsy sneered. "I can't very well look at them with you holding them."

Jana's eyes narrowed, but she went to the bed and placed the towels on top. "They're Egyptian cotton and we offer free monogramming."

Both women snorted, but it was Mitsy who snidely said, "I could afford to have everything in this store monogrammed if I wanted."

"On the other hand, *you* couldn't afford to have a handkerchief monogrammed with your initials—b-i-t-c-h," Sherilyn giggled as if she'd said the funniest thing in the world.

Mitsy joined her. "I'd pay to see that."

Jana picked up the towels. "Mitsy, would that be cash, check, or charge?"

"What?" Mitsy's hazel eyes widened.

Jana didn't even try to keep the satisfied smile off her face. "You said you'd pay to see that. I have to ring up the sale first before I can send them out to be monogrammed."

"I'm not buying those," Mitsy huffed. "Bring me those satin slippers on display over there."

"Is there a problem?" Olivia, her brow puckered, came up to them.

Jana shook her head. "Nothing I can't handle." She turned to Mitsy. "Is there anything else you would like to see?"

"If there were, I would have asked you."

"Perhaps—" Olivia began, but stopped when Jana touched her arm.

"It's all right. Really. Why don't you see if that couple has any questions or are they still browsing?"

Olivia looked at Mitsy and Sherilyn a long time, then moved away. Jana now had friends. The knowledge erased the nasty thoughts running through her head. Once upon a time she would have made a point of enticing their husbands and making sure they later found out about it. But now, Tyler was the only man she wanted to be with.

Calmly, Jana faced the women. "I can take anything you dish out and you know why? Because I'm just beginning to know and treasure what real friends mean." She smiled and spread her arms wide. "So bring it on. You can run me all over the store until I have things ten feet high, but you won't break me. But I have to warn you, I'll only bend so much."

Her smile growing, she went to get the slippers and then returned, surprised to see that Sherilyn was leaving the store. She placed the slippers beside the towels. "Here you are."

Mitsy picked up the slippers. "I can't see the size."

"Seven," Jana told her.

"I'll see for myself." Slipping the bag off her shoulder, she placed it on the bed and took the slippers to the window, examining the embroidered shoe in detail.

Jana caught Olivia's gaze and smiled to reassure her. Another customer came in and Jana nodded her head for Olivia to assist her. Jana could handle Mitsy.

After a long two minutes, Mitsy returned, tossing the slipper down. "It's not what I want." She picked up her purse. "I'll take the towels."

Jana couldn't hide her surprise. She'd thought Mitsy would rather wear flannel in public than purchase anything from her. "If you'll come with me, I'll write the receipt." Rounding the desk, Jana set down and reached for the receipt book.

"Where's my wallet? Where's my wallet?"

Jana looked up, a lump settling in the pit of her stomach like lead. Mitsy was looking directly her.

"You stole my wallet! Give it back!" she shrilled, the black Chloé bag gapping open.

Jana slowly came to her feet. "I don't have your wallet."

"What is it?" Olivia asked, rushing over.

"Your sales clerk stole my wallet!" Mitsy repeated. "It was in my purse when I came in here. She took it when I went to the window to check the slipper's size."

Olivia didn't even look at Jana. "You must have lost it someplace else."

"I distinctly remember seeing it after I came in here when I opened my purse to check my lipstick." Mitsy turned her angry gaze on Jana. "You're a slut and a thief!"

Jana clenched her hands instead of slapping Mitsy. "I don't steal."

She sneered. "I notice you didn't deny you have the morals of an alley cat."

"I don't have your wallet," Jana repeated. Then she saw something that made the floor shift beneath her feet. Tyler was entering the store. How much more could he hear about her and not be disgusted by the sight of her?

"Call the police," Mitsy ordered, staring hard at Olivia. "As the owner, you have a responsibility to your customers."

"My sister is well aware of her responsibility," Tyler said, coming to stand beside Olivia. "What's going on?"

Every eye in the shop converged on Tyler. Jana wanted to disappear. She didn't have any doubt the missing wallet was planned. Mitsy would play this out to the hilt and that meant Jana would soon be in handcuffs.

"Jana stole my wallet. I demand the police be called," Mitsy said.

"I agree," Tyler said.

Jana began to tremble. She hadn't realized how much she wanted his blind faith in her. She didn't bother with defending herself again. What was the use?

"First, however, I want to look at the tape from the security cameras," Tyler said, his expression thoughtful.

"W-what?" Mitsy asked, her fingers tightening on the handbag.

"Security cameras," Tyler explained, his voice neutral. "They're strategically located throughout the store. They'll tell us who stole the wallet."

Mitsy swallowed, but said nothing.

Tyler pulled out his cell. "I'll call the police, but maybe you should check your purse again before I do. Filing a false police report is a crime too. Jana could sue you for slander when the real culprit is discovered."

He pressed in one number. Mitsy grabbed his wrist. "I don't want to get anyone in trouble."

"If she stole your wallet, she deserves to be in jail. My sister has the reputation of the shop to consider," Tyler said. "Jana won't be able to deny what happened once we view the tape."

Mitsy released Tyler's arm and fiddled with the pearls at her throat. "Maybe, maybe I dropped it and my friend picked it up." She pulled out her own cell phone. "I'll call her."

"If you're sure," Tyler drawled, deactivating his phone. "I want you to get exactly what's due you."

"Sherilyn, do you by chance have my wallet?" Mitsy's face creased into a semblance of a smile. "Oh, good, I'll meet you at Hermès." She disconnected the phone and dropped it into her bag. "She has it. I was mistaken. I left it on the table where we had lunch. She forgot to tell me. I better go."

Mitsy started for the door and Tyler caught her arm. "Don't you think you owe Jana an apology?" Her mouth tightened. "I'd hate to see you sued for slander. Isn't your husband thinking of a political career?"

"That's the least you can do," said the woman Jana had helped earlier. "She certainly has grounds."

"Who are you?" Mitsy asked, her lips pursed in annoyance.

"No one you'd know. I'm just doing some shopping while my husband is in town. Perhaps you've heard of him: Winston Strong."

"The Fifth Circuit judge?" Tyler asked.

"Yes," The woman smiled. "You know Winston?"

"No, ma'am. Just heard of him," Tyler said, a thoughtful look on his face. "He has quite a reputation for integrity."

"Yes. I'm very proud of him." Mrs. Strong turned her attention to Mitsy. She was no longer smiling. "We both detest injustice of any type."

"Mrs. Strong, this is a pleasure," Mitsy gushed, extending her hand. "I'm a member of the Junior League. We're having a reception in the home of our president for you tomorrow."

The handshake was brief. "I was looking forward to it until now."

Mitsy eyes widened as the words sank in. She gulped and turned to Jana. "I'm sorry. Please accept my apology."

Jana was still looking with bewilderment at Mrs. Strong. "You don't know me."

Mrs. Strong smiled again. "It doesn't take me long to size up a person. You struck me immediately as a woman of substance."

Jana was touched. "Thank you." She turned to Mitsy. Being gracious wasn't as difficult as she once thought. "I accept your apology," she told Mitsy.

Relief swept across Mitsy's thin face. She faced Mrs. Strong. "I'll see you tomorrow. Good-bye." She hurried from the store.

Jana brought her full attention back to Mrs. Strong. "I deeply appreciate your help, but Mitsy has valid reasons for not liking me. At one time I wasn't very likable."

The elderly woman didn't bat a lash. "Many people have pasts they'd rather forget. To me, they are the most interesting and strongest. It takes courage to change. I don't suppose I'll see either of you ladies at the luncheon tomorrow?"

"No," Olivia and Jana said in unison.

"Too bad. It would have been interesting." She extended her hand. "Good-bye."

Jana closed her hand around the other woman's. "Good-bye."

The door had barely closed before Olivia gave Jana a brief hug, then went to help the couple that had stopped browsing to watch the drama unfold.

"You all right?" Tyler asked.

"Wonderful. It's a good thing Olivia has security cameras."

"She doesn't."

Jana blinked. "What?"

Smiling, Tyler lifted her chin to close her mouth. "I was bluffing."

Her throat tightened. "You believed me."

"Did you doubt that I would?" he asked, the smile gone from his face.

She considered lying, then said, "Yes."

"Then I'll have to work harder at getting you to trust me." Curling his hand behind her neck, Tyler pulled Jana closer for a brief kiss. "That's for starters. I'll be back tonight around eleven."

She trembled. "Would you like to come up?"

"Yes, but I better not." His thumb grazed across her lips. "You're too tempting. Stay safe."

Jana watched as Tyler waved to Olivia on his way out the door. Their relationship had definitely added another dimension and although it was scary she couldn't wait to see him again.

"Where are we all going on our next date?" Griffin asked the moment Julian came through the front door Wednesday night.

Olivia was sure the expression on her face was as stunned as Julian's. She'd let Griffin stay up to say hello to Julian because she'd known he wouldn't have gone to sleep otherwise. Helpless, she looked down at the expectant face of her son and didn't know quite what to say.

"I'm open to suggestions," Julian said, hunkering down so that he was eye level with Griffin.

"Well," Griffin drew the word out. "We could go to Game Works." He spread his small arms as wide as they would go. "It's this big arcade with two floors of video games." He giggled and folded his arms. "I bet there's one where you can beat me."

"Griffin," Olivia admonished, but since Jana, who was babysitting Griffin, and Julian were laughing, she didn't think her reprimand had done much good. "It isn't nice to brag."

Her son looked up at her with innocence shining in his eyes. "But Uncle Tyler and Grandpa Maxwell always said if it's fact it isn't bragging."

"I can't possible pass up that challenge, especially since I'm trying to impress your mother," Julian said, the corners of his mouth tilted upward. "I suppose this place has a restaurant."

"A whole floor with different foods," Griffin said, some of his excitement subdued. "Since I had pizza Sunday I can't have any for a while now."

Julian put his hand on Griffin's shoulder and looked up at Olivia. "Any plans for Friday afternoon?"

"We don't have any, do we, Mama?" Griffin asked, his eyes wide and hopeful.

Seeing the two of them together, Olivia felt a lump lodge in her throat. "No," she finally managed.

"Yippee!" Griffin impulsively launched himself into Julian's arms, then laughed louder as Julian rose to his feet while still holding Griffin.

"I guess we have a date," Julian said as he set Griffin down. "I expect your mother to get a good report from Jana. I wouldn't want anything to stop us from going out Friday night."

Griffin headed for the stairs, then stopped midway and called, "Good night," before continuing up the stairs.

Smiling, Jana followed. "He'll be in bed by the time I get there."

A tremulous smile on her face, Olivia turned to Julian. "Thank you."

On seeing the tears in her eyes, the warmth in them, Julian felt tightness in his chest he'd never experienced before. "I care about him, too," he said, meaning every word. "Besides, its bad form to let the son of a woman you're interested in always beat you."

Olivia's heart quickened. It would be so very easy to let herself care too deeply for Julian. "I'm far more impressed with a man's other qualities." She reached for his hand. "Come on. I'm ready for my ice cream."

Like teenagers, they'd shared a banana split loaded with chocolate syrup, strawberry and caramel topping, nuts, and whipped cream. Sitting at the far end of the patio at the Marble Creamery, they took turns feeding each other. They laughed and talked in between bites. Julian insisted on offering the plump cherry to Olivia. Opening her mouth, she leaned forward to eagerly accept the ripe fruit. The laughter died when she stared into Julian's hooded eyes. *He wanted her.*

She felt her body clench with the first faint stirrings of desire. Surprised, a bit embarrassed, and yes, pleased, because her ex-husband hadn't taken this away from her as well. She glanced away.

Strong fingers turned her head. "What is it?"

She felt her face heat and hoped he wouldn't know the cause. She didn't like lying, but the alternative was unthinkable. She leaned away from the disturbing warmth of Julian's hand when she had the crazy urge to turn her head and bite. "Just thinking."

"Thinking, huh," he said. "Wonder if it was the same thing I was thinking?"

Olivia flushed deeply, her eyes widened in alarm. Speechless, she stared across the small table at Julian. She didn't have to see the smoldering look in his dark eyes to know they had been, and still were, thinking the same thing. Her breath snagged. She didn't mind thinking about intimacy, but she wasn't ready to put action to those thoughts. "Jul—"

"It's all right," he said, standing and reaching for her hand.

Unsure of what he meant, she automatically placed her hand in his and walked beside him to where his car was parked. "I—" she started, but had no idea of what she meant to say.

Julian, who had been reaching for the door handle on the passenger's side, curved his arm around her waist instead, effectively trapping her body between his and the car. She trembled from the heat and hardness of his body, from the feel of his unmistakable desire.

His hand cupped her cheek. "It's not hard to figure out that since you haven't been dating, you haven't been doing other things either."

She would have tucked her head in embarrassment if his strong hand hadn't gently kept it in place. It didn't enter her mind to close her eyes. His gaze was too intent.

"We'll take this one step at a time."

She moistened her lower lip with the tip of her tongue. "What if we never get to step two?"

His grin was slow, sexy, and self-assured. "You let me worry about that."

Laughter bubbled from her lips. "You're as bad as Griffin."

"I like the sound of that." His thumb grazed her lips, making her tremble. "I like tasting your lips even more." His mouth boldly took hers, his tongue mating with hers, thrusting deeply. Trembling, she held on, kissing him back, feeling desire once again sweep over her.

He lifted his head, his breathing as labored as hers. Shivering in his arms, she knew what he already knew. One day they wouldn't pull back.

Tonight was the night.

Jana sensed it the moment she opened her door Friday night and saw Tyler. When they arrived home, Julian had been waiting for Olivia and Griffin. They'd quickly changed and left. Tyler had been in his office. Jana had stared longingly at the closed door before going to her apartment.

Now, seeing him, her pulse raced, her breath quickened in anticipation. The hot desire in his eyes ignited her own.

She'd never wanted to please a man as much as she wanted to please Tyler nor been so afraid that she wouldn't be able to. Before she'd met him, her actions toward men had been cold and calculated. Her emotions were never involved. With Tyler all of her senses were sharpened and attuned to him. With every breath she drew, every fiber of her being, she wanted him to be as caught up in their lovemaking as she.

"May I come in?" Tyler asked.

Fear and exhilaration swept through her. She had to swallow before she could answer him. "Yes." She stepped back on legs that trembled and refused to steady.

Coming inside, he closed the door behind him, his gaze still locked with hers. His hands tenderly cupped her cheeks, then slid to her shoulders and drew her into his arms. Warm lips skimmed along her neck. "I could kiss you all night."

Eternally grateful that she'd taken her bath early, Jana gave herself up to the pleasure of being held. "I'd let you too."

"Let's see." His mouth took hers in a hot, open-mouth kiss that stole her breath and made her body ache. She strained closer, her arms locking around his neck. Hungrily he feasted on her mouth and she on his.

Soon it wasn't enough. Her impatient hands went to his shirt and tugged it free. The muscled warmth of his skin only made her want to touch his more. Her lips brushed across his nipples. He shuddered, his hands clenching on her arm. She froze.

Had she offended him? Was she too bold? The one thing she dreaded was seeing distaste in his eyes. She couldn't bear that.

"Jana?" Her name was a hoarse thread of sound.

She didn't want to look, but she lifted her head. Oddly, Tyler's faith in her gave her the courage to do so.

Finally their gaze met. Tears sprang to her eyes. In his eyes she saw the tenderness and warmth she'd yearned for all her life. And something else: a burning desire that shook her to the core.

"Tyler," she whispered, a call that he answered. His mouth fused with hers, gentle at first then ravenous. She was with him all the way. The terry cloth robe slipped from her shoulders. She wore nothing underneath.

His sharp intake of breath caused her eyes to open. His expression was filled with reverence. He didn't take time to unbutton his shirt, just reached for the tail and pulled it over his head. It was still in the air when he pulled her back into his embrace.

A bubble of laughter slipped past her lips at his impatience. It became a whimpering moan of pleasure as his mouth closed on her taut nipple and sucked. Her legs turned to water.

Tyler swung her up in his arms and strode quickly to the bedroom and placed her on the bed. With trembling hands she reached for the button on his jeans.

"I'll do it faster." He proved he was right. Kicking the jeans aside, he covered her body with his. It was glorious and arousing. She wanted more. A small, needy whimper slipped past her lips.

"I'm going to love every incredible inch of you, then start all over again," he promised.

He was good as his word, slowing driving her crazy with wanting him where her body ached the most. He lavished her body with kisses, took teasing love bites, stroked her until her skin was hot and sensitized. "Tyler, please."

He was relentless. Kisses trailed from the slope of her shoulder, past the thrust of her breasts to her stomach until he reached the essence of her. She cried out, arching off the bed, and shattered. When she was still coming down, he began to enter her.

"Jana."

She fought through the sensual haze and opened her eyes. She kept them open as he filled her completely. Then he began to move, a slow rocking at first that caused a coil of heat in her stomach to radiate outward. She locked her legs around his hips, her arms around his neck and gave herself up to his lovemaking. She gave him her all and he gave in return until they were both racing for completion. They finished together in a wild shout of exhilaration.

Tyler breath was coming in spurts. He'd never experienced such ecstasy. He started to roll, but Jana's arms tightened around him. He brushed a tender kiss against her damp temple. "I'm heavy."

"You're not," she said, nuzzling the side of his neck.

He returned the favor. He couldn't seem to get enough of her. "Yes, I am."

"In a good way," she murmured, then nipped his earlobe.

His body that had begun to cool stirred. "I want you again."

"Then take me."

He joined them, then rolled. He stared up into Jana's flushed face. Her hair was mussed, her nipples pouting. He grew harder just looking at her, but looking could never be enough.

Her hands splayed on his chest, she began to move, a slow circular motion of her hips. He closed his eyes, enjoying her driving him to the edge of sanity. Like a blind man, his hands touched her wherever they could until one covered her breast and one hand slipped between her legs.

His finger sought the sensitive nub in her body and stroked. Her body began to move faster. His eyes opened. Her head thrown back, her eyes closed, her lips slightly parted, she gave herself to him holding nothing back.

He'd never seen anything more beautiful or more humbling. He tried to prolong their joining, but their bodies refused to be denied. Wrapping his arms around her, he kissed her and felt them go over together.

Later they lay facing each other in silence, content for the moment. "I don't want to leave you," Tyler said.

"Then don't," Jana whispered. "Stay with me."

"For as long as you'll let me." Kissing her forehead, he hooked his arm around her and drew her closer. "For as long as you'll let me."

15

Olivia and Jana weren't having a good night. They were used to being with Julian and Tyler, and used to talking with them frequently. Now they'd been alone for the past three days. Once Griffin had gone to bed, they'd given each other manicures. After their nails dried they watched a movie and ate popcorn.

"At least we'll see them tomorrow," Olivia said. "Tyler did say he'd be finished, didn't he?"

"Yes." Jana grabbed a handful of popcorn she didn't want. It was sheer torture having Tyler so close and being unable to be with him. He came to her almost every night. They'd make love, talk then sleep in each other's arms. She'd never known such contentment. "Why didn't you go to the medical dinner tonight with Julian?"

"I wanted to." Olivia sipped her cola. "But Griffin's schedule is getting so out of whack. Plus I don't want him thinking Julian means more to me than he does."

"He's too smart for that." Jana tossed popcorn into her mouth. "He's crazy about Julian."

"Caring for Julian is easy," Olivia admitted.

"The same with Tyler." She turned to Olivia. "I don't want you to betray his trust, but this Courtney woman still worries me."

Olivia set up, placing the glass on a coaster on the coffee table. "He's over her."

Jana closed her eyes briefly. "I guess it's payback time. I tried to take my first ex-husband away from the woman he was seeing."

"What happened?" Olivia asked quietly.

"He told me to get lost," Jana said, then sat up beaming. "Tyler has just as much integrity as Gray, maybe more so. He wouldn't run a game on me."

"Of course not."

Jana plopped back on the sofa. "We are two very lucky women."

"We're blessed," Olivia corrected.

"Blessed," Jana said. This time she believed.

Jana was an asset to Midnight Dreams. She loved the shop and helping customers. Olivia said she was a natural and Jana believed her. The store was bustling and she couldn't be happier.

"Hello, Midnight Dreams," Jana said into the receiver, a smile on her face.

"I want to see you."

"Father?" She almost screamed aloud. Happiness swept though her. "Of course. There's so much to tell you."

"Where can we meet?"

"Anytime. You can come to the garage apartment where I live or you can come to the place where I work. Whichever is best for you," she told him. She'd hoped and prayed, but never let herself believe he'd actually call her. She'd sent him two letters since she couldn't get him on the phone.

"I prefer the house," he said. "I'll be there at seven."

"I'll be waiting," she quickly said. "Father, I'm so glad you called. I want things to be different between us."

"They will be. Good-bye."

Jana felt like twirling around with her arms outstretched. *Her father had finally forgiven her.* She'd almost stopped hoping that that would ever happen.

"What put that smile on your face?" Olivia asked.

"I just got off the phone with my father. He wants to see me." Even saying the words made butterflies take flight in her stomach.

Olivia's smile almost matched Jana's. "That's wonderful. I'm so pleased for you."

"I owe it all to you and Tyler." Jana shook her head. "If the both of you hadn't stepped in to help me change my life it might not have happened."

"We simply gave you the opportunity." Olivia leaned against the desk. "You were the one courageous enough to turn your life around."

"For a while I didn't think I'd make it." Jana glanced around the shop. "I like working here. I like my life."

"Very few people can say that and mean it," Olivia told her.

"As much as Julian has been hanging around, I'd say I'm not the only one who can say that," Jana teased.

Olivia blushed. Jana laughed. "A handsome, attentive man can certainly make a woman's life interesting."

"Like Tyler?" Olivia bantered.

"Especially Tyler. To think I was scared of him. He's the most sensitive, honest man I've ever known."

"He thinks you're pretty special."

Jana sobered. "My past doesn't bother him. It's almost as if it never happened."

"To Tyler, it didn't. That was your life before."

"That what he says, but . . ."

"But what?" Olivia asked.

"What if one day something happens and he changes his mind? Or we're out and I meet one of the men I used to know? What then? Could he still look at me the same way?"

Olivia placed her hand on Jana's arm. "Tyler is rock steady. He firmly believes it's not what the person was but who they are now, just as I do. He won't change."

"No, I guess not," Jana answered, but deep down she wasn't sure. Tyler was dependable, but he had also stopped caring for Courtney. They'd made no promises. In any case, long ago Jana had promised herself that she'd never fall in love. It was too painful when they didn't love you back, and no one ever had.

"You're going to wear out your new shoes if you don't stop pacing and come back inside."

Jana glanced over her shoulder at Tyler and continued to pace on the sidewalk in front of the house. "He's late. What if he doesn't come?"

"He'll come." Tyler walked to her and slid his arm around her waist. "Traffic from Frisco is terrible this time of day."

"Maybe." Jana bit her lip.

"Stop worrying." Tyler tightened his hold. "If he hadn't wanted to meet you, he wouldn't have called."

"That's what I keep telling myself." She glanced up into Tyler's strong face. "I've waited so long for him to forgive me, for him to love me."

"He couldn't help but love you," Tyler told her.

Jana turned away without saying anything. Tyler's family was so different from hers. He'd grown up with loving parents. Hers couldn't or wouldn't love her.

"Here comes another car."

Jana whipped her head around. A white Mercedes cruised toward them. Her heart began to beat faster. She stepped out of Tyler's arms and started toward the car.

Tyler caught her arm. "Wait here, Jana."

Her stomach somersaulted as the sports sedan stopped directly in front of the curved walkway. The windows were tinted so she couldn't see inside.

The door on the driver's side opened. Her palms dampened. The moment the man came into sight, the years and harsh words tumbled away. "Father." She rushed to him, throwing her arms around him before he reached the sidewalk. "I missed you so much."

"Let's go inside." He pulled her arms firmly from around his neck.

"Of course." She'd forgotten that he had never liked public display of affections, perhaps because her mother was so demonstrative, especially with men. "Father, I'd like you to meet Tyler Maxwell, the brother of the woman I work for. Tyler, this is my father, Thomas Carpenter."

"Pleased to meet you, Mr. Carpenter." Tyler extended his hand. For a moment he didn't think Jana's father would shake his, then he slowly lifted his hand.

"Mr. Maxwell."

"Please come inside," Jana said, still bubbling. "I want you to meet Olivia Sanders, my boss and friend, and her son, Griffin." She laughed self-consciously. "Olivia insisted you stay for dinner. I tried to call you back, but got the machine."

"I've been busy. Can we go inside?" he asked tightly, his mouth pinched.

Jana's smile slipped. "Of course. This way." She started to take his arm, then thought better of it. She led the way up the sidewalk.

Tyler stepped in front of her and opened the door. "Please come in, Mr. Carpenter."

Olivia appeared almost immediately. "You must be Jana's father. We're so pleased you could make it and hope you can stay for dinner."

"Not if my life depended on it," came the harsh reply.

Jana was stunned. Anguish almost sent her to her knees. "Fath—"

He rounded on her, cutting her off. "Don't ever refer to me as your father again. I disowned you long ago."

"Mr. Carpenter, that's no way to talk to your daughter," Tyler admonished, his voice hard.

"You can't tell me what to do," he riled. "From that display I witnessed outside, it's plain to see why you let her stay. You're just like all the other men in her life."

"Father, please."

"With all the men your mother was sleeping with I don't know why I was the one caught. She's trash and you're just like her. Money and power only gives it a classier name and address." He stepped toward her. "I came here to *tell* you to leave town. Because of the sordid past of you and your mother, I had to leave Richmond. I won't leave Frisco. I have a wife and daughter I respect. I can hold my head up."

With each condemning word, the ache inside Jana grew. "Fa— I'm sorry."

"Too little, too late." His hands clenched. "Do you have any idea how it feels to hear men discussing your wife and daughter like high-class tramps?"

Tyler had heard more than enough. "Mr. Carpenter, it's best that you leave."

Jana's father brought the full force of his anger on Tyler. "I had you checked out. You're not the usual type. Neither was her first husband. She nearly destroyed him. Don't let her do the same to you." He strode to the door. "I'm changing my phone number. If you come near me or my family, I'll have a restraining order put on you."

"Please!" Jana cried.

"If you're looking for forgiveness, you won't find it here." He looked first at Tyler, then at Olivia. "Did she tell you that she picked up my sister-in-law's husband at a birthday party she'd crashed? She did it to get back at me for not inviting her. I didn't because I was ashamed of her and with good reason, as she proved. If you know what's good for you, you'll kick her out." Opening the door, he left.

Jana stood there, trembling, aching, wishing she was numb instead of hurting so deeply. Her father had never loved her and he never would.

"Jana."

She jerked away from Tyler. She felt too brittle to be touched.

"Jana, why don't you come upstairs and lie down for a while in your old room?" Olivia asked gently.

How? She could never look either of them in the face again. She was trash. How had she let herself believe that she could change? She raced to the door. Tyler caught her before she had gone five feet. "Please," she begged, refusing to look at him.

"He was wrong."

She shook her head. "If only he was."

"Jana—"

"Please, I need to be alone for a little while."

His hands tightened, then Tyler released her and stepped back. "I'll give you an hour."

Jana continued out the door, across the lawn, then up the stairs into her apartment. She only went a few steps before heart-wrenching sobs tore from her throat. She crumpled to the floor. Her father hated her. Could she blame him?

She'd done things, had things done to her that would make a streetwalker blush. How had she thought she could be happy when her past would always be there, waiting to trip her up and bring her back down again?

She was what she was. She'd never be able to outrun her past or live a life good enough for people to see her and not the old Jana.

So why keep trying?

Pushing up, she went to her bedroom and stared at herself in the mirror. Tonight she was going to be just what her father thought she was, amoral and heartless. Turning away, she went to get dressed.

Tonight, she was going on the hunt.

Tyler tried to stick to his promise to wait an hour, but lasted only forty-seven minutes before he went to the apartment. Jana had sounded so broken it had torn him up inside. His fists clenched. It had been all he could do not to drag her father from the house. Each step Jana made away from the old life was difficult enough. She was still too unsure of herself.

He rapped on the door. "Jana. Open up. I brought you a tray. Jana?" No answer. "I'm coming in." Using the spare key, he opened the door and saw the bedroom door open. He walked quietly in that direction. If she was asleep he didn't want to wake her.

The room was empty. The perfume he'd given her wafted in the air. The mirror in the bathroom was foggy with steam. She'd dressed and gone out. She'd never done that before. He didn't like to think of the possible reason for her doing so now.

People were quick to pass judgment on her. He wouldn't fall in that category. Going to the kitchen, he put the plate of food in the refrigerator, then straightened. The roses he'd cut from the garden and given her that morning were on the breakfast table. One long finger touched the petal.

"Come home, Jana. Be as strong as I know you can be. Come home. Come home to me."

Nightlife in Dallas, like most big cities, didn't start to swing until midnight. Aware of this, Jana sat through a couple of movies, then went to lower Greenville Avenue where the trendiest of the private nightclubs were located. This was the most likely place to be patronized by the type of man she was looking for. She wouldn't get past the velvet rope without being on the list, but she planned to interest a man before he went inside.

Paying the cab, she got out. Late-model luxury cars lined the streets and crowded the small parking lot. She staked out a darkened corner of the parking lot and waited, ignoring the men who arrived in a Lexus, a Infinity. When the Porsche Cabrera roared into the parking lot, she moved to a white Mercedes she had already picked out, that was several cars from the end of the parking lot, and began digging through her purse.

"Is everything all right?"

She started and turned around, sizing up the man in one quick glance. Late fifties, wanting to be thirty, with a cream-colored Ralph Lauren sports jacket, tobacco-colored tailored slacks, Cole Haan loafers. She caught a whiff of Creed cologne that cost four hundred dollars for eight ounces.

She pressed her hand against the Hermes scarf she hadn't been able to part with that she'd worn as a top, exposing several inches of skin. The man's gaze lingered on her breasts, just as she'd planned, then dropped to the bare skin. She waited for his gaze to lift, trying to keep the irritation from her face as she did so. "I seem to have locked my keys in the car."

He stepped closer. She caught his arm. "Don't. The alarm might go off." She sighed, running her hand though her hair, tightening the scarf across her breasts. "To make matters worse, I left my cell phone charging at home. I can't even call service or go home since my house keys are on the key ring."

He pulled out his cell as she'd known he would do. "Please use mine."

"You're a lifesaver." The cell phone was top-of-the-line. She dialed a false number, paced, then sighed and left a frantic message that she was locked out of her car and where she was. "My brother must be out." She handed him the phone. "Thanks."

"You don't plan to wait out here, do you?" he asked.

"I don't have much choice. I need to be here in case my brother comes."

His gaze touched her breasts again. "I hate to leave you out here. Please, just come inside for one drink at least. Your brother would understand, and it's hot out here."

She couldn't take the chance of the real owner of the car coming out and driving away. "I'm afraid I can't. Although I'd love to. It's so refreshing meeting a courteous man like you."

"There are a few of us left. I've got an idea." He laughed self-consciously. "I guess we better introduce ourselves first. I'm Harry Former."

"Janet Street." The name just slipped out. She wasn't sure why she didn't want to use her real name. Wasn't she doing this so she could throw it in her father's face?

"Janet, why don't we leave a note on the car with my cell number. That way your brother could reach you," he said.

"That's sweet of you, but what if we get separated inside? It's always packed and jumping."

"We won't if we go to my place."

It was a bold move on his part, but hadn't she laid the groundwork for just that invitation. She took a cautious step back.

"Please don't take offense," he said quickly. "You'll be perfectly safe." Going into the breast pocket of his jacket, he pulled out his wallet and showed her his driver's license. "See, you can trust me."

Since she planned on going home with him, she refrained from pointing out that if he was an ax murderer her seeing his license wouldn't make a hell of a lot difference. The address at the new W apartments meant he had money. The units started at half a million.

"You can trust me," he repeated.

"All right," Jana finally said, allowing him to lead her to his car. She started to get in, then stopped. She knew this would end in his bed as well as he did. Most people who went clubbing wanted sex for the night and no lingering good-byes in the morning.

"Just a drink and conversation," he cajoled.

She got in the car. This was what she came for, what she wanted.

The drive to Harry's place took less than fifteen minutes. He pulled into the underground parking lot and parked near the elevator, which quickly and silently took them to the penthouse floor.

Unlocking the door, Harry stepped aside so she could enter. The penthouse was beautiful and tastefully decorated with artwork, sleek furniture, and hardwood flooring. The more she knew of Harry, the more it appeared as if he could keep her in the manner in which she had once been accustomed.

He went to the bar and splashed whiskey in a glass she knew was Baccarat. "What would you like?"

For me to have lived my life differently. The words came to her so strongly that she thought she had spoken them aloud.

Frowning, he came around the bar. "You're not afraid, are you?"

"Not the way you think."

"Good. Drink this. It will help you relax."

And lose any inhibitions about tumbling into bed with him. She downed the whiskey in one gulp.

His smile was slow. "I like a woman who can handle her liquor." He took her glass. Let me get you another one." At the bar, he poured another drink. On the way back to her, he picked up a control on the glass coffee table. Lights dimmed, a fire started in the fireplace, soft music began to play. "That's better."

Jana didn't say anything as he handed her glass to her. Just don't think, she ordered herself.

"Why don't we sit down?" Taking her arm, he led her to an immense chaise with a carved wood frame near the fireplace. She didn't want to think of all the women who had been there before her and who would come after her.

They were barely sitting before his arm went around her, his lips pressing against her bare arm, his free hand on her knee and sliding higher.

Jana shut her eyes. *Just go for it. This is all you'll ever be.*

His hand reached the edge of her skirt and began to inch higher. His mouth moved to the curve of her jaw, the same place Tyler had brushed with his fingers.

"No!" she bounded up.

"What's the matter with you?" He stood, glaring at her. "You're old enough to know the score."

"Yes, but tonight I don't want to play the game." She started for the door.

"Then why did you come up here? You knew where it would lead."

Her hand on the doorknob, Jana turned. "Every man wouldn't expect sex for helping a woman." She knew one in particular. "If you hurry, perhaps you'll be able to pick up a more accommodating woman." Opening the door, she made good her escape.

———

The security light on the garage and at the corner of the apartment allowed Tyler to see Jana when she was a good distance away. He made himself remain on the third step leading up to her apartment rather than going to her as he badly wanted to do. She stopped when she saw him, then slowly continued until she stood over him. The wrapped top was just wide enough to cover her breasts.

"I picked up a man. He took me to his penthouse."

Tyler's gut clenched. So many emotions were running though him he couldn't sort them all out.

"I tried to shut my mind down to what was going to happen, but I couldn't."

He caught her hand. "You're a different woman now."

"I want to be," she said quietly.

"Your father threw you a curve, but you didn't cave in."

Tyler knew her so well. "I was going to show him that I was as amoral as he said. Then I realized that I would only be hurting myself again, just as I've done all these years." Her hand clenched in his. "All my life I've tried to make my parents love me. My mother's twisted sense of values became my own. I kept hoping my father would step in and stop me. After a while I didn't care. Being in control over such powerful men was its own lure, and I was always in control. I never let myself care too much for any of them."

His thumb grazed the top of her hand. He didn't want to hear this, but realized she had to talk about her painful past before she could put it completely behind her.

"I can't go back to that lifestyle. From now on, I'm going to live for myself."

Tyler came to his feet, his hand tenderly cupping Jana's face. "I knew you could do it. You're right. You have changed from the first time I saw you."

"I was deceitful, desperate, and a pain."

His thumb grazed over her lower lip, felt her shiver. "Not then. In Seattle at the nightclub."

Her eyes widened.

"I'm the man who carried you to safety. I was there with a client, unwinding after a busy day."

She was momentarily speechless. "Why didn't you ever say anything?"

"I didn't place where I had seen you until the cookout a week after you came. Then too, I was enjoying getting to know the woman you were becoming, the new Jana."

Her trembling hand covered his. No words had ever meant more. Her forehead touched his. "You are an amazing man, Tyler Maxwell."

"You're an amazing woman."

Her head lifted. "Not yet, but one day I hope to be. There's another reason why I came home. You."

He was momentarily speechless. "You make a man weak and feel like he can lift a mountain at the same time."

"You make me believe." She wanted so badly to make love with him, but not with some other man's cologne clinging to her. "Good night."

"Good night."

Halfway up the stairs, she stopped. "Thanks for waiting up for me. No one ever has before," she said then continued up the stairs. Opening the door she went inside. *The new Jana.*

She felt new and it was wonderful.

"Quick. Lock the door and turn over the open sign before anther customer comes in," Olivia said, hanging up the phone.

Jana laughed and did as she requested. "Is this the woman who wasn't sure about dating Julian a month ago?"

Olivia made a face. "As I've always said, a woman can change her mind."

"You won't get an argument from me." Jana followed Olivia into the back. "Where are you two going tonight?"

Olivia blushed. "He's cooking dinner for me at his place."

Jana's eyebrows slowly rose. Olivia's blush deepened. She ducked her head.

"I like Julian," Jana said. "I'd say go for it."

Olivia's head lifted. "He kissed me and my brain turned to fuzz."

"It's kind of scary knowing a man can do that to you." Jana grabbed their purses from the cabinet.

Olivia laughed. "It's kind of difficult to imagine Tyler that way."

"Your brother is the most complex man I've ever known." They started for the front. "He can be so laid back one minute, then dangerous and compelling the next. The minutes race when I'm with him and drag when we're apart."

"The same thing with Julian," Olivia admitted, digging in her purse for her keys. "That's why we're staying in tonight. Thank you and Tyler for babysitting Griffin."

"We enjoy him. With Tyler, I'm learning that staying at home has it privileges," Jana said, and then, "Looks like we have a determined customer."

Her hand still in her big purse Olivia lifted her head and froze. "God, no!"

Jana looked from the angelically beautiful, well-dressed man to Olivia. Her face was pale, her entire body trembling. Instinctively, Jana wrapped her arms around Olivia and stepped in front of her to block out the angry-looking man. "The door is locked. Whoever he is, he can't hurt you. All we have to do is walk back to the phone and call Tyler and he'll be here in minutes."

"I—" Olivia began, then closed her eyes. "Why did he have to come back?"

"Come on. Sit down." Supporting Olivia, Jana started toward the back. The glass on the door rattled. Olivia flinched and stopped, seemingly as if her strength was gone. This Olivia frightened Jana. "I'm calling Tyler." Removing the phone from its holder, she hit the speed dial. He answered on the second ring.

"Tyler, we need you at the shop. A man frightened Olivia."

"Aaron," Olivia said softly. "Tell him it's Aaron."

Olivia looked back over her shoulder. "It's Griffin's father."

Tyler's curse said it all.

16

Hanging up the phone, Jana helped Olivia to the chair in front of the desk, thankful it was facing away from the door. "Tyler will take care of everything. I'll get you a glass of water."

"He can't see Griffin. He can't!" Her eyes widened. She fumbled for the phone. "I've got to call Wanda and warn her."

Jana stayed Olivia's nervous hands. "Griffin was going home with Xavier after day camp today. He won't be home until after seven."

Olivia relaxed immediately. "I forgot."

Those two words told Jana how much the appearance of her ex-husband had affected Olivia. "Griffin is probably trying to talk Xavier's mother into letting him have another dessert."

The strain around Olivia's mouth lessened. "Carol is a good mother. She won't let him get away with anything."

"Of course she won't. You'd never entrust Griffin to anyone who didn't have his best interest at heart."

Olivia set upright, her nails digging into Jana's hand. "He couldn't have come back for my baby. I won't let him ruin Griffin's life the way he wanted to ruin mine." She rose to her feet and turned, the paleness gone and in its place fierce determination. "There's no way in hell I'll let him get close to my son."

"Tyler's here." Jana went to the door with Olivia directly behind her. Jana could hear the two men arguing before she unlocked the door. "Tyler, maybe it's best you come inside to Olivia's office."

Tyler's mouth tightened.

"If he wants to cause a scene, it's all right with me," Aaron said, picture perfect in Armani.

"It's all right, Tyler," Olivia said. She started for her office.

With a triumphant smirk, Aaron followed.

Tyler flexed his hands, a muscle leaping in his jaw. Jana caught his hand as he passed. "She needs you to stay in control and help her."

His sharp gaze sliced into her. Once it would have made her cower, now she squeezed his hand. "Go. I'll lock the back up."

"Sorry. Thanks." He caught up with Aaron. Both disappeared through the swinging doors.

Jana locked the front door and called Wanda. "We might be here awhile."

"That devil is back."

No translation was needed. "They're in Olivia's office."

"She never wanted him near her again. This must be hard for her," Wanda said. "You stay close by her in case she needs you."

"Wanda, what they're saying is private. I have no right to be in there."

"Olivia stuck by you. Tyler's sweet on you. Can you do any less?"

No, she couldn't. "You play dirty," Jana said.

"Don't waste any more time." The phone went dead.

Jana hung up the receiver, took a breath and went to the back, very much aware that it was going to get rough.

Olivia felt more in control behind her desk. Having Tyler by her side helped. So did Jana's presence. She'd just come inside, closing the door softly behind her.

"What do you want?"

"Not even a hello after almost eight years, Olivia? What happened to all that Southern hospitality and Christianity?" Aaron asked with a smirk on his face.

"Spit it out, Aaron, then get the hell out of my sister's life." Tyler took a threatening step from around the desk.

Aaron's light brown eyes narrowed. "It's not Olivia's life I'm concerned about, but that of my son."

"No!" Olivia shouted, coming around the desk to face her ex-husband. "You're not coming near my son."

"He's mine too or did you forget that?"

Her cold gaze held his. "No, but believe me I've tried."

The nasty smile slid from his face. "My lawyer will call tomorrow with a date, time, and place to meet. I advise you to be there."

"Why?" she asked "The divorce is final. I made sure all the papers were filed and I have the decree."

"Which might not have been granted if the judge had known you were pregnant."

"You couldn't have cared less!" Her fists clenched. "You were sleeping with Edward more than you were sleeping with me."

The nasty smile reappeared. "And enjoying it more."

Tyler moved fast . . . but Olivia was faster. The slap across Aaron's face echoed across the room. His hand lifted and swung. Tyler caught his hand, slinging it away violently, causing Aaron to stumble and fall.

Fists clench, legs apart, Tyler stood over him. "Get up and get out."

Aaron slowly came to his feet. "You'll pay for this."

"Not as much as you if you raise your hand to anyone in my family again," Tyler promised.

Jana opened the door. "I'll show you out."

Aaron looked at her as if he was seeing her for the first time, then his eyes narrowed as if trying to place her. Straightening his tailored jacket he left without another word. Jana followed him out, locking the front door behind him. Olivia not dating and her insecurity with men now made perfect sense. Such a betrayal would cut deeply.

Jana closed her eyes, but the picture of Gray's face filled with pain and shock wouldn't go away. She realized how deeply her betrayal of her first husband had wounded him. His grandmother had a right to hate her. In a sense she was no better than Aaron. They were both cheaters and liars, both had hid their deviousness from the person they married.

She turned as Olivia and Tyler emerged from the back. "Tyler and I are going to pick up Griffin. Can you drive my SUV home?"

"All right." Jana accepted the keys. "If there . . ." Her voice trailed off. Nothing she could do or say would help.

Olivia tucked her head. "Thank you."

Jana's hand clenched around the keys. She wished she hadn't listened to Wanda. Her gaze settled on the middle of Tyler's wide chest. "Drive carefully."

"You all right?"

Her head came up. Tears stung her throat. With all he and Olivia were going through, he still thought of her. Perhaps if she had met him years ago her life might have been different. "Yes."

His eyes narrowed as if he didn't believe her. "See you later."

"All right." Jana looked at them moving slowly, as if each step was an effort. Aaron's threat to Griffin was taking a toll on them both.

Griffin thought it was cool that his mother and uncle joined them at Chuck E. Cheese's for pizza and fun. He couldn't believe his luck when he was able to get another dessert and play all the games he wanted. He was having one of the best times of his life. But on the drive home he began to realize that his mother was quieter than usual.

"You feel all right, Mama?"

"Of course, honey." She turned to look into the backseat of the truck where he sat. "Just a little tired. I think I'll stay home tonight and you and I can play a couple of your new games."

"Wow." He almost jumped up and down in the seat. It was already past his bedtime. This day was coming close to the wonderful times of his birthday and Christmas all rolled into one. Her spotted Julian's car when they turned onto their street. Griffin giggled. "I'll beat him as usual."

"I thought it would be just the two of us," his mother told him.

He liked playing games with his mother, but Julian was cool. He never treated him like a little kid or acted if he was imposing when he and his mother were sitting on the sofa together. "Sure."

Tyler pulled into the garage and cut the motor. "Are you positive you want to handle it this way?"

"Yes."

Griffin climbed out of the back seat of his uncle's truck. He'd learned long ago not to try and figure out what adults were talking about. "I'm thirsty. Can I have a soft drink?"

"Yes."

Before she changed her mind, Griffin raced toward the kitchen.

"You can't make it up to him by letting him have his way," Tyler said, gazing down at his sister.

"I know." She rubbed her temple. "I better go tell Julian I'm not going."

Julian stood when Olivia came into the media room. All Jana would tell him was that she was running late. He frowned and crossed to Olivia. She was trembling. Her eyes were red, her lids puffy as if she'd been crying. "Olivia, what is it?"

"I'll be going." Jana came to her feet. "Good night."

"I'll walk you out," Tyler said as she neared.

Jana's smile was brittle. "That's not necessary."

"I think it is." Without waiting for an answer Tyler laced his fingers with Jana's and left the room.

Julian took Olivia's cold hands in his. "Please tell me what's the matter."

She pulled her hands free, inexplicably feeling lonely already. "We can't see each other again."

"What?"

Olivia picked up a framed crystal picture of her and Griffin with his cap and gown on when he'd graduated from kindergarten. "It's best for everyone."

"How can you say that? Something's happened and I want to know."

"My ex-husband is back." She swallowed before she could continue. "I think he wants custody of Griffin."

"Honey, no." He tried to pull her into his arms, but she pushed away. Her rejection hurt.

"I hate to be rude, but I'm very tired."

He didn't move. "I don't get it. Your ex shows up and you're ready to turn your back on me, on us?"

She placed the picture back on the table. "There is no us."

That infuriated him. Catching her arms, Julian turned her around. "Look at me. What has this to do with us?"

"Just let it go."

"Not until you tell me."

Angry, more frightened than she had ever been, she shouted, "I won't make a fool of myself again."

"Just because he cheated on you with some woman is no reason to think I will."

A pained expression crossed her face. "If only he had."

"What?"

"My ex-husband is gay. Only he failed to tell me at the time of our marriage. I can see you're shocked. Imagine how I felt when I read his e-mail from his lover, his best friend and the best man at our wedding." This time she was able to push out his arms.

"I was so stupid. If I hadn't seen those e-mails he never would have admitted his secret life. And you know what he said? That he only married me because I was so gullible and innocent. He never cared about me. He just used me."

"Olivia . . ." Julian began, then discovered he didn't know what to say to help her. She had a right to be angry and frightened.

"Leaves you speechless, doesn't it? Took me almost four months to tell my family. Then I had to be tested for AIDS, subject Griffin to the same tests, then waiting each time for the results." She closed her eyes momentarily. "The fear is indescribable. He put me and Griffin at risk for his own selfish pleasure."

"Olivia, no woman should ever have to go through what you had to endure, but you can't paint me with the same brush."

"He's almost as handsome as you are," she said.

"I'm not gay," Julian quickly told her.

"But you're beautiful. It's only a matter of time before another woman catches your attention." She looked him in the eyes. "I won't go though that again."

"You're not pushing me out of your life."

"Leave, Julian."

"I'm not leaving until you start making sense."

"You leave my mother alone." Griffin rushed into the room, his small fists balled.

"Honey, no!" Olivia wrapped her arms around her son before he reached Julian, holding his trembling body close to hers.

"Griffin, I'd never hurt your mother or you," Julian told the little boy, regretting that he had handled things so badly.

"You were yelling at her," Griffin accused.

"I'm sorry, but sometimes when grown-ups feel passionate about something they yell, like playing sports."

Griffin looked as if he didn't believe him.

"Good night, Julian."

With her arms wrapped protectively around her son, Olivia was close to tears again. Julian had no choice but to leave quietly. "This isn't over," he told her.

He left the room without another word, carrying with him the picture of Olivia's frightened face. He had a low opinion of men or women who weren't honest about their sexual orientation. Their partners had a right to know, but Julian was aware that gay men, more than gay women, sometimes led a double life.

Outside, he looked back at the house. He'd leave for now, but he had no intention of staying away. Olivia *and* Griffin meant too much to him to be shut out of their lives.

Tyler hadn't gotten to where he was by taking no for an answer. He'd overridden or ignored every one of Jana's objections to him following her inside her apartment. He didn't know if she was upset because of what she'd learned about Olivia's husband or some other problem. He just knew he was going to find out why before he left.

"You going to tell me what's bothering you, or do I have to guess?"

Her hand threaded through her hair, shiny and fashionably cut, vastly different than when he had first seen her. "Tyler, I'm rather tired."

"So you want me to guess." He took a seat on the sofa.

Jana blew out a breath. "Shouldn't you be with Olivia?"

Crossing his legs, he placed his arms on the back of the sofa. "She wants time with Griffin."

Twin furrows ran across Jana's forehead. "What about Julian?"

"Griffin has to come first." His mouth flattening into a thin line, Tyler pulled his arms from the back of the sofa and clasped them between his knees.

Jana went to stand in front of him. "You can't mean that she doesn't plan to see him again?"

"Olivia will make the right decision."

Jana started for the front door. Tyler caught her just before she could grab the doorknob. "It's her decision to make."

"But it's wrong. He cares about her," she said.

"Then he'll understand that she's reliving a lot of pain and heartache, and let her work though it." Tyler headed for the kitchen.

She shot him a look. "You wouldn't."

"I'm not as patient about some things." He opened the refrigerator. "Did you eat?"

"I wasn't hungry."

He reached in and pulled out a plastic-covered container. "We'll have ham sandwiches."

Jana reached around him for the mayonnaise, lettuce, and tomatoes. "Have a seat. I'll fix them."

He smiled.

"What?" she asked, placing everything on the spotless white formica counter.

Tyler took a seat at the small wooden table in the kitchen. "I distinctly remember the time you wouldn't have offered or known how."

Jana paused in reaching for a knife. "Sometimes that life seems so far removed from me, almost as if someone else lived it, then other times . . ." Sliding the knife out of the holder, she whacked the lettuce.

"Then others times . . ." he prompted

She opened the bread sack and paused. "I feel as if I'm only a step away from what I was." She went back to fixing the sandwiches. "Olivia's ex reminded me so much of myself, so selfish and arrogant in what I wanted no matter how it might hurt anyone. I always came first."

"The difference is, he's still the same prick."

She whirled back. "But he made me remember those times I carelessly ruined people's lives."

Tyler went to her, not touching, just looking deeply into her pain-filled eyes. "You're not the woman you were yesterday or even a day ago. Each day you learn more about yourself. Painful to look at, but if you don't, you won't become the woman I know you can be."

"And what kind of woman is that? One that picks up strange men and goes with them to their apartment?" she asked.

He touched her then. "A woman, like most of us, who's not perfect or blameless or sinless, but trying to find her way. A woman with enough courage to admit her mistakes and try to learn from them. A woman I'm glad picked Midnight Dreams to enter."

"It was the only store open."

"Guess we were both lucky." He pulled her into his arms, their bodies aligning.

Her hands trembled on his chest. "How is it that you always manage to smooth out the rough places in my soul?"

His eyes darkened. "Because you deserve happiness, you deserve to know you have value."

"As long as I'm in your arms, I believe."

"Then I'll just have to hold you more often."

"Please."

His mouth brushed across hers in a gentle kiss. Slowly he lifted his head. "You make my head swim."

She snuggled closed, feeling strong and weak at the same time that she could bring a man like Tyler such pleasure. "Same here." She took a deep breath and took another precious step. "With you being in control no longer matters. With you, I can't wait for the mindlessness, the fluttering in my stomach when you're near." She lifted her head. "Strange, but it's liberating."

He groaned and pulled her closer. "You're making it difficult to turn you loose."

She didn't want him to, but Olivia needed him tonight more than she did. Slowly she pushed out of his arms. "Have a seat while I finish fixing the sandwiches."

"Why can't I nibble on your neck while you're doing it?" he asked, his mouth curved into a winsome smile.

"Because I wouldn't be able to think and there's no telling what I'd put in the sandwiches or how long it would take." She went to the counter.

"Just fix one for you. I already ate."

She glanced over her shoulder. "Taking care of me again?"

"Always."

The word went straight to her heart. Having a man like Tyler around almost made her believe in forever.

Olivia hadn't been able to eat more than a few bites since Aaron showed up on Saturday. Today was Tuesday. Her stomach was tied in knots. It didn't help that Griffin kept asking about Julian. Aaron had taken something else from them.

Seeing Aaron across the table with not a care in the world made her want to go over the table and wipe that smug smile off his face. He didn't care that he was disrupting his son's life. As usual, he only cared about himself.

"Thank you for coming, Mrs. Sanders," Aaron's layer, Ben Barnes, said. "You have your lawyer, so there's no reason for your brother's presence."

"There's every reason in view of the fact that, if not for Mrs. Sanders's brother, your client would have struck her," Brianna Ireland, Olivia's lawyer, stated.

"She slapped me," Aaron snapped.

"And your response was to hit back?" Brianna asked. Brianna was brainy, beautiful, and resourceful. And depending on the situation, she could be ruthless and relentless. She was the best divorce lawyer in the state.

Aaron opened his mouth, but his lawyer touched his arm and spoke for him. "Of course not. My client's emotions have been running high since he's been separated from his son."

Brainna's brow rose. "That's strange since Mrs. Sanders has not heard from him since she informed his parents of her son's birth as she was unaware of his whereabouts."

Aaron's lawyer laced his fingers on the polished cherry table in the conference room of Brianna's office. "Second-hand knowledge at best and unproven."

Opening a folder in front of her, Brianna removed seven Christmas cards and seven birthday cards, then shoved them across the polished surface. "As you can see from the return address, date on the envelope, and the writing on the cards, Mrs. Sanders did indeed notify her son's grandparents of his birth."

"We'll have those analyzed for authenticity of course." Aaron's lawyer barely glanced at the cards.

"Of course." Brianna turned to Aaron. "Mr. Sanders has expressed no interest in his son. Frankly, Mrs. Sanders is concerned that any association may be detrimental to the child."

"Because I'm gay?" Aaron asked sharply.

"Because you're a liar, a cheat, and have the morals of an alley cat," Olivia said, unable to remain quiet. "You knew you were gay with multiple partners and that your lifestyle put me and any children we might have at risk, yet you said nothing."

"Slanderous hearsay," Mr. Barnes said. "Might I point out that the divorce degrees cited irreconcilable differences?"

"Because I was too ashamed to tell anyone the truth," Olivia admitted.

"Don't say any more, Olivia," her lawyer cautioned.

"Please let her continue," Mr. Barnes said, his smile slick. "You admit to being ashamed. Might you also have been angry with Mr. Sanders? So angry that you failed to let him know that you were carrying his child?"

"Don't answer that," Brianna told her.

Aaron's layer smiled like a cat that just spotted a bird's nest on the ground. "She doesn't have to. Since both parties wanted the divorce it went through three months after papers were filed. Five months and two weeks later birth records show Griffin Maxwell Sanders was born, weighing seven pounds, eight ounces with an Apgar score of ten. He was full term and healthy. She deliberately kept the pregnancy a secret, depriving my client of almost eight precious years of his son's life. We want joint custody."

"No!" Olivia shot to her feet. "You're not taking my son."

"Olivia." Tyler wrapped his arms around her, but he felt the same. "Name your price. I'll pay it, whatever it is."

Aaron stood, managing to look offended. "How dare you think I'd put a price on my son's head. If that's the way you think, perhaps I should sue for full custody."

"You can't do this!" Olivia cried. "Hate me, but don't take it out on my son!"

"*My* son as well."

Mr. Barnes stood. "In anticipation that an amicable agreement could not be worked out I filed papers last week petitioning the court for joint custody. We'll let the courts decide. Good day." Mr. Barnes picked up his briefcase and left with Aaron.

The door closed behind them. Olivia trembled in Tyler's arms. "He can't take my baby."

Tyler looked over her head at the lawyer's solemn face. "We'll fight."

Olivia gazed at her lawyer. "Brianna, you don't look hopeful."

She placed the greeting cards in hers folder before she spoke. "The Family Court's judge is not going to look at his sexual orientation as a deterrent to joint custody, because the court can't openly discriminate. And you can bet his lawyer is going to make sure the case is heard before a liberal judge. But any judge will want some very good answers as to why you kept your pregnancy a secret."

"I wasn't sure at first," she said slowly.

"And when you were?" her lawyer asked, watching her closely.

"I wanted to protect my child from a man who lied as easily as he breathed, an adulterer." Olivia straightened. "I still feel the same way."

"Because of his sexual preference?" Brianna asked.

"I'm not homophobic, if that's what you're asking. Some of my best clients are gay men." She shook her head. "It wasn't the fact he was gay, it was because he lied to me and used me."

"That was the answer I was hoping for." Brianna tapped the folders on the table. "But why did he come back now?"

"We've been asking ourselves the same thing," Tyler said. "He didn't suddenly feel paternal and get an urge to be Griffin's father. There has to be a reason, and I'm going to find out."

"Do that, and keep me posted," Brianna told him. "Be prepared for this to move quickly because a young child is involved."

Olivia swallowed the lump in her throat. "There's a chance he could win, isn't there?"

"I won't lie to you, but the court strongly favors the mother in custody cases. You're a wonderful, well-respected woman in the community with a spotless reputation and nothing to hide." Her eyes hardened. "If we have to, we'll fill the court with people who'll testify on your behalf."

"But that might not be enough," Olivia said, her stomach knotting when Brianna didn't disagree. She could lose her son to a selfish, disreputable man, and there was nothing she could do about it.

Aware that Olivia needed to keep her mind occupied, Tyler didn't object when Olivia insisted he drop her off at Midnight Dreams. While she was in the back putting up her things, he spoke briefly with Jana who assured him she'd keep an eye on Olivia. He didn't have a doubt she would. She'd changed from the selfish woman to a caring individual who thought of others first. He hoped he was one of those lucky individuals. Kissing her on the cheek, he drove home and went straight to his computer.

If one knew where to look there was a wealth of information to be had in cyberspace. He'd try to get it legally, but if he had to bend a law or two he wasn't going to lose any sleep over it. Tyler's fingers raced over the computer keys. First, he wanted to check to see if there had been anything about the earning status of Sanders, LLC, in the news lately. Aaron liked money and the privileged lifestyle it granted.

But the manicured nails, tailored suit and perfect diction couldn't hide the fact that he was a sleaze. He'd suckered Olivia into a marriage to hide his homosexuality. He hadn't cared about her then or later. The divorce had been quiet because he hadn't wanted knowledge of his sexuality to get out.

It had been almost eight years since Tyler had seen him, but he hadn't changed from the self-centered man he'd proven to be during his short marriage to Olivia. There had to be a reason for his sudden decision to seek joint custody.

Tyler located an interview in the *Washington Post* dated fifteen months ago. Harold Sanders, Aaron's father, had been interviewed about the growth potential of the private equity firm he'd started. They had taken a hit after 9/11, and like many companies were trying to come out of a tailspin.

Further digging revealed Aaron's father, the CEO of the firm, had been diagnosed with prostate cancer seven months ago. He'd gone into remission after chemotherapy and radiation. An article in *Black Enterprise* magazine four months ago revealed the cancer had reappeared in his lungs, then spread to his liver. He wasn't expected to recover.

Tyler leaned back in his chair. He'd only met Harold Sanders once, the day his son married Olivia. He had struck Tyler as a rather quiet man. His wife was the same way. They'd acknowledged Griffin after Olivia had notified them, sent birthday cards and Christmas cards with money, but nothing personal. They'd made no move to make him a part of their lives.

It was only after Griffin started asking about why his father didn't visit like his friends' dads and asking if it was his fault that his father didn't live with them that Olivia had begun sending gifts in Aaron's name. She'd wanted to spare her son the pain of knowing his father didn't care about him, but it had made Griffin idolize his absent father all the more. If there was the slightest chance for him to see his father, Griffin would take it.

And that would break Olivia's heart.

Olivia added not sleeping well to not eating well since Aaron's lawyer had called to tell them of the date to meet in the judge's chambers. It was set for Friday. Aaron was moving quickly. She didn't mind. She wanted him out of her life as soon as possible.

This time for good.

Sitting in the judge's chambers next to her lawyer, with Aaron and his lawyer less than two feet away, it was difficult to keep her anger and fear under control as Brianna had warned her to do. Her nails dug into the purse in her lap.

"Thank you, Judge Watkins, for agreeing to meet in your chambers to discuss the custody of Griffin Maxwell Sanders," Aaron's lawyer said. "You'll see by the papers before you that at the time of my client's divorce, he was not aware of his wife's pregnancy."

"Neither was my client, Judge Watkins," Brianna stated. "The divorce and the reason for it had put her under great emotional stress."

"We are not here to discuss the divorce, but the wrongful withholding of my client's right and privilege to share in the joy and pride of raising his only child," Aaron's lawyer said.

"He never wanted Griffin. He doesn't want him now."

"Olivia, please," Brianna cautioned. "I'm sorry. Your Honor, but, like any caring mother, my client loves her son deeply and wants what is best for him."

"Keeping him away from his father isn't best for him," Aaron's lawyer quickly pointed out.

"That's debatable," Brianna was just as quick to say.

Aaron came out of his chair. "What's that supposed to mean?"

"Sit down," Judge Watkins ordered. "I don't want another word out of anyone unless I ask you directly." Aaron glared at Brianna, but he took his seat.

"Mrs. Sanders, Mr. Barnes raised a good question. Once you knew you were pregnant, didn't you consider the child's father had a right to know?"

Olivia's hands tightened on the purse. "After I learned he was having an affair with his best man at our wedding along with several other men, I felt so stupid and gullible, that I tried to think of him as little as possible. My pregnancy was the only thing that sustained me during the darkest period in my life."

The judge didn't even glance at Aaron. "Did you keep the pregnancy from your ex-husband because of his sexual orientation?"

Olivia was glad Brianna had already posed the question and that she could answer it truthfully. "It wasn't that he was gay, it was because he'd lied to me and used me. After the divorce I didn't know how to locate him, so I contacted his parents. Since his birth, Aaron hasn't made any contact with Griffin."

Judge Watkins turned to Aaron. "Mr. Sanders, what do you have to say on your behalf?"

"I love my son. I want to make that clear, but I was afraid that she had turned him against me. Also, I didn't want to disrupt his life." Aaron briefly bowed his head "But my own father is ill and I see now how important the relationship is between a father and a son. I want to be a part of Griffin's life, to let him know his grandfather before it is too late. Nothing is as important to me."

Brianna pressed her hand against Olivia's to keep her quiet. "Mr. Sanders, according to the staff at the hospital, you seldom visited your father while he was hospitalized."

Aaron's cold stare drilled into her. "They're mistaken."

"Is the house staff mistaken as well?" she asked. "You've visited your father only twice in the past two weeks."

"I've been busy running the company and preparing to gain custody of my son," he defended. "My parents understand and support me in this."

"My client has a prosperous business and finds time for her son," Brianna put in smoothly. "He is and always will be her first priority."

"Not quite," Aaron's layer said.

"What are you talking about? I can have witness lined up within the hour that will collaborate what I've said," Brianna said.

"I wonder what those witnesses think of Mrs. Sanders hiring Jana Franklin, a woman known to live off the generosity of men and that's putting it nicely," Mr. Barnes said. "More importantly, why is this same woman living in the garage apartment on the grounds of Mrs. Sanders home and allowed to be in daily contact with an impressionable child? Ms. Franklin's reputation is so debased that her own father wants nothing to do with her. In fact, he is only too willing to testify to the fact."

Olivia didn't need to feel Brianna's hand clench on her arm to know Aaron's lawyer had dealt them a setback. "Jana has changed."

"Not according to her father," Aaron's lawyer said. "Haven't some customers canceled orders or stopped patronizing your store because they don't wish to associate with her?"

"One customer canceled an order, then reinstated it," Olivia told him.

"Sales have gone up since Jana has come to work from me. I have the records to prove it. She's a valuable asset."

"From male customers, no doubt." He placed a folder in front of the judge. "You'll see that she has been married three times and moved from man to man with appalling regularity. She's also been seen embracing Mrs. Sander's brother. There is no telling what else is going on before that young child."

"The only thing going on is what's in people's narrow and nasty minds," Olivia said. "Jana goes to church and has helped with community projects. My pastor and his wife, as well as other members of my church, will testify as much." She glared at Aaron. "Some people can learn from their mistakes, other revel in them."

"What about your client's lifestyle?" Brianna questioned.

"My client's sexual preference is and should not be of concern in this matter. Only his fitness as a parent, which, unlike your client's, is unquestionable. His only focus at this time is gaining joint custody of his child," his lawyer pointed out. "He is a responsible citizen and respected in the community. He has been deprived from watching his son grow up or developing a relationship with him." He faced the judge.

"In an effort to partially end the suffering my client has had to endure, I ask you to grant him visitation rights until a custody decision can be made."

"No!" Olivia came up out of her chair, shaking off Brianna's hand on her arm. "He doesn't want Griffin. He's incapable of loving anyone but himself."

"Mrs. Sanders, your objections have been noted, but studies have shown again and again that children raised with the influence of both parents grow up to be emotionally healthier and productive over their counterparts," the judge said. "Please take your seat."

Olivia responded to her lawyer's determined hand more than the judge's order. She dropped into her chair.

"Your Honor, might I reiterate that Griffin's paternal grandfather is gravely ill and is not expected to recover. He has expressed his wish to see his grandson before dying." Mr. Barnes placed another folder in front of the judge. "His deposition and his doctor's statement. The quick resolution of this matter is paramount."

Brianna leaned forward. "My client also asks a quick resolution because she doesn't want her son's life disrupted. It should also be pointed out that his paternal grandparents have contacted their grandson only with birthday and Christmas cards since his birth. On the other hand, Griffin's uncle, Tyler Maxwell, a respected businessman, and Griffin's maternal grandparents have had an integral and positive effect on his young life. He's happy and well adjusted."

"Mrs. Sanders," the judge said, "Has Griffin expressed an interest in seeing his father?"

Olivia didn't want to answer the question. Griffin would be over the moon if he knew his father wanted to see him, but he only knew the lies she'd told him, lies she thought would protect him.

"Mrs. Sanders?"

"He thinks his father loves him," she finally said.

"I do," Aaron piped up. "We deserve to be together."

Olivia turned on him. "You deserve to rot in hell for what you put us though. I had to hold him while he screamed in pain when they drew blood to make sure he wasn't HIV positive, then endure the agonizing wait for the test results."

"You b—"

"Aaron," his lawyer quickly cut him off. "Your outrage is understandable. She put Griffin through a lot of needless pain."

"Not according to studies at that time," the judge said. "It shows she was smart and concerned. Obviously she has done what she felt best for her child."

Olivia tried to take heart in what the judge said, but Brianna's hand remained clamped on hers. It wasn't over.

"I need time to go over what was presented before me today. In the interim, however, Mrs. Sanders you will have Griffin available and ready to spend the weekend with his father. He can pick him up at twelve tomorrow. He will be returned no later than five Sunday afternoon."

Stunned, Olivia stared. "No."

"Griffin deserves to know he has a father who loves him," the judge said.

"Let me go with him," she pleaded. "Aaron is a stranger to him."

"That may be your fault," the judge said with disapproval. "Don't let your prejudices blind you to what's best for Griffin."

"You're the one who's blind," Olivia protested.

"Olivia," Brianna cautioned.

Judge Watkins stiffened. "Ms. Ireland, I advise you to instruct your client to conduct herself better when we meet again." She closed the folder. "All parties, including Griffin, will meet in my chambers a week from today for my final decision. And Mrs. Sanders, I suggest you spend your time wisely in preparing Griffin for the visit with his father. Don't even think of defying my order."

"He'll be ready, Judge Watkins," Brianna said.

Olivia said nothing as tears rolled down her cheeks.

Jana knew when she saw Olivia's pale face that evening the news wasn't good. She also knew her first concern would be her son. "Griffin is in the kitchen helping Wanda prepare dinner." Jana didn't add the cook had remained because she had wanted to learn what the judge had decided. Olivia was already aware that they all supported her.

"Are you Jana Franklin?" the woman who came in behind Olivia asked.

Jana got a funny feeling in the pit of her stomach. The attaché case denoted she was probably Olivia's lawyer, the Dolce & Gabanna white suit that she was probably very successful. "Yes."

"Why? What's going on?" Tyler asked, joining them.

The woman's gaze went to him. "So sources were correct."

"Make sense, Brianna," Tyler told her.

"Let's go into the library." Olivia led the way, as if every step was more difficult than the last.

Jana didn't move. Brianna stopped and looked back at her. "This concerns you as well."

"What is it?" Tyler asked again.

Jana already knew. Her past had caught up with her.

17

Less than five minutes later Jana realized how right she was and how much her father truly hated her. She felt chilled and wondered if she'd ever get warm again.

"Jana, I'm sorry."

Jana's head snapped up on hearing Olivia's softly spoken words. "They're trying to take your son away from you and using me to do it, and you're sorry?" Too keyed up to sit any longer, she stood. "You should be berating me and helping me pack."

"I won't turn my back on my friend," Olivia said. "I need to go see Griffin." Coming to her feet, she was gone.

Jana might have known that would be Olivia's response. It was up to her. "It won't take me long to pack."

Tyler stepped in front of her. "I thought we already had this conversation."

She wrapped her arms around her waist when she wanted to wrap them around him and weep. "They'll use me to take Griffin."

His knuckles caressed her cheeks. "They can try. You're not the same woman."

Tears clogged her throat. "My father thinks so."

Tyler's face filled with rage. "He's about as much of a father as Griffin's father is, and that's as nothing as it gets."

Jana turned to the lawyer. "You know I have to go. Tell them."

Brianna crossed her long legs and looked Jana in the eyes. "I've heard your name recently mentioned a couple of times, and it has never been good."

Jana didn't flinch, didn't hang her head. She'd done enough of that. This was the kind of woman, smart, successful, beautiful, respected, that Tyler could be proud of. She envied her when she'd never envied anyone. "How boring for you."

"Actually, it was," Brianna agreed. "Personally, I wouldn't get mad at the woman for taking my man, I'd try to figure out what he got from her that he wasn't getting from me and make sure he didn't stray again. Or hang him up by his balls."

Jana looked at the woman with surprise and a grudging respect. That's exactly what she would have done . . . if she cared enough, which she never had until she met Tyler.

Brianna leaned back in her leather chair. "If I thought you'd hurt this case, I'd help you pack. The fact that you're more concerned with Griffin's happiness than your own is in your favor. And sleeping in a garage apartment isn't exactly what you're used to, yet I don't get the feeling that you're unhappy about it."

"I'm not," Jana said. "Olivia helped me when I had no place to go."

Brianna nodded. "Olivia is well known for being a nurturer with a strong faith. The fact that, knowing your reputation, she still helped you turn your life around is a major point in her favor. You're father's unwillingness to forgive makes Olivia's kindness all the more commendable."

"See," Tyler said, sliding his arm around her waist.

Brianna's arched brows quirked at the motion. "Is there any point in asking if you're dating anyone besides Tyler?"

Jana flushed. "No."

Tyler smiled, his arm tightened.

"Well, Aaron's lawyer believes your relationship might affect Griffin," Brianna told them.

The smile died on Tyler's face. "He should be more worried about his client."

"His problem." Brianna looked from one to the other. "Then I take it you two haven't gotten hot and heavy in front of Griffin."

"What do you think?" Tyler asked, his body tense.

Holding up her hands, Brianna stood. "Just asking. I'll see myself out. The next forty-eight hours won't be easy for Olivia."

"We'll be there for her," Tyler said. "She's gone through enough."

"I couldn't agree more." Brianna went to the door. "Nice meeting you, Jana." It took Jana a moment to respond.

"Thank you." Nodding Brianna was gone.

Tyler pulled Jana into his arms. "You are going to be sensible aren't you?"

Jana asked a question of her own. "Will there ever come a time when people will forget my past?"

He had to be honest with her. She deserved nothing less. "For some, yes. For others, no."

She looked out the atrium doors to the gardens beyond. "I wish I had the power to change the past."

"You can't. You can only learn from it," he told her.

She faced him. "Some lessons are too hard." Her voice trembled as much as her body.

"Not if you don't have to learn them alone."

"Tyler, I . . ."

"What?" he asked.

"Nothing." She placed her head on his chest and curved her arms around his waist.

Needing to hold her as much as she seemed to need him, Tyler held her, hoping that was enough, yet afraid it wouldn't be.

Olivia had put off the conversation with Griffin as long as she could. In an hour Aaron would be there to pick him up. Tyler had offered to talk with Griffin, but she needed to do this herself. But it was going to be the hardest conversation she had ever had.

"Griffin, I need to talk to you." She put her joysticks aside. She had needed to be close to him, to touch him as much as possible. She refused to think that there might be a time when she couldn't.

He'd been overjoyed that she had stayed home from work, just as he had been last night when she'd allowed him to stay up an hour longer, reading to him until he fell asleep. He hadn't known that she hadn't left his room until that morning.

"Sure," he said, with his usual bubbling laughter. "I was creaming you anyway." He put his controls aside and turned to her. "I was thinking, since you stayed home today, we could go to the Chuck E. Cheese's for lunch. Maybe Julian could meet us there."

Her trembling hand ran over his head, then curved around his shoulder. Would either of them ever forget Julian? Probably not. He'd left a void in their lives. She'd tried not to care too deeply, but the pain of their separation proved that she'd failed. But now wasn't the time to dwell on it. Griffin welfare was what mattered most. "You remember when I explained to you that even when two people are in love and get married, they might not stay in love like your grandparents and they get a divorce."

The animation left his face. "Like you and my father."

"Yes."

His fingers plucked at the hem of his shorts. "Some of my friends' parents are divorced, but they still see their fathers and get to do things with them."

Olivia's heart clenched at the hurt in her son's voice, the droop of his shoulders. Aaron had a lot to answer for. No matter how unchristian, Olivia hated him with every fiber of her being, but she wouldn't let those feelings spill over and hurt Griffin. "Your father loves you. He's just been busy, especially now since his father is ill."

Griffin's small head came up. "Granddad Sanders?"

Although Griffin had never met his paternal grandparents, he remembered them nightly in his prayers. "Yes." Olivia swallowed. "Your father wants to see you."

The spurt of joy on Griffin's face tore at her heart. "Like now? He's coming to see me even before my birthday or Christmas?"

She swallowed again. "He's in town."

"Wow!" Griffin took her hand and bounded up. "Come on, Mama, let's go see him."

Although she felt a giant weight on her chest, Olivia allowed herself to be pulled up. "He's coming here to pick you up."

His dark brown eyes rounded. "Here?"

Her hand ran over his head. "He'll be here at noon."

Griffin jerked his head toward the wall clock. "That's in thirty minutes."

And much too soon. "That . . . that gives us enough time to pack."

"He's taking us with him?"

Her hands fisted. "Just you. You two are going to spend some time together. He'll bring you back tomorrow at six."

Some of the happiness left his face. "You're not coming with us?"

Olivia hated herself for being glad then, as always, she thought of Griffin first as she had since she felt the first flutters in her stomach. "It will be wonderful with just the two of you getting to know each other. It will be just like a sleepover and I'll be as close as the phone."

She could see the appeal of the idea taking root in his quick-thinking brain. "Just the two of us having fun?"

"You could go to Chuck E. Cheese's with him."

"We could, couldn't we?" He grabbed her hand again. "Let's go pack. I want to be ready when my father gets here."

"Do I look all right, Uncle Tyler?" Griffin asked for the umpteenth time.

"Never better," Tyler said, sitting beside Olivia on the living room sofa. "Any man would be proud to call you his son."

Griffin went back to staring out the window. "You sure he has the right address, Mama?"

"Yes," Olivia mumbled.

"It's not twelve yet," Tyler pointed out. He almost wished Aaron wouldn't show up, but that would be too cruel. Whatever Aaron was, Griffin loved him and wanted him to be a part of his life. Trouble was, Aaron had proved that he didn't care about his son.

"Boy. A limousine just pulled up." Griffin glanced over his shoulder. "Do you think that's him?" He raced over and took her hand. "Come see if that's him."

Tyler took Olivia's trembling arm and went to the window. Aaron strolled up the walkway as if he owned the world.

"Is it him?" Griffin asked.

"Yes," Olivia said, one strangled word.

Griffin took off for the front door. Tyler didn't try to stop him.

Griffin opened the door and stared up at his father for the first time. He wasn't as tall as his uncle or Julian and his shoulders weren't as wide, but the smile on his face was all that mattered. He squatted down so they were eye level.

"Griffin?"

Too full to speak, Griffin nodded

Aaron opened his arms. "Come to your father, son."

Used to hugs and roughhousing from his uncle, and lately Julian, Griffin launched himself into his father's arms, expecting him to catch him and maybe swing him around as they did. Instead his father grunted and almost toppled over.

Griffin heard his father say a bad word a workman had used when he hit his thumb instead of the nail. The man had been angry. Tears sprang to Griffin's eyes. He'd messed up. He'd made his father mad.

He felt himself lifted and stared into his uncle's face. "Is he mad?" Griffin whispered, afraid to look and see for himself. The workman had gone to his truck and hadn't returned for a long time.

"No." Uncle Tyler said. "You're just as glad to see Griffin as he is you. Aren't you, Aaron?"

"Of course," Griffin heard his father say, but he didn't sound happy.

Griffin cautiously looked over his shoulder to see his father flicking his fingers over his suit. "I didn't mean to make you fall."

"You did nothing wrong," his mother said, but she wasn't smiling either.

"No one said he did." His father's smile returned. He held out his hand. "Are you ready to go?"

Griffin scrambled down, careful this time to curb his happiness. He took his father's hand. "Yes, sir."

"Where are his things?" his father asked.

Uncle Tyler hunkered down to Griffin, reached into his pocket and handed him a small cell phone. "The charger is in your backpack. Call anytime. You know how mothers worry."

His father looked as if he'd eaten something that didn't agree with him. "That isn't necessary."

Uncle Tyler ignored him and handed him the backpack. "Have him back tomorrow no later than six."

Without a word, his father started toward the waiting limousine. Griffin wanted to ask him to stop. He hadn't kissed his mother good-bye and she looked so sad. She started after them. Uncle Tyler put his arms around her.

"I love you, Griffin. Always remember that," she called.

Although he didn't like saying it in public, he didn't like seeing his mother cry either. "I love you too, Mother. I'll call." He held up the phone, just before his father opened the door and urged him into the limousine. The door shut. Through the tinted window he saw his mother leaning against his uncle with tears streaming down her cheeks.

"Something is wrong with my mother. I need to get out." He tried to reach for the door handle, but his father wouldn't let him.

"She's fine. Let's go," he ordered the driver and the car took off. "And you won't need this." He took the phone, slipping it into his coat pocket.

"I can't call my mother," Griffin said.

"Don't be a baby," his father chastised. "Maybe now she'll know how it feels."

Griffin didn't understand what his father was talking about. He just knew something was wrong with his mother. He clearly recalled the time she'd cried because she'd been worried about him at Water World.

Disobeying two rules he'd always been taught, Griffin didn't fasten his seat belt nor did he remain seated while the car was moving; instead he got on his knees and looked out the back window of the speeding vehicle at his mother and felt like crying too.

"He took my baby," Olivia cried.

Olivia wouldn't move until the limo disappeared. "I know it hurt." Tyler hugged her to him as they entered the house. He led her to a chair in the living room and knelt beside her. "It's hard, but he'll be back. You'll talk to him tonight."

Tears streamed down her cheek. "Aaron is too mean and selfish to let Griffin keep the phone."

"That's why I slipped another one in his backpack when neither of you were looking." He squeezed her hands. "Aaron isn't the type to help Griffin unpack. He'll call."

She hugged him. "Thank you."

"I love him too," he said, his voice suspiciously rough.

She stared down into his face. "In feeling sorry for myself I'd forgotten that."

Tyler brushed the last of her tears away. "You're entitled."

Olivia shook her head. "Feeling sorry for myself won't get Griffin back in my arms sooner. I better get to the shop."

Straightening, Tyler pulled her to her feet. "Jana and the new part-time clerk can handle things."

"It might make the time go by faster," she told him.

He didn't believe her, but let it go. "In the meantime I'll keep searching the Internet. Maybe the private investigator I hired has come up with a reason for Aaron's sudden interest in Griffin."

Olivia's eyes narrowed. "Whatever the reason it's for his own good. He's only out for himself."

Tyler nodded. "I agree. We'll find the answer and be ready for the next hearing."

"If the judge rules against—"

"She won't," Tyler interrupted.

"If she does," Olivia continued, her face set, "I'll do whatever it takes to keep Griffin away from his father permanently."

Tyler had already figured as much. There was no way in hell he'd allow Aaron more than temporary visitation of his nephew. "I'll make the arrangements."

She squeezed his hands. "I'll run upstairs to get my purse. Please let me know if you find out anything."

"You'll know the second after I do."

"Courtney was a fool to let you go," Olivia said. "Jana has more sense."

"But she's a whole lot harder to catch," Tyler said.

"My money's on you." Patting his arm, she went to her room.

Tyler stared after her, then went to his office, wishing he felt as confident about Jana. No matter how hard he tried, he knew that, in the back of her mind, her past still haunted her. He'd be the biggest liar in the word if he didn't admit it had given him some sleepless nights as well.

Sitting at his desk, Tyler turned on the computer and waited for it to boot up. What he had to remember, what he hoped Jana remembered, was that there were no little or big sins in the eyes of God. Sin was sin and once a person repented, in God's eyes, the sin was forgotten and cast into the sea of forgetfulness. Tyler was of the same opinion.

Jana was a different person, and he wanted her in his life. This time he didn't plan to lose.

Olivia had powdered her nose twice since she'd parked several car lengths down from Midnight Dreams. She looked at her reflection in the compact. There was nothing she could do about her red eyes and puffy lids. She couldn't stay in the SUV all afternoon, but she didn't want to alarm her clients.

Closing her eyes, she leaned her head back against the headrest, unable to keep her mind off Griffin. Was Aaron watching him carefully enough? Griffin was an inquisitive young boy. He needed guidance and perimeters set. Aaron had about as much parenting skill as a fly.

Opening her eyes, she reached for the door and got out. She'd go crazy if she kept thinking about it. Shoving the straps of the satchel bag over her shoulder, she strode down the street and into the shop.

Both Jana and the new clerk glanced around. Olivia smiled at them despite the fact she wanted to scream out her anger and pain. "I'll put my purse up and be right back out to help you."

Jana crossed to her. Her gaze didn't miss a thing. "You don't have to be brave. If you need to cry, cry."

Olivia blinked. "I don't seem able to do anything else."

"He's the smartest boy I've ever met."

"But he's just a boy." Biting her lip, Olivia went to her office and sat behind her desk. "Please, God. Take care of Griffin."

"I don't feel well." Griffin shoved what was left of his fifth large slice of pepperoni pizza across the table from him. He had thought it was so cool that his father had let him decide where they ate dinner. Griffin had chosen a pizza parlor where he'd proceeded to eat his way though a large pizza accompanied by three strawberry sodas.

Aaron frowned across the wooden table. He hadn't taken one bite of food. "What's wrong with you?"

Griffin's arms circled his waist. "I think I ate too much."

"Don't you have more sense than that?" Aaron snapped. "Didn't your mother teach you anything?"

Griffin's eyes filled with tears. This wasn't turning out like he thought. All his father did was fuss. Nothing Griffin did pleased him.

"Your mother turned you into a crybaby. Stop sniveling," his father ordered.

"Yes, sir," Griffin managed, but somehow a tear slid down his cheek.

"Let's go." Standing, his father grabbed him by the arm and almost dragged him to the limo. "Get in, and don't you dare throw up."

Griffin did as he was told. He wanted his mother, but one look at the angry face of his father and he knew better than to ask to go home. "Can I call my mother?"

The anger on his father's face disappeared. "We don't want to worry your mother." Scooting closer, he pulled Griffin to him. "You'll be fine."

Griffin snuggled closer. Maybe his father didn't dislike him after all, but he still wanted his mother.

Olivia was fighting a losing battle. Expecting the knock on her door to be Jana or Ann, the new clerk, she reached for another tissue. "Come in."

The door opened and Julian stood there, tall and more handsome than any man she'd ever seen. "Hello, Olivia."

Her hands clenched. "What are you doing here? I don't want to see you anymore."

"I can't stop thinking about you, worrying about you and Griffin."

Tears filled her eyes and ran down her cheeks. "Please go."

Julian strode across the room, blatantly ignoring her words. "You're not shutting me out. I care about Griffin, too."

She lost the battle against the tears and her determination to avoid Julian. "Oh, Julian."

"I'm here, honey. I'm here." His arms tightened. He never wanted to let her go. Worrying about Olivia and Griffin, not being able to see them, or comfort her, was a hell he never wanted to go through again. "We'll fight to keep Griffin where he belongs."

"I can't stop worrying about him," she confessed. "Aaron will be more concerned about winning Griffin's affection than in setting limits. You know how Griffin likes having his way."

Julian tenderly brushed the tears from her face. "He's also smart and loves his mother."

"Please tell me he'll be all right."

"He'll come home to you tomorrow and that's where he'll remain."

"I don't think I could stand it if he didn't," she told him.

Julian plucked tissue from the box on her desk. "Dry your eyes. You have a customer."

She did as he said. "I haven't been much help since I came in. I'll probably cry all over whoever it is."

Julian kissed both of her hands. "He won't mind."

"You?"

He looked a bit embarrassed. "I need another set of those sheets. I miss sleeping on the ones I bought since they are in the laundry."

Olivia felt a smile curve her mouth upward. "Oh, Julian, thank you."

"Good night, Griffin."

"Good night, Father," Griffin dutifully said from beside his father on the sofa in the sitting room of his father's suite in the downtown hotel.

"I'll see you in the morning," his father told him, making no motion to get up to help him get ready for bed like his mother did.

"Yes, sir." Griffin went to his bedroom and quietly closed the door. He supposed the room was all right, but he missed his own room with his books and games. He missed his mother most of all. She always helped him run his bath, listened to his prayers, and read him a story afterwards. Maybe he should tell his father.

Griffin took a couple of steps toward the door, then stopped. His father had called him a crybaby. He didn't want him to think he couldn't take a bath by himself. He wasn't a baby.

Going to his backpack, he began taking out his clothes. He pulled out his pajamas and was reaching for the next item when he saw the phone. He grabbed it, began punching in his home phone number. Suddenly he stopped and went into the bathroom and closed the door before continuing. The phone was picked up before it rang the second time.

"Griffin, is that you baby?" his mother asked, her voice sounded like the time he had become separated from her in the grocery store.

"Yes, ma'am."

"You're all right, aren't you?"

He didn't want her to think badly of him like his father did. "Yes, ma'am. I'm going to run my own bath."

"Where's your father?"

Griffin let the lid of the toilet down and sat on top. "I guess he's still watching TV."

There was a pause, then, "I don't want you running hot water. You can wait until you get home tomorrow night to take a bath."

He perked up a bit. "I can?"

"One night won't hurt. Have you eaten dinner?"

"Yes, ma'am. We had pizza for dinner and afterwards we came back to the hotel and looked at a couple of Disney movies. I didn't want to tell him I'd already seen them."

"Griffin, you sound different. Are you sure you're all right?"

He wanted to go home, but he didn't want his father mad at him. "Yes ma'am. I better get ready for bed." Before he started crying like the baby his father had called him.

"All right, just remember I love you, will always love you no matter what. I want you to remember that we can always talk about anything. If you find out you're not sleepy and want to talk, all you have to do is call."

"Good night, Mama. I love you."

"Good night, sweetheart. I love you too. I'll see you tomorrow. I made your favorite dessert."

Griffin rubbed his stomach. He didn't want to think about food. "Yes, ma'am. Good night."

"Good night."

Griffin disconnected the phone and went to change into his pj's. Tomorrow he was going home.

Olivia's eyes tightly closed, she clutched the receiver even after the only sound was the droning dial tone. Tears seeped from beneath her closed lids.

Tyler finally took the receiver from her. "Olivia?"

Shaking her head she turned, burrowing into the comfort and security of Julian's arms, but even as she did so she thought of Griffin alone. Ever since she had come home, she'd sat by the phone in the media room, watching the phone, waiting and praying for her child to call.

"He was trying to be so brave." She lifted her head because the people surrounding her loved Griffin as well and were just as worried about him. Tyler, Julian and Jana had waited with her since she came home from Midnight Dreams, doing their best to keep her mind off the silent phone.

"Aaron sent Griffin to get ready for bed by himself. Griffin says he's all right, but he wanted to get off the phone so he could go to bed." She wiped her eyes with the handkerchief Julian gave her. "Griffin has never willingly gone to bed."

"Wanna bet he reverts to his old ways tomorrow night?" Tyler said.

A slow smile formed on Olivia's face. "He'll probably have a thousand things to tell me."

Julian stroked her hair. "And you'll listen patiently to every one of them even if he's already told you twice before."

"Probably more times than that. That's Griffin's favorite tactic," Olivia said, her heart lighter. "He'll say, 'are you sure I told you this before?' with the innocence of an angel."

"He came by that honestly," Tyler said. "Both of us hated to go to bed."

"You're still a night owl," Jana remarked.

"I think better at night." Taking her hand, Tyler pulled her up from the love seat. "Julian, see if you can get Olivia to do more than pick at her food. I'm going to see Jana home. Good night."

"Good night," Julian called, his gaze on Olivia. "You really should eat something."

"I'm fine. Thank you for staying with me," she said.

His hand squeezed hers. "You've already thanked me a dozen times or more, and as I told you before, it's not necessary."

"But sitting with distraught mothers can't be how you usually spend your time."

"You're the only mother I've ever dated," he said, not quite sure why he revealed that about himself.

She frowned. "I'm honored and puzzled."

He shrugged carelessly. "It's just that a lot of single mothers are usually looking for husbands."

"And you were honest enough to know you weren't going to be around for the long haul."

She'd hit the nail on the head. "Something like that."

"I can see why you picked me than," she said. "I have no intention of marrying again."

Her words shouldn't have bothered him, but they did. "Just because Aaron broke your trust is no reason to think every man will."

"I think we've had this conversation. Thanks for coming." She came to her feet.

He didn't move. "We have. Complete with you trying to toss me out."

"And Griffin came to my rescue," she said, her voice trembling.

He came out of the chair, wrapping his arms around her. "Don't go there. Stay annoyed with me."

She almost smiled. "Which can be so easy to do."

His hand stroked her back. "Part of my charming bedside manner."

Olivia pushed out of his arms. "Are you really so horrible?"

"Used to be." His hand cupped her face. "But since a certain woman took me to task in the emergency room, I'm almost completely reformed."

"You needed it," she said.

He chuckled, hugging her. "You talk about Griffin being opinionated. You and Tyler are the same way." He gave her a quick kiss. "Griffin will come through this and figure out a way to stay up later, eat more junk food, and get that new game he wanted."

She bit her lip. "I planned on picking it up after church tomorrow."

Julian tsked. "Well, I certainly hope you don't plan on giving it to him until he's been home at least an hour."

"I was thinking of giving it to him at bedtime so he wouldn't remember being alone tonight," she said.

Julian sobered. "You're a fabulous mother, and if you think I'm leaving *you* tonight, you don't know me very well."

"Julian, I couldn't—" She trailed off and placed her head on his shoulder.

"If I didn't know how upset you are, I might revert to my old self and become angry that you thought I expected sex." He set her free and turned to stare down at the sofa. "Griffin says this turns into a bed. I thought we'd watch movies until you fell asleep. Then in the morning you can cook me breakfast."

She folded her arms. "Why can't you cook me breakfast?"

"Because I asked you first." He began taking the cushions from the sofa.

"I'll go get the linen."

He straightened. "What thread count?"

She grinned. "One thousand two hundred."

"You certainly know how to tempt a man."

"Don't I though," Olivia said, and headed for the stairs.

"You must really like Julian," Jana said as hand in hand she and Tyler slowly made their way to her apartment.

"He cares about Olivia and Griffin," Tyler answered.

She slanted a look at him. "Is that why you gave them time to be alone?"

"Yeah." He paused and looked back at the black Maserati at the curb. "I hope he doesn't make me regret trusting him."

Jana tugged him forward. "He just wants to be there for her."

"That's what I thought, but if I'm wrong . . ."

"Olivia is old enough to make her own decisions." Jana started up the stairs with Tyler slowly following.

"Sometimes women don't make the right decision when a good-looking man is involved."

Jana turned from opening the door. "If Olivia heard you insult her like that, she'd probably infect your precious computers with some super virus or spyware."

He shuddered and followed her into the house. "Don't even joke about something like that."

"I wasn't joking."

"You certainly know how to hurt a man."

Once she might have taken offense at such a statement. "Don't you forget it. You want iced tea or lemonade?"

"Lemonade." He plopped on the sofa. "How long do you think it will take for them to say good night?"

"I didn't get the impression Julian was in any hurry to leave."

"What?" Tyler paused in reaching for the remote. He'd talked Jana into letting him buy her a small television so they could watch movies together.

"He only left her side to go check on his patients at the hospital," Jana reminded him. "He's very perceptive. He realized that the more Olivia is alone, the more time she has to think of Griffin and get depressed. Julian doesn't want that to happen and he's there to comfort her."

"She has me."

Jana turned with the glasses of lemonade and rolled her eyes. "Tyler, come on."

He stared at her a few moments, then launched himself out of the chair. "He's dead meat."

"Tyler, come back here." She hurriedly sat the glasses down and caught up with him, her hand slipping behind the belt buckle of his jeans. "Don't you dare go over there and embarrass her with all she's going through."

"He's not taking advantage of Olivia," he said.

"Who says he is?" Jana asked. "There are good men left in the world."

He simply looked at her.

"Yes, I said it. I'm looking at one."

His smile was slow. "Hallelujah."

She let go when she wanted to tug him closer. "Don't get a big head."

"Wouldn't dream of it," he said, then started toward her.

Jana backed up a step. "Don't you want your lemonade?"

"I got something better in mind." He kept coming until their bodies touched. His hand settled on her hips, keeping her in place. "Since you don't want me to go back to the house, I have to keep busy doing something."

"Like what?"

"Why don't I show you?"

It was after twelve when Tyler left Jana. He hadn't wanted to leave her at all, but he's been worried about Olivia. Seeing Julian's car still there, Tyler's eyes narrowed, then he thought of what Jana had said and what Olivia was going though. If Julian could help her, Tyler would try to stay out of it. But if he was playing with his sister, then *he* was going to need a doctor.

Opening the front door, Tyler headed for the stairs, telling himself he was going to be sensible and an adult, but he didn't realize his hands were clenched into fists until he heard muted voices coming from the media room. He swiped a hand across his face. He didn't want to look if anything was going on, yet he didn't want to leave his sister to be taken advantage of.

Slowly, cautiously he went to the half-closed door, took a breath, then peered around the door. Olivia and Julian, both fully clothed, were on the sofa bed. Olivia had changed into sweats. She had her head on his shoulder, his arm was around her and they were watching a movie. He left as quietly as he had come.

Jana had been right. There were good men in the world and it looked like his sister had found one. Assured Olivia was all right, he left as quietly as he had come. There were also good women and he was going back to his.

18

Jana and Olivia cooked breakfast together. They ate on the terrace. Julian left soon afterwards to check on his patients in the hospital. Olivia, afraid that if she went to church she might miss Griffin's call, had stayed at home to prepare Griffin's favorite meal. Jana helped while Tyler worked on designing the computer program for his latest client.

It was after lunch when Tyler received the call he'd been waiting for. As soon as he hung up he went to find Olivia. She was in the kitchen grinding out noodles while Jana stirred the homemade pasta sauce.

"I know why Aaron wants Griffin so badly." Both women stopped what they were doing.

"The private investigator learned from one of the people working at Aaron's father's house that his father passed over Aaron and plans to leave the company to Griffin. The employee heard them arguing," Tyler said. "Aaron is an only child. He and his father aren't on good terms because Aaron wants to sell the business, but his father is adamantly against it. As guardian of Griffin, Aaron will have control of the company."

"I don't want the money," Olivia said. "I'll tell him as much when he brings Griffin back this afternoon."

"It's not that simple. According to the servant, Griffin has been entitled to a share of the profits since his birth," Tyler said. "You refused spousal support, but once Griffin was born he was a legal heir. His grandfather was giving Aaron the money to send, but he spent it. Griffin is due a sizable chunk of the company's assets, and considering they haven't been doing well since his grandfather's illness, there might not be that much left."

"Then that's it." Olivia said. "All we have to do is tell the judge."

"He'll deny it and probably turn it around as a reason for wanting Griffin, to ensure he has his inheritance," Tyler said. "Or say he invested the money to help Griffin and lost it in the stock market."

"You're right. He's sly and devious." Olivia swallowed. "I won't let him come anywhere near Griffin after today."

Tyler put his hand on her shoulder. "We'll do whatever it takes."

"This has been so much fun, Griffin, hasn't it?" his father asked as he sat across the limousine from him. "Soon you'll be with me to have more."

"Yes, sir," Griffin answered. He'd quickly learned his father didn't become impatient with him if he agreed with everything he said. Griffin had also been careful not to ask for seconds during breakfast or lunch.

"You'll tell your mother that, won't you?"

"Yes, sir." Looking out the window Griffin saw his street sign as the limo turned the corner. He began counting the houses.

The limo pulled up to the curb. Through the window Griffin saw his mother, Uncle Tyler, and Julian. Forgetting they couldn't see him he waved.

"Don't forget, Griffin, you had a wonderful time."

"Yes, sir."

Opening the door, Aaron emerged from the vehicle. Griffin came out of the car in a flash. He didn't stop until he was in his mother's arms. He didn't care who saw him. He held her as tight as she held him. They went into the house and Julian followed.

Aaron turned up his nose at the rudeness of Olivia and the man with her. Obviously he was as uncouth as she was. They could have been cordial enough to speak. If they had he could have learned the identity of the gorgeous man with her and tried to get a feel if he swung both ways. Perhaps it was for the best. Money first; pleasure later.

And when he had Griffin in his custody, all that pampering nonsense would cease. A good boys' school, preferably one as far away from him as possible, would help shape him up. As soon as he got home, he'd have his secretary do some research on the matter.

Tyler held out his hand. "My phone."

"I don't have it," Aaron told him. No matter how much money Tyler had, he remained unpolished.

Tyler got in his face. "Then you better find it or I'm going to press charges for theft."

Aaron almost laughed in his face. "You can't be serious."

"As a heart attack. The phone cost three hundred dollars. I have friends at the police department. Want to bet I can file a complaint and they arrest you before your plane leaves?" Tyler said with entirely too much glee in his voice for comfort.

Aaron's clenched his teeth. "I'll leave it at the hotel."

"Make sure you do. Or the police will be waiting for you when you return." Dismissing Aaron as if he were nothing, Tyler started for the house. Aaron's dislike for Tyler escalated. He knew the perfect way to take him down a peg or two.

"You're awfully nonchalant for a man who is interested in a woman who is known to crawl into the pants of any man—" Aaron stopped abruptly when Tyler whirled, fist clenched. Aaron stumbled back.

"Say another word and you'll be picking your teeth up off the ground."

Aaron opened his mouth, then shut it. He rushed back to the limo and climbed inside. He'd make them all pay.

Tyler didn't move until he felt his anger was under control. He'd only gone a few steps when he glanced to his left. Jana stood on the walkway coming from her apartment. From the stricken look on her face, he knew she'd heard Aaron.

Head bowed, she started back to her apartment. Tyler wished he had Aaron in front of him for five seconds. How much more could Jana take?

Jana knew he'd come.

She'd made him an offer he couldn't refuse. After overhearing Aaron, she'd taken a cab to a pay phone and called him. This time he'd taken her call.

Her father looked like a respected businessman in his tailored sports jacket and slacks. He had always made a point of never being out in public looking less than his best. Public perception meant a lot to him. Perhaps that's why she meant so little.

"You said on the phone you were ready to discuss leaving," he said the instant he slid into the booth across from her at the dimly lit restaurant where he insisted they meet. He wasn't taking a chance that they might be seen together.

"If you promise not to testify at Griffin's custody hearing," she said. "His mother loves him more than anything."

He tsked. "You can't tell me you care."

"Despite having grown up without love from either parent, I can recognize it."

His facial expression harshened. "You brought it on yourself."

"Did you ever stop and ask yourself why?" She braced her arms on the wooden table. "I'll tell you. It was because first I wanted my mother's love and thought if I was like her, she might pay more attention to me than she did to the latest fashion or her latest lover."

He started to rise. "I don't have to listen to this."

"You do if you want me to leave and never come back," she told him.

He sat. "Say it and get out of my life."

Once the words would have taken her to her knees. But she'd learned her opinion of herself mattered more than what her parents thought. Her mother had yet to call.

"Did you hear what you just said? To you, I'm too vile to even be in your presence. But did you ever make an effort to spend time with me? To try to teach me right from wrong? Encourage me? I'll tell you. Not once. Instead you ignored, then criticized, then shunned me. Not once did you do or say anything to let me know you cared when I was growing up."

"I was busy earning a living."

"Stop lying. At least be honest enough to admit the truth," she told him. "You hated my mother for trapping you into marriage, and that hatred spilled over to me. Neither of you wanted me. I tried to get Mother to love me by imitating her lifestyle. I thought if I acted out enough, you would pay attention to me. You never did."

"I've got the only family I ever want."

Her laugh was brittle. "So you have. I just hope neither of then turns their backs on you the way you have me. Good-bye, Thomas." Picking up her purse, she walked away, her eyes dry.

She expected to find the note from Tyler stuck under her door when she arrived home. He knew she'd heard Aaron and would be troubled when she didn't answer the door. No one had ever worried about her before. He was working on another project yet he was concerned about her. Putting her purse away, she went to the house and knocked on his door.

The door opened. Relief spread across Tyler's face. He pulled her into his arms. "Please tell me if you decide to go off again."

"I didn't mean to worry you," she said, hoping he didn't realize she hadn't answered him directly. She never wanted to lie to him.

"It took a lot of willpower not to go into your room and see if your suitcase was missing."

Somehow she'd gained his trust and his affection. "You about ready to take a break?"

Lifting his head, he stared down at her. Desire leaped in his eyes. "Julian took Olivia and Griffin to see a Disney movie."

Her hands went to the buttons of his shirt. She'd take every precious moment with him. They had to last a lifetime. "Perfect."

Julian had looked forward to the impromptu outing Tuesday afternoon with Olivia and Griffin, which didn't surprise him. He enjoyed challenging Griffin, trying to outwit him, being with him. The kid was smart and fun.

"I'm going to try and do something with this hair," Olivia said. They'd just come out of the wind tunnel. "I'll be back in a minute."

"May I have a soda while you're gone?" Griffin asked. "I'm thirsty."

Olivia leaned down to within an inch of his face. "No." Kissing him on the cheek, she went into the ladies room.

Griffin turned to Julian. "I bet you're thirsty."

Julian smiled and put his arm around Griffin's shoulder without think-ing and started for an empty bench. "You are not getting me in trouble with your mother."

"She can't stay mad at people for long," he said. "Uncle Tyler and my granddad are always telling her she'd too soft-hearted."

"Probably, but that's what makes her such a wonderful woman and mother." Julian sat and stretched his long legs out in front of him. The cor-ners of his mouth kicked up when Griffin tried to copy the pose. "She loves you very much."

Griffin drew his legs up. "I don't think my father does."

Julian's gaze went to the ladies room. He needed help on this one.

"He was smiling when I first saw him, then I almost knocked him down. And when we went out to eat I got sick." Griffin turned and stared up at Julian with eyes exactly like his mother's and as wounded as when she had to let Griffin leave to visit his father. "Maybe he left because of me."

Julian's heart went out to Griffin. He recalled all too well his own doubts and insecurities about his father. "Griffin, you had nothing to do with your father leaving. Some marriages just don't work."

"That's what Mother said, but he didn't seem to like me much."

"Griffin," Julian placed his hand on the young boy's shoulder. "Fathers are supposed to love their children as much as mothers do, but it doesn't al-ways happen. My father was in the military and was very strict with us and was often gone. My younger brother and I learned to stay out of his way on those brief furloughs home." He took a deep breath and let himself remem-ber the good times and not the bad.

"My mother was as sweet and loving as your mother. Having her love made up for my father not loving me. It's not your fault or mine that our fa-thers aren't the way we'd like for them to be."

"Where's your mother?" Griffin asked.

"She died when I was sixteen, but I still remember her love. It's gotten me though some rough times."

Griffin leaned closer and whispered. "When I was scared the other night at the hotel with my father, I thought of my mother."

Julian hugged him. "We're blessed to have mothers who love and loved us." He looked up and saw Olivia coming toward him. Another blessing. He hadn't realized how much of one until he'd almost lost her.

Jana knew it wouldn't be easy. Knowing she was right wasn't any consolation. Each word of her resignation tore at her heart. Yet, there was a strange kind of comfort in that. She genuinely cared about people without expecting anything in return. She wasn't the heartless, bitter woman she once was. She had Olivia and Tyler to thank for that, for giving her a second chance.

Finished, she put the letter in her purse and placed her suitcase by the door. Her hand on the knob, she took one last look around the room. She'd had more happiness while living here than all the years she had foolishly wasted her life. Despite everything, she had found a measure of contentment here. She didn't know if it was possible anywhere else because Tyler wouldn't be there.

She had become one of those foolish people she'd always laughed at. She'd fallen in love. She'd never regret loving Tyler. It was probably one of the few unselfish acts she'd ever done. The other was leaving Olivia and Griffin as happy and secure as she had met them. Opening the door, she started for the house.

As usual, the front door was left open for her in the morning. That amount of trust and welcome meant more than she could ever say. Closing then locking the door, she headed for the kitchen. Warm laughter welcomed her into the room. Tyler, Olivia, and Griffin were at the breakfast table and Wanda was at the stove. "Good morning."

A chorus of greetings welcomed her. She was wanted.

"Morning." Tyler immediately rose and came to her, kissing her on the cheek. "I was beginning to worry about you."

"Sorry." She took the chair he pulled out for her. She wasn't hungry, but she said her blessings, then placed her napkin in her lap.

"Pancakes all right, Jana?" Wanda asked.

"Just one or I won't be able to fit into any of my clothes," Jana managed.

"You look fine to me." Tyler looked at her over the rim of his coffee cup. "But then I'm prejudiced."

Jana tried to smile, but her facial muscles wouldn't work.

Tyler put his cup down. "What's the matter?"

"Nothing. I didn't sleep very much last night," she told him truthfully, then blushed at his slow grin. He hadn't left until nearly dawn.

"If you want to rest a bit before you come in, I'll go in by myself." Olivia smiled at Griffin. "You and Ann have been wonderful about me taking off with Griffin."

Jana looked at Griffin's happy face, saw the love shining in his mother's eyes. "We were both happy to do it."

"Still, I appreciate it." Olivia sipped her coffee.

Griffin chewed and swallowed his blueberry pancakes. "Julian is coming over tonight to teach me chess. I bet once I learn I'll beat him."

Olivia shook her head. "I honestly don't know if I should try and curb his self-confidence or not."

"It's not self-centered or vicious. Griffin is going to grow up to be a wonderful man. You've taught him what's important, what to value. You're the type of mother all children should have," she said, unable to keep the longing and regret from her quiet voice.

Suddenly aware that she had unwittingly drawn the attention of the adults, Jana busied herself adding cream and sugar to her coffee. They'd felt sorry for her long enough. So had she.

Under the table, she felt Tyler's hand gently touch her leg, reassuring her. For him, for the love she could never give him, she gave him the smile he waited patiently for. There would be time enough for tears later.

Jana took the excuse Olivia had given her and returned to her room instead of riding to work with her. That way she could take a cab to work and have her suitcase with her when she turned in her resignation so she wouldn't have to come back. If she did she knew she'd find Tyler waiting for her. He was as stubborn as he was loyal.

"Jana?"

Jana stopped pacing in the front room on hearing Tyler's voice. "Just a minute." Picking up the suitcase, she placed it in the closet in the bedroom. Tyler might become suspicious if the door was closed.

Rubbing her sweaty hands over her slacks, she opened the door. "Hi."

He stepped over the threshold, closing the door behind him, and pulled her into his arms, his warm lips finding hers. Her arms circled his neck, her body sank against his, and she let the kiss empty her mind, enjoying the hum of her body, the strength of his arms around her, the hard muscles.

"Hi," he finally said on lifting his head. "Now what going on in that beautiful head of yours?"

He knew her so well, and liked her in spite of what he knew. He was both her salvation and her penitence. "You're an amazing man."

Puckers ran across his brow. "Was that meant to throw me off track?"

"Just stating a fact." Her thumb traced the strong line of his jaw, the sensual lower lip. "You have an amazing mouth, an amazing body."

Tyler's breathing quickened. "You're going to make me forget my good intentions if you keep that up."

"Let's see." Jana took the kiss she desperately wanted. There was a maelstrom of fire and burning desire from the moment their mouths touched.

Tyler's hand was hot on her skin: his fingers gentle and rough as he plucked at her nipple. They hardened even more.

Her hands went to his shirt. She wanted him. Her body was on fire.

He moaned. "If I didn't have to meet the team for a new installation, I'd take you back to bed."

"You can't be a few minutes late?" she asked, tugging at his shirt.

His laugh was rough. "It would be more than that and you know it. See you tonight." He sobered. "Tomorrow is the hearing. I'll be glad when this is all over. The judge has to rule in Olivia's favor."

"She will." Without her father's damaging testimony to harm Olivia's case, Griffin would remain where he belonged, with his mother.

"That's what we're all praying for." He kissed her again, then he was gone.

Shivering, Jana stared at the closed door. She was doing the right thing. She just hated that it hurt so much.

"I'm leaving." Jana handed the letter to Olivia shortly after the store opened and watched the stunned expression race across her face.

Olivia didn't even look at it. "Why? I thought you were happy here."

Jana swallowed. "It's better this way."

"How can you say that?" Olivia asked, suspicion in her eyes.

"My taxi is waiting," Jana said, tears stinging her throat. "I'll miss you."

"Then stay," Olivia said.

"I can't," Jana said, turning and going to the front door.

"Tyler won't let you walk out of his life," Olivia warned as she followed.

Jana stopped abruptly. "I'm not the right woman for him."

"Bull." Olivia turned her around. "You once accused me of being a coward and you were right. Who's the coward now?"

"Don't you think I'd stay if I could? I'd give anything to be able to erase my past, erase the things I've done." She gulped. "Tyler deserves a woman he doesn't have to be ashamed of or wonder how many of the men in a social gathering she's slept with."

"He also deserves a woman who'll love him. He deserves you."

Her throat too full to speak, Jana gave Olivia a quick hug, then hurried out the door, only to bump into Julian. The smile on his face died when he saw how upset Olivia was. "What's going on?"

"She resigned. Maybe you can talk some sense into her head." Olivia sniffled. "She won't listen to me."

"Come on." Taking Jana's arm he led her a wooden bench beneath a mature elm tree a short distance away from the store. "You picked the worst possible time to leave with the hearing tomorrow."

"I'm doing it to help." She glanced away. "My father won't testify if I leave town."

Julian cursed softly under his breath. "Do you know how much guilt this is going to put on Olivia's shoulders?"

Her head whipped back around. "I didn't tell her the reason."

"She'll figure it out," Julian said. "What about Tyler? He loves you."

The words pierced Jana's heart. "He cares, but he doesn't love me."

Julian tsked. "You're wrong. Or are you kidding yourself so you won't have to take the blame for hurting two people who helped you when no one else cared."

"I wouldn't do that. I love them," Jana cried.

"Then stay and prove it." Julian stood. "Tell your father to take a flying leap. He has his family and people who love him. He's leaving you with nothing. Your choice. Love or loneliness?"

Jana stared after him. "Why do you care?"

He turned. "Because I've come to know you, and I like the woman you've become. Others feel the same way. You can have a life here or you can keep running."

Jana briefly closed her eyes, then went to the parked taxi and got in.

Late that afternoon Tyler was back in his office and in the middle of im-putting data when there was knock on his door. Since Wanda didn't disturb him unless it was important, he hit save, went to the door, and opened it.

Surprise, then alarm hit him on seeing Jana standing there, trembling, biting her lip. His heart almost stopped when he saw the suitcase by her feet. "You're not leaving me."

"No, I'm not." She launched herself into his arms. "I know you're busy, but I need you to come with me to see my father."

The bastard would only hurt her more. "Honey, maybe you should think about this."

Loosening her hold, Jana stepped back a fraction. "I have. I'm going to tell him I've changed my mind about leaving town so he won't testify, and assure him that he won't have to ever worry about me trying to contact him again."

"Not testify? You mean you're telling me you agreed to leave so he wouldn't testify?" he asked, his eyes growing cold.

"Yes, but I've changed my mind," Jana answered.

"Thank God," Tyler said, cupping her cheek. "I'm sorry. I know he hurt you again."

"Not as much as leaving you and Olivia. Julian made me see that."

"Julian?"

"I was leaving the store after turning in my resignation and bumped into him," she explained.

"I owe him. Let me get my keys." With the keys in one hand and Jana's in the other, they went to the garage. A trailer home pulled up and a good-looking older couple emerged.

"What great timing! I knew you'd make it," Tyler said, greeting his parents with a hug, then pulling Jana forward. "Mama and Daddy, I want you to meet a very special woman, Jana Franklin."

Jana very much wanted Tyler and Olivia's parents to like her. She was extremely nervous, but soon found that they were genuinely warm and as outgoing as their daughter. They were going to the store to see Olivia while Tyler took Jana to Frisco to see her father.

"You sure?" Tyler asked when he parked in front of her father's sprawling ranch house. Homes in the swank development started at two million dollars, then rose sharply in price.

"Positive."

He squeezed her hand and then released her. Jana went to the double recessed doors and rang the doorbell almost hidden by English Ivy. The man she came to see answered. His eyes filled with anger when he saw Jana.

"I'm not leaving town, but you don't have to worry that I'll ever try to contact you again in any manner. If you're low enough to try and get back at me by testifying tomorrow, that will be on your conscience. I have people who care about me and I'm not giving that up. Good-bye."

Jana's father stood speechless in the doorway as she turned and went to Tyler waiting by the truck.

Tyler caught her hand again. "Well done."

"Could you do something else for me?"

"Anything," he answered.

"Take me to the store. I want my job back."

Olivia tried to be happy that her parents were there, but she couldn't keep worrying about tomorrow. She had yet to speak with Griffin about him having to talk to the judge. After dinner she excused herself and went out to the pool. Julian followed, sliding his arms around her from behind and pulling her to him.

"Tomorrow he'll come home with you."

"But will he stay? I've prayed, but I know God's answer isn't always the one we want to hear." Her voice trembled. "It's telling that he hasn't mentioned his father since he returned. Did you hear him tell my parents about you?"

Julian grunted. "Yeah. How badly he beat me."

Olivia turned around. "That's just it. He enjoys being with you."

"I feel the same." He kissed her forehead. "Of course I'm extra partial to his mother."

"Thank you for being here for us," she whispered.

"Where else would I be except here with you and Griffin?" The words were barely out of his mouth before he realized their implication.

"We appreciate it."

Julian didn't want her appreciation, he wanted, he needed her love. Instead of shock the realization brought a calming peace.

She stepped back. "I need to talk to Griffin about tomorrow." She kissed his cheek, then walked away.

Julian wanted to go after her, but she had enough to deal with. After the hearing tomorrow was time enough. With Griffin home, Julian hoped they'd have something else to celebrate.

The next day Olivia discovered that talking with Griffin wasn't as difficult as letting him go alone into the judge's chambers. "I'll be here when you come out," she told him, trying to smile.

"Your Honor, you should take into consideration that she may have influenced the boy," Aaron's lawyer said.

Judge Watkins cut him a look. "Are you presuming to tell me how to conduct this interview?"

"No. No," Aaron's lawyer quickly said.

"Good." She held her hand out to Griffin. "Griffin, we're going into my chambers. You have nothing to be afraid of."

He nodded and took her hand. At the door, he looked back at his mother. Julian was there as well.

"We'll go get pizza when this is over," Julian called.

Griffin wanted to smile, but he couldn't. His mother looked sad and his father looked angry. Tucking his head, he continued though the door.

"I want you to know that you can trust me," Judge Watkins told the boy. She sat on the sofa and patted the seat beside her. "I just want to ask you some questions. There are no right and wrong answers."

"Yes, ma'am." Griffin sat beside her. His teachers said the same thing and never meant it.

"How did the visit with your father go?" she asked.

"All right."

She smiled, reminding him of his teacher last year. He'd liked her. "Just all right? You mother told me how much you cared for your father."

"I do."

She leaned back. "What did you do?"

"We went to dinner at a pizza place, then went to his hotel and watched Disney movies." He kicked his feet. "I got myself ready for bed."

"You certainly are a big boy. You mother and father must be very proud."

"My mama is," he confided. "She and Uncle Tyler and my grandparents always come to awards assembly at my school."

"You father might like to attend as well."

Griffin glanced up than lowered his head. "I don't think he likes me."

"Why?"

Lifting his head, Griffin told her about how he had made his father angry, how he called him a crybaby. "But that's all right because Julian told me that his father didn't like him very much, but his mother loved him so much and it made up for his father not loving him. My mother loves me a lot too."

"Julian is the man with your mother? The one who said you were going out for pizza?"

Griffin grinned. "We're dating."

She frowned. "We?"

"I get to go with them sometimes. We went to Six Flags the other day. Julian's cool."

"So you like Julian?"

His shoulders drooped. "I wish . . ."

"What?"

"That he was my father," whispered Griffin.

"I see. Griffin, you're a very fortunate young man. I want to talk with your parents while you stay with your grandparents and uncle." The judge stood and went to the door. "Everyone please come in. I've made my decision."

Cheers went up in the judge's chamber amid protests. "My decision is final. Permanent custody is awarded to Griffin's mother, Olivia Sanders. Mr. Sanders, you had your chance."

"I love my son!" Aaron yelled.

"According to the documents before me, your newfound love is a result of his being in line to inherit the family firm," she said with disapproval. "I only hope you learn to value him as much as his mother and his extended family does."

Without a word, Aaron left the court, his lawyer behind him.

"He's mine forever." Olivia rushed back outside to her son.

"You think you have room enough for me?" Julian asked.

Olivia turned to him. "What . . . what did you say?"

His arms circled her waist. "Will you marry me?"

"Oh, Julian. Yes!" She flew into his arms.

He held out his other arm for Griffin. "You too."

Griffin wrapped his arms around Julian as far as they would go. "Are we still going to get pizza?"

Everyone laughed as they piled out of the courthouse. They were coming down the steps when a black limousine pulled up at the curb. A uniformed driver jumped out and opened the door. Out stepped a tall, distinguished man with silver hair.

Beside Tyler Jana gasped. "What is it?"

The well-dressed man started up the steps, saw her and quickly went to her. "I found you at last."

"Frederick," Jana said, making the introductions. His family owned several oil tankers. He was one of the richest men in the country and one of the men who had begged her to stay. "What are you doing here?"

"I've come for you, of course." He caught her arm. "Come, the car is waiting." He'd already turned back when he felt resistance.

"She's not going anyplace with you," Tyler said, his voice hard.

"Do not be angry because I didn't take your calls," he said. "I was furious at you for leaving me, but I have come to my senses. I want you back."

"She's not going with you," Tyler said, his arm sliding possessively around Jana's slim waist.

Up went Frederick's aristocratic nose. He dismissed Tyler with a glance. "You'll want for nothing, Jana, my darling. I'll take an extended holiday and we can go to San Tropez or Morocco or anyplace you desire."

"She's rather stay with me and be my wife," Tyler said bluntly, his face as harsh as his voice. No one was taking Jana away from him.

Jana gasped. She stared at Tyler. "You want to marry me?"

"I planned to ask you later. I love you." His face softened, his voice gentled.

Tears crested in her eyes. "I love you, too. So much it almost scares me." She turned to Frederick, "Nothing can compare to what I have here. Goodbye, Frederick."

"If you change—"

"I won't. This time it's forever." She gazed up at Tyler with love shining in her eyes. "Only this man will do."

To the cheering approval of his family, Tyler took Jana into his arms and kissed her. For him, only she would do.

Epilogue

Jana had thought her wedding day had been the happiest day of her life. She'd been wrong. Since then, each day with Tyler was more incredible than the one before.

Waiting for Tyler to finish working and come upstairs, she sat in bed with a forgotten book and stared at their wedding picture on the nightstand. Both of them were beaming. The "small" garden wedding six weeks ago had had a hundred well-wishers. The number swelled to over three hundred for their reception at Hotel ZaZa because Tyler was well respected and had so many friends. Many of those in attendance were now her friends, too. She was doubly blessed to have found Tyler and that, miraculously, he loved her.

Olivia's wedding was to be a more formal affair, and was scheduled to take place in two weeks. Afterward, Julian was moving in. Since Olivia and Tyler each had a separate wing in the three-story house, there was enough room for both families. *Family.* Jana hugged the book to her chest. At last she belonged, and had a family of her own.

The bedroom door opened. Tyler, a broad grin on his face, began unbuttoning his shirt before he was two steps inside their room. Laughing, she jumped out of bed and ran to him.

Kissing her, he picked her up. "You're going in the wrong direction."

She kissed, then nuzzled, the strong line of his jaw. "It got me in your arms faster."

"Point taken." He sat on the side of the bed with Jana in his arms and stared deeply into her eyes. "I love you, Jana Maxwell."

Her hands, palming his face, trembled as much as her body. "I'll never grow tired of hearing those words or take for granted how blessed I am. I love you, Tyler Maxwell, for now and for always."

"I know," he said, his voice deep and raspy just before his mouth covered hers.

Jana gave herself up to the rapture of loving Tyler, the first and only man she'd ever love unconditionally, the first and only man who knew her faults and loved her back the same way.

READING GROUP GUIDE

1. Jana disrupted a number of relationships with her wanton behavior. Was it entirely her fault for luring the men away or should the men share the blame equally?

2. If you had proof positive that the man you loved cheated with another man/woman, could you forgive and forget? Would you give him another chance or pack your bags? How difficult would it be to trust him again?

3. A woman's sexual history is judged more harshly than a man's. Why is this and do you think it's fair?

4. Many men have loved women despite their dubious sexual pasts. Would you feel threatened if such a woman was around your significant other a great deal? If so, how would you handle those feelings?

5. Jana started on the difficult road to redemption when she hit rock bottom and finally saw what her self-centered life had cost her. However, there were those who weren't ready to forgive or forget her past. Could you have been as forgiving as Tyler and Olivia?

6. If the unthinkable happened and a woman somehow persuaded your man to stray, and years later you met the now-reformed woman, could you forgive her or would she need a hair transplant?

For more reading group suggestions visit
www.stmartins.com/smp/rgg.html

St. Martin's Griffin